ATTACK ON AUREON IV

There was a roaring sound from somewhere above the palace. Then a second roar joining it, and a third. Then a roaring whoop and an explosion.

The Princess screamed, *''Skyraiders!''*

There was another whoop, another explosion, nearer this time; the floor vibrated. Then a whooping sound coming right at us.

I reacted, leaped across the room catching the Princess around the waist, and held onto her as we hit the floor and rolled under the bed. The room jumped with the sound of the explosion and chunks of stone fell from the ceiling.

''How will we get out of here?'' the Princess asked.

I held up one of the Bullets. ''These. I don't have time to explain. Put it between your teeth. Bite down. Swallow.''

A screaming whoop closed in on us.

''NOW!'' I shouted.

The Princess bit and swallowed. There was a pop and she was gone.

Then the room exploded, with me in it, and all I saw for a while was blackness.

Bantam Science Fiction
Ask your bookseller for the books you have missed

ALAS, BABYLON by Pat Frank
BEFORE THE UNIVERSE by Frederik Pohl & C. M. Kornbluth
CAMP CONCENTRATION by Thomas M. Disch
A CANTICLE FOR LEIBOWITZ by Walter Miller, Jr.
THE CENTAURI DEVICE by Harry Harrison
CRYSTAL PHOENIX by Michael Berlyn
ENGINE SUMMER by John Crowley
THE FEMALE MAN by Joanna Russ
FUNDAMENTAL DISCH by Thomas M. Disch
THE GATES OF HEAVEN by Paul Preuss
HOMEWORLD by Harry Harrison
THE JANUS SYNDROME by Steven E. McDonald
JEM by Frederik Pohl
MAN PLUS by Frederik Pohl
THE MAN WHO FELL TO EARTH by Walter Tevis
MOCKINGBIRD by Walter Tevis
ON WINGS OF SONG by Thomas M. Disch
THE PARADISE PLOT by Ed Naha
RE-ENTRY by Paul Preuss
SLOW FALL TO DAWN by Stephen Leigh
SPACE ON MY HANDS by Frederic Brown
THE STAINLESS STEEL RAT WANTS YOU! by Harry Harrison
SUNDIVER by David Brin
TALES FROM GAVAGAN'S BAR by L. Sprague de Camp & Fletcher Pratt
THE TIME MACHINE by H. G. Wells
TIME STORM by Gordon Dickson
UNDER THE CITY OF ANGELS by Jerry Earl Brown
VALIS by Philip K. Dick
WHEELWORLD by Harry Harrison

THE JANUS SYNDROME

Steven E. McDonald

BANTAM BOOKS
TORONTO · NEW YORK · LONDON · SYDNEY

THE JANUS SYNDROME

A Bantam Book/October 1981

ISBN 0-553-14993-8

Published simultaneously in the United States and Canada

Bantam Books are published by Bantam Books, Inc. Its trademark, consisting of the words "Bantam Books" and the portrayal of a rooster, is Registered in U.S. Patent and Trademark Office and in other countries. Marca Registrada. Bantam Books, Inc., 666 Fifth Avenue, New York, New York 10103.

PRINTED IN THE UNITED STATES OF AMERICA

0 9 8 7 6 5 4 3 2 1

Dedicated to Pam and Sandy for the 'toons, the DNA, the cookies, and the giraffe.

Thanks to Dirty Dick's No Pap Records for the records, and to Ben Bova for guidance, foresight, and inspiration.

1 St. Louis Blues

Click.

The TV set I'd been staring at for twenty minutes suddenly shut down, leaving me to search for quarters while checking my watch. Seeing the time, I stopped checking the watch. Your time is up, number three. At least mine was.

I looked up and pulled a face, picked up a can of crapawful soda that I'd bought twenty minutes ago, and tried it. Still crapawful. I wasn't exactly comfortable either; the TV seats the Greyhound Bus people had put into the various terminals, including the St. Louis terminal, were designed to make you so uncomfortable you didn't notice the crappy quality of the TV signal.

Show-me. The goddamned *show-me* state. Missouri didn't have much to show. I wasn't particularly interested in looking, either. Area Fourteen had set one of his favorite midway contacts on me, cloak and dagger and all, and I wasn't amused. He refused to tell me why I was here, the assumption being I'd be able to pick up things for myself, looking at everything, rather than having preconceptions.

So show me, Missouri.

I was approximately in the middle of the terminal, with a good view all around of a modern gray-and-black urban plastic rat-hole. Wide windows all along one side, ticket desks at the other, exit 'way in the distance, at the bottom end, left luggage right behind me, lights 'way overhead, pillars at skewed intervals from one end to the other, exit out to the buses back and on my right. I'd almost memorized the layout at the start. I'd had to.

On my left, an alcove filled with pinball machines and

automatic soda vendors; I'd gotten the soda from there. There was no one in there at the moment. Further down the terminal hall, there was a larger game room for less transient people, and a cafeteria.

I watched the exit at the bottom, and the exit from the game room and cafe. My contact was a remarkable young creature called Kerry Fossen, and it would be like her to sneak up in back of me and shout boo, making me piss my pants, and thanks, Area Fourteen. He'd love that. I'd damn near made a total physical wreck of myself traveling Greyhound all the way from Fresno to St. Louis. And now, just to use a simple and highly descriptive phrase:

I was pissed off.

Area Fourteen loves handing me need-to-know assignments. Usually the stuff I didn't need to know was the crucial stuff. I did a lot of fast talking and even faster running. I wasn't meeting Kerry to arrange for her to be shipped up to Area Fourteen, nor was I the one to be shipped. All the damn Mastercomputer had to do there was ship either of us a Bullet; instant zap, and there we are. Fortunately for my disposition, the midway contact had brought me something to allow me to get a decent, if short, sleep.

I quit bitching at myself and watched harder, checking faces and looking for anything unusual. Kerry was a damn good agent, one of the most reliable—some of them were garbage, barely capable of growing fat and old at the same time. If Kerry had a contact time set, she'd do her damnedest not to undershoot or overshoot it.

I sighed and gave my eyes a test swing to make sure I could keep her in line of sight. Lady has a walk would kill an octogenarian at fifty paces. More than the physical attraction, though, there was the attraction of knowledge: she could point me in the right direction and tell me to go.

Need-to-know. Show-me. *Whirrrr.*

There are days I hate, and this was one.

I was worried, all the same. Situations like this could mean Enemy in the area. On occasion, silence is the only possible route; too many ears and eyes watching out for wisps of information. If there was an Enemy tag on Kerry, it could mean trouble. And if Kerry was in trouble, better break out the shining knights—or at least a slightly overdone one. Enter Kevven Tomari.

I checked my watch, checked the terminal clock, noted the positions of the big hand and little hand on the terminal clock, and the shape of the figures on my expensive watch. Love my expense account, even if Area Fourteen hates it.

Show-me.

He liked that motto, did Area Fourteen. Causing me trouble.

If the Enemy had tagged Kerry, though, they'd kill her. I was wary. We'd lost a lot of agents recently to Enemy work. Too many.

I untensed when I saw her coming through the entranceway at the bottom of the terminal; five feet of her, plus afro, plus pantsuit. It was impossible to mistake her, even from this distance; there is simply no one else like Kerry in an assortment of planets.

I got ready to go meet her, then stopped and dropped back into the seat.

Kerry was crossing the distance rapidly; she wasn't looking for me. For good reason.

Two of them, trailing her. They hadn't made any move on her yet; that had to mean they were aware that she was here to make a connection. So they were going to hit contact and connection together, a neat double-header.

And for me, ugly as hell.

I watched them carefully, scanning side to side to check for others. None. Both white types, hair cut in similar fashion, similar casual suits—it prevents part of your team getting iced if you have a few identifying points in the scrimmage—one blue serge, one business gray. They were flanking her on either side, some distance behind, hands in their pockets.

I tried to juggle strategy while watching them. If they followed pattern, they'd try to corner us, and then shoot. A couple of shots from .38 snubnoses would do the trick, cartridges only half-filled with cordite to cut the noise. Silencers were too clumsy. After the hit, a fast escape through a nearby exit, and personal transmission back to home base.

Kerry didn't look at me as she went by, and neither did they.

I took out a pack of cigarettes and made a show of looking for a match. Kerry was aware of her shadows, and she'd passed the ball to me; I was going to have to work fast not to fumble the play, and I didn't have the barest shred of a plan.

I was going to have to think on the fly.

I hate working blind.

I stood up with the air of a True addict without a light, looked around in desperation, and settled on the nice gent in gray walking by on my left. I picked up the heaviest of the two carryalls—the one that held my cassette recorder and headphones—as I started off.

I caught up with him and plucked at his sleeve, slouching back a bit as he stopped and turned.

"You got a light, buddy?" I said

His mouth opened slightly, and his eyes shifted to take in his partner, who was moving away from us, still trailing Kerry.

"Well, actually—" he started.

I brought the bag up sharply into his groin, doubling him over, took his hair in my free hand, slammed his face into my knee, smashing his nose with a sound like an apple being smacked into a wall, dragged his head back as I dropped the bag, and punched him in the throat with my fingers bent under.

I held him up for a moment while I checked his clothes with a fast frisk, slapping his pockets. Nothing. His weaponry was elsewhere, and I didn't have time to search him properly.

I let him drop, swung, and shouted, "KERRY! GO!"

And then I was off and running myself, diving for cover in the annex where the Greyhound people had hidden the soda and pinball machines; I'd memorized possible cover just for this sort of thing. I'd only been near Enemy on Earth once before, and had escaped unscathed easily enough. This time it was different.

Out of the corner of my eye, I saw Kerry running for a row of seats; she vaulted over the row, shoulderbag still in place, one small hand on the back of a seat, movements as lithe as a cat's.

I left the ground in a flying dive, and felt a breath of fire across my back, smelling ozone and smoke; adrenalin surged. I hit the polished floor, slid a way, and rolled under a pinball table, crawling to take up position behind a large soda machine. I was weaponless, and about as much use as a hula-hoop during the goldrush. And judging by the heat across my back and the smell of ozone, the Enemy were packing a lot more than .38 revolvers.

Another laser shot sliced into the soda machine next down the row from mine, melting a chunk of the façade to slag. It broke away from the machine, molten-white and glaring, cooled rapidly on the way down, and splashed onto the floor, blistering the wax and rapidly turning solid.

I shivered and drew back. If that guy caught me, I'd be as dead as a dog I'd seen run down in Columbia.

There was a low plopping sound, like corks being pulled from wine bottles. A needlegun. That had to be Kerry; either someone had warned her or she'd come to the conclusion that she needed extra-powerful weaponry, and had gotten it somehow. And I was supposed to be reinforcements.

I didn't like Area Fourteen's jokes.

At least Kerry would distract the other hit man, even if she didn't kill him. The other one was dead for sure; a punch in the throat doesn't lend itself to survival on the part of the victim.

I peered cautiously from my cover. I could barely see Kerry; she was hidden behind the seats. And the only way I could judge where the hit man was hiding was from the direction of his beams.

One of the seats flared up.

I pulled back, wondering what to do. Kerry had all the weaponry, and I couldn't risk making a break for the corpse out in the main area, if it was still there. Somebody would have called the cops, and they'd be in easy reach of the place. And I'd be an easy target.

Kerry solved the problem with a fast group of needles. There was a yell, then a thud and clatter.

I checked, carefully. Kerry was rising from behind the burned seats, her gun held in both small hands, turning in a slow circle, scanning the area, ready to fire. She was still wearing her shoulderbag.

The other body would be gone by now. Enemy never leave their losers lying around.

I broke my cover and started jogging out; I'd have to retrieve my bags, join Kerry, and then get us out of this place. There'd probably be more Enemy hanging around to make sure, and getting us to someplace safe so she could hand me a Bullet transporter was going to be the hard part.

As I started across the terminal building toward her, I looked down toward the entrance. A group of cops was on its way toward us at a fast trot, guns at the ready.

I signaled Kerry with a wave; there was a parking lot behind the building, and a nearby exit. Area Fourteen was going to have to sort out the mess himself; he'd gotten us into it, and I was damned if I was going to get screwed trying to clear it up myself.

Kerry dropped her gun back into her bag and signaled that she'd meet me on the outside. I followed her reasoning. She was closer to another exit.

She started running, and I started to change direction.

And the third man started firing.

A tight shot caught Kerry in her left shoulder, flaring her jacket up. She screamed and lost balance, hitting the floor hard.

I had a flash of the dead dog.

People started hitting the floor again—something I'd thought they did only in New York City—and I skidded around, almost losing my balance, starting toward Kerry.

She made it up from the floor just in time to avoid another shot. The beam singed her jacket as she staggered away.

I dived behind the row of seats that she'd left, and rolled, flattening. Three shots struck the row, making the plastic bubble, throwing up dark, oily smoke that made my eyes tear; I gagged. Kerry was almost at the exit; as I watched, she stumbled and hit the doors with her good arm thrown out. Her aim was good enough; her hand contacted metal instead of glass, and pushed the doors open as she fell through. She'd be safe enough on the other side, if she stayed behind concrete.

My turn now.

I came up and started running, zig-zagging. I knew where the sniper was now, behind the ticket desks, under plenty of cover. He could keep moving about to prevent being shot down before he completed his mission.

I heard sounds of firing as I closed on the doors, and blessed a couple of thousand fates. I'd forgotten the cops when Kerry had been hit; they were creating a distraction, unwittingly.

I hit the door, my arms held out, and stumbled through, slipping on the damp concrete. It had been raining when I came into St. Louis; I'd been looking for the Arch, but hadn't seen much.

I rolled as I hit the concrete sidewalk, pulled into the wall, and crawled along it until I reached Kerry. I felt silly, but if anyone wanted to use me for target practice, they'd have one hell of an awkward target.

Kerry was slumped against the wall; her needlegun was back in her hand. She was using her gun hand to clutch the wound in her shoulder, which was pointless. The wound would have been instantly cauterized.

I hunkered down next to her, gently pulled her hand away from her shoulder, and took the gun from her. There was no resistance.

The beam had gone straight through, leaving a neat hole and some serious burning.

She didn't say anything; she couldn't speak. She was in agony; her skin was a dirty gray under the light reflecting from the parking area, and her teeth were clenched together.

I stripped her jacket off carefully and laid it aside; I was going to need it in a minute. Then I unbuttoned her blouse.

"You know something, honey," I said, as I pulled it away from her shoulder, "here we are, everybody's getting shot at, and all I'm doing is undressing you."

I bit a wince in half, clamping my teeth together as I peeled the cloth away from the wound; sympathy or empathy. I'm lousy with it, most times. I start feeling like it's me who's been shot.

Kerry's face twisted; it was worse for her. I could have used a telepath to bleed off the sensations. I still had to get at the entrance wound.

"Better grit your teeth, lady," I said.

And ripped the blouse from the burn-holes all the way around.

"That's gonna go first—" I picked a section of bra strap off her shoulder; it had been cut neatly at both ends, leaving a short white piece and two charred tags—"on your expense account, I guess." I dropped the piece in Kerry's lap as I picked up her jacket. "I spend months trying to charm you out of this rig, and when I finally get started, I have to turn—" ripped the lining from the jacket with a grunt, checking the contents—"nurse and doctor. Kept telling you about how you were so attractive. And you get shot."

The beam had cut through the top of a strip of explosive F, but nothing else had been touched. And the explosive was useless without the detonators.

I stripped out the flat medipak and depressed the function key at the bottom, stretching the 'pak out to enough length to fit over Kerry's double wound. I bent back to her and applied it to her shoulder like a giant white Band-Aid, pressing it down gently.

As I set the last edge into place, a blue strip lit across the middle of the 'pak; treatment had started. Kerry relaxed with a sigh while I unclipped a medical transponder from the jacket and clipped it to her bra.

I sat back on my heels and looked at her. "How do you feel now?"

"I feel incredibly good," she said, in a weak voice. "I've just been shot, and I *obviously* feel wonderful."

I laughed, and she smiled wanly. "You're coming back to normal."

She sat up and got into a more comfortable position; the 'pak would have administered painkillers and stimulants at least.

She said, "Uh-huh. I wouldn't mind so much if you didn't chatter while doctoring me."

"That's to stop me from fainting," I said. Not quite true, but my nerves always managed to let me down when forced into things like this. If I didn't talk to myself, I'd probably slip up.

Kerry said, "No wonder, is it, that I ignore you in favor of stronger men?" She grinned. "Tomari, you're a fake. What's happening with the guy that shot me?"

"Just a minute." I crept around to a window, getting street mud on my hands; the knees of my pants were finished already, and my knees sore from crawling on the sidewalk.

I wiped my hands down the sides of my pants and looked through the glass, watching for a moment. The cops weren't doing too well; a couple of them were stretched out, and the rest were simply blasting away with no hope of hitting him. They needed a tactical squad, and, if my guess was good, one might even be gearing up now. But they didn't know what they were up against.

I did.

I dropped down and crept back to Kerry, passing on the situation as I settled down. I added, "He's going to massacre those cops unless somebody takes a bomb to him."

She looked at me. "You offering?"

"Well, you aren't." I picked up her jacket and ripped out two Bullets, passed one to her. "There's your ticket home."

"Hoo-hah, Area Fourteen is going to have words for me." She took the Bullet, held it up to look at it. "I wasn't supposed to have that needle-spitter, you know."

"Those Enemy cats weren't supposed to have those lasers either," I said, as I stripped out the explosive F strips from her jacket.

"You've hit the same point as me, you horrible black bastard, you."

"You've been reading Richard Prather again."

I turned her jacket over, pulled the buttons off, collecting them in one hand. When I had them all, I dropped them into my pocket, handed her jacket to her, and dropped the needlegun into her lap.

She folded the jacket, clumsily, and dropped it into her lap, over the gun. "That goes on the expense account as well."

"Uh-huh. I'll see you when I get upstairs. Then we can match accounts. That damn computer owes me for—" I started wadding the explosive, with the buttons inside—"a complete outfit." The explosive was as soft as molding wax in my hands.

"Aren't you going to kiss me goodbye, wounded heroine and all?" Kerry said.

I looked up at her and grinned. "Next you'll be fussing with your hair and clothes every time you get into a scrape."

"My hair's unmussable," she said.

"Okay, so I can't ruffle it."

Under the light, the bomb turned from gray to blue-green; activated.

"Ah, you're no fun, and I hate you for it."

I dropped the bomb into my pocket and kissed her. We were good friends; we hadn't really had time to get together much—her manor was Planet Earth, mine was anywhere Area Fourteen wanted to send me.

But I loved her all the same; she was my kind of Beautiful People.

We broke, and she winked, put the Bullet between her teeth, bit, swallowed, and waited for a moment.

Then, with a loud popping sound, she was gone. Air plucked at my clothes.

I looked up, for the moon; I couldn't see it for the buildings. Area Fourteen was a hundred twenty degrees ahead of it, at the forward Trojan point, screened from detection.

A kind of home for me.

I stood up, took the bomb out of my pocket, kneaded it a little more, and walked to the door; I hadn't been shot at out here, and I probably wouldn't be. They hadn't put much power into this hit, and they'd blown it.

I pushed the doors open warily, slipping inside and taking cover behind a pillar, watching. No one looked in my direction; the civilians had run for safety and the cops were too busy trying to flush the sniper; they were making a mess of the desks and walls.

I looked for the two dead Enemy; no sign. I hadn't expected to see any trace of them. The Enemy made a point of picking up their own garbage. We hadn't laid hands on a single Enemy casualty so far, and the same applied to us where the Enemy were concerned.

I wished that somebody would see fit to haul a living, breathing Kevven Tomari out of the firing line right now. But Area Fourteen wouldn't do that. I had a job to finish, and I was supposed to take care of myself.

The red beam from the sniper's weapon snapped through the air, took a cop in the chest, transfixed him, vanished, and let him fall, smoldering.

I broke cover, zig-zagged to more cover closer to the sniper, got down, and pulled out the Bullet I'd taken from Kerry's jacket, putting it between my teeth.

I charted my course carefully; this was going to be the shortest part of it, but also the most dangerous. I could easily get caught in a crossfire and cut to pieces.

I hefted the bomb, considered trying a throw from here, but I probably wouldn't be able to make it. I hadn't a clue about throwing anything, never mind a bomb that wasn't quite round.

I shook off nerves and broke.

My feet cracked hard on the floor, running with balance pulling me ahead. There was a shout from my right, a cop spotting me, and most of the firing ceased.

I slammed the bomb against my empty hand, sparking it into timing to detonation. Eight seconds.

. . . brought it back as I thudded zig-zag at the ticket desks, weaved away to avoid being targeted.

. . . hurled it with five feet to go; it didn't matter if it didn't land on his nose, the bang would get him anyway.

. . . twisted and dropped flat, biting the Bullet and swallowing, curling up in case I'd mistimed.

There was a pain in my side; I'd hit the desks while dropping, hadn't noticed it.

And then—

St. Louis Greyhound Bus Terminal vanished from around me.

I was flattened out on the receiving deck of Area Fourteen, two hundred forty thousand plus miles out in space.

I rolled over and stood up, grinning at the curious faces, alien and human, that looked down on me from various catwalks over and under my position.

And I heard Area Fourteen say, "When you have seen to your shoddy state, Kevven, report for debriefing in room eleven."

I pulled a sour face.

I was home again.

2 Base Brief

The figures on the screen were doing a frenzied dance, scuttling this way, that way, all ways together, bluecoats and civilians—

And Kevven Tomari.

There was no explosion, and the police caught the sniper as he emerged from cover.

Area Fourteen's voice said, "That is the way it should have been handled. There was no need to cause an explosion, with the destruction you should have known would follow."

I sighed. "You're a damned, tin-plated, transistorized two-star general. I didn't have much time to think. I used the nearest means to hand, and it went boom, and that's that."

"Mademoiselle Fossen was in possession of a needlegun, which you could have used."

"Oh sure, sure. Except the cops would have started popping 'em at me as well. And then there's your rules—"

"Mademoiselle Fossen had already utilized the weapon."

I hated debriefings, because it always meant I'd be told my mistakes, and have them demonstrated to me in the process, usually by simulation. Even when I thought I'd done a good job, Area Fourteen would pick holes in my operations, with infinite patience.

"Look, I don't have your brainpower, or your sheer intellect," I said, "Nor did I have the time to consider forty thousand ways of flushing a sniper before moving. He'd have shot every one of those cops and then me, if I'd given him time."

"You should have been aware of the third man," Area Fourteen said. His voice would have suited a mousy little accountant. Picky bastard. "Even the Enemy have more intelligence than to simply pursue and strike. The trap was simple. It caused you to show your hand, and quite neatly bracketed you."

I sighed again. "Dammit, you iron maiden, I didn't even know what I was walking into. You didn't tell me anything."

"To make you more aware of the possibility."

"I wasn't told I was going to be bracketed like that. Standing rule in that case is to expect a tag on the contact, and that's what I watched for. Now how the hell—"

"I would have expected a little more cautious thought on your part, Kevven."

The screen blanked out.

"And I'd have expected a damn sight more consideration on your part, you computerized idiot! For Christ's sake, I'm not a goddamned Builder."

He was silent for a moment. Then: "Very well. Perhaps I have been overestimating your abilities."

"You bet."

"Sarcasm is unnecessary."

"Oh, sure it is, solid-state."

I started getting out of my floating seat.

Area Fourteen said, "You did assist in saving the life of one of our best agents."

"And my own as well."

"I am not worried about your life, Kevven, as it is perfectly obvious that you achieved that aim, especially as I can see you quite well, standing and smirking at your silly sense of humor."

I pulled a face. "Yes sir, wise master djinni. Is that all?"

"No. I estimate the cost of repairing the damage you caused at approximately one half million dollars. The funding will have to be provided."

"I'll take 'em a check the next time I go through," I said, helpfully.

"You shall not. I calculate—"

"I noticed. Don't bother telling me what the result would be. I can guess. I was making a joke."

"You were?"

I sat down again, shaking my head. "You wouldn't notice."

"Perhaps not. However, to return to the subject, I was forced to reroute funds through a total of one thousand, three hundred fifty-one pathways, a waste of both my abilities and our own funds, said funds paying for your lifestyle, as well as journeys such as the one you undertook from Fresno.''

''Yeah, I gotcha. A waste, right?''

There was a sigh. ''Humans seem to have a capacity for destruction and violence that far exceeds anything else in my experience.''

''I don't think you have much experience then. I can name you a half-dozen other places where they get nastier, and more often too.''

''I can do very little with you while you insist on being obstreperous.''

I grinned. ''When we make the movie, Leonard Nimoy gets your part, solid state.''

There was a sigh. Area Fourteen loves theatrical gestures, all of which tend to be a little on the weird side, as he appears to address you from a point about five feet six inches from the floor, four feet in front of you. Incongruous; you start thinking he's a little invisible man after a while. Eventually you even start assigning him looks, characteristics, gestures, and so on.

He said, ''I am afraid I do not understand your humor. Nor do I wish to understand it. You appear to enjoy changing its parameters constantly, momentarily, and without warning.''

''Boy, oh boy,'' I said. ''Are you in *trouble*.''

''Explain, Kevven.''

I shrugged. ''I always got that the whole point of humor was changing it—kinda like a surprise, opening the jack-in-the-box and getting a custard pie in the face instead of—''

''No,'' Area Fourteen said, interrupting the explanation; he was probably way ahead of me anyway. ''I doubt that I need to know. I may investigate more thoroughly later.''

He paused for a moment, another gesture. Then, ''This Leonard Nimoy is an actor, correct?''

''Yep. Stage, screen, TV, radio. you name it.'' I grinned. ''Famous for his ears.''

''Hmm. I expect there was sarcasm intended. . . .''

I laughed. ''Precisely, Captain. Vanity isn't good for you.''

''Neither is it good for you, Kevven, though you may believe it is. I much prefer that you attempt to remain quiet on missions, though you may believe otherwise.''

I shook my head. ''Each to his own, m' man. I could lecture you on the importance of *baaad*ness, but you wouldn't be impressed. 'Sides, L.A.'s my gig not Harlem.'' I stood up again, smoothing a wrinkle out of my pants; I'd put clean ones on—the others had wound up damaged. ''Is there anything other than the lecture on the futility and expense inherent in using a quarter-pound of explosive F on snipers?''

''No. You might as well return to your quarters.''

''Wonderful,'' I said, and started to head for the door.

''Kevven.''

I stopped. ''What now, monocircuits?''

''I apologize for the shortness of your stay here this time.''

Don't believe the sentiment; there was a smirk in the SOB's voice, and I could hear it. Area Fourteen just had to have an accountant's mind—sneaky, nasty, evil, various other epithets.

''And your mother, too,'' I said.

And left before he could say anything else there.

Not that running out of a briefing room would stop him. It just made me feel better.

My quarters were located on the opposite side of the base; I'd never seen it from the outside, and I wasn't sure I knew my way around the inside all that well. I could reach the emergency boats—some lifeboats they were, Dustpipes; anywhere a personel transmission beam could get, so could they—as fast as anybody inside, but that was because of training. I hadn't spent all that much time on the base, despite being born on it. One of the disadvantages of setting up a legitimate and solid cover. University on Earth, even . . .

The part that strained my mind was trying to work out where the hell the bases had come from—they were everywhere in the universe, as far as I knew; as far as *anybody* knew, come to think of it. Mostly, they were located—still are—centrally; Area Fourteen was just in a convenient location within his sector, which includes a few assorted civilizations in a two hundred light-year span.

And you can bet, wherever the Builders' bases were, there was also a bunch of Enemy skulking around. I once tried checking back in records for the first appearance of the Enemy, and gave up after five hours and thirty thousand years. I could have asked, but that would have been cheating. And it wasn't just us little old humans getting it; from what I'd learned—and Enemy-ID was kindergarten stuff for us—the rest of the Universe had Enemy around them, looking like the natives.

The worst of it was, one Enemy hit-attempt wouldn't be the only one. I could guarantee another one, and more afterwards if that failed. We lost agents regularly.

It made life painful, not knowing what to expect from the people who didn't like us much. It made it even more so not knowing who or what the Builders were; we didn't even know what they looked like. But the Builders' mystery could be lived with; the Enemy preferred us dead.

That was the Enemy for you.

I slipped my comkey into my left hand and put my thumb over the plate, and went through my door as it irised open.

As the door irised shut again, the linkscreen at the bottom of the room flicked on with a message for me from Area Fourteen.

It said: *WELCOME HOME, MR. SPOCK*. SIGNED: *CAPTAIN KIRK*.

I grinned and said, "I didn't think it would last long, Area Fourteen."

"Highly illogical in the first place," his voice said from my comkey. "A momentary review of my storage was all that was required."

"I thought you didn't understand jokes." I clipped my comkey back onto my belt and went over to the wall, touching the bedbutton. The bed obligingly slid out for me. There wasn't much to speak of in the place; it wasn't required, as I generally didn't stay around for long.

"I understand them all too well—your idea of humor, however, I prefer not to understand."

"Good for you."

"Indeed."

He paused while I went and got myself a glass of water; I'm not much for alcohol. My vices are sex and smoking, no drugs of any sort. Fussy little me.

Then he said, "In the next one hundred twenty seconds, mark, you shall have a visitor." I groaned, loudly. That meant a mission, and, if I knew Area Fourteen, I'd end up somewhere or other getting shot at, or ducking spears, or just running like hell with something twice as fast, twice as heavy, and twenty times as mean right behind me and gaining.

"Your visit *was* rather short, wasn't it?" he finished.

I looked at the linkscreen for lack of anything else, and grunted something awkward that had roots in Harlem. It served well enough.

I waited.

Drily, Area Fourteen said, "I didn't have a mother."

I raised both eyebrows and Uncle Tommed the screen.

"And furthermore, I don't find your parody of your genetic and ancestral roots to be very becoming. It makes you look like a sauerkraut pudding covered in chocolate sauce: a most unsavory-looking thing indeed."

That did it. The combination of droll tone and apparently idiotic comment cracked me up. I almost doubled up, whooping. I made it to the bed before falling over, still howling.

Let me tell you, I've never been one for subtle appreciation.

I was starting the downhill slide when the doorboy bleeped. I slapped the comkey to open the door, and rolled over.

Annabelle Freeman walked in and stopped just inside the door, as it closed again, hands on her hips; she was wearing one of her white zip-up jump suits, the zipper ring halfway down, probably left there, forgotten, when she got distracted by something. Annabelle's like that; never all here. Not a surprising mental state for an expert telepath.

She looked at me for a moment, then said, "What in the hell are you laughing at?"

I didn't get the chance to answer right away.

Area Fourteen said, "He is displaying the total illogic of his species, Mademoiselle Freeman." The "Mademoiselle" was as theatrical as anything else; Anna was slated, like me, as an American. "I shouldn't really waste my time informing you, as you, too, are of that species."

I sat up, with a Cheshire Cat grin, and turned to Annabelle. "I think he sounds more like Mr. Spock every time I come up here."

She grinned back. "I suppose you've told him that already."

"Yeah, I have," I said. I could feel the giggles coming again. "But he thinks he's Captain Kirk!"

And I collapsed again, shaking with laughter that hurt more with each shudder. Annabelle just stood there, shaking her head and grinning at the sight of me.

Finally I managed to stop gasping and whooping, and settled

back, breathing deeply to steady myself, wiping my eyes with the back of my hand.

Area Fourteen, never missing a chance at putting a damper on something, said, ''If you'd continued another half minute, I would have called sick bay and had you taken away for examination and treatment.''

Meaning, I assumed, he wished I'd continued so he could have had me carted off. Computers are efficient enough, but give them half a chance and they'll be dissecting everything within reach for new ideas. The problem is that they don't get queasy or have to eat.

Hooboy, I thought, as my stomach lurched—that dead dog was still playing hell with my digestion.

I said, ''Sorry I spoiled your fun.''

''Hmm,'' he said. ''However, as you are now in control of yourself, I will leave you with Mademoiselle Freeman.''

''You do that. You're just the type to leave us big baaad buck nigger bastards with a po' liddle white trash girl.''

Who is also a black belt in karate, can read minds when she really wants to—she usually leaves mine alone out of courtesy, although her regular companion, who looks like a cauliflower, often takes a peep—and who could probably flatten me with a mindshot.

Annabelle is also almost as tall as me, shaped nicely—after all, being tall doesn't mean being weirdly shaped necessarily, look at Margaux Hemingway—long haired, raven division, and looks thin-faced; somebody once compared her to a ferret in looks, although that's a bit extreme. She's not bad looking when you think about it.

Anna said, ''If you ever saw that mythical buck nigger, you'd go so white the Ultrabrite people would be after you for the secret.''

''Yass, Missy,'' I said with a grin. ''So what has Special Abilities got to do with me this time?''

She pulled a face and strolled to the wall furniture panel, punching for an easy chair. She settled into it as it popped up, crossed her legs, and smoothed the knee of her jump suit.

She said, ''Nothing much. It's really just a matter of information-gathering.'' She changed position, curling up, getting comfortable. ''But I'm required as a link, so that you can understand the background you'll be getting. The sentient at the other end of the link was on the scene just recently—she made the arrangements, although I'm not sure how. I think some sort of hypnosis was used to avoid trouble.''

That meant telepathic hijinks on the part of the sentient in question; Annabelle's trouble was that she used ''hypnosis'' in the telepathic sense—direct mental jiggery-pokery, mainly pokery, with the jiggery for extras.

She went on, ''The other thing is that you have abilities as an operator that will probably assist you on the mission. In case there's any trouble.''

She ran a hand through her long black hair, and looked around at my quarters.

''They aren't much,'' I said, ''but they're all I was given. Someone decided that, being a natural transient who never sticks in place, I didn't need anything fancy.'' I stretched a leg out along the bed, wriggling to get comfortable on the lumps, and gave it a mighty whack with my heel. It thudded dully. ''Or comfortable, for that matter.'' I returned my attention to Anna. ''So I have a mission that requires some little help from SAS. What're my chances of coming back in a rubber bag?''

Anna blinked and wrinkled her nose at me. ''None at all.'' She shrugged. ''It's a fairly easy mission.''

I sighed and shook my head. ''Anna, my little love-dove, the last time anybody told me that I nearly came home in a *doggy*-bag. The friendly natives were, in order, cannibalistic, advanced, and hungry for the latest foreign food; me, in case you don't get the idea.''

''I mean it,'' she said, sounding offended.

''So did they.''

She stood up and walked to the door, standing with her back against it and looking at me, smiling a little wickedly.

''Look who's complaining,'' she said. ''Weren't your ancestors cannibals?''

I got up off the bed and joined her at the door, leaning against it with my arms to either side of her and looking lovingly into her eyes. Grinning, naturally.

''Nope, they weren't. They were all vegetarians.''

''You and an oversexed Shiktabria, Tomari.''

I made a face and she made one back.

''At least they always kept away from fatty foods,'' I said, and projected a feeling of desire at her. I wasn't sure whether it would register; it didn't work most of the time, but sometimes she'd be in the right frame of mind to pick it up.

She was this time. She pulled a rueful face.

She said, "I told you about that mythical big buck, Tomari."

"Well, Missy, Luba me hear tell you is unloved around this place."

She grinned. "That's my secret."

I smiled. "Yours and Area Fourteen's, you mean. It gives him a thrill in his rectifiers."

"I don't have rectifiers," Area Fourteen said.

He sounded a little wistful.

I said, "Poor you. Would you mind not peeking through the keyhole? I'm trying to seduce this woman here, and I have to concentrate."

"Should you succeed—"

"You'll be surprised. Now go away."

He didn't say anything more.

I turned back to Anna, who was leaning with her arms folded.

"Where was I?"

"You were trying to talk yourself into stealing a kiss from me."

I gave her an offended look.

"Talk myself into it? I was actually trying to assuage your fears, my dear Annabelle."

She grinned. Wickedly.

"I'm waiting, Tomari. I have to have something to tell Sweet Jane about."

Sweet Jane was Anna's constant companion, in most places. The cauliflower.

I said, "Where is she?"

"Sleeping. Silly thing was up for a week researching."

"You'd better tell Jane cauliflower's good for her."

"That was not a funny remark."

"And the same to you, Bubble-belle."

"Why does my heart become solid concrete when you try endearments like that?"

"Uh-uh, the liquid concrete just sets, that's all."

She wrinkled her nose. "Anybody ever tell you that you're a mushbag?"

"Once in a while."

There was a space of silence, and then she said. "I knew it. You're just leading me on again, Tomari."

So I kissed her.

And that computerized sonofabitch who was watching—blew a bronx cheer.

It was protoplasmic.

It was a protoplasmic *lump*.

Colored a sort of putty gray.

It stood in the corner of Annabelle's office, like a potted plant.

It shuddered.

And burped.

Then shivered and jumped.

I counted another two shudders, seven shivers, and four jumps—it left the ground only slightly, never moving from its spot—before it burped again. When the report came, it came with the sprouting of a dark blister on the surface of the lump.

The blister extruded a round eye, which stared blankly at us; the eye looked a little like the multi-faceted eye of an insect blown up to giant proportions, and was attached to a thick tentacle.

I looked from the Lump to Annabelle, who was watching my reactions. Naturally.

I said, "What the hell *is* it, Bubbles?"

She grinned and looked at the Lump. "It's a pet."

Blurrrp!

I looked back to the Lump, and a warm blob hit me in the face, feeling around and patting my cheeks. After a moment, it developed fingers and attempted to twist my nose off.

Then it dropped away, apparently finished checking out my face.

Anna said, "It's a mimic. We've got a couple in for study. I keep this one in here to impress the visitors."

Boorrrch!

Hand and eye vanished together.

I said, "I'm impressed, I think. Any practical value?"

Anna went around her desk and settled down into her chair, pushing it back and putting her feet up on her desk, her hands behind her head.

She said, "So far, not really. We're trying to work out what it uses as a chameleon mechanism, to adapt it for use, but all we can tell so far is that it needs a fully malleable form. Plus a lot of energy." She nodded at the lump in the corner, as it quivered. "It isn't too good at imitations unless it has a template to hand. Added to that, having developed the central ability to mimic forms, it hasn't developed any real sentience. It's a protoplasmic plant."

"You were hoping for something to balance with the Enemy, huh?"

She shrugged. "More or less. Special Abilities needs something like it, even if only for spying purposes."

"Good luck with it."

She nodded.

Special Abilities Section is the place to find the particular oddity you need; the Builders' bases aren't normal by most standards, but SAS goes a bit further than even that. The main aim is to locate certain abilities in sentient forms, or, failing that, in forms without sentience, as long as they're alive. Name it, and SAS will try to find it—a tank capable of knocking over a city before breakfast, also capable of raising a family of little tanks—that's SAS's department; you can tell by the clatter of little tank treads in the nursery; want something that'll sit on your desk and process bauxite for you, without mess? Ask SAS for details, and figure on reasonable profits. I hadn't dared to go through SAS's records—I'm too easily fascinated, and I have to work now and then. But watch out, because the lissome young thing next to you could have, in her handbag, something that looks like one of those hairy key rings; it's liable to be a mixture of cigarette lighter, trash disposer, and flame-thrower. And it breathes, as well. SAS, naturally.

I said, "Well, seeing as I'm here, why don't we get on with what you have to do?"

Anna swung her feet down, nodding. "I'd better give Jane a call."

I groaned. "*Sweet* Jane?" Anna nodded again. "What the hell does Sweet Jane have to do with this?"

Anna looked slightly offended. "She's best suited to handle the other side of the mindlock."

"And why, may I ask?"

Anna smiled. "Your digestion. The sentient involved isn't exactly pleasant to look at, Kevven."

"So? I've seen some pretty ugly things in my life, including a bunch of characters out to eat me."

"That's *their* digestion they're playing with. I know you. You're queasy."

"Sure I am, Bubbles, sure I am." I sighed and shook my head. "Okay, send in the troops. If it's Jane, it's Jane."

"Good." She tapped a plate on her desk and spoke into the intercom. Then, looking up at me. "Jane's bringing the sentient. Honest to a pink giraffe, Tomari, I don't know why I like you—I expect my subconscious senses a man underneath the wimp."

"You want to find out?" I said.

"One kiss doth not a night in paradise make." She smiled. "Until the end of time, Kev, we'll upbraid each other."

I shrugged.

"Well, you know how it goes. Ships passing in the night, with nary a hoot of a foghorn to acknowledge the other's existence."

"And you're getting sentimental."

"A sentimental slob, yes, that's me."

We were prevented from taking *that* any further by,* =*What's a slob?*

Sweet Jane had arrived.

I'm not sure why I don't like Jane; perhaps it has something to do with her being built along the lines of an oversized cauliflower. My mother used to force-feed cauliflower to me as a youngster, and I've hated it from the first. Perhaps it's Jane's talent for sarcasm and summing up everything immediately after everybody else; generally, she does it to me to annoy me. Anyway, if it's because of the force-fed cauliflower, I'd say it was a lousy prejudice. Jane's a perfectly normal cauliflower, and often inseparable from Annabelle. The sticking-close attitude is typical of telepaths.

Jane went on,* =*If it is a negative that applies to Tomari, then I am probably in agreement with his self-description.*

Jane was enclosed in her normal survival bubble, riding a floater plate attached to her underside. Her home environment was something on the order of a planetary smog as thick as the proverbial pea-soup, pressures to match, composed in the main of ammonia; the mobile survival bubble she used had a clearer view, and I wished, every now and then, that whoever had built it had used the smog instead.

In front of her was a closed environment, a dark green, squarish box, about a meter and a half on a side. She guided it over to Anna's desk and let it settle down slowly.

I said, "Hello, Jane, and how are you?"

*=*Not well for seeing you, Tomari. I hear you boffed a mission downside.*

I was glad nobody would be able to tell I was blushing.

Anna looked at me curiously.

"I didn't screw up, Bubbles. That computerized goof-up ticked me off for working fast."

"What the hell did you do?" she asked.

"Blew up a sniper with a handful of F. In a Greyhound terminal."

She laughed. "I never did like those places."

"Yeah." I waved a hand at the box on the desk between us. "Let's have a look."

"It's your lunch, Tomari."

She opened it up as I stood up. I looked down into the red-lit environment.

Anna was almost right. But I didn't lose my lunch. Not quite. I did say, "Oh man, is he shit-ugly."

"She," Anna corrected.

"Yeah."

There was an eye, the size of a football, which seemed lidless; around it, blobs of protoplasm that looked like gray-green marbles. *Slimy* marbles. Enough tentacles to make Medusa feel cheated, from the size of tiny writhing worms to long, thin cables. A beak like an octopus, and a sickening color to match. The eye appeared blood-red in the light of the environment.

We looked at each other for a moment, probably feeling about the same at stomach level.

The alien opened her beak, gave a rasping hiss, and writhed.

With a sizz, the lid went down, and, THUD! closed.

I looked up, and, with venom, said, "you sonofabitch, Area Fourteen."

He chuckled happily; whether or not that heap of circuits felt *any* emotion was another matter entirely

Anna said, "I told you."

Sweet Jane floated over the desk, went around Anna's back,

and stopped over the box, apparently looking at me. But she was blind in my range of sight. She saw mainly in radar fashion, all around. *Sensitive* radar, though. It saw features when she concentrated.

She said,* =*Didn't like her, hmmmmm?*

I ignored her and said to Anna, "I won't be working with her people, will I? I don't think my stomach's that strong."

Annabelle shook her head. "You'll be working on a humanoid planet. It's a pickup; this is just to give you the details of the arrangements."

I looked at the tank, and at Jane. No movement. Jane was probably discussing me with dark, green, and ugly.

I scowled at Anna. "That puts me out of our sector, then. There isn't a humanoid race around here. Where am I going?"

Area Fourteen said, "Area Ten Seventy-Four. I feel sorry for them, I really do."

"Oh, shut up," I said, testily. Area Fourteen has a talent for getting under my skin. "No, cancel that. Where the hell's Ten Seventy-Four?"

"M31 in Andromeda." He said that innocently.

I sighed and shook my head. "Jesus, you sure as hell do pick 'em. I suppose this one is even tougher than the last thing you had me do? That one you told me *nothing* about!"

"Which one was that?" Anna asked.

"Earth," I said. "I'll tell you later."

Jane said,* =*You'll be a long way from home.*

I looked at the cauliflower inside the survival bubble, and said, "Jane, I wasn't aware you really cared about me." I noticed that Annabelle was grinning. "Now that's a surprise to me."

* =*Surprise? I didn't say anything about caring for you. Just that you'll be a long way from home. . . .*

3 How to Kidnap a Princess

I had to hand it to Area Fourteen. He was, at least, imaginative. Very. He picked some interesting places, and then let me get into trouble in them.

Take Aureon IV, the sole populated planet in a group of twelve, plus assorted asteroids. It has a 1.09 gravity, a bit more than Earth's, but not enough to bother me; I'd trained for heavier gravities.

Neither did the weather bother me, even if it was dry enough to suck water from the skin; I was dressed for that, looking a bit like an Arab. Temperature was up around a hundred ten Fahrenheit in the shade; I'd been in worse.

Nor was it the fact that I'd had to pass up riding to my destination—the riding animals around here looked like a cross between a dragon and a kangaroo, big, mean, and bouncy. I'd walked long distances before, even run them. And it was only about five miles across the desert to Kathalya.

I wasn't even bothered by the fact that, though the Aureons were at the level of crude weaponry that went bang instead of slash, I wasn't armed all that well—the weapon I had was a disguised gun that went bang rather than zap, and I prefer the zap types over the bang types, and it was in a weirdly designed pouch hanging on the belt of my robe. I also had a bunch of Bullets and some explosive F and detonators in the robe.

It wasn't even that this whole thing was a cross-eyed arrangement that forced me to act as a one-man kidnap squad rather than a normal, sane envoy.

None of that. Nope.

Nervously, I looked down again, and, feeling remarkably

disassociated from everything, felt my stomach scrabble furiously for safer ground.

Lots of sharp rocks down there.

Maybe a thousand meters *straight* down the side of the mountain.

My toes, in sandals, were perhaps a millimeter from the edge.

Fighting vertigo and an urge to flail my arms frantically, I looked back up, trying to make my feet grow roots as I stared out at the horizon. I reached behind me with one hand, trying not to quiver, feeling for a surface. I didn't contact rock.

I hoped it *was* a mountain. If it was a rock bridge, my fortunes were going to take one hell of a plunge.

I slid my left foot back, slowly, wanting to scream, heard it and felt it scrape over the rock and grit, and stopped it. I slid my other foot back to join it, then reached back again. No rock face yet.

I slid my left foot back again, carefully. There could be a crevice behind, even—

Nothing.

I slid my other foot back, and turned in the space I had, trying to avoid a radius any larger than a dime; I was scared badly. It's no fun to come out of shift on the edge of a sheer drop down the side of a mountain, without any warning.

I was starting to think that the Builders had programmed the Mastercomps to be as evil as possible. . .

The side of the mountain was three feet away. Crossing that space was about the best time I've had in my life.

I put my back against it and slid down until my butt touched rock, then relaxed, looking out over the sky and the horizon. I couldn't see Kathalya, but that was because it was off in another direction. There was mainly desert, otherwise.

The Aureons were lucky. All their populated areas were linked by land bridges. So there was one ruling clan, with branches all over the place, one of them in Kathalya. A segment of which I was to kidnap, a young Oriental thing six feet tall, with lovely, long, black hair and a taste for knife-fighting. Told you about those Mastercomputers, didn't I?

The lady was a princess, and had the name of Meheilahn M'jura ka Opul, which, presumably, she used to run through attackers; she was around twenty-three Terran years old.

I was supposed to charm her and remind her of her agreement, then spirit her away, assuming she didn't cut me up for practice before I said anything.

I checked my equipment and supplies again, for something to do—yep, Bullets all there, medical transponders, medipaks, explosive F, transceiver, powerpack, lockpick, knife kit, vitamin supplements, reduced rations, gun and assorted ammunition clips—knockouts, explosive bullets, and so on—thin cord usable for tying recalcitrant guards, toothbrush.

My supplies were intact, as well, consisting of water bottles attached to my belt, and money of assorted denominations. The Mastercomputer had given me a somnicourse in language and general customs; I didn't expect to be here long enough to require anything else.

I stood up again and stretched, unclipping a water bottle and taking a swig. Ice rattled in the bottom—I prefer to take my drinks with ice.

I clipped the bottle back and looked at the edge of the plateau.

That drop was sharper than a whore's neckline.

I glanced around, located the downslope, and started walking. The path narrowed after a hundred yards, but there was enough room to stay calm; I still had to hug the wall to feel more or less safe.

It wouldn't be long before dusk; I would reach Kathalya just as night was starting to fall.

They were dressed in light armor the color of the desert, and they approached me on either side, cautiously, crude, blunderbuss-like weapons raised, not quite aimed at me. I was wary; those horns might be crude and noisy, but what came out of them could shred me like a combine harvester cutting wheat.

I'd expected something like this; civilizations below the age of true technology tend toward protectionism. The sun goes down, the barriers go up.

Well, I could go in another way, and get the drop on the guards, if any.

I halted five feet from the two, and kept my face lowered; my head was covered by the hood of the long robe.

The one to my left said, "Your business, stranger?"

I said, "I wish to enter the city, praised warrior. I have important business to conduct tomorrowday."

"You must remain without, honored stranger. There are lodgings for latecomers." I raised my eyes as he pointed to the east. "That, or you may spend the night in the gatehouse."

The meaning was clear; I'd get a cell for the night.

I said, "My thanks, praised warrior."

And looked up.

Their metal masks covered their faces, hiding their expressions, but it was easy enough to imagine what they looked like.

They stared at me for a moment, while I stood there looking stupid instead of dropping flat. I could have been killed there and then.

Instead of firing, they both dropped their weapons, turned tail, and fled towards the city, screaming in terror. Amongst the noise, as they vanished into the distance, I could make out something that one of them was screaming over and over.

It was *"Black Devil!"*

I object to it, I really do. My mother gave me a good upbringing, and I only eat people who've been well-cooked first. I had a *good* mother.

I shook my head and changed course, taking gun out of the pouch. It was a squat creation, made along the lines of the Aureon's own weaponry. Except: better balance, more accurate, more powerful, and fitted with a laser sight, which made aiming simple.

The next two guards found that out as they approached me. I'd loaded the knockout clip, and as they came towards me, I looked up, gave them a big smile, and said, "I'm a Black Devil."

That froze them both for just long enough.

I centered the red dot on the exposed flesh of one, fired, changed my aim to the other, who'd started running already, and centered the red dot on his tailbone. He yelled as the knockout stung his butt, and fell forward.

He tried to get up once, then fell back, unconscious. Whether from fright or the knockout I wasn't sure. Whatever the mamas of these boys told them in youth, it was pretty powerful stuff. All I got was Mr. Nobody.

I rolled the face-down guard over, so he could breathe, and left them both as they were. They wouldn't wake up for some time, and it was unlikely anybody would find them in the sand, especially at night.

Getting into the city itself was a piece of cake. They'd built a wall with plenty of gaps in it, for guards to go through. I simply walked through one.

Oh, yeah.

After laying the guards out with the knockouts. . . . .

I'm unsubtle, but I get the job done.

Kathalya's nightlife was in full swing when I went through the city. I took back alleys until I reached what seemed to be a high-class tavern, and prowled around until I found something that looked like local transportation for single Aureons, and, in the name of universal peace and justice, commandeered it.

Or, if you like, I stole something that looked like a bicycle from behind something that looked like a tavern, and didn't get shot in the ass for doing it.

I pedaled through the back alleys—the effort wasn't much less than walking, really, as the Aureons hadn't thought of gear trains yet—and stopped near a wide boulevard to recheck my mental map. From the direction I was heading, and the place I was, I wasn't too far from the main palace. It was set inside a circular park, like a jewel in a ring; it was one of the few places in Kathalya with any real plumbing to speak of. The damned city smelled like a cesspool to me, the city-bred spacehopper.

Or maybe it smelled like a skunk works.

Whatever, it *stank*.

I started pedaling again, and eventually ran out of back alleys to pedal down. Now it was a matter of crossing the wide road that hemmed in the park, getting over the railings into it, and avoiding the guards. Which meant a wait, because the road still had a lot of people using it, even at this late hour.

I hid the bike in an alley, settled down in a section of another that smelled less like the skunk works than the rest, and sipped water, taking a vitamin supplement and a bite of concentrated food while thinking over what I had to do.

It was typically silly. Sneak in, get this princess Meheilahn M'jura ka Opul to bite a Bullet, and take her back to Area Fourteen with me. It would have been easier to have a Bullet delivered by envoy and pick her up that way, instead of playing games and getting me messed up.

Oh well, they never do anything the easy way. Bureaucracy.

More interesting was the resemblance of the Aureons to Earthers; parallel evolution was a possibility, for sure—I'd studied instances of it in base school. But the odds against said evolution producing *strictly* similar biological arrangements were in the number areas where my mind couldn't go.

Fact: Aureons were biologically almost identical to Earthers; discount the one or two slightly different placements of internal organs, because if you start far enough back, normal race adaptation will account for it. An Earther could interbreed with an Aureon, easily, without the problem of biological alteration.

Assumption: the Builders had been seeding planets here and there, not necessarily with *homo sapiens*, but with all kinds of life forms, from the basic bug in the goop on primordial worlds to sentient creatures. So, if one, there would be others to match.

Possibility: the bases manned by sentients from all over the universe—we had sentients from other sectors at Area Fourteen—could be watch stations.

Which made me think up—

Question: what the hell is going on?

Answer: *I don't know.*

And didn't; I must have asked myself that question a half-million times from the time I was able to think of it.

Thinking of the Builders made me think of the old man with the big book; gathering knowledge and events from all over, a universal keeper of records. Perhaps . . . But that made it futile when there was so much we could do yet. . . .

And we hadn't done a thing.

I recognized where my thoughts were leading. Frustration. *I* wanted to do more, but I was just one sentient among millions, probably billions, most of whom were more experienced than me, more intelligent, better qualified physically, or everything there plus other things.

The fact that everything seemed to be designed to go against me didn't help—after being outfitted for this jaunt, it would have to turn out that the damn computer hadn't bothered with superstitions. Leaving me to find out that something called a Black Devil was looked on as a Vile And Nasty Thing down here.

I made myself comfortable amongst the garbage, dirt, and skunk works smell in the alley, and tried to ignore the stench as I dozed off. Sleep for a couple of hours wouldn't hurt.

When I woke up, the skunk smell had grown about fifteen skunks stronger, and one arm was asleep, resting in some garbage. It woke up painfully; the worst part of it. Otherwise, I felt relaxed and wide awake. An advantage of sleeping well;

snatch a couple of hours here and there on a mission, and I'm usually fine.

I stood up and brushed dirt and garbage off the robe, walking back to my vantage point. The main ringroad had emptied of people by now; my worry was the patrols around the park. They moved in a set pattern, and I'd been given both patterns and timings; one two-man patrol would pass opposite my position, and I could expect around twenty minutes dead time. I'd have to wait five to let them get out of sight before moving.

It was fifteen minutes before I dared move; the patrol had passed by around eight minutes before. The extra three minutes was for luck.

I gathered up my robes and sprinted across the road, watching for people, and leapt, grasping the top spikes of the railings. They weren't much use for keeping people out—that was the job of the patrols.

I hauled myself up and over, landing in a crouch on the grass inside, scanning side to side quickly, the gun in my hand; knockouts only. When there's no need to put the final touch on a job . . .

I started through the park, keeping to high cover and shadow, watching for patrols. It wasn't that I didn't trust Area Ten Seventy-Four; I just didn't trust the patrols to stick to the pattern and times given. A break for a pee, or a crap, or a drink, or dawdling, or boredom making them speed up, any one of a thousand things, and my black hide would be displayed as the first Black Devil caught for show, and sorry we couldn't keep him alive—they eat people, you know.

Which was what kept me alive when I found that one of the patrols had gone anti-clockwise instead of clockwise, for a break in the monotony.

I flattened into the grass, hood over my head, breathing as quietly as possible, which was still too loud for my nerves, as was my heartbeat.

A plant by the side of my head blinked suddenly.

I almost jumped up, screaming, but managed to grit my teeth and hold my breath, hardly even quivering. It had given me a hell of a fright; I hadn't met any plants that had blinked at me before, although I'd spoken to a tank.

The "eyes" that had blinked were photosensitive organs;

probably a response to my landing. There was a little light around . . .

The guards tramped by, a short distance away, on one of the pathways through the palace grounds.

I stayed where I was until I was certain they were some distance away, then broke cover.

I made it to the side of the palace without any trouble; but it proved what I believed about plans. You can't trust a damn one of them.

I found an ornamental water spigot, probably for the gardeners, and used it to clean the worst dirt from my robe and hands. The flow was only a trickle at best, and not at all noisy.

A bit damp, but cleaner than I would have been without it, I started looking for a door.

There was a lone guard walking around the side of the palace. He was in front of me, facing away, with plenty of exposed neck.

I raised the gun, and fired.

He didn't make a sound as he folded to the ground.

I dragged him into cover, and shifted brush over him; it would hide him long enough, I hoped. He'd be in for it the day after, though.

I found a way in soon after that. You can't beat going in the front door, I'll tell you . . .

I picked the lock in seconds flat, eased the door open, tensing for the sound of alarms, gunfire, or just plain yelling, and slipped inside, shutting the door behind me. It was dark; no lights in the corridor. It didn't matter that much.

I relocked the door behind me. I wasn't going to need it again.

I paused for a moment, orienting myself against the blueprint in my mind, then started walking, feeling along the wall. There was a branch corridor somewhere along here, first turning to my right . . .

My hand fell into empty space, and I turned the corner. There was a light at the end of the branch; good enough. I sped up, watching for the next turn, caught it, and walked even faster, gun in hand.

Nobody jumped on me, shouted at me, or tried to shred me with a blunderbuss. It was as easy as dropping a brick on my foot. I was well within my time limits.

The princess's apartments were behind a pair of ornate wooden doors; from the look of them, they were thick wood. And if I knew my palaces, they were probably triple-layered. Wood, iron core, wood. It makes for efficient defense.

I set to work on the lock, had it picked in seconds—simple locks, these Aureons had—and opened the door, slipping through and relocking it behind me.

I put the gun back in its pouch, straightened my still-damp robe, and marched stolidly across the massive room I was in, to the bedchamber door, opening it and walking through.

Home free, just like that.

Well . . .

Maybe not just like that.

Area Ten Seventy-Four had mentioned the princess's proclivity for knives, and I'd probably walked in a little too boldly.

The princess herself was as pretty as promised; heck, beautiful by a long shot. Her hair was unbound, and she wasn't wearing much. But I wasn't concerned with that, despite it being one of my main interests.

The most interesting thing right now was long, thin, fitted with an ornate hilt, silvery, and very sharp.

A knife.

With the point neatly placed against my throat, just *waiting . . .*

And the eyes of a princess fixed coldly and darkly on my face.

I raised my hands and placed them on top of the hood, locking my fingers. I didn't want to make that knife angry; there is no fury like a knife scorned, no matter what they say about women.

It pricked.

"Who are you?" the princess asked coldly.

I smiled and said the first thing that came to mind.

"A Black Devil."

Ooooops.

The knife pricked again, threatening to go *slash.*

She said, "I have no interest in the petty idiocies of the commoners. Who are you?"

I resolved that the next time I saw Annabelle it wasn't going to be kisses and cuddles for her; kicking and clobbering was in mind. At least. *If* I lived through this.

Well, the lady questioning was pretty nice, and had a marvelously musical voice. Pity she had to be nasty with me.

I smiled even wider—ah, the Ultrabrite people should have seen me then . . . well, lost chances.

I said, "My name is Kevven Tomari, my good lady." She didn't say anything to that; it wasn't an Aureon's name, for certain. I went on, "I have been sent to bring you to the place where I live—"

Prick.

I stopped and took a deep breath.

I tried again with, "An agreement was made between you and an agent associated with me to have you accompany me to Area Fourteen. I am here to pick you up—"

Prick.

I stopped trying, watching her. She was frowning, but her eyes didn't leave my face for an instant. Such pretty eyes, too; almost almond-shaped, flared with expert traces of makeup around the edges. But she didn't really need much; she was beautiful from painted toenails to dark, shining hair.

And she knew it, too, the sultry bitch.

That knife was worrying me even more at the moment; with its owner getting distracted, the damn thing was starting to press in without being supposed to. Any second now, I was going to swallow to get rid of the constriction in my throat, and my adam's apple was going to get sliced in two going up and down.

While I waited for the slicing of my main vocal attribute, she puzzled over me.

It was unnerving.

Eventually, she said, "I do not understand. What are you talking about?"

Her eyes narrowed, giving her an unpleasantly vicious look.

I moved my lips, keeping my teeth gritted, and let air whistle out; I'd been holding my breath. As it was, I had my head pulled back as far as possible.

I whispered, "Uh, listen, if it's anything to you, I talk better when there's no knife in my throat."

"I think you may talk too much as it is, and not enough of that of which you should talk. But—" The blade left my throat, although she didn't put it away; she was keeping it handy to throw at me.

As I relaxed, she added, "I hope that you are not so foolish as to play games with a *ryah*-sticker."

I grimaced; a *ryah* wasn't a pig-analog. It was a beastie the size of a rhinoceros, and twice as mean.

"Do you mind if I sit down?" I asked.

She shook her head and I located a place on the floor to seat myself. She sat on the giant bed across from me, knife held in throwing grip in her lap. It was still a bad situation, but not as bad as trying to explain something to someone who has a knife at your throat.

While I recovered my poise, such as it was, the princess said, "You had better explain yourself coherently, unless you wish me to call a guard."

That she hadn't called one already was a pretty good sign; she was curious about me—after all, it isn't every day that a superstition walks in your bedroom.

"I've already told you *who* I am," I said. "*What* I am is for you to decide."

She watched me while I looked for a way to phrase what I wanted to say; I needed a way that wouldn't push her into yelling for guards, or whatever she did to get guards in here.

"Okay," I said. "I'm from a place called Area Fourteen. That's my home. I'm a kind of agent for them—"

"A spy?" she said.

I shrugged. "Not really. More of a special soldier."

She nodded. She understood that well enough.

I went on, "The thing is, I was sent here to fetch you back to my home." I held up my hand as she started up, reaching for a cord. "I'm not supposed to kidnap you, Princess. You've already agreed to go. Or so I was told when I started out."

She sat down on the big bed again, tugging at her lower lip with her free hand, watching me suspicously. She seemed puzzled, but said nothing. It was beginning to get on my nerves; if something wasn't done about this idiotic situation soon, I was going to have a go at putting her out with a knockout shot and carrying her off that way. I should have done it in the first place—but, no, I'd had just a *little* faith in the arrangements.

"Look," I went on, "I don't know how the arrangements were made, but I know who—*what*—made them. And it probably came in a big box, brought to you by a deliveryman who probably looked stupid." Her eyebrows rose slightly at that; either she was tickled by my description, or I'd struck a memory square on the nose. The memory, I hoped. "You might not have seen anything particularly ugly in the box, but the creature has a lot of tentacles, a beak, and one massive eye, and is enough to make you throw up just by looking at it once.''

It wasn't exactly the most concise description, but it seemed to be sufficient; it started the princess nodding thoughtfully. She also relaxed her knife-hand a little more, laying the blade in her lap. After a few moments of that, she stood up, looking at me, and pointing with the knife blade.

She said, ''You speak of the *Fra Fra Seyoh*.'' I probably did, too. ''I begin to understand you now. You speak in a confusing way.''

I spent a few spare seconds damning solder out of Ten Seventy-Four; I'd been fed the right language, and the wrong conversion program. I should have been given a speech-habit program, preferably upper-class bigwig. I was speaking in my usual way, even in Aureon's language. I was only getting a little of it through the customs program I'd been fed—it takes time to learn to use a language correctly, even *with* a proper program. Damned stupid computers.

I said, without thinking, ''Well, I think you've got it.'' She looked puzzled again. I corrected quickly for it. ''I believe, Princess, that we understand each other now.''

She nodded. ''I believe we do. But whoever you work for must prefer to gamble clumsily—this seems a strange way in which to work. To me.''

I stood up and stretched. ''That's two of us, Princess. I'm a little annoyed by it.'' I paused. ''Seems it leaves me with my foot in my mouth every so often, and that's more often than I'd like.''

She smiled sarcastically; she'd gotten that unpleasantly vicious look back, and it played hell with those aristocratically beautiful features—I liked her looks from the start, once we'd gotten the knife out of the way.

She said, ''Perhaps it would be well for your foot to be placed firmly in your mouth. It might keep you from jabbering.''

That one *hurt*.

''Whatever,'' I said, stepping quickly on a retort—those retorts get in *everywhere*, don't you know—''we had better get you ready to—''

''I must prepare that which I am taking with me,'' she interrupted.

I shook my head. "You won't need to take anything. We've got all you need where you're going to." I had a sudden thought about all of this; she wasn't going just for the joyride. Not her. "What are you getting out of this?"

She crossed her legs, running a slim hand down one thigh; the movement was made all the more interesting by the knife that was in the hand she used.

She said, "I am to receive protection for my people, and help for my farmers." She paused momentarily, then added, "Do they tell you nothing?"

I grinned. "That's right." I mulled over it a moment; agricultural help I could understand. Aureon had a lot of desert, and something could be done about that. But protection? Aureon wasn't on any star-routes as far as I knew; the starjumping races only jumped to planets where other starjumpers were, so they wouldn't be a problem to the Aureons. And the planet was under one rule, so it wasn't one country against another—about the worst problems they had in that direction were caused by the usual run of malcontents, would-be dictators, and misfits who couldn't be bothered to stick with one political system, never mind that said system had operated smoothly for around six hundred Aureon years. They'd get around to developing later.

So, if all that was out, *what?*

Of course, I'm not dumb. I had an idea.

I just didn't *like* the idea.

The Enemy.

I said, "Protection from whom?"

The princess had been watching me while I thought about it. She seemed to be trusting me, but obviously didn't think I had many brains in my head, looking like a Black Devil or not.

She said, "From the Skyraiders."

"Skyraiders?"

"They fly the Skyships, to steal my people and destroy my cities."

Pompous bitch; she only had control of a part of Aureon; the main power was centered around the other side of the planet. Well, she *did* have a few cities here and there, Kathalya for one.

I said, "These . . . Skyships. They're shaped like jewels?"

She stared at me for a moment, then nodded. "You know them?"

"Yes." I shook my head. "Wherever we go, they are there. But we call them the Enemy, Princess."

"I see." She paused momentarily; it seemed to be habit. "Then you only agreed to our protection so that you might attack from another point?"

I nodded. "Something like that, I expect. They'll try to do the job, though. For your people, not just for themselves."

"It is all right, whichever way. It is a help."

"Sure," I said, and didn't believe for a second that we could do much against the Enemy; the first training in Enemy history consists of two words: *the Enemy,* followed by a couple of pictures of worlds they've destroyed, and a sentence: *This is what they have done*.

You get scared right there.

I shook my head. "Anyway, Princess, we had better get you ready to leave." I took two Bullets out of one of the robe's pouches and held them in one hand. "Get a full set of clothes on, and select whatever items are of personal value to you; anything else you want, or need, can be supplied at Area Fourteen."

Apparently, clothes were in the forefront of her mind, because she said, "Handmade?"

"Well . . ."

"I dislike the cheap rubbish the machine spinners make," she said, a little snottily. I made a mental note to remind Ten Seventy-Four to investigate the invention of the spinning jenny on Aureon. Their history was as cockeyed as Earth's.

Anyway, it would be safer to avoid the truth; she wouldn't be able to tell.

I said, "As you wish, Princess. We have people at the base who can produce the material from their own bodies."

"Very well," she said, and clapped her hands. "I shall leave that with you."

I nodded. "Fine. The same thing also applies to oils, perfumes, jewelry, and other cosmetic items. I think you'll be rather surprised by what we can give you."

"But—"

She didn't get any further than that.

There was a roaring sound from somewhere above the palace; it sounded like a giant bullroarer. Then there was a second roar joining it, and a third.

Then a roaring whoop.

And an explosion.

The princess screamed, *"Skyraiders!"*

There was another whoop, another explosion, nearer this time; the floor vibrated.

A whooping sound came at us.

I reacted, leaped across the room from a frozen start, caught the princess around the waist and held onto her as we hit the floor; rolled under the bed, pulling the sheets over us. Not much protection, but enough, if we were—

Hit.

The room jumped with the sound of the explosion, settled, jumped again. The explosion had been in another part of the palace.

One of the bullroarer sounds ended suddenly; one of the ships was down, probably in another part of the city.

Another explosion, distant.

I pulled myself from under the bed, pulling the princess with me; she had dropped her knife when I pushed her under the bed.

I looked around the room. Some of the ornate hangings had come down with the explosion, but there didn't seem to be anything else seriously wrong with the room; I'd messed up the neatly-made bed, though.

Somebody started banging on the main door, and shouting.

"Princess?" I said.

"I am all right," she said. I turned to look at her. She was at a clothes closet, taking down a heavy robe. "My retainers will be coming to take me to safety. How will you get us away from here?"

I held up one of the Bullets. "These. A type of magic, if you like. I don't have time to explain. We'll just vanish."

She gave me a slightly suspicious look, and pulled the robe on, without belting it; clever woman. One of the best defenses against stone shrapnel is a heavy robe, left loose.

I said, "Your people are here, and they'll start cutting down the doors any second now." I flipped her the Bullet, and she caught it. "It isn't a poison pill, and you'll have to take my word for that. You're too valuable, if you like." I demonstrated how to use the thing; between teeth, bite down, swallow.

The banging on the doors was getting louder.

I said, "We'll both go together," and put my own Bullet between my teeth. I had spares . . .

Lucky for me.

As I heard wood splinter, a screaming whoop closed in on us.

I shouted, "NOW!"

And the princess bit and swallowed.

A pop, and she was gone.

Then the room exploded, with me in it, and all I saw for a while was blackness.

I came to with my head pounding, and an immense weight across my back. There was something wet on my face, and the whole of one side of my robe felt wet, drenchingly so.

Carefully I felt down my side, checking for a wound. After a few moments my hand touched a ragged leather tear, then smooth surface. That explained that. Some, or all, of my water bottles had burst, soaking me.

I checked my face, and stopped when my fingers touched pulped flesh on my forehead, wincing because of stinging pain. Not a bad gash, but messy. I was bruised along one side of my face, probably from falling on it. I'd probably missed out on pain because whatever had knocked me out had done it before I registered injury.

I strained my neck to look behind me, saw that part of the big bed was lying across my back, mattress on wood, with stone lying across the mattress; I blessed my luck. If the stone had hit first, my back would have been broken. Not that I would have noticed.

Something exploded in the distance.

Carefully, I eased myself from under the wreckage, feeling badly bruised along my back—it probably wasn't too serious if it was hurting like that—and sat down on a heap of stone, untensing cramped muscles and working out what sort of condition I was in. Annabelle was definitely in for it . . . at the very least, a clinically applied program of bruises in the same order as mine. . . .

Whoever had been knocking the doors down had been discouraged by now, at least.

I took the gun out of the pouch and checked it; it was still in working order. I ejected the knockout clip and slotted in a clip of explosive bullets, jacking one into the firing chamber. The laser sight was intact, which was fine by me; maybe I was a little crazy from the aftereffects of the concussion, but I wanted to get a couple of Enemy before I ran for home. We'd promised protection for the Aureons, so . . . well, Agent Commander Tomari, here's your chance to play hero first-class and impress that humbug Uriah Heep of a computer.

I wobbled unsteadily to my feet.

A Jet Jumper blasted through the wall.

Reaction: automatic.

The gun snapped up, the laser target point centered on the junction between the suit of the Jumper and his pogo stick transportation, and I fired.

The explosion separated suit from platform; the pogo stick shot into a wall, went dead with a flash of flame. The Jumper crashed into the wreckage, and lay still, suit smoking, thick legs blasted away. I couldn't see anything behind the heavy full-face visor.

Then the suit, and the machine, were gone.

I staggered toward the break in the wall, clung to the stone as I peered outside. More Jet Jumpers, suits bronze in spotlights from the jewel-shaped troopship that had put down in the park.

Three Jumpers broke away from the main group, heading toward my position, the blast from the Jumper sticks flattening the grass that they traveled over. I knew it wasn't personal, but . . .

I raised the gun, centered the dot on the leading Jumper, fired, switched to the next Jumper before even wondering if I'd hit the first, fired again, targeted the third, fired a third time, switched back to the lead Jumper, fired at the head.

The three were flung from the Jumper sticks by the impacts of the bullets, shaken by the miniature explosions; the bullets were designed for power enough to kill a Jet Jumper's suit, if not the Jumper himself.

A riderless stick hit the wall next to me and dropped, one edge of the platform digging into the ground. It was cutting a furrow, slowly.

I didn't think. I grabbed it, pulled it upright as I fell back through the break in the wall, and climbed on it. The controls were simple; just steering, rise, and speed. The weapons were all in the suits; if I could get one of those, I'd be unstoppable. But the damn suits all vanished the minute one was killed.

Still, a Jumper stick was a pretty good catch.

I gave it full speed ahead, lifted about three feet as I did so, and hurtled through the gap in the wall, twisting the steering bar hard left, sticking close to the wall. My exit seemed to catch them by surprise; they fired, but hit only stone.

I shouldn't have been surprised; the Jumper I'd shot first hadn't expected me, either. They were used to being left unmolested. Not too surprising; the blunderbusses used on Aureon might shred me like a Nixon document, but they wouldn't impress a Jumper that much.

Pile of wreckage coming up ahead, I saw; I hit the rise control and went over it, steered right to take me away from the palace buildings.

The wreckage vanished behind me as I looked back, hit by an Enemy beam.

I steered between the trees, cutting my speed to accommodate, and staying high enough to avoid hitting anything low on the ground. The Jumper stick platform was superbly balanced, easy to ride, no vibration from the jets.

It was nice while it lasted.

The next moment, I was sailing through the air, momentum supplied by the now-vanished Jumper stick, twelve or fifteen feet up.

Reaction was automatic; I curled into a ball, twisting down, crashing through brush, rolling, impact cushioned by brush and soft soil, keeping hold of my weapon as I slammed down flat, the wind knocked out of me; at least I'd rolled all right; I could have slammed into a tree, or something equally unyielding.

I spotted a bronze suit heading for me, raised the gun, fired as the dot centered. The Jumper suit flew backwards, crashing through a bush as the pogo stick slammed into a tree, swerving sideways.

Both vanished.

Nightmare symptoms: the concussion was playing hell with me; I was seeing things here and there, acting delirious, and staggering around. No Jumpers came at me.

Eventually I collapsed into thick undergrowth, crawling into hiding, waiting for the attack to pass, stomach churning. Hell, they wouldn't come looking. I wasn't a threat now. They'd neutralized me by taking away the platform from under me; my head had done the rest.

I passed out for a while.

I couldn't have been under for long; explosions were still going off in the distance, and I could hear Jet Jumpers nearby, crunching through brush.

My head seemed like empty space, not a good sign; at least I seemed to be thinking clearly enough.

I crawled out of my hiding-space, gun in hand, and started across the park; I didn't want to get up yet. Down, I had a better chance of getting away with what I now intended to do.

I was going to blow up one of the Enemy troopships, shatter a dark jewel.

Thinking about that, I struck my head on a hard surface, and my hands touched stone.

4 Down the Dustpipe

I backed up a little and got to my knees to see what I'd run into.

It was an ornamental stone pot.

A *big* pot.

Well, I needed a place to stop and rest for a moment, so I could check what I had, and check my condition.

And pots . . .

Are for putting things in.

I complimented myself on my genius-level mentality, tucked the gun securely into the belt of the robe, and scrambled up the side of the thing; it was easy enough, with plenty of room and plenty of handholds. It was around ten feet tall and wide, with a lid.

I pushed the lid up, straining and grunting, and squeezed down inside, dropping to the bottom. I left the lid as it was; I needed something to grab when I went out again, and I could use the handhold to lever the lid further off later.

I settled into the bottom of the pot, with my back against the cold stone, and made a quick check of my equipment. Everything was there, except two bullets; I'd lost mine when the roof fell in on me. Hell, I even still had my toothbrush.

Everything seemed in order, anyway.

I still had a couple of water bottles intact; I opened one and drank half what was in it, using up some of the concentrated rations. One of the bars tasted a bit dusty; not too surprising, in the circumstances, but the water was still cold. I hadn't realized I was so thirsty—the next thing to worry about was shock. But I didn't think I'd suffer it—I hadn't been damaged that badly.

I settled back again and stripped the explosive pack out of my robe, molding it while I waited. The pot provided plenty of cover, and it didn't seem likely that it would be hit by a stray shot from one of the ships. They were raising less hell than the time before I passed out in the grass. It wouldn't be long before they left.

It was one hell of an attack, for sure, even with only three ships. The city would be a shambles when they left. And it was possible that they were attacking other parts of the planet.

Well, I couldn't do much, but I could do a little damage.

And probably get myself killed in the process, like the fool I am.

I took out the little cube-shaped detonators—no need for disguise on Aureon, I guess—and stuck them into the explosive, just pushing them in far enough to make them stay in place.

I gave it a few more minutes, then stood up, looking up at the top of the pot; not very far away.

Rumbles of explosions in the distance, like faraway thunder.

I put the bomb in the gun pouch, making sure it was safe, then tensed and jumped; my hands caught the rim of the pot, my sandals scraped against the rough stone, pressing in and pushing me up as I pulled with my arms. I halted the climb, swung around, grasped the lid, and pushed, grunting. With a loud scraping noise it slid over, leaving plenty of room for me to climb out.

I hauled myself up onto the edge of the lid, swinging around and into empty air, kicking back against the stone while pushing out with my hands—

Orange light of burning to the north.

—sailing into space, and down onto grass, impacting and rolling straight into cover.

Scraping sound from behind, hissing, and the sound of the lid smashing on the base of the pot; not to worry, the other noise would cover it.

I crawled away, rapidly, drawing the gun. I was heading, I hoped, back to the ship that had put down in the park; it might have moved, or I might have gotten myself lost. But there was that map in my mind, ingrained and standing out like lightning at midnight, with a little mental mark pointing where the ship was.

I stopped and took out one of the spare Bullets, holding it with the gun; slid the bomb from the pouch, holding it carefully, ready to finish the molding job.

I got up and started running, dodging from tree to tree, breathing steadily and using long, loping strides. I saw the ship as I left a close group of trees, and dropped flat, watching the terrain ahead.

It was clear; no sign of any Jet Jumpers.

I molded the detonators into the explosive, wadding them right down. Eight seconds; I'd have to be well clear before it went.

I lifted the bomb and looked at it; blue-green in active condition, dull surfaced, weighing maybe a half-pound. Inside it, enough blast to take out a wall, or destroy a bank vault.

Or blow up a spacecraft.

I broke cover and ran hell-for-leather at the ship, thinking, heroes don't die, they get remembered forever, and wondering when I'd get it, and where, feet thudding on grass; explosions in the distance, fire still burning in the north, palace dark and destroyed nearby—

Palace!

Damn.

There was my cover, if I could reach it.

I saw the troop ramp leading out of the Enemy troopship like a gray metal tongue licking the grass, saw a Jet Jumper flying down it, sliding off the edge towards me, raised the gun on the run, fired twice, ran by the dead suit and hissing Jumper stick, leapt onto the ramp and up, fired twice more at a second Jumper, slammed gun butt and bomb together, flung the bomb as far down the gray corridor as I could, turned tail while the thing was still in the air, hurtled outside, leaped from the ramp towards the ruins of the palace—

Ran, ragged breath ripping from gagging throat, feet thumping against grass, then stone, nerves ragged, head pounding and paining, vision blurring, thighs hurting, I was *never* a good distance runner, gun in hand with bullet jammed between sweaty palm and slippery gunbutt—

Jumper—

five

—coming at me from the side of the palace—

four

—seeing me as I saw him and raised the gun—

three

—and targeted red dot bullseye on the weak point found through plain accident and pulled the trigger still on the run gun bucking pulling out of recoil and firing second time in eyeblink split-second before the first shot struck and pulling out of recoil again still running—

two

—and going through the break in the wall as the Jumper crashes down not seeing where he lands and leaping over rubble going for the door hanging off its hinges and through and seeing the poor bastards caught by the explosion that knocked me out and—

one

—breaking out into corridor strewn with rubble and dodging down it until I find a wall-hanging half down and jamming Bullet between teeth one-handed dragging down the tapestry and falling rolling into it and covering head with arms and *praying to hell and gone that the bang doesn't bring the rest of this place down around my ass—*

zero

—hearing the dull thump as it goes.

And the second, louder, detonation as the rest of the ship caught from the first.

The floor shuddered violently as the explosion roared out; I curled up more, waiting for the wall to come down on me, then realized—

What the hell am I waiting for?

Bit the Bullet and swallowed.

And the ruins of the palace of Kathalya, and the explosions, and the falling debris, and the Enemy, above all—

Were gone.

And I was back on Ten Seventy-Four, rolled in an ornate tapestry.

Ringing, whooping, blinding, flashing, jangling lightning—

All in my head.

I was awake immediately; I registered the alarms on the way out of sleep, waking startled.

That was the way it was meant to happen.

Ten Seventy-Four was under attack by the Enemy.

I kicked the sheets aside and rolled out of bed, grabbing my clothes from the floor as I stood; they were standard issue coveralls, with a wide belt that could be used for weaponry if needed, or instruments of various sorts. I was glad for them. It didn't take more than a few seconds to get into them and zip them up; likewise the boots, which were pull-ons with zippers.

I crossed the transient apartment I'd been given for the night, flipped open a locker, and took out the compact weapon that was inside. The locker had been keyed open by the attack alert.

I clipped the laser to my belt, turned, and ran for the door, slipping through while it was still opening, and joining the mass of sentient life that was moving swiftly down the corridor, towards the center of the base. In a few minutes, all the Dustpipes would have been boarded; if the attack was for sure—and, I thought, it would be—the Dustpipes would be flipped into assorted parts of the universe, and left to find their way to other bases.

The evacuation was orderly; there wouldn't be any kind of panic—all who worked on Builders' bases were given subconscious instruction for such an emergency. The alarms were designed to trigger all sentients awake immediately, and get them moving.

Along the walls of the corridor, the alarm signals changed color from blue to white, flashing alternately with orange; the Mastercomputer had decided the attack was going to take place.

It was then that I remembered the princess; she was in transient quarters, where she'd been placed after arrival. I'd been fed through to sickbay for repairs, and I hadn't thought about her at all, except during the fast debriefing. After all, she was only a part of another job. . . .

I stopped and turned back the way I'd come, pushing through the surging flow of aliens; most of them moved out of my way. I'd seen a rack of floater trucks on my way down—we were about halfway to the Dustpipes now. Ten Seventy-Four would be taken up with co-ordinating defense and evacuation, and probably wouldn't have assigned anyone to go fetch the woman.

I found the row of trucks and pulled one free, climbing on the back and hitting the lift control; as I started it moving forward into the corridor, sentients moving aside to give me a clear path, I had a thought that the trouble I generally got into was my own fault. I should have left Aureon the moment I woke up, instead of playing hero—that, apparently, *had* been due to the crack on the head. But I wasn't so sure. I'm normally pretty addled anyway.

I spotted an unused door to a set of emergency stairs—I'd come up through one of the big float-lifts, with a massive group—and swerved the truck at it, leaning back as the front hit, steadying myself by getting my center of gravity lower than the floor.

Then I gradually dropped the height of travel as I sailed out into empty space, until I met level floor again; I went down the next flight in the same way, taking it faster.

As I dropped through further levels—damning the neat design that prevented long falls and also emergency drops like this—I hit the com plate on the control board of the truck.

"This is Agent Commander Tomari, Ten Seventy-Four; I need directions to my subject charge for Area Fourteen."

"Acknowledged, Agent Tomari," the computer said, and listed a corridor and apartment in the transient section. Then he added, "You have very little time. I am assigning a sentient to assist. You will evacuate together."

"Acknowledged," I said, and aimed the truck at the exit to the level I wanted; it opened for me, under Ten Seventy-Four's direction.

The corridor was empty when I reached it; the transients' section was in one of the outermost segments of the base. It had been evacuated a while before the alert was triggered for the innermost sections. It made for an easier evacuation.

I hit top speed going down, then hit the stop control as I saw the door coming up, letting the floater skid around on its brakefield, until it was facing backwards. As I stepped off, I could see a dark blur coming around the corner towards me.

I pulled my comkey from my belt, hit the talk switch, and said "Override."

The door irised and I jumped through.

The princess was cowering in a corner, with all her blankets pulled up to her; she was half-naked and terrified. She might have been able to handle anything that came on her home world, but the alert's cacophony, mental, aural, and visual, had frightened the hell out of her.

I said, "Princess—"

She screamed.

I didn't have time to waste trying to calm her down carefully; I went across the room, grabbed her hair, pulled her up, and slapped her face, hard, each side.

She sobbed, then straightened up, taking a shuddering deep breath.

I started to tell her to get moving.

She hit me.

It was a fist blow, very expert, and it caught me on the jaw; I barely saw it coming, but managed to ride most if it. It still threw me backwards, with one hell of a pain exploding in the lower half of my face.

I didn't bother trying to sort her out; I came up and ran across the distance between us, leaping and pinning her down, thumbs on carotid arteries: one advantage of the Aureon physiology being close to human.

She struggled for a moment, then went under. I held on for a few more seconds, then let go. She'd stay under until I got her to the Dustpipe.

I crossed the room again, to a clothes closet; she'd been fitted out with clothing here—not much, but enough to last her for a few days, while Area Fourteen made other arrangements for her.

If and when we got there.

I took down four long gowns, one of them the gown she'd brought with her, and slung them over my arm; I could feel something heavy in each of them; if my guess was right, each gown was fitted with a knife. Why, I couldn't think—she probably felt safer with weaponry to hand. The damn computer wouldn't argue.

The floater truck hummed through the open doorway, piloted by the sentient Ten Seventy-Four had assigned to follow me.

I wasn't going to argue; even something as ugly as him was a blessing right now. Even if he did have a remarkable number of tentacles, four large circular eyes, a large, meaty, greenish body, and a large orifice on his front underside that could have been a mouth.

It stopped the floater truck by the bed where the unconscious princess was spread out, face down. I threw the cloaks on the back, grabbed the woman, and hauled her up and over, in a fireman's lift, balancing her carefully on my left shoulder.

The octopus-thing on the truck controls said, telepathically, *=*Hurry. There is little time left.*

"Coming," I said, and climbed on the back of the truck as

fast as I dared. Two tentacles flicked out and looped into my belt, locking against each other as the truck lifted and started for the door. I swayed to keep balanced.

As we hurtled along the corridor, I said, "You sure you can hold onto me like that?"

*=*I am quite strong enough. You might as well utilize both arms to retain your burden.*

One of the eyes swiveled to look at me.

I grinned and said, "Okay. Thanks for the assist."

*=*It was necessary, and I was nearby.*

A lift was waiting at the end of one of the corridors, and the sentient flying the truck swerved it into a fast turn, swinging it around and braking to a stop facing the doors as they closed.

Ten Seventy-Four was handling everything, it seemed. The lift took off as soon as the doors closed, using five or six times the acceleration of normal transport. I felt my legs buckle slightly.

The octopus-thing was akin to a Helldriver gone power-mad; the doors were barely half-open when he powered up and took off, almost dragging me off the back end. The tentacles, though, didn't budge.

He kept the speed all the way up as he flew down the corridors toward the lifeboats, skidding the floater around the corners on its field, level to the floor. The corridors were empty; we were going to be the last out. The impression of a dead place hadn't quite taken hold yet; the systems of the base were still in operation, all lights up, and the alert signals still running.

It was a picture of unreality; empty and echo, but not yet dead.

I knew, though, that as soon as we were settled inside the Dustpipe—that was the name given to the lifeboats by myself and some confederates at Area Fourteen—unnecessary base systems would be cut off and all power diverted to defensive systems: weaponry and shields. If the Enemy made it through—as was likely—the Dustpipes would be warped out to programmed points and the base would destroy itself. Depending on the location, the bang could be from a hundred thousand miles in diameter to two or three million; the energy required was formidable. And available.

We slid around a final corner into the last stretch of the run; the door at the bottom led to the boarding area for the lifeboats;

it was a null-gravity area, rigged to provide fast and efficient access. Boarding was handled by tractor beams, and the sentients assigned to each lifeboat module were simply picked up and tossed there.

Thingummy skidded the floater to a halt inside the doorway and left the controls, flying; a personal floater plate, most likely—I couldn't see that he could easily move around otherwise. He was probably a converted water-worlder.

I stepped off the truck and bent down to pick up the gowns, throwing them over the princess; her hair had fallen straight down and was swinging against my legs as I moved.

I followed Thingummy into the main section of the boarding area, and watched as he was suddenly lit by the blue glow of a tractor beam and pulled forward; he curled all of his tentacles around himself as he went, forming himself into a ball.

Then it was my turn.

I stepped forward, keeping my hold on the princess. The beam caught me, tugging, and I floated forward in null-gravity, my feet leaving the floor. Then I was into a wide-open spherical space, disorientated, floating.

The entrances to the Dustpipe modules were arranged evenly around the entire area of a big spherical chamber; all but one of them were dark. The last one was lit a bright red, flashing insistently. I was heading towards that one, with Thingummy some way ahead of me.

Thingummy vanished through the entrance; he would be heading down a corridor on the other side, to be placed in front of the Dustpipe itself.

I passed through the doorway and found myself flying with feet down towards a floor; in here, there was a recognizable up and down—definitely imaginary, as there was no gravity. But it helped.

Gravity returned at the Dustpipe; Thingummy was already inside, probably getting settled in. I moved carefully; the gravity was low, for speed. The module was big enough for a complement of fifteen or so, but designed oversized—if an attack knocked out some Dustpipes, personnel could be rearranged.

This Dustpipe was arranged for only three of us.

I found a crash-tank for the princess and dumped her into it, with her gowns; I plucked them out and tossed them over the side. The tanks were emergency-designed, and unnecessary unless we hit something in the wrong place; acceleration was countered by gravity equalization fields.

The linkscreen/control board over the tank started to slide down on its arm; I hit the function-cancel switch to disconnect the control segment, then punched the return plate to raise it again.

The last switch I wanted was set into the side of the tank itself; sleep-stimulation. I wanted the princess to stay under sleepstim until we reached another base. Thingummy was easy enough for me to bear—the Fra Fra Seyoh was horrible; this guy was much nicer to look at—but I didn't think the princess would be too happy to see him.

I left her in the tank, and crossed to another spare one, vaulting the low wall and settling in as the padding contoured for human proportions. My own linkscreen started sliding down, and I glanced over to the tank that Thingummy had settled into. His own screen was in place. I couldn't see him—he was settled right down, it seemed.

The screen was lit with a warning to prepare for departure; this part of it was as normal as waiting for a plane to leave on an intercity flight on Earth, and probably any other planet that utilised that form of transportation.

I hit the com switch, and said, "Computer, can we see what's happening outside?"

There was no verbal answer. Instead, the warning of the screen blanked out, to be replaced immediately by a sensor plot in three dimensions; the plot showed at least twenty points—Enemy ships—closing in on the centerpoint, the base. It stayed for a moment, then vanished, replaced by a view of the jewel-shaped Enemy ships; I wasn't sure, but they looked like heavy destroyers. A kill-mission, if so. Once they were in range—judging from the plot, they were still around forty lights away, and closing carefully—they'd start firing; they wouldn't stop for some time. No finesse, no fancy tactics, just a lot of heavy weaponry being used at once.

Whatever doubts I'd had were gone now; this was an attack all right.

Not that the Builders would care that much; one day they might even get around to replacing Ten Seventy-Four. Until then, they'd be happy to let another base dep.

The ships vanished from the screen; they'd made a fast jump.

The picture had come from a buoy, I guessed; we didn't use ships for much other than escape. It was one of our biggest failings—and saying so didn't make a damn bit of difference. Everything just went on the same way.

Violence, said the wise computer, *is no answer.*

Sure. Meanwhile, we get stomped on.

I said, "Leave it off. I don't need to see any more."

The screen blanked to show the jump-imminent warning. There was a countdown in the corner, now.

I watched as the figures flicked down from two minutes to one minute, fifty-nine seconds.

The ventilation systems were making a slight hissing noise, the other ship systems humming, barely noticeable; the silence made them all the more prominent.

It would be the same in the other Dustpipes; groups of sentients with atmosphere and a few other things in common, such as a home about to be destroyed, would be waiting in silence to be tossed anywhere from the next star system to a galaxy a billion light-years distant. They wouldn't know where they were going until they got there. Then they'd have to pilot for a base.

As far as I recalled, there'd only been one Dustpipe filled with refugees landed at Area Fourteen in my lifetime, but bases were being destroyed all the time. Too many of them. New ones appeared, too, but there didn't seem to be any system for replacement, any coherent form of defense. It was so futile that I hated to waste time and energy thinking about it.

I closed my eyes at fifty-nine seconds and settled back.

Seconds ticked away.

A dull reverberation from somewhere beneath me.

They had arrived; the attack was starting. That one had hit our shields.

I opened my eyes to see: PREPARE FOR TRANSFER

I shut my eyes again. This was the mind-straining part.

Another dull reverberation, followed closely by a third.

Then everything went black
white
rainbow-colored
solarized
and I felt myself torn apart molecule by molecule at an incredibly high speed and

thrown to the winds of space with my mind flailing for a handhold when

it all went solarized

rainbow-colored

white

black

and I came back to normal, feeling solid, with the local universe stabilized around me once more.

I hit touchplates on my control panel and did a fast check of the ship; subconscious impulse through training. Everything was in order; the burst of interstellar overdrive hadn't caused anything to bust loose, as I'd half-expected.

Thingummy was working on his own board with three tentacles; the controls would have shaped to his needs. Generally, they stayed in forms that humanoids with flexible digits similar to my own could use, but the design allowed extra parameters for possible situations.

I said, "Everything alright on your side, Thingummy?"

There was a mental grunt, and he said, *=*Yes. Don't call me Thingummy.*

"Well, hell, nobody told me your name," I said, settling back into my crash padding. "So what do I call you?"

*=*I would prefer my given name. Shreekor. And yours is . . . ?*

"Kevven Tomari. Call me Kev. I kind of prefer it, and it saves time."

*=*Very well, and right on.*

"Mindpicker pickermind," I said, surprised. From associating with telepaths, I knew they didn't communicate so much in conscious language; the recipient converted. But Shreekor was the first one who'd been able to trigger me with my own natural usage of language. "No offense intended, Shreekor. I was surprised."

Apparently, he'd caught some of my thinking. He said *=*I understand. Now I would prefer to begin locating us so that we can find another base. Orientation should take little time.*

"We near any planetary systems?" I asked.

I saw Shreekor's tentacles flicker out of the corner of my eyes.

*=*Unlikely. The odds are none too good for it. Why?*

"I guess I just expected it underneath. Seemed the best thing to do in case there was any trouble."

*=*I see. No, the lifeboat is designed for such emergencies. In*

such a case, a beacon would be switched on, at the risk of Enemy approach.

"Uh-huh. Okay, I'll take your word for it." I straightened up and watched the control board. "Shall we find out where we are and get a new set of vectors programmed in?"

*=*The lifeboat requires only one pilot for normal operations. I suggest that, as we may be operative for some time, I take command now, while you rest. You will take over during the next time-sector, and your companion in the third.*

"She isn't trained for it," I said, looking over at Shreekor's crash-tank.

There was a startled feeling.

*=*Is not trained?*

I shook my head. "She isn't part of a base complement. I was supposed to be taking her from Aureon IV to Area Fourteen when we got hit."

*=*I believe I see why you had to carry her.*

I nodded. "Yeah. She panicked and attacked me. I had to knock her out." That reminded me. I programmed in the automatic medical systems and set them to work on the princess; it would prevent her having a headache when she woke up. "Thanks for the help, anyway."

*=*It was nothing. But perhaps you should have transferred her back, or left her where she was.*

I looked sharply over at the tank the alien was in. "Listen, my good friend, I am not so crazy as to go messing about trying to ship her back in the middle of an attack. Also, I risked skin getting her off Aureon, and wound up stuffing Jumper sticks down Jet Jumper throats as well, so I am not going to let her get killed now. Plus, my good friend, I am not anti-life and wasn't going to abandon her for no good reason. So you are thanked for the suggestions, but you can take 'em and stuff 'em right up what you use for an ass. Okay?"

*=*Oooops. Apologies, gentlebeing Tomari. A Shimo-sh'sasai I am, and less tactful than even the usual.*

Shreekor's wry tone made me smile; as it was, I hadn't really taken offense. I just hate trying to be subtle and falling down in the process. At least he'd understood what I was saying; you can't always reach a level of communication with aliens. Trying to explain to a female Krr'Hrshraa, for example, that you do not wish to spend the night with her husband—who is the weaker of the mating pair—and at the same time attempting to avoid offending her, is a task suited only to the staunchest and sneakiest diplomat; anyone with even the smallest capability of being ruffled will be.

Shreekor, by comparison, was as nice as me.

I said, "You're forgiven, Shreekor."

*=*Thank you. As for the story, I would be glad to hear it as soon as I have dealt with the mundane matters of navigation and orientation.*

Someone should have been watching the sensors and radar screens, but we were too busy jawing at each other, blithely unconcerned about such minor things.

I said, "I'll be happy to tell you it. I'm kind of proud of it."

Before Shreekor had a chance to add anything, I looked up at the radar screen. There was a small blob of reflected signal merging with the center point, our lifeboat.

Merging.

A bell-like bong echoed throughout our compartment. In the silence after it, I heard a thin keening sound, metal on metal. A drill.

We were being boarded.

5 Sasha-Ra

I stared at the screen and listened to the whining sound of the drill at our hull.

Shreekor said, *=*What is it?*

"We're being boarded," I said.

*=*Enemy?*

I shook my head, forgetting for a moment that Shreekor was a telepath, remembered and corrected. "No. I've never heard them of boarding anything except a base."

*=*We may have something new to say.*

"Except for one minor fact: the Enemy aren't renowned for leaving anything alive nearby."

*=*Hmm.*

I stood up in the crash-tank and climbed over the edge, checking my comkey. "Get me an estimate on how long the hull's going to last before it gives way completely, and tie a translator into the intraship communications for me. If nothing else, I can try talking to them."

*=*What are you going to do?*

"I've absolutely no idea, m' man. But something." I started for the door to the next compartment, stopped, turned to look back. "And wake up the princess."

*=*The sentient you brought with you?*

"Yeah, that's her." I hit the switch on the key to open the door. "Keep her under low-level. She may come in handy. You any good at mindgames?"

*=*Disguise?*

"Yeah."

*=*Why?*

I shrugged. "She'll probably have an adverse reaction if you aren't careful about it. Just keep a tag on where I am and get her to me if I need her. Got that?"

*-*Indeed I have. But plunging into possible danger, regardless, is a little drastic.*

"Well," I said, "it's a chance for you. The way we're going, we aren't defending ourselves all that well."

I cut it short there and ducked through the door; from the sound level, they were drilling one end of the lifeboat open. Three compartments down. As far as I knew, they weren't drilling in vacuum; that had definitely been a boarding tube. It made it easier for spaceside scavengers to strip ships.

What I didn't like was the sudden contact; it seemed too convenient that we'd arrived in the same general area as another ship.

I found the general area of the drilling, located the exact point by feeling along the bulkheads until the vibration reached highest pitch.

Shreekor's telepathic voice said, *=*We have approximately five of your minutes until breakthrough.*

Sub-vocally, I said, "Surprises me they aren't using an energy drill."

*=*There are numerous possible reasons.*

I closed the door I'd come through, opened the next one down and let it close most of the way, jamming it with the key's signal, so that there was a gap I could shoot through if need be.

"Such as?"

*=*The possibility that our hull might be of a volatile material. The Khrdira utilise an alloy in their spacecraft hulls that has been known to explode violently on contact with certain energy wavelengths.*

Through the gap, I surveyed the area the other ship was drilling into. It was mostly empty, excepting couches and a table, plus some lockers and other equipment along the walls; it was a duplicate of the next compartment along, a lounge.

I said, "That's silly of them."

*=*Attempt talking sense into sentients and you generally get nowhere.*

"That sounds like a comment on me."

*=*Well . . . I have been scanning the exterior. They are cutting an entrance with an open-mouth edge-drill rather than a bore. I*

also doubt that they intend to decompress the compartment—

"You don't know how happy that makes me."

*=—*as they are working in a no-suits condition with a force-field in case we decompress.*

"Mind-reading?"

*=*Comparing actions and making qualified judgments.*

"Uh-huh."

*=*The sentients manipulating the equipment are humanoid, somewhat taller than yourself, slim, but well-muscled, with a somewhat greenish complexion.*

"Pointed ears?"

There was a mental reflex of mild surprise and puzzlement.

*=*I don't understand. Is it important?*

"You never know."

I could see the vibrations on the wall itself now; a slight blurring. The drill they were using had to have a high rotational speed; the alloy the bulkhead was made of was pretty tough.

*=*Whether they can hear or not might be pertinent . . . never mind. We do not have the time. They lack external auditory sensors such as yours. They have antennae. What purpose they serve, I do not know.*

"Fine."

I unclipped the gun and sat down, making myself comfortable; I'd been scrunching myself up against the door, which made it a possibility that I might not be able to move fast enough when the time came. Cramped muscles and such. I'd know when they came through the hull.

It occurred to me that my luck was running into trouble lately; I'd been hit by enough coincidences for the odds to be listed as a record—I could imagine a googol or two being mixed up with said odds—in the *Guiness Book Of Records*. I'd been hit by three Enemy attacks in a row, in a couple of days. And now this had come along as well.

*=*One other thing about the drillers. From the scanners, I see that they appear remarkably similar.*

"Clones?"

*=*It appears so.*

"Good Christ."

*=*I also have another contact. Different species, completely. Very interesting.*

"In what way?"

**=It's unusual to find two entirely different species aboard a single spacefaring craft.*

"Bite your auditory lobe, or whatever it is, Shreekor. Unusual my third leg."

**=You are beginning to feel the strain?*

"You noticed the poor humor? Go on; the details?"

**=Female, a little shorter than you, complexion a shade of gold, humanoid. Odd . . .*

There was a feeling of weary surprise; he'd spotted something else.

"What now?"

**=She is armed, but under guard. Further humanoid sentients . . . But while physiologically identical, they appear to be of different planetary origins. I suspect a physically mutated species.*

"I'll give you another one as well. Those green-skinned drillers are slaves. That's about the only explanation for cloning in this case. You can use them for dirty and heavy work and replace them as necessary. Especially if they have a fast maturation rate."

**=I follow the reasoning. But I am at a loss here. The female appears to be a prisoner, but not unfriendly towards her guards.*

"And armed?" I frowned. "Uh-huh, it's strange, for sure. I think we'll have to ride it out by feel. I'd like to get out now, though. But—"

**=I know.*

"Yeah."

We couldn't skip out while we were in contact with the other ship; our jump-field would wrap itself neatly around the other can as well as ours, and wherever we wound up, we would still be in contact with them. And if they pulled out and left a hole in our side, we couldn't move—the field would encounter distortion, wrap itself both inside and outside the lifeboat, with the result that we'd be inverted in relation to the normal universe. Without a chance of being brought back to normal—all that would be left would be a widely-scattered collection of simple atoms in some sub-universe.

I got up and rested my back against the wall of the short passageway I was in, watching the other compartment through the gap, hoping for divine intervention; going by experience, none was forthcoming.

Shreekor said, *=*I have briefed your, ah, ward. She has accepted the situation as it stands, although she does not understand it. If she is needed, I will send her.*

"Good enough. Let's see what happens next."

What happened next was that a large circle appeared in a fluff of metallic powder. It was almost wide enough to drive a small tank through, leaving only five centimeters or so between itself and the join of wall and ceiling; there was hardly any space at all between it and the floor.

The section of bulkhead slid back with a sharp hiss of metal on metal, tilted, vanished into the gloom behind. I could hear voices now, deep and guttural, and then high-pitched chittering.

One of the big, thin humanoids leaned through the hole, moved back. It looked about two and a half meters tall, and its skin was a dull, pale green; it had a long face and hangdog eyes with protruding orbs. From quick observation, I guessed that the orbs themselves didn't move, that they had a floating iris. In low light that could allow night-vision with around a hundred and ten degrees of view.

More importantly, one of those could probably break me in half with one hand, as an afterthought, and without more than a token squeeze.

It moved out of line of sight, back into the gloom.

I brought my gun hand up to rest against my belt, watching. So far everything had proceeded without any fuss; if this went on for much longer, I'd start shooting to liven things up. It was positively boring.

A head poked through the hole, then an arm, the hand of which grasped the edge. The head appeared more or less homo sap, with a lot of long hair that seemed to be thicker than normal, a shade of dark gray. The skin was golden, the eyes hidden beneath the shadow cast by protruding bony ridges.

The head turned from side to side a couple of times, probably checking for anything with Truly Awful Designs on boarders, then withdrew.

Sub-vocally, I said, "They bringing up heavy weaponry and a raiding party, Shreekor?"

*= *No sign of either. It appears that proper boarding is not their intention.*

"Well, it's a hell of a way to come ask for a cup of sugar."

*= *??*

"Never mind."

There was more movement at the hole, and the female humanoid Shreekor had mentioned stepped through.

I'd been half-expecting her to look like this; apart from a few details, the head and arm I'd seen a few moments before had been near homo sap.

She was even nearer to homo sap; her skin was golden, with a hint of sparkle to it, and her hair was flame red, streaked with stripes of white that appeared to be perfectly natural. Physically, she was shaped like a homo sap female, sub-species *Playboy* centerfold, dressed to suit it: tank, vest, and shorts of a light, close-fitting shimmering material, sandals, a wide belt around her waist with a large holster attached on the right, butt facing forward which meant she was a left-hander. That was a combat uniform for tropical areas without jungle, or shipboard fighting. The belt had a number of attachments, probably instruments.

She stopped after she stepped through the hole, and turned to face back the way she'd come, reaching out with her right hand. It stopped at the level of the bulkhead.

Shreekor said, *= *Curious. They have erected the force-field again.*

She stepped away from the hole and turned ninety degrees, looking at my position; seeing her face placed the necessary alienness. Her eyes were oval, with arched eyebrows; her eyes literally shone, almost like cat's eyes. I wasn't sure about mechanism; I couldn't see any sign of iris or pupil.

Her face was oval as well; she was beautiful enough to me, but then, I was brought up in a way that allowed me to see beauty within something that someone else might immediately dislike on a gut level. Like appreciating Mondrian or Picasso, or Bartok or Ligeti, or the innate beauty of a Japanese woman in traditional surroundings, or an Ashanti princess standing six foot two in crashingly modern Western surroundings. Not the eye of the beholder, but the eye, mind, and gut all working together.

She had enough homo sap evolution, as was—probably from a much earlier stage—to let me see that the look on her face was a combination of curiosity and fear.

She looked at the door I was hiding behind for a moment—she was probably wondering why it was slightly open; I didn't think she could see me—and then, attention attracted by something I couldn't see, turned back to the hole.

After a few moments, I saw what she was looking at.

The chunk they'd taken out of the wall was being slid back into place.

With a hint of puzzlement, Shreekor said, *=*They are apparently replacing—*

"I can see it, Shreekor. It's weird."

*=*They are marooning her.*

"Looks like, yeah."

The circular section was neatly slid back into place; a moment later, the gap between plate and bulkhead started to fill with some kind of sealant.

I said, "Any idea how strong that seal's going to be?"

*=*There is no way to test it. It is unfamiliar. It is, though, probably utilised by that particular ship for sealing damage areas.*

"Hope it holds."

The woman stepped back from the resealed wall, and turned in a slow circle, scanning the room. When she stopped again, she flipped up the flap of the holster with her right hand and drew out a large, flat, weapon; gun-shaped, probably some form of laser or other energy weapon. It didn't have the right design for a projectile weapon, and looked too light to absorb recoil from anything effective.

I was a little disappointed; I'd almost been looking forward to a big battle against the pirates of whatever, with Tomari as the pure-hearted hero. Instead: one woman with a gun, frightened and apparently dumped on us.

I sighed as she turned toward me, and hit the comkey to open the door, lifting it and my own weapon as I stepped through; just to make sure she got the idea, I aimed carefully at her head.

She didn't get the idea.

She brought her own weapon up to aim at my head, holding it in both hands and going into a two-point balance, legs apart, feet at ninety degrees to each other.

I said, "Drop your weapon," heard the comkey start translating it, and dived to one side, fast, rolling around fast, resighting as soon as I was stable again, and fired.

The front quarter of her weapon melted away, and she dropped it with a startled yelp, her mass of waist-length hair swinging with her movement; she'd been off-balanced by my actions.

I kept the laser aimed at her as I got up; she stared at me, eyes flashing, rubbing her gun hand. Even though she'd dropped the thing fast, she'd felt heat.

I hooked the comkey to my coverall so that it could pick up my voice and do the honors in translating; if I lost it, we'd be reduced to grunting and making gestures at each other.

I said, "You had better follow my commands for the moment, whoever you are. Explanations can be held for the moment." I did my best to be precise; the computer would be a while getting the hang of her language, although it operated more or less telepathically when translating—it allow Shreekor to program and use it directly; SAS sections on all bases have totally telepathic units of their own, which allow fast access for telepaths connected with the bases.

The woman seemed puzzled for a moment, probably attempting to work out how it was done. It startles at first, but they eventually get the hang of it.

She hesitated for a moment, then said something.

The comkey said, in her light tones, "Yes."

I smiled. "Good. Turn around and walk ahead of me through that door."

She hesitated again; either the computer was screwing up syntax, or she wasn't sure whether or not I intended to shoot her in the back.

She turned and walked forward. I touched the comkey switch and the door opened as I followed her. If it startled her, she didn't show it; she probably assumed it was triggered by electric eye or some such device.

I knew one thing for certain: no matter what sort of good intentions the rest of her people had, I wasn't going to start feeling safe until I was out of the way. After all, they hadn't sent any luggage through with her.

I gave her plenty of room ahead of me as we went through the passage and into the next compartment; she seemed ready to follow instructions, but the rule is always to take care.

I stepped through and let the door close behind me, then leaned against it.

I said, "Take a seat and make yourself comfortable."

Again she hesitated, looking at me.

I said, "Go on. I don't intend hurting you."

She nodded curtly and sat down on one of the couches; she sat tensely.

''Shreekor,'' I said, ''is there anything going out from here as far as communication is concerned?''

*=*One moment. Computer will have to scan.*

''Okay.'' I glanced at the woman, saw she was watching me with those strange eyes. ''One more thing. Seal off the boarding area and depressurize it.''

*=*Done already. You may be a man of action, but I am a Shimo-sh'sasai of many plans.*

''Ah, dat ol' patriotic spirit there.'' Our boarder was watching me apparently speaking to myself with a touch of puzzlement. I raised the comkey and said, ''I'm speaking to a telepath, and I have to vocalize to do it.''

She absorbed that and then said, ''I see.''

*=*There is a carrier wave emanating from your area. Occasional modulation.*

I half-smiled, raised the key. ''Where's the transceiver?''

The woman didn't move; she didn't need to say. The thing could be part of the belt, or part of decorations—I'd worn transceivers as jewelry.

She was wearing an ornamental choker, with an inlaid jewel in the center section, and long, dangling earrings, although I couldn't see her ears under the mass of hair.

I crossed over to her, bent down, and reached out for the choker; she jumped.

Without touching her, I yanked the choker away from her throat; yep, that was it. It made a neat throat-mike. The earrings could be left for the moment.

I stepped back and said, ''Shreekor, link our coms up with my key, and put me on their wavelength.''

*=*I have already attempted communication with—*

''It takes charm, my good man.''

*=*Hmmph. Very well. You are connected.*

It was my turn to hesitate a little now; I hadn't any idea of what I was going to say—I couldn't threaten them, after all, as we weren't exactly well armed. And their actions weren't exactly logical by my standards—or, it seemed, by Shreekor's either.

Well, I could ask a question.

I raised the comkey and said, ''Lifeboat to boarding ship. Are you receiving this?''

From the comkey, a soft voice said, ''We are receiving. Continue.''

I looked at the unit for a moment, an eyebrow raised. They seemed reasonable enough.

I said, "We have your agent under guard. Explain your purpose."

The soft voice said, "Your prisoner is not our agent. Our purpose was to rid ourselves of her. We regret any damage caused. Repairs will be completed shortly."

"What do you expect us to do with her? You *are* telling me you're leaving her with us?"

"That is correct. As for what you will do with her, that is up to you." There was a few moments' pause. "Your translation equipment is excellent, especially for a . . . lifeboat. There will be no further communication."

Dead air.

I lowered the comkey, puzzled. That explained a little of it—about one percent. The marooning we'd already assumed. But it was a strange way to go about it, alien motivation or no alien motivation.

I turned to the woman, and raised the comkey. "Take off the earrings. I'm not certain of you yet, and without contact I feel you are that much more harmless."

I think I was taking out some of my annoyance on her. I'd had a tense few minutes back there, and I was starting the come-down, and getting irritable with it.

She moved a little faster this time, reaching up and unclipping the earrings one after the other, shaking her hair back. I held my hand out for them.

She dropped the earrings into my hand, chains and all, then, as I closed my hand over them, snapped her legs up and launched her feet in my direction.

The soles of her feet slammed into my chest before I could get out of the way; I was off balance already, and the double-foot kick sent me half-way across the compartment, and into a table, gun and comkey both flying in different directions.

I came to a painful halt with my legs wrapped around table legs, and my shoulders pressed awkwardly against the base of a couch.

I started to get up, and Pretty Baby's voice said, "*Kalru!*"

I assumed it meant I wasn't supposed to do that, and stopped trying, simply because she'd dived on my gun after kicking me across the room, and was now keeping it aimed squarely at my chest. Her aim was steady enough, even if she was lying prone; she was using her elbows as support.

While I watched, she got up from the floor; saying her movement was slinky would be doing an injustice to her. She *flowed*, each part of her moving the way necessary, no excess expenditure, no unnecessary movement.

"Lee-ka oh su sarra!"

She motioned with the weapon for me to get up.

I stood up, facing her, watching her carefully. She frowned at me.

"Dya?"

It was a question; what it meant, I had no idea. There's a limit to guesswork.

I shook my head. *"No comprende,* Pretty Baby."

**=Tch, tch, you're forgetting alien relations. Do you think she'll shoot you?*

I let him know my feelings on that score by thinking of a football. Being kicked for fifty.

"Su-tha, eh d'quar?"

I pointed at the comkey lying near the door to the next compartment.

"I need that. I can't understand you."

"D'taan, k'ehr?—Eh, w'tha?"

I pointed to my mouth, to the key, to my ear; then tried another tack, pointing to my mouth, the key and her. She frowned at me.

"D'taan—"

I pointed to her, to the key, to my ear, trying to mime understanding. Then had a thought.

Shreekor said, *=*Help is coming.*

I said, "Shreekor, I don't need physical—"

The door hissed open and the princess charged through, knife in hand. I didn't see what she intended to do with it; the distraction was enough.

Pretty Baby turned to take a shot at the princess and I dived at her, hitting her at waist level and bruising my shoulder on something hard that was connected to the belt. We thudded into the couch at the other side, knocking the wind out of the woman and making her drop the gun.

Wind brushed my ear and something went *shutch!* into the couch.

I turned my head to see a black hilt joined to the couch padding; there was no sign of the blade.

I looked at the princess, who was watching me haughtily, and said, in her language, "All I needed was the distraction, not a display of prowess with a blade, Princess."

One elegant eyebrow rose. "You have no manners. I saved your life."

I got up, picking up gun and knife with one hand and Pretty Baby with the other, by the vest. She didn't struggle.

I said, "Princess, as far as I'm concerned, the only danger to my life came from your direction. You nearly hit me. I could have settled this quietly, without trying to gut anybody."

*=*My, my, my, what an assumption of ability, my friend.*

"Nuts," I said.

The princess sniffed and turned on her heel, stalking out again. The door closed behind her.

I dropped Pretty Baby on the couch and scooped up the comkey, clipping it on the coverall to leave my hands free, and clipped my weapon back on my belt.

I said, "I don't know what you hoped to gain by knocking me over and holding me hostage. If what your ship says is true, then they're leaving you with us."

She sat tensely, staring at me.

I gave her a moment, then said, "If I hadn't flattened you, you'd now probably be dead."

"You intend to kill me as it is," she said.

I raised an eyebrow. "No. All this runaround was because this ship was boarded by the crew of an unknown ship. Technically, I suppose I'm entitled to toss you out into space, but I don't see any reason to. Added to that, you've just threatened my life, and come very close to getting killed for it." I pointed at her with the hilt of the knife, and she flinched a little. "What I'd like are some coherent explanations. Some pretty peculiar things have been happening recently, and I don't like them. This, particularly."

She didn't say anything.

"Look," I went on, "this is a lifeboat. The place it was sent from, no matter where it is, was destroyed a short time ago by a squadron of exceptionally powerful ships. We were dumped here, only to find, against all kinds of odds that we were practically next to another ship. Yours. Which immediately boarded us. See why we're a little over-careful?''

She looked down into her lap for a moment, then back up at me.

''It is fitting.''

I heaved a sigh and shook my head.

''That,'' I said, ''tells me nothing.''

She gave a semblance of a shrug. ''My people have abandoned me.''

''You do something wrong on board?''

''No.'' When she looked up at me, her eyes were dull. ''I was in command of the ship that put me here.''

There was a sliding crunch from the hull, then silence.

Shreekor's calm voice said, *=*The other ship has detached and is accelerating away.*

Pretty Baby was looking down at her hands. I didn't disturb her.

''Intending to jump, or something?'' I asked Shreekor.

*=*There is some evidence of building spatial distortion . . . yes, they have accelerated beyond light speed. A crude drive. It leaves a severe distortion path for some distance.*

''Chances of them keeping track of us to possibly trail us to wherever we're going?''

*=*Going by what we know, negligible.*

''I'll take your word for it,'' I said, and turned back to the woman. ''What's your name?''

''Nikoi L'aan,'' she said, looking up. Her eyes remained dry—tear ducts possibly unnecessary—but there was a deep sadness in her face. ''I am *Sasha-Ra,* one with no family bond. A mutant and an outcast.''

That was a mouthful; it promised interesting connections, as well.

''What happened inside the ship to get you thrown out that way?'' I asked.

Her eyes flashed; a pale amber luminescence.

She said, ''Politics.''

''I'd have thought a ship was too small to feature an item like that.''

She shook her head. ''No. The *Sasha-Ra* crafts are prone to internal conflict. As are the few *Sasha-Ra* worlds, where the nomad ships make landfall.'' She paused, shrugged. ''Few *Sasha-Ra* settle. We feel unwanted, wherever we are, often even frightened of an open planet.''

That figured; agoraphobia would be a problem where multiple generations of space-wanderers were concerned.

''So you had a mutiny?'' I said.

''Yes. Led by—'' her eyes flashed—''my first officer. I had always thought him loyal.'' Her eyes dimmed, dulled. ''My ship was one of the newer ones. I was made *Sasha-Ra* at an early age, planetside, on a world that I do not know the name of.''

''And the clones you used?''

She seemed surprised. ''*Mya-Wei*. They are used for many kinds of work, beasts of burden. They have developed little intelligence.'' Her eyes flashed again. ''Kardran B'aik used them, and well. There was little fighting—a full battle would have destroyed us all, with the ship.''

I nodded. ''Okay, so we know what happened. So why did they put you here? For all you knew, we could have been waiting with enough firepower to atomize you and your ship.''

She shook her head. ''Your ship is not a warship. We scanned you as you appeared, to be certain.'' She stretched, luxuriously. ''I would otherwise have been marooned on a world where survival would have been possible, either empty or civilized. Perhaps one of the space-worlds.'' She shook her head, smoothed her hair with one hand. Nervous gestures, and some weariness; she was trying to keep her mind off what had happened, probably. ''It was decided that there was no need to kill me. At least it would assure some popularity among the loyal members of the crew for Kardran B'aik.''

I crossed the compartment and set the table upright again, sitting down with the knife in my lap.

I said, ''Well, that sounds truthful enough. Whatever, it looks like you're going to be with us for the time being.''

She watched me for a moment, then said, ''What is to be done with me?''

I shrugged. ''We're supposed to be on the way to another base, so I guess you and Shreekor—that's the telepath I keep speaking to—will be looked after there. I think you'll be all right. We can use extra people anyway.'' I paused for a moment, leaned back and sighed. ''Me, I'll be moving on, with the princess. I'm supposed to be taking her back to my home base, and I'm overdue already, I think. Like I said before, we hit some tangles. This part of it I'll have to put down to a weird coincidence.''

She gave me a puzzled look. ''Why are you apparently so certain that your people will accept me?''

I grinned. ''The day has yet to arrive when I see any base that has one single bunch of sentients on it. You'll be fine, as long as you don't mind traveling around. And sarcastic computers.''

''Sarcastic—these computers are sentient?''

''Oboy, do you have something to learn, Nikoi L'aan. Sentient, yes, and mean with it.''

She sat back, eyes shining.

And a harsh whooping started up.

Nikoi said, ''What?''

I came straight up. ''That's an alarm. You'd better follow me.''

I hit the comkey switch and went through the door as it opened, Nikoi L'aan coming after me.

She said, ''Where are we going?''

I didn't look back as we went through compartments into the first offshoot into the crash-tank sections; she'd be okay in a tank.

I said, as I keyed a tank on, ''I have to get you ready for running. I think we've just hit another crazy coincidence.''

I almost shoved her into the tank. She got the idea and settled down into it, the linkscreen and control section sliding down into place. I hit disconnects selectively. She might as well see what we did, and be in communication with us as well, but I didn't want her able to mess around with anything that could cause disaster.

I said, ''Shreekor, what's going on?''

That was probably the point at which I started appreciating Shreekor's talent for understating things.

He said, *=*Enemy attack. That's what.*

6 The Sleeper

Four points on a dark screen, at the far edge of the scan range.

Sitting still.

On the linkscreen, a stretched-scanner picture, four fuzzy jewels, recognizable even so.

Enemy fighters.

I said, "Shreekor?"

I was back in my own crash-tank, waiting for something to happen. If we'd picked them up, they'd picked us up as well. The only reason for the waiting was probably that they weren't sure exactly what we were. It wouldn't be long.

*=*Vectors set.*

"What are we waiting for?" I asked, looking over at his tank.

*=*I am curious.*

"About what?"

*=*This situation. Doesn't it puzzle you, Kevven?*

"Yeah, my good friend, it puzzles me all right. But if we stay around too long, those things are going to come turn our little old lifeboat into a colander."

*=*Point taken. One other thing: there is a possibility that the seal made by the people of Nikoi L'aan's ship might give way.*

I grunted. "Thank you kindly for presenting that possibility for consumption by my more-than-normally paranoid mind."

*=*I'll play you off for the chance to space the lady.*

My mind gave a reflexive twitch, and I snapped, "The *hell—*" and stopped again, rotated through righteous indignation/anger to suspicion, and went on, "I hope you were joking with me, Shreekor, because if you weren't, and you try anything like that,

I'll tie every one of your tentacles into one big knot and use you for a soccer ball. Got that?''

*=*Not with a crash of thunder, but with a snuffle. Whatever happened to good old alien relations?*

I grinned, relieved. ''They all got arrested for xeno-incest. So how about getting us out of here?''

*=*Hmmm . . . well, cross your fingers, shut your eyes, leap in the air—metaphorically, of course—and pray that I know what I'm doing.*

''Yassuh baas,'' I said. ''I prayin', baas, I prayin' you knowin' what you doin', yassuh I is.''

*=*Well, I thought it might make you feel better. Apparently, though, it simply changes your attitude . . .*

''Well, m' man, *do* you know what you're doing?''

*=*Of course I do. But I bet you don't.*

''Ouch.'' My eyes flickered to the screen, registered a new trace. ''Well, get doing, they're starting to move.''

*=*So they are.*

And he threw us into overdrive, and my mind was pounded on by the overdrive effects, mental distortion amongst the spacial.

When it settled out, we were in clear space—

Well, almost clear, anyway. There was a trace on the screen, too large to be a ship.

Shreekor said, *=*That is Base 908. We are reasonably safe. It is set within a Stellar nebula. We will have to travel slowly.*

''Uh-huh. So let's give 'em a call, octopus.''

*=*They didn't teach you much, did they?*

''Huh?'' I said, showing off my personal genius.

*=*If they had taught you much, you'd be aware that we can't call them. The background noise is intense, for one thing, and we have no five-space transmission equipment aboard.*

''Shreekor,'' I said, ''you're a telepath. Can't you even give them a squeak to say hello?''

There was dead air for a few seconds. Then he said, *=*There are apparently no telepaths aboard. Long distance telepathic communication on my part requires a sensitive at the receiving end.*

I went cold at hearing that, almost stopping breathing.

''Shreekor, there isn't *one* base that doesn't have telepaths. They're too damned common, for one thing, and too useful for another.''

Dead air again.

Then, *=*I know, I* know. *I am trying to avoid the necessary explanation.*

More dead air, while I stared at his tank. The coincidences again. I didn't like them, never have, never will. And the one serious possibility we both had in mind. We shouldn't be out of contact at all with a base this close; telepathic links mostly avoided normal space, like five-space communication equipment.

And no contact from 908 meant one ugly thing.

It was a dead base.

And it hadn't had a chance to blow.

"Let's just make sure."

*=*As you wish.*

Readouts changing on the board.

We didn't exchange any comments for a while; the atmosphere had changed. We didn't know what we'd find at 908—there was no sign of Enemy around the base, but that didn't mean much. For all we knew, there could be a dozen ships hanging in the radar shadow of the base.

Grim visions . . .

I ran a check on the princess; she wouldn't have been expecting the overdrive.

She was in shock, almost unconscious.

I gritted my teeth, annoyed at myself. I should have expected that and put her under before we jumped.

I hit the medical and sleepstim keys together. That would bring her out of it fairly soon. If there was anything still operating on board 908, I could get her back to Area Fourteen via shifter.

But that was a vain hope, and I was all too aware of the fact.

I let my hand drop away from the board, resting it on the side of the crash tank. The padding was warm, smooth. Nikoi L'aan wouldn't have expected the overdrive either; no logical reason to expect the drive of her own ship to work in the same way as ours.

A pity the Builders hadn't seen fit to use a jump method that was less traumatic. But we used shifters most of the time; the lifeboats were simply more capable of handling a full evacuation.

"I'm going to talk to Nikoi," I said.

*=*It might be more advisable to remain where you are.*

I climbed out of the tank, my feet thumping the deck together, jarring me; bad landing.

I said, "Sure. There isn't much that can go wrong right now."

*=*Very well, do what you want, see if I care.*

I opened the door with the comkey, went through into the next compartment and then into Nikoi's area.

I said, "How long before we reach 908 anyway, Shreekor?"

*=*Approximately . . . allow me to check. I need to translate to your timescale.*

Mental silence echoed in my head; I waited.

*=*Approximately four of your hours. We are traveling under impulse power, with something on the order of four point one seven nine gravities thrust, your scale.*

"Shades of *Star Trek*." I raised an eyebrow and looked around at Nikoi. She was lounging in her tank—wide-awake and apparently unconcerned about overdrive effects—watching me curiously. Her eyes were glowing again, moderately. "Maybe if we shake a Roddenberry at 'em they'll quit."

*=*What is a Roddenberry?*

"Something you wouldn't understand," I said. "Leave it until later."

I hooked the comkey onto my overalls and shook my head.

Nikoi said, "The telepath irritates you?"

"No," I said. "We haven't been together long enough for that."

The glow in her eyes flickered a little.

"You seem sarcastic towards him."

"Oh, that's natural. I'm the same way with everybody." I grinned. "Want to go take a look at him?"

"This telepath looks nothing like you?"

"No." I paused and sniffed; there was a smell—more like a definite presence at the edge of sensing—of some kind of perfume in the compartment. I looked curiously at Nikoi. "That smell you? The perfume?"

There was a flicker of an expression that I interpreted as amusement.

"Yes," she said. "On many worlds they call it the smell of the *Sasha-Ra*. It is worn because of the life on the ships. The odors would otherwise drive all aboard insane."

I shook my head. "Well, our life-support tends to work more efficiently. Tends more to the antiseptic."

"That is why there is only a trace," she said. She stood up in the crash tank and touched one of the instruments on her belt.

A moment later, the compartment took on the stink of an Avon warehouse with all the stinkum bottles shattered. It was enough to make my eyes sting. If that was the way they let that stuff go on their ships, the things must stink pretty bad. All they'd have to do was put down on some world or other, blow the hatches, and everybody within a hundred miles would know about it.

The smell of the *Sasha-Ra,* for sure.

I coughed and said, "Okay, turn it off and let the ventilation mop it up, otherwise I'm going to choke."

She shook her head and touched the belt again. The cloud didn't go away, but it didn't get any stronger either.

She climbed out of the tank and went to stand by the door; I touched the comkey and opened it. The perfume smell immediately diminished in strength, but the whole lifeboat would be smelling of it for as long as we were on it.

I led her through to the compartment occupied by Shreekor and myself; the princess was still out of it, under sleepstim, while the med units worked on the shock she'd had.

The perfume smell dissipated until it was again only at the edge of awareness.

I pointed to Shreekor's tank and said, "That's him, it, or whatever. He's piloting us at the moment, or, if you prefer, he's watching the computers piloting."

*=*Hmph.*

I grinned. "Sounds like you've got an ego, my—"

There was a metallic thump from the bulkheads; I felt it simultaneously with my feet.

The Dustpipe lurched crazily, throwing Nikoi into me as I lost balance. Together we slid along the floor and piled up against Shreekor's crash-tank, tangled up; there was a sharp pain in my shoulder, and another in my butt—I hadn't been able to roll because of Nikoi.

I untangled myself from Nikoi and sat up against Shreekor's tank.

"What the hell happened?" I asked.

*=*The seal gave way. You see, there is an advantage in staying in the crash-tanks.*

Shreekor's tone was dry.

I said, "Yeah, sure. Go on."

*=*I presume that the bonding element in the seal was strained during the jump to here. We are probably fortunate that it lasted so long. The disruption of our gravitational fields was responsible for the lurch. The same disruption is also responsible for the plug being repelled. Said plug is currently moving away from us on a perpendicular from our present course. The situation is a little more complicated, but I won't strain your mind.*

I rubbed my sore shoulder and leaned back against Shreekor's tank; Nikoi was already stood up, looking down at me with a puzzled expression. Shreekor was probably piping it through to her as well.

I said, "Well, let's go and get it back."

*=*Why?*

I raised myself a little so I could peer down into the tank. Shreekor's multiple eyes looked back up at me impassively—well, I guess they were impassive. I'm not much good with alien expression.

I said, "Why? Well, how about, as an example, so we can put it back in place, seal it again, and get the hell out once we've gotten all the information we need?"

*=*Presumably you will remove the numerous warps from the plating, and replace the crystallized and torn sections of the plate?*

I sighed and slid back down the side of the tank until my butt thumped floor.

*=*Never mind. Your training probably would not cover such things.*

"Yeah," I said. "Sure. Next time, tell everything first, okay?"

*=*Apologies. But we are disabled until repairs are carried out.*

"Obviously." I got to my feet, dusted myself off; my back was warm where I'd been sat against the side of the tank. "There isn't an Enemy ship around, is there?"

*=*No. But if there was, it would be too bad.*

I turned around and glared at the tank. "You know something, Shreekor? You're really a fun person to be around. Really *positive*, y'know?"

A bunch of tentacles flopped over the side of Shreekor's tank, with a shuffling noise. They lay still.

"That's right, play dead, *shvartzer,* and I might let you off."

*=*You really know how to hurt a Shimo-sh'sasai, don't you?*

There was a history of torture and exceptionally vicious pogroms in that statement; that was all I needed. An alien with a Jewish background.

I said, "Come off it, Shreekor, you've got a thicker skin than me."

*=*Sniffle. Sniffle. Sob. Waaaaaaaaah!*

"Bet you're trying not to laugh."

*=*The pain, the pain, the—*

I shut him off, ignoring him, and turned back to Nikoi.

"How do you feel?"

She looked down at herself, then back up at me. "A little bruised, but no worse." She paused for a moment. "I think that Shreekor has a good point. It would be safer to remain within the safety berths."

"Crash-tanks," I corrected. "But yeah, he's right. I'd better take you back."

Her eyes flared a little, very briefly.

I led her back to her compartment; it wasn't all that lonely, as she could call up for a chat anytime.

As she settled down and I sorted out her control board for her, she said, "This . . . enemy you spoke about. Who is it?"

I turned away from the board and leaned against the tank, looking down at her.

I said, "We just call them the Enemy. They've been around quite a while, and I don't think anybody knows who they are. I don't, for sure. All I do is run and hide when they're around."

"Every time?"

I shook my head. "Not every time. Once in a while I have to stand and fight." I sighed, and rubbed a hand over the edge of the tank. "I'll explain it in a while. Do you have some sort of timepiece with you?"

"Yes." She checked her belt, hands moving with trained precision, and held up a small gray cube. She pressed the side of it with one finger and it lit up, showing multiple cube-shaped figures with linear designs set into them. "But why?"

I took it from her. "I want to rig this into the computer so you can get a countdown for our arrival." I closed my fist around it; it fitted neatly. "I'll bring it back, and then explain the Enemy to you. Or, at least, what I know about them."

I turned and left.

Thinking, *how do you explain a bunch of vicious killers like the Enemy?*

I slept for a couple of hours after talking to Nikoi; Shreekor woke me after parking the lifeboat relative to the base. I'd been snoring peacefully, and waking was a bit of a shock; I came to with the immediate realization that we were in trouble as far as the lifeboat itself went, and as far as the base went.

As for knowing I was snoring:

I said, "How do you know I was snoring, Shreekor?"

*=*My training covers many things, my friend. And, despite my being a natural telepath, I can hear auditorily. And quite well, too, thank you, and not just in your limited range.*

I couldn't help a grin; Shimo-sh'sasai he might be, but that didn't stop my appreciation of the humor, bad situation or not.

"Yeah, well," I said, "my mother always said I snored."

*=*Your mother was quite correct. In fact, I had computer correlate the sound. You snore like a ratchet.*

"So said Shreekor, ever the scientist despite the most terrible of stresses. Speaking of which—"I touched the on switch and watched the control board and linkscreen swing down toward me—"let's take a look at things as they are."

The screen lit; the base hung in the middle of it, surrounded by the slight luminescence of the nebula we were in.

I leaned sideways and looked at the princess's crash-tank; she was still under, which was unusual.

Shreekor said, *=*I have kept her under sleep stimulation for the while. It makes work much easier on our part.*

I nodded. "Okay. But let her up in a while. Otherwise she'll be bitching when she *does* wake up. These royal types get feisty about pains in the head, and that's what I get from oversleeping."

*=*Hmm.*

I studied the picture of the base; I could make out some spots on the beach ball shape where there was probably damage; there was a pucker, like the scar from a heavy-caliber bullet wound, in the north-east section on my screen. It was possible that something had gone right through, and that something else had sealed the hole right afterwards. If that was the case, the base would have an entire section blown away.

I said, "No chance 908 was unmanned?"

*=*Records list it as a manned station.*

It had been a pretty vain hope, any way I looked at it. I'd been brought up as part of a base complement, as had my parents and my grandparents. My line took up in Bantu country on Earth; my ancestors were pureblood Mala, a tribe—typically—that no one has ever heard of. For a good reason. Except for those few ancestors hauled off to Area Fourteen, the tribe had been wiped out by slavers.

The thing was I'd never heard of an unmanned Builder's base.

"Records," I said, "should have listed this base as destroyed when it was attacked."

*=*They don't. Which I personally find very odd. The damage appears old—notice the lack of debris—and there should have been some form of contact attempted. It is possible that the attack was carried out so swiftly that there was no time for defense and transmission of the message.*

"Bullshit." I sighed and settled in the tank, rubbing my face with both hands; dark backs and light palms, looking clean. Feeling tired. "The lifeboats carry . . ." I stopped and shook my head.

There was an empty feeling in my mind, instead of Shreekor's voice.

I said, "Yeah."

There was that puckered scar in the hide of the base.

Whatever it was had gone straight through, for sure.

Taking the Mastercomputer and all the lifeboats with it.

*=*It is unlikely that anyone would have visited this area for some time.*

"Yeah, I guess you're right."

I gave the base a final long look, then punched the switch angrily, turning it off. Why the hell this sort of thing had to happen was beyond me; the fact that no one seemed to *know* hurt even more.

I shook my head, trying to clear out the anger; it wasn't going to do anyone any good.

I said, "Okay, Shreekor, what do we do next?"

*=*You and our new passenger had better take life-support packs and board the base. We will need information as well as supplies for repair.*

"And what about you?" I said, looking over at his tank.

*=*I will direct you. From here. I possess none of the physical requirements. And your princess has no training for this sort of mission. As you and Nikoi L'aan are best suited, you go.*

His logic was impeccable; it left the heavy work to Nikoi and myself.

"Lazy bum," I said.

*=*Your commentary will not change the situation one little bit. You go, with Nikoi L'aan.*

The Dustpipe, from outside: a long, silvery cylinder with flat ends, no glaring signs of drives, just a series of grids at the rear.

And a ragged hole in the silver surface, where the plug had ripped loose. There was no doubt about it; the distortion encountered during our last jump had played havoc with the seal and the surrounding metal, crystallizing it and generally ruining it.

We'd been lucky.

I thought about that as Nikoi—I'd now taken to anglicizing her name and calling her Nikky—and I dropped away from the Dustpipe towards the dead base.

We could have been hit by distortion during jump; the usual effects were bad enough, and death during jump would probably be the worst set of sensations ever felt. Not that anyone would have cared much.

Nikky moved ahead of me, the pale yellow glow of her life-support field blotting out some of the background glow. We were both wearing the same equipment—I'd spent an hour teaching Nikky to use some of it— and that consisted mainly of the dual life-support and propulsion packs across our shoulders, a heavy power belt, cutting torches, a sensor pack, medipaks, communications equipment, and high-power strip lights; the lights themselves were strapped to our shoulders, and raised over our heads, angled so that whatever we happened to be looking at would be lit. Nikky would probably see more than I would anyway; her eyesight extended into the infra-red and ultra-violet.

The beach ball shape of the base hung before us; space plays tricks with the mind, and we hardly seemed to be closing on it. It took an effort to realize that, in fact, the base was closer than it had been a minute ago, and larger, filling out more of my sightline, blocking out more of the background.

The silence was awful.

I looked back at the tiny shape of the lifeboat, hanging against the background of glowing dust; so far away. If anything attacked, we'd probably be better off hiding in the base.

But nothing attacked.

I watched the base; I'd thought of them as being built like a wheel for a long time, an illogical assumption, as the wheel design is built for gravity by centrifugal force, and the bases used generators. The engineering problems involved must have been incredible—the bases were massive—but the Builders, whoever they were, had apparently had no trouble. For all I knew, anyway. As far as Area Fourteen was concerned, my guess was that homo sap—and sap he is—probably wasn't around when it was built. Just a convenient position.

So why build around the third planet?

I dropped the question; I'd asked it too many times before.

I said, "It doesn't look dead." It broke the silence, at least.

"True," Nikoi replied. I accelerated and caught up with her, traveling level. "But I can see traces of damage from here."

Without the lifeboat computer enhancing the image, I couldn't see much; just a few darker patches on the skin of the base. To me, they looked like beerstains on a dark beach ball. Nikky could probably see the damage more easily

We turned turtle, decelerated, halted hanging twenty centimeters above the surface of the base, the dark metal filling the view in the silence; dead and cold.

I said, "Our main problem is finding a way in." I looked over at Nikky; her hair, floating in free fall, swirled around her; she had a glow in her eyes, apparently produced by interest. "I think that's Shreekor's part," I went on. "And with luck, he should have his sensors together."

Nikky's eyebrows gave a twitch, the motion distorted slightly by the shimmering of her life support field.

She said, "You sound as though you dislike the other alien."

I grinned, hoping it was reassuring rather than frightening—there was at least one race with a tendency to take fright at a show of teeth.

I said, "He isn't the only other alien. Besides which, he's okay. To quote one of our famous poets, 'You're a better man than I am, Gunga Din.' Shreekor's just better suited to direction and piloting, as he pointed out. Without wasting time."

She turned away with a nod, scanning the surface of the base.

There were entrances scattered around the exterior, but all of them were flush with the surface; the biggest of them could take a number of lifeboats, or a big ship, with ease. Others allowed exit for EVA work, or just plain practice.

Shreekor said, *=*I have, as you put it, got my sensors together. So please follow my instructions.*

He guided us around the outside of the base, giving precise instructions on how much acceleration was to be used, until we reached a point where he claimed there was a hatch.

On the way, we'd passed over some of the more serious damage to the base; a crater gouged out of the skin, filled with solidified slag. The moon had similar features, worn by meteorites and time; the crater here was still more or less in the same shape it had been when first formed, with a central, jagged spike pointing lopsidedly from the center. I could see other damage fairly clearly now, as well. The puckered scar was north of our position, a ragged crater that had been filled in by a second shot, blocking off access that way. Whatever had produced it had done some very serious damage. I could also see some of the burn scars from energy weaponry, ragged dark lines across the skin of the base, and great chunks chewed away.

The Enemy made a hell of a job of wrecking bases.

The base had lost all of its gravity during the wrecking session, by the look of it; there wasn't even a trace of spin to help out. Which I didn't mind too much; I wasn't sure I could bear walking on walls all that easily. Any debris flung off in the attack had vanished into the depths of space a long time ago, without trace; some surprised system would find it traveling through some time in the future, millions of years away. Given enough time, and provided said debris didn't either encounter a sun or get hooked up by a stellar system, it could eventually leave this particular galaxy entirely.

I turned my attention back to finding a way in; it would be easy enough if there was still some power on the base—certain sections, such as the locks, had independent power—but if everything was dead, we would probably have to cut our way in. Which wouldn't matter too much, as Shreekor's main plan was to cut a chunk of the base surface away, weld it into place over the hole in the Dustpipe, then seal it in place with a flood of sealant, if we could find any.

Nikky was searching an area above me, her face close to the

metal. I started looking a distance below her; it would be harder for me—she could see things I'd normally miss.

It was a few minutes before Nikky stopped searching; she waited for a moment, then, activating her flight pack to hold her in place, pressed down on a section of the surface.

Silence, and an eerie quality with it: a section of the surface slowly folded inwards, vanishing into darkness as smoothly as a curling snake. A huge black hole in the base's surface waited for us.

I looked at Nikoi as she looked at me, then at the hole. The lock didn't show any signs of moving back into place.

I said, "After you, Mademoiselle L'aan."

She didn't say anything to that; insteaed, she activated her flight pack and guided herself into the darkness, vanishing into shadow.

There was a light, breathless feeling throughout my entire body, a kind of nervous sensation; I recognized certain symptoms of it: fear of the dark. I was experiencing a nightmare close up.

I took a deep breath and let it out, hissing, between my teeth, took another, activated the flight pack, and followed Nikky into darkness.

Ahead of me, her lights flashed into brilliance. I reached up and touched the controls for my own lights, saw them illuminate Nikky, her life-support field barely visible under the glare, her hair floating around her.

I stopped beside her; she was looking at the inner door of the lock. It was frozen open. No sign of atmosphere. Not too surprising, as the attack would have gotten rid of it. And there hadn't been any atmosphere trapped in the lock; I'd been half-expecting something wrong with the inner door, more along the lines of it being jammed into place.

"Let's get a move on," I said.

"You are frightened?" Nikoi said, as she looked around.

"Yeah," I said. "I know the Enemy. I wouldn't be surprised if they left something nasty behind."

Nikky started ahead of me, moving slowly. "I am very frightened. Such a dark place . . . so dead. It seems unnatural."

I moved off after her, careful with the flight pack controls; an impact with a bulkhead, even gentle, could be fatal if I wrecked my life-support. The field wasn't designed for anything more than meteorite deflection.

I said, "The bases are pretty unnatural anyway."

"This Enemy is a terrible opponent. Why do you allow them to continue destroying like this?"

I sighed. "It isn't my decision. I just work for this crazy bunch." I stopped in front of a door, unhinged a cutter. I tried the opening mechanism first; nothing. I started cutting. "So far as I know, we haven't got the weaponry to take them on one to one. We just watch and collect material and information. We're purely on the defensive."

The glowing red line produced by the cutter's bright emerald beam slowly tracked around the edge of the door; it was effective enough. It wasn't long before I'd cut my way in. I was hoping for something important first try, but all I got was a games room. The equipment—much of it I didn't recognize—was scattered around, overturned, some of it broken, a few pieces floating against the bulkheads.

I backed out, and turned. "Nothing in there. We aren't going to find much at all. What damage there is, is too extensive."

Nikky looked pained.

I said, "I told you. They're bastards. By the looks of things, the base took a heap of them with it. Otherwise they'd probably have destroyed it completely."

She started down the corridor without replying to that; she hadn't quite believed most of the things I told her about the Enemy, although she believed most of the detail about the Builders; she'd had plenty of objective proof. Compared to her technology, what was involved in our lifeboats made most of their ships look awkward. But one of our directives included leaving other technologies to develop in their own way, without inflicting ours on them.

We moved through the base, checking occasional doorways; we had to burn through almost all of them, and most of the locks we encountered on the way. Eventually we came to the area of the base that had been blasted through. The hole was straight enough, and the corridor we were in had been blocked off by solidified slag and melted debris; the only way through was to burn or blast.

We trained the torches on the metal from a distance, with filters over our eyes; the effect from the burning would be enough to blind both of us otherwise.

We switched the cutters on and left them to do the necessary work, huddling behind a bulkhead for the few minutes needed.

While we waited, Nikky said, "I have heard tales . . ."

I looked around at her; talk about anything was welcome right now. I hated empty silences, and silence in vacuum most of all. Long enough in it, and you could go mad. It's almost as bad as sensory deprivation.

I said, "What about?"

She made herself more comfortable. "Many of the travelers at the ports were the *Sasha-Ra* are made welcome speak of forces beyond mortality fighting within the universe."

"That isn't so surprising. I wouldn't be surprised at some sort of noise about the Builders getting around."

"But they say that these forces vie for supremacy."

I felt my eyebrows draw together; it could be distortion—after all, the Builders and the Enemy had to be fighting for something, or else it came down to a battle of delinquents on an incredible scale. Supremacy was as good as anything else. What the hell the Enemy intended to do with the universe once they'd mopped up the Builders—if ever—I didn't know. But force seems always to be intended to result in something lording it over something else.

I said, "Yeah, I guess it figures. Not that I'm in this to control anything or anybody."

"There was a rumor of an organization," Nikky went on, almost as if she hadn't heard. "It was supposed to be battling one of these forces."

"I don't blame 'em a bit for trying, Nikky. We aren't much use." I sighed and peered out of our cover. The cutters were still at work. "For all I know, the Builders built the bases to protect developing worlds from the Enemy. They didn't do much of a job, if so."

"You sound bitter about it."

"Hell, I try to do my job, and every time somebody forgets a little bit of information and I wind up nearly getting my ass shot off. Of course I'm bitter about it. I don't like getting shot at, and I don't like seeing my friends getting shot down because somebody thought I'd get along better without being warned."

Nikky looked surprised. "That has happened recently?"

"Yeah. Days ago. A lady I was supposed to contact got wounded pretty badly by the Enemy. I had to blow up a commercial transportation station to get the sniper." I slapped my hands together, watched the field surfaces join, felt the reflex of the field preventing contact as it was meant to. "I got told off for extreme measures. At the time, I didn't have the chance to consider alternatives. I was trying to save lives."

"Ignore the others, then. At least you have the courage to follow the line you believe in."

"Not courage, necessarily," I said, surprising myself with the untypical modesty/honesty. "I just didn't have much choice. The guy was slaughtering people. I had to do something. And, also, I owed him for shooting my contact. She's a good friend."

"A lover?"

I chuckled at that. "Hell, no. We never get together long enough. She usually has something to do on Earth—that's my home planet—and I usually get missions out on some crappy planet or other. Just isn't like living aboard a tin can."

Neither of us had noticed that we'd moved off the original track. Not that it mattered just then.

I looked around the side of our cover, and saw that the torches had cut off after burning away the wreckage in the corridor. The edges were still red-hot, but that heat would radiate off fairly soon. In the meantime, the life-support fields would protect us.

I waved for Nikoi to follow me, and floated the length of the corridor to the torches, swinging the filter up out of the way. I unhooked them and clipped my own back to my belt while Nikoi stopped and picked hers up.

I started forward again, went through the ragged hole the torches had made, avoiding the glowing edges automatically, and turned over.

The light from my shoulder rig reflected from a multitude of slagged edges, some of them reflective, others dull. It wasn't a perfect shaft, but close enough. Maybe fifty meters at the widest point; probably a number of c-speed shells had torn straight through.

I turned over, looked downwards. The same story as before, except that the shells had obviously exploded; there was a massive end-hole below me, where the lifeboats had been originally. The radiation might have been contained, and possibly the concussion effects—that would have been enough to knock out the gravity generators—but the blast effect was devastating enough. Not enough to total the base. Just the lifeboats and the Mastercomputer. A lucky shot, probably. For them.

It must have been a pretty well-planned sneak attack. Or the detectors on board had been screwed up by the nebula.

Nikky was silent as she viewed the destruction. As was I; there was no use in pointing out things to each other. It was all too plain that we weren't going to get anything from this part of the base.

I didn't know how many sentients the base had had; but if there hadn't been any kind of report from an escaped lifeboat about this base, then the entire complement was dead, so much energy and hot gas escaping into space to become a part of the nebula.

We turned and left; as far as that part was concerned, we'd seen enough. The blast hadn't gone completely through the base. Just far enough.

I was beginning to hate the Enemy more than anything I'd ever come across.

We started moving through the base again, slowly; we didn't expect to find anything—a strange fatalism had gripped both of us. This was a dead place, and all traces of information as to its death had vanished at the time of dying.

In my time of dying, Lord . . .

I'd never liked viewing the remains; it made me feel sick.

It was an hour after looking down into the hole through the base that Nikoi spotted heat radiating from one of the bulkheads; it wasn't a trace from anything we'd done, and there wasn't very much of it. Shreekor's sensors wouldn't normally have noticed it, and it was only because of Nikoi's range of vision that it had been found at all.

We stopped and I picked up my sensor pack, slapping it up against the doorway.

I said, "Shreekor, we've found something weird. I've got my sensor pack up nearby, so you'd better scan through and tell us what the hell's hiding on the other side."

*=*One moment. Take cover.*

He didn't have to tell us; by that time, Nikky and I were scooting back down the corridor and around a bend; I had my laser out, and Nikky was holding her cutter in a presumably offensive way. The thing would make a pretty effective weapon.

We'd covered a great deal of the base already; there was so much destruction that sections we'd normally have checked out were closed off, mostly destroyed. One of the computer rooms had remained intact, mostly. All we'd found in there had been the normal blank panels, partially pulled away, and a few components drifting around. Someone had taken it apart, probably Enemy. Although it didn't seem to fit the pattern. There was also a lab section that had apparently been used, but we couldn't be sure whether that was before or after the attack. Not that it seemed to matter. There wasn't a trace of Enemy around.

We'd finally located some materials for repairing the Dustpipe as well; sealant, mainly, and spray hoses. I'd found an operative floater truck, which would ease transportation considerably. Most of the equipment was unusable because of damage, so we could consider ourselves lucky. In part. We didn't know yet what was going to be on the other side of that bulkhead; or, in fact, whether what was in those sealant tanks was going to be usable after all this time.

A few minutes later, Shreekor said, **=I have completed the scan. There are no life-forms behind the bulkhead. There* is *a mechanism of sort sort, a combination of electronic and electromechanical systems. The nearest correlations are a complex refrigeration unit or a crude cryogenics apparatus.*

"Suspended animation?" I said.

Nikky looked at me with one eyebrow cocked.

**=It is quite possible. However, I detect no sign of life. But the equipment is operative.*

"I didn't know the bases were equipped for cryogenic suspension," I said, moving out of cover.

**=They aren't. But anyone with the requisite knowledge of biophysics and the materials, plus a moderate skill at assembly, should be able to construct a cryogenic unit that could be used in a situation such as this. Also, barring accident and catastrophe, such a unit is able to maintain suspension for millennia. Until power gives out.*

I signaled Nikky to follow me, and started back down the corridor. Shreekor hadn't said it would go bang if we started fooling around, so it looked like it was safe enough to check up on it.

"So the poor bastard who built it is most likely dead."

**=Indeed. I detect no lifesigns, and unless the suspension is complete there should be something.*

"Well, oh wise captain, do we burn in or not?" I tucked away the gun and readied my cutter.

**=You may as well go in. I am interested in seeing what sort of unit was constructed.*

I directed Nikky to start cutting at the top; she swung her filter down and kicked the deck, floating up and over, hair not quite caught up with the rest of her. The effect was fascinating, a great swirl of shining red and white hair around her.

She thumbed the power stud of her torch and the beam lanced out, eating into the edge of the doorframe.

I leveled the thin tip of my own cutter at the other side of the door, near the lower edge, and started cutting it away.

When we had the door cut away, I made a point of pulling the chunk back; I didn't want to wreck whatever was in there. It took a moment to get the thing to floor level; I kept it in place by welding one edge to the floor.

Then we stepped inside.

There was a maze of jury-rigged equipment; masses of wiring that had been neatly collected together so anybody entering wouldn't break any of it. From the equipment I could see, this was where the bits taken from the computer had gone. Also, probably, the result of the use of the lab that Nikoi and I had visited.

I turned full circle, slowly, looking at everything; it had to be a cryogenics set-up. There was no other excuse for the incredible rig that had been fitted in here.

There was a control unit set about three feet from the ground, on a dais. I went over to it, looked it over. It was covered by a screwed-on sheet of heavy plastic, protecting various switches. Except, I saw, as I leaned closer, a section where the plastic was thin enough to break easily.

I cleaned dirt and ice crystals from the plastic to make out better what was underneath. The particular switch was marked clearly enough; my guess was that the lunk who'd built it wanted to make sure there were no mistakes.

This switch means OFF!

I didn't bother to try it; I'd been wrong before, and I'd seen examples of complex minds producing complex solutions. This could be one. Easily.

I couldn't understand the symbols on the console. Better to leave it for now.

I stepped back from it, giving it a last few looks, it set at a thirty-degree or so slope from the horizontal, on a large plinth.

The wiring from it was protected by heavy tubing, splitting in a number of directions. One direction had a massive atomic battery at the end of the conduit; it was a standard unit, and, if my teaching had been right, probably still capable of operating for a few millennia.

So that covered function and power.

The cryogenic coffin itself—I was feeling a bit morbid about the situation by now—was placed over near a bulkhead; fairly small, and pretty scruffy. It hadn't been jury-rigged; neither had the functions console. Both had been engineered for this particular use.

I leaned over the unit, and used the life-support field to clear away dirt and frost; the top was the same thick, transparent plastic that had been screwed over the functions console. Curved gracefully, as thick as a wood plank, probably a thousand times as tough.

There was a small, humanoid alien inside, long, thin hands crossed over a scrawny chest, face composed as if it was sleeping. Mottled blue skin—the mottling probably due to the suspension process—no more than three and a half feet tall. Gracefully curving antennae looking like thin worms with oversized suckers on the end, probably hearing organs as there was no sign of anything I'd normally think of as ears.

The fingers were triple jointed, as were the twin thumbs to each hand, one either side of the main group of five fingers per hand; feet bare, more or less the same as the hands, with five toes, all triple jointed, and a large thumb-like toe per foot. Not symmetrical; the sleeper could have been genetically redesigned.

The arms and legs were covered by the thin white gown that ran from throat to ankles. So I couldn't make any guesses about the arms and legs.

But I suspected they'd have just as many capabilities as the hands and feet. The sleeper would be as limber as an acrobatic monkey, and capable of handling miniature work with absolute ease. The proof was in the rig around me.

That meant he was an engineer/scientist, and probably one of the best of all the bases.

I said, "He doesn't look dead."

*=*It seems not.*

"You're getting what I'm seeing?"

*=*Yes. I also have an identification. It's an Aldebaranian.*

And 'he' appears to be the correct designation. He's definitely a long way from home.

"So're you, my man. Don't complain about it." I turned and looked back at the functions console. "You make anything of that yet?"

*=*Functions control console. I have set the computer to translation. The symbols are Aldebaranian.*

"I guessed already," I said.

*=*While we are waiting, why don't you take a closer look at the equipment? The information may be useful if we have to bypass the control unit.*

Nikky floated up to me, resting a hand on my shoulder through the field, and looking at the Aldebaranian in the cryogenic box. Her eyes flashed.

I said, "I've a better idea. Nikoi ought to look it over. She has better vision than me."

*=*For once, a good idea. You should have more of them.*

"I do. But I thought you were the brains of the crew."

I grasped Nikoi around the waist and swung her around, floating her into first position; she started scanning closely immediately. It didn't require any real concentration on her part, just a slow scanning pattern that didn't miss anything.

While she went over the rig, I went back outside and retrieved the sensor pack I'd left hooked on the bulkhead.

When she was finished, a few minutes later, she floated back over to me, and settled in an apparently comfortable floating position a few feet away.

"Do you think the one in the casket is still alive?" she asked.

I shrugged. "Could be. But I'm not putting any money on it right now."

"The console is operative."

"Yeah, but we don't know yet whether the rest of it is."

She started to float away from me, back towards the casket. I followed her.

She said, "I wonder how long it took him to construct this? It must have been a difficult task."

I halted my flight and looked down on the peacefully sleeping alien—or peacefully dead alien—a few feet below.

I said, "I'd be surprised if it took too much time. He's built for this sort of job."

Shreekor interrupted with:

*=*It seems that he is most likely still alive. The equipment, going by scan analysis, is in perfect condition. According to the computer, the mechanism produces a stasis effect as far as life functions are concerned. There isn't even the slightest trace of brain function.*

I looked over at Nikky; her eyes flashed as she glanced up from the casket.

"You sure that isn't because the brain's deteriorated?" I said. "Or that he's simply died off in the meantime and been preserved?"

*=*I'm quite certain.*

I sighed. "Okay, I'll trust your judgment and blame you later. So, Doctor Octopus, can we wake him up?"

*=*But of course! Why else would I have you waiting there?*

Why else indeed?

"Okay," I said. "Just say when, and what, and where, and how, and I'll throw the switch."

*=*And bang goes my surprise. You worked it out already.*

I didn't spoil the illusion for him.

7 The Ship

I dropped the miniature biomonitors on the functions panel, pushing them down to make them stay in place, and gave the compressed emergency life-support pack a good shove to push it over to Nikky; she was waiting by the cryogenic casket. Shreekor had sent the equipment over for us, as nobody expected the midget Aldebaranian to be in any real condition to go flying around the place.

Nikky caught the square unit in both hands, and turned it over, looking at it. I kept forgetting: she wasn't one of the Builders' crew. That sort of thing happens when you meet somebody else who's spent a lifetime in space.

I floated over to Nikky and opened the pack for her, showing her how to fix it in place over the coffin, then went back for the biomonitors; Nikky would have to stay within the support area to get the alien into the pack for transport across to the lifeboat; I was going to have to stay outside to flip the switch.

But I could see through the transparent material easily enough. This would be something to watch.

Nikky attached the biomonitors, then stepped back, her eyes on them.

I said, ''Shreekor?''

*=*Go ahead.*

I picked up the cutter, turned it over, and rapped the thin plastic over the switch; it shattered easily, brittle. I'd had a sensor pack on the board a while ago; Shreekor had come back with the news that only one switch was working anyway; the rest were all fused at the contacts, probably after use. The whole thing was automatic, but had to be activated manually.

I took a breath, then flicked the switch.

The row of lights that had been glowing under the heavy plastic, along the top of the console, went out; a three-by-three square of white lights in the bottom right corner lit in place of the row, flashing steadily in sequence, probably some sort of computer code to say A-OK. I hoped so.

The whole arrangement had been very logically set up; anybody not understanding the language and symbols used would be quickly directed to the one obvious switch—in fact, too obvious. At least for my comfort. I'd only been reassured by Shreekor's insistence.

The entire bank of lights started pulsing steadily, all together; then they settled down into steady output.

Other lights flicked on; various functions in operation.

I was beginning to feel useless; I'd thrown the switch, and that was the last thing I could do until the Aldebaranian woke up, if he did. Nikky, even, didn't have much to do. The computer had sorted out most of her language, so the readings she was getting on the biomonitor screens were understandable, but Shreekor was the one who was directing this, and only he could say what to do, if anything.

I was bored stiff.

And I continued to be bored stiff for the next hour and a half, while the machinery continued to work on the Aldebaranian.

A light flickered out, another one lit, flashing as if it had achieved something by lighting up.

In a way, I suppose it had.

Shreekor said, *=*Brain functions are beginning to return. Heart is functioning, albeit slowly.*

Nikky turned to look at me. She seemed pleased.

So he was alive; I hoped his brain hadn't turned to spinach in the meantime.

*=*Interior temperature continues to rise; blood temperature rising.*

"Alive, huh?" I said.

*=*Of course. By tomorrow evening he'll be ready for cooking. I'm told roast Aldebaranian is exceptionally tasty.*

"Don't tell me you're a cannibal?"

*=*Heh, heh, heh. Don't worry, you're lunch, my friend. Whoooorr!*

I laughed. "Shreekor, you ought to know that isn't effective without the visuals. You've been reading my mind too much."

*=*Only the impulsive links with horror stories and such that tend to be brought up when you think of me. And we all have our monsters.*

Nikky looked at me again, for a moment; she looked bored now. The whole thing had settled back into simplicity; so bland it made sleeping look exciting.

I said, "We do?"

*=*Of course. Ours look like you.*

"So do most of ours."

*=*Do you have to spoil my fun?*

"Yeah, of course I do. It's the local 'hate a Shimo-sh'sasai' week, don't you know?"

*=*Hmph.*

A series of lights went out on the board; another series lit, flashing. Judging by the previous flashing light, these were probably also positive.

*=*All life-systems approaching normal.*

There was suddenly a feeling of tension; I wasn't sure whether it was from myself, or coming broadcast from Shreekor. I felt my hands close into fists, and I realized I was gritting my teeth so hard that my jaw muscles were cramping. I took a deep breath and untensed myself as best I could. It wasn't quite enough.

I looked from the casket, where Nikoi was concentrating on the biomonitors, to the console.

All the lights blanked out at once.

"Shreekor!" I said; it was almost a shout.

*=*He's awake.*

I relaxed, for a moment, then stiffened up again as the lid of the casket popped up. But that seemed natural enough. Nikky stepped back in surprise and glanced at me, then back at the casket.

The Aldebaranian sat up and clapped his hands.

Then passed out, falling back.

Shreekor said, *=*Biomonitors indicate exhaustion.*

I wasn't too surprised.

Nikky started arranging the equipment for transport.

The alien's stay in the cold casket had caused the exhaustion; the waking procedure was complicated, and, even with the required operations fully carried out by the equipment, was a strain on the alien. Added to that, he probably hadn't been living and working under the best of conditions while building the equipment. He'd left out exercisers, for one thing; that meant he'd have a cramp or two while getting reoriented. The lifeboat's equipment would solve most of the problem, though. I hoped.

At least his brain was in better condition than the rest of him.

After we loaded him into a crash tank, Nikky and I went off to change; Shreekor and the medical equipment could take care of him. It wouldn't be too long before we could speak to him.

While I relaxed in the lounge, with the princess curled up combing and braiding her hair, I pondered the journey so far; it was a series of mild cataclysms, probably against all odds. Somebody was going to get hell from me when I got back to Area Fourteen. Nobody had told me about Enemy attacks on Aureon, or the probability that Ten Seventy-Four would be hit; no notice of the wrecking of 908 was bad enough.

It probably wouldn't do me any good; I'd just wind up assigned for the return trip.

I pushed the pessimism out of my mind; I'd helped save a life today, so not everything had gone wrong. Besides, it would be a couple of weeks before we got moving again; the work ahead was going to be tough. Cutting out a section of the base and welding it to the lifeboat, then sealing it well enough so that jump-distortion wouldn't do any damage. With two of us suited for the job.

I sighed and winked at the princess.

She stopped brushing her hair for a few moments, looking at me from under half-closed eyelids, half-smiling, a little playful.

I should have taken her up on that part of it.

After all, it isn't every day a Black Devil and a princess get so close . . .

The little alien was sitting up in his tank when I went back to the compartment we'd put him in. He was sipping from a large cup; steam rose from the top. The heat didn't seem to bother him.

I sniffed at the air to see if I could recognize it.

And thereafter attempted to stay out of range.

I noticed that the princess and Nikoi were both attempting to do the same, as politely as possible.

The Aldebaranian, blissfully unaware of that, kept on sipping, now and then looking up with lively round eyes, with vertical-slit irises.

Shreekor was hovering over the tank, most of his tentacles hanging down around him; he was using three to make last adjustments to a flying mike; that was obviously for translation without fuss, for our benefit. Shreekor, naturally, didn't need anything electronic to do the work.

He said, *=*You can begin the interview soon. Our guest requires a few more moments to finish his dinner.*

"Dinner?" I pulled a face, trying to avoid breathing through my nose. "Where I come from, that stuff comes out the hind end of animals, instead of going in the top end as fuel."

*=*Is his physiology reversed, or is yours?*

I grinned; nice question, the sort they teach us to avoid. I said, "I wouldn't care to say. It's a good question for the philosophers."

There was a deep mental chuckle.

*=*You saved yourself* just *in time.*

Nikoi braved the fumes coming from the crash tank, and leaned over the Aldebaranian, inspecting his antennae. His eyes rolled up to look at her, giving him a babyish-cute look, and the antennae wriggled.

She looked up at Shreekor and said, "How is he?"

*=*He is in reasonable condition. There is no crystallization damage. The worst appears to be some atrophying of unimportant muscles.*

The Aldebaranian looked around at us, holding the cup away from him with one arm; he held the other up, letting the sleeve of his gown—a new one, I saw, probably produced by the lifeboat—fall back; his arm was thin, with a trio of joints, including a lumpy one at the wrist that seemed to be ball-and-socket style, giving him a swivel capability. He flexed the arm, showing off, then tested the shoulder joint by swinging the arm right around until it stopped, in three or four directions. Another ball-and-socket joint.

He folded the arm up again and proceeded to ignore everyone while he finished the contents of the cup; once he'd made sure he'd gotten the last drops, peering into the cup intently, he put the cup between his hands, wrapped his long fingers right around, and pressed.

With a popping sound, the cup flattened out. Foam plastic.

Without pausing, the Aldebaranian stuffed one end of the crushed cup into his mouth, bit down, and started chewing. Three more bites, and the entire cup was gone.

That was some trash disposal system.

He patted his stomach, sighed contentedly, and settled back into the padding in his tank, relaxing, as we all gaped at him—all except Shreekor, that is. I couldn't tell whether he was gaping or not.

Shreekor obviously asked him if he wanted any more, as he shook his head in a circular motion and said, "No, my thanks to yourself, kindly as you surely are, and all of your friends, family, and associates."

At least, that's how the translator put it. Not that I wasn't happy with the refusal; the ventilators were just clearing the last gasps of the previous drink. But the speech had a ritual air to it.

Shreekor said, *=*That's nothing. When I woke him, he spoke for so long that I forgave you all your chatter immediately.*

I blew a bronx cheer in Shreekor's direction, drawing a surprised stare from the Aldebaranian and a disgusted look from the princess.

Shreekor was more of a humorist; being telepathic, he got the basic sense of it.

He started bobbing up and down, tentacles flapping, oversized mouth working, all eyes rolling. As all the tentacles went up together, I saw the floater plate beneath him, and the squarish implant unit partially covered by his skin. The implant was probably what allowed him to operate in air.

"That's cheating," I said, with a laugh. "I thought all this time that you used your tentacles for flying."

Shreekor settled down and turned all his eyes on me.

*=*Liar. Shall we get on with it?*

"Yeah." I swung away from Shreekor and went to lean on the bottom of the tank, looking down at the little sentient. He watched back, curiously. It was like watching a peculiar little kid; except that this little kid had as much IQ as the rest of us combined, and then some.

The mottling was gone from his skin, and he was a healthier shade of blue. We were getting to be a pretty colorful crew.

I said, "What do they call you?" The computer quickly translated it for the alien, blanking my normal speech with a damper field.

The alien looked thoughtful, then nodded sharply. "I am known to all those who know me, and was named by those who conceived and birthed me as—"

The next seventy-eight syllables were his name.

I looked over at the two women. Nikoi was looking moderately amused, and the princess was laughing behind a hand, her eyes on me.

It was one hell of a way to get started.

I caught a couple of syllables out of the stream and formed a familiar word from them, converting—*zhwelluh*—to the English *jeweler,* changing the pronunciation a little. It fitted his design, at least.

I said, shaking my head to clear the waffle set up by the stream of syllables, "If you don't mind me saying so, your complete name is probably too long to use all of the time. So, if you have no objections, we will call you the Jeweler."

The Jeweler considered that, then gave a bounce with his entire body. He seemed pleased. He said, "That will do as well as any other name that you might give this one. It is always better to have a name of any kind, shortened though it may be, than to have no name at all. Therefore I thank you for the honor of a name."

I looked towards the ceiling, although any direction would have done as well—I just needed somewhere to aim eyeborne exasperation. I sighed and looked over at Nikoi. She was grinning like the Cheshire Cat, and not attempting to hide it. The princess was off in a corner, leaning against the bulkhead and smirking in my direction.

Shreekor was watching as well; I thought I could detect a tinge of amusement coming from his direction.

I said, "Yeah."

And turned back to the Jeweler.

Hell, nobody else was going to do the damn job; they were all too busy having a laugh at me. And I was beginning to talk like the Jeweler myself.

I said, "If the Jeweler does not mind, I would be much happier if answers were kept as short as possible, to facilitate a short interview. Considering your health . . ."

The Jeweler bobbed happily and chirped, ‘‘Affirmative.’’

I couldn’t believe it. One word? I echoed him, saying, ‘‘Affirmative?’’ with a startled rise to the end of it.

The little alien’s eyes rolled around and then fixed on me. ‘‘Indeed. Lingua technical. Time save. Short answer. Short talk.’’

I think he’d decided I was a little thick between the ears.

I looked over at Nikky, whose eyes were resembling the lights of a Christmas tree, flashing multiple colors. I said, ‘‘I think we’re going to lose something in the translation.’’

She looked intently at the Jeweler. ‘‘It is not so hard to translate the concept.’’

‘‘Maybe you get it in an easier form,’’ I said.

‘‘Perhaps.’’ She moved up to the side of the Jeweler’s crash tank, and looked down at him. He removed his attention from me after a space, and transfered it to Nikky with a preoccupied chirp. He probably hadn’t seen any of the various homo sap forms before; a number of the bases had homo sap personnel, but as a percentage of the whole, very few.

Nikky looked up at the flying mike for a moment, then said, ‘‘Base destroyed when time yours?’’

I raised both eyebrows, surprised; it sounded right, but compared to normal speech it came out backwards. It was possible the translators were acting up; I didn’t fully trust them.

The Jeweler answered snappily with a stream of chirrups; the translator didn’t bother to translate into speech.

Shreekor said, *=*That’s about four and a half thousand years ago on your scale*.

Neither the princess nor Nikky showed any signs of having heard that; presumably Shreekor only intended it for me.

I said, ‘‘Probably before Christ and Moses, then.’’

*=*Who?*

‘‘Christ and Moses. A couple of Terran mythological personalities. Religious symbols, but they probably have a factual basis.’’

There was a surge of interest.

*=*I’ll have to return to that later. Mythology and religion are my two central hobby-interests*.

I looked over at him; he was floating away from the tank, just watching.

I said, ‘‘Yeah. You ever get around to Area Fourteen, you’ll get plenty of material to work with. Half of Earth is religious fanatics, and the other half's just plain nuts." I paused. "Guess which half I belong to."

There was a mental chuckle.

I grinned and turned back to the work at hand.

"Who destroy base?" I said.

The alien looked at me. "Enemy. Close jump cover attack. Systems dead fast. Lifeboats dead. All dead except this one. I hide. Enemy go. I build machine. I sleep. You come. Wake I. I tell."

*=*All in one choppy go.*

"Yeah," I said. "I'd kind of hate to hear his life story told like that. Or the other way. He'd drop dead before he got past the first month."

But we'd got most of what we'd been after; a date and a doer. Without asking for details—he'd run off the choppy version without a flicker of emotion—it seemed that the attack had been carried out by Enemy ships coming out with cover, an easily applied maneuver here; they'd have come in close and started blasting without warning. The results: visible.

I said, "Jeweler's status?"

"Scientist-engineer class one," he chirruped with a bounce. Then he added, modestly, "I *clever.*"

Yup. So he was.

In fact, we could use his help getting the Dustpipe back on the way to somewhere alive.

I looked over at Nikoi and saw that she'd activated a link-screen for the exterior view. But she wasn't looking at the few visible stars, or the nebula background.

She was looking at the dead hulk of 908, hanging in the middle of the screen.

She was beginning to believe in the Enemy.

After the sleep period, Nikky and I took the torches back to the base and started cutting a chunk out of the hide; it was a tough job, because we had to cut through exceptionally resistant metal—it had been designed to stand up to more than a couple of heavy torches, after all. It look us almost five days to finish the cutting alone, a long, lonely job with only each other and Shreekor's telepathic voice for company; space closed in quickly, and we both had to fight the jitters now and then.

But we finally got it cut away; getting it over to the Dustpipe was the easiest part of the job, even with problems accelerating the mass and then decelerating it to a stop near the lifeboat. We left it attached by a number of lines before taking off to sleep. We'd been spending up to fourteen hours cutting; the final day was a twenty-hour stretch, and exhausted both of us. We were glad it was over.

The next day we were up again, with the Jeweler joining us outside to direct us in playing molecular football to straighten out the plate. We had to fetch a pile of components for him, which he spent some time turning into the necessary equipment. Bulky, but usable. Once the plate was knocked out of its original curvature, it had to be folded over the hole in the Dustpipe. That finished up another exhausting day.

The princess watched us stagger back on board and wander off to our crash-tanks; none of us needed sleep stimulation to get a good night's rest.

That was a touch over six days; I'd told the princess that we'd be laying in for repairs for around two weeks. She'd been fretting then; she was even worse now. Without training, she was practically useless, and she had very little to keep her entertained. The computer could provide music to taste, but that quickly bored her, as it required sitting around and listening. The computer's stock of translated fiction wasn't much good either; most of it was totally incomprehensible to her, just as it was to me.

There was a small number of Dusicilian participation-dramas; you haven't really been entertained until you've been involved in one of those, with sight, sound, touch, smell, empathy, and taste in three dimensions plus time.

But if you can work out what's going on, you're doing better than me; being a participant in the drama can produce any number of plots, which can be changed at any point by reaction.

The best we could do for her was to set up the computer with one of her home games; that, at least, took up some of her time. And she was able to play around with the food banks.

With distressing effects.

We spent the seventh day resting up from the previous six—like a well-known deity.

The computer, by this time, had switched to a random program based on an odd series of musical tones; more or less strange chromatic scales being modulated and keyed at variable intervals. It was keeping time with pops and sizzles, the time signature being an electronic 11/4.

I reprogrammed it and did a little composition; nothing spectacular, just a bunch of flutes and windchimes, with some wind to go with it. The computer, being a computer, wanted to get fancy. I was too weary for that. It took some convincing, but it eventually got the idea.

Not exactly Bartok, but pleasant enough to listen to while stretched out on a couch in the surviving Dustpipe lounge and making eyes at the princess; a touch of déjà vu, even. She was braiding her hair again.

The peace lasted an hour; very entertaining—I almost dropped off to sleep during it. The princess was probably getting frustrated with me by that time, as I kept letting my attention drift away from her, despite marvelous attempts at keeping me riveted by dextrous use of body language. I was just a bit sleepy. . . .

I would either have been jumped on by the princess or finally dropped off with thoughts of being upbraided by either Area Fourteen or darling Annabelle for doing extra-curricular things with SAS biology specimens if Shreekor hadn't blithely entered, floater and all, ordering the computer to be silent for a while.

It turned out he didn't like my idea of music at all.

So he thought he'd try *his* idea of music on us.

Shreekor, a cappella, proceeded to sing.

*=*I'm a bit tone-deaf, actually,* he admitted, when he'd finished screaming and yowling.

I took my hands away from my ears and wiped the grimace from my face. The princess, looking distressed, looked at me; she kept her hands in place.

The Jeweler was applauding.

I said, "I did kind of notice you were off-key. Just a notion."

Four large eyes swiveled to look in my direction.

"And don't try intimidation, either," I said. "It won't work on me."

*=*Hmph. I go so far as to undergo performance-terrors to sing you the love song of the Shimo-sh'sasai god Chelch, and you react like that.*

Deadpan, I said, "Poor Chelch."

*=*Ah, you're no use to anybody, Kevven Tomari. So you sing. And* I'll *comment.*

I pulled another face. "No, thanks."

The Jeweler leaned forward in his curled-up position on the floor and said, "This one is of the opinion that Shreekor provided a most excellent combination of tones and scales, providing an interesting variety of complex harmonies for the most joyously-minded and spirited of listeners to many unusual types of music,"

That was brief, for him. It didn't stop him sounding like a pleased critic who'd just been zapped by the latest Stockhausen or Cage.

I turned around fully to look at him; he turned his cat-iris eyes on me, blinking slowly. You couldn't really take offense at him; he was too cute.

I said, "It sounded like a couple of rabid dogs having a fight on a hot tin roof with a thousand cats."

The Jeweler made a slight moue. "Kevven appears not to understand the subtle nuances of such a beautifully arranged piece of music, where the most subtle harmonies lie in the range you call ultrasonic. That is to say, above the range of your hearing. Such nuances are what makes such a piece of music a delight to the prepared and conscientious listener. Such a listener, indeed, as this one is."

He swirled his head in a circle, his eyes still on me, his antennae dancing. He seemed to be indicating sorrow at my deficiencies.

I stretched and looked at the princess. She was looking annoyed.

I said, "It's a matter of personal opinion." I slapped my knees, sitting up. "I may disagree with what you say, but I will defend unto the death—or almost, anyway—your right to say it."

The princess gave me a haughty look. "That is an interesting sentiment."

I grinned at her. "Of course it is. I said it, didn't I?"

Her lips twitched slightly; she was either annoyed at me or trying to hide a smile.

She said, "However," and leaned forward, brushing her hair forward over her shoulders, stroking the sheen carefully, looking up at me "on Aureon, the royal family reserves the right to say what may or may not be opined."

Which promptly started an argument about the freedom of speech; it stopped the princess from chafing for a while, anyway.

It almost got violent; and that pleased her.

Typically enough.

The next day was taken up with making final adjustments to the plate and checking the curvature; once we were sure it was properly in place, we started welding it down; we got the job a quarter done before breaking for sleep. It was hard work. If we'd been able to use molecular bonding, we'd have had the job done in no time, and the plate would have fitted neatly in place without any possibility of upsetting the jump-field and being twisted out of place. We'd tried bonding it; it wouldn't work. The alloys involved refused to flow together, which left us with the poor second choice of welding the thing in place and then sealing it with as much sealant as could be sprayed on.

The final bit of welding took us most of the ninth day; we started spraying on the sealant brought from the base, getting a layer down on each side of the plug. We had to use lines to hold us in place; the force with which the sealant barreled out of the hoses threatened to make us victims of Newton's third law of motion. The sealant itself spread neatly before turning solid; it had been designed for spaceside work.

In all, hard work but worthwhile; we were getting somewhere.

The tenth day saw us up and spraying with a vengeance; in the first hour, we emptied two sealant canisters, getting down five or six layers on the outside. The Jeweler and Shreekor had decided between them that fifteen to twenty layers would be enough to keep us safe; we'd probably be okay with a half-dozen layers inside and outside, but Shreekor wanted to play it safe. And all we were losing was time.

I was just connecting a spray hose to a canister, and trying to hold the canister against me with my legs to prevent it floating off every time I bumped it, when the ship appeared.

I didn't see it. None of us did.

We *felt* it.

We couldn't help but feel it.

I looked for Nikky and the Jeweler—the Jeweler had been watching us spray—and saw them looking at each other; the Jeweler was bubbled in a life-support field on the hull of the lifeboat. Nikky was floating a distance away with a spray hose in her hands.

She looked at me.

And then we all swung around to look.

And there it was.

Two cubes, linked by a long, thin rod. Distance plays tricks with your eyes in space, and it's almost impossible to estimate sizes and distances. I wasn't going to try guessing with this monster.

The leading cube seemed immense, and the rod protruding from it seemed fairly thick; it slid off into space at an angle, vanished against the background. The other cube was minuscule in comparison, but visible. If anything happened to that, whatever was in the leading cube would hardly notice it.

It was a dinosaur of a ship.

I felt a little silly, floating outside the Dustpipe; here we were, trying to repair an insignificant little hole in an insignificant little spacecraft, and this bastard had popped out of nowhere next to us.

*=*The central question is: who are they? Also: where did they come from, why are they here—perhaps the appearance is perfectly innocent, but the appearance of the ship at this particular location makes that very dubious. So: what do they want?*

Shreekor sounded dejected; he'd run through the entire catalog of known ship types—a sort of *Jane's,* Builders' style—to try and find the ship, and come up with nothing. Then he'd tried getting the computer to speculate a little—which any of the Mastercomputers would have done immediately—and received a *no data* answer for his pains. And he couldn't answer his own questions with anything.

I looked around the lounge; the Jeweler was curled up in the middle of the floor, arms wrapped around his thin body, playing with Big Thinks by the invisible dozen; his toes jiggled absently. Any other time, I might have been amused, but there wasn't room for amusement right now.

We were all too scared.

Nikky was settled in a corner, curled up, hugging herself; she'd gotten involved in something she'd thought was too big to be possible.

So had I; I just didn't want to admit it.

It was another one of those weird coincidences.

Nikky said, "Perhaps it is a colony ship."

*=*There are no planets within half a thousand light-years of this point. Base 908 was here for study purposes only.*

"Besides," I put in, "that damned thing's too big. By the looks of it, you could cram half a planet's population inside there and still run races."

The princess, huddled up on one edge of a couch, said, "I am frightened."

I went over to her and sat down next to her, putting an arm around her; she was as tense as a guitar string, shivering, although warm.

I looked at Shreekor; he didn't have any real outward signs of fear, but I could feel him feeling scared, just a little. He seemed to be keeping it on a tight band to avoid panicking the others. He trusted me to keep quiet about it.

The Jeweler was the only one not really worried; he was having too much of a good time with those Big Thinks of his. Lucky him.

Despondently, Shreekor said, *=*We don't seem to be getting anywhere. Any more suggestions?*

"Perhaps a scientific vessel?" Nikoi said.

I shook my head. "Still too big. You don't need that much room for scientific work, unless you're going the multi-generation route like the bases. And judging by the way he appeared, that would probably be a waste of time."

I looked at the linkscreen that was on in the lounge; the ship was on it, the base barely visible as a dark spot in one corner.

I said, "Just how big is that thing anyway, Shreekor? My scale."

He didn't hesitate. *=*The cube sections are eight hundred and twelve point seven nine kilometers on a side. The connecting strut is one thousand five hundred twenty-seven kilometers long, with a square cross-section of three hundred thirty seven square kilometers. Total volume involved: one thousand seventy-four million, four hundred and eighteen thousand, five hundred and ninety-four point nine five cubic kilometers. More or less approximately.*

I shuddered. The bases were miniature planets, designed to be self-sustaining multi-generation enviroments; even so, the biggest I knew of would have fit into a corner of one of those cubes.

"He just waits and waits," Nikoi whispered. "Why? I wish he would do something."

I said, "Why don't we just get the hell out of here, Shreekor?"

*=*The seal is not complete yet. There is—*

I shook my head, impatient with him. "Just move. We can finish the job later."

*=*What good will normal space flight be? We can't move swiftly enough to avoid anything it may send at us. We are as well off here as anywhere.*

"Well, hell, let's get the goddamned seal *finished*. The princess can heave a hose around as well as anybody else, and the Jeweler won't have much trouble in zero-gee—"

*=*Inform him when he wakes up, then.*

I'd forgotten; the Jeweler was juggling Big Thinks. What the hell about, I didn't know; the ship outside didn't necessitate much brainpower.

Then again, I was letting my body think for me, instead of my head.

I said, "Guess he's going through the ninety-nine percent perspiration part of being a genius." And half smiled.

There was a mental chuckle from Shreekor.

*=*A little hope leavens the gloom, doesn't it?*

"Yeah," I said. "It does." I got up and turned toward the door to the repair section. "No sense sitting around. We'd better get some—"

*=Kev! *The screen!*

I whirled at the mental shout, turning on one heel and immediately planting myself in fighting stance, arms moving to hold the balance; I was pumping adrenalin suddenly.

It was all for nothing, at least in here.

When I saw the screen, I said, "Oh my God."

The big ship was moving, turning ponderously, the leading cube swinging toward us.

The hatchway leading back to our control section opened under Shreekor's command. He went through like a bullet, followed by myself, Nikky, the princess, and the suddenly wide-awake Jeweler, in that order.

Shreekor vanished into his tank while I vaulted over the edge of mine and dropped flat, reaching for my controls, turning on the linkscreen over the tank.

I looked away from the screen for a moment, saw the princess rooted to the spot a meter from the door.

I called, in her language, "Princess! Get in the tank!"

She snapped out of it, moved lithely across the compartment, and got in, settling back.

I punched up remote sleepstim and watched her go under; I didn't want her panicking.

"Nikoi," I said.

"I will stay," she answered, from behind me. I turned to look over my shoulder; she was watching my linkscreen, her eyes glowing. "That craft . . . Enemy?"

I shook my head. "I don't think so. Shreekor?"

*=*If that is an Enemy ship, they have no more need for other ships. The speculation is illogical.*

"Better watch those Spock pills, guy." I looked for the Jeweler. He was curled up again, on the floor, watching Shreekor's screen intently. He seemed to have come to some conclusion that he wasn't quite ready to share. But he didn't seem worried. "That sonofabitch coming for us?"

*=*No. What's a "spock pill"?*

"Later." I looked from screen to Shreekor's tank. "Why no?"

*=*The leading section has passed already. And some degrees away.*

I checked the radar plot; I had to boost the scale to prevent the ship blocking too much. Then checked the screen. Shreekor was right.

Nikoi said, "The base. It is moving over the base."

She was right.

"Shreekor, get us the hell away from here!"

We started moving immediately; if that ship was going to explode the base, the blast could possibly take us with it.

A flash of blue at the base of the rear-end cube; a thin thread of azure splitting the background glow.

A halo of blue light wrapping itself around the hulk of 908.

*=*Tractor.*

"Jesus Christ almighty," I said. "They're swiping the base."

*=*I'm holding acceleration at maximum.*

The base started moving slowly, towards the cube; the ship had stopped. The hulk slowly gathered speed; I checked the radar screen, saw that it was crossing the distance at a pretty good clip.

A could of miles before it ran into the cube, a red spark lit; the blue one went out.

*=*Pressor.*

I'd caught on before Shreekor mentioned it.

I checked the radar screen again; we weren't moving away fast enough for my preference.

The hulk of 908 vanished beneath the cube, vanished from the entire radar scan area.

The ship had swallowed the base.

I said, "Shreekor, I get this weird feeling we're going to be next."

*=*I, too.*

Another blue spark at the base of the cube.

The lifeboat shuddered violently.

Nikky grabbed my coverall with one hand to stop herself falling. I heard the Jeweler chirp surprise.

"Whaddya know, I was right," I said, through my teeth.

*=*I'm trying to break the hold with emergency power.*

I watched the board and saw the readout climbing into the danger area.

I said, "It's not doing any good."

We were slowing quickly; too much drag from the tractor, and there was the entire mass of the other ship behind it. Plus their power.

Fear clawing into my throat; what the hell were we going into?

*=*Well, we'll at least find out what's going on here.*

"Oh, shut up," I hissed.

Full stop; starting backwards. The readout was in the danger area now. We were going to burn out every system on board the lifeboat soon.

My board went dead.

"Shreekor?"

*=*Mine too.*

Gathering velocity; or speed, trying to remember which was which through fear.

Listening; my breathing harsh, Nikoi gasping. The Jeweler chirped. No sound from the ventilation or other ship systems; silence so dead and cold—

—sweat was breaking out on my face.

The cube was growing larger on the linkscreen; the systems were intact. They'd just been blanked. But we needed life support more than a screen.

The Jeweler chirped again.

Buzzing in my head, a muzzy feeling; not bad air, not enough time.

*= *We can't even attempt a jump now.*

"Positive, ain't ya?"

"What is happening?" Nikoi asked. "I feel so—"

A slithering noise from behind me, and a thud. I struggled up, looked over the edge of the tank; Nikoi was unconscious, piled up like a heap of washing forgotten on a rainy day—

—Dizzy.

I gasped, *"Shreekor."*

Silence.

"Shreekor! Shreekorrrrrrrr!"

The Jeweler chirped at me, standing below my tank; he hadn't been there a moment before.

I hadn't been sprawled over the edge of the tank either.

The Jeweler pulling at my clothes; I watched him fuzzily. *Funny little alien.*

I picked him up; he was light. He had my comkey in his hands.

He didn't struggle.

I said, "Wha' want, funny man?"

Chirrup!

The comkey said slowly, "Ship."

"Yuh. Ship. Big."

His head moved in a cirle and his eyes started to close.

Chirra-chirrp!

The comkey said, "Builders." Then, more chirps. "Ship. Builders."

I dropped him and he sprawled on the floor, the comkey skidding away. He looked at me mildly with his half-closed cat-eyes.

And slumped over sideways.

I was the only one left.

I struggled to my feet, determined to do *something* that was nebulous—

Fell.

Hit the floor hard with distant pain in my face and shoulder.

And let the world slip away from me, swearing as I fell into empty, starless space.

8 The Enforcers

Sensations of floating free—

Absolutely wonderful.

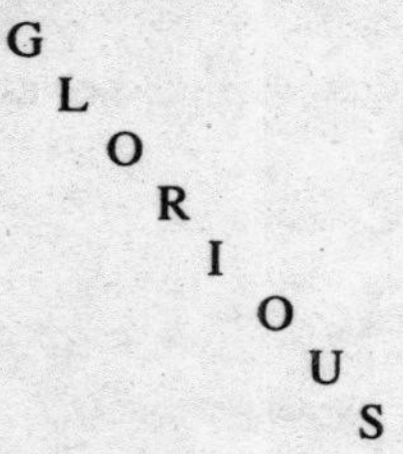

—totally unhindered by form or feeling.

Great fun.

Like a sunshine high; without a downer to come.

I should have panicked there and then, and fled wailing into the innermost recesses of whatever holes I could find. But I felt too good to bother with such nebulous things as fleeing with a scream on my dissolute lips. Everything around me was saying: don't panic, you're welcome here, you belong. Formlessness was a minor matter, all it meant was that I didn't have a *corpus*. And *corpus:* capable of getting sick, of getting hurt. I was in the best possible condition.

A diffused form-trapped glow over me—

B
E
A
U
T
I
F
U
L

—like a face looking down; I tried to get a good look, but the fuzz refused to resolve.

*= *Poot,* I said.

In this dim diffusion—

Waves of light and sound pulsed through me, washed over my mind.

Mind.

The *key.*

I opened my mind, said:

W
E
L
C
O
M
E

(enter freely and of your own will).

Something rushed by, evading my lazy grab.

A heavy door said: *slam!*

Thunderously silent, but startlingly stated:

slam!

Something there, but intangible; letting it feed me.

Not that important, is it, if I can't get to hear what you're telling me?

I turned away from the fuzz—

P
E
A
C
E
F
U
L

—and floated happily off on the tide of time, looking for flower-laden exploration, a soul-jungle, searching for something to

* =*poot!*

at.

I didn't explore far.

I was taken gently by the scruff of my id and neatly pulled back into place; a cosmic truant officer returning a wandering pupil to school.

(stay)

Can't make head or tail of the story, Teach.

(wait)

If I bring an apple will you let me listen in?

(patience, child)

Wanna play.

(soon)

Okay, Teach.

(good)

I settled back into place before the fuzz—

T
I
M
E
L
E
S
S

—and let the waves of light/sound sweep over me, soothing me and gentling me.

The fuzzy yellow thing emitted love; I was a good pupil, and I hadn't really *meant* to play hookey. . . .

Peace.

Love.

Sunshine high in space.

Master of the Universe—

Crazy dreamer—

Child of the sun—

A baby, learning, a flower growing towards the sun, uncurling and unfurling my petals, twisting my stem, reaching for—

—my control board.

I stopped, frowning; just a flicker before I'd been dreaming . . .?

It flooded back; I understood what the Jeweler had been trying to tell me: *Ship. Builders.*

Or: *Builders' ship*

We were probably the first of any of the sentients on the various bases to see the Builders at work. And they worked slowly; four and a half thousand years that base had been waiting to be repaired or replaced. I'd heard of bases being destroyed before, many times. This was the first I knew of that had been repaired.

Where the hell had they been all that time?

They could have been repairing other wrecked bases, replacing those destroyed; maybe it took them a long time to rebuild the things. With the sort of repair ship they used, they really didn't need good defenses. They'd simply rebuild later, a hundred years after the fact, or a thousand, or a million, as it suited them.

It looked like we might have been picked up by accident, and checked over to make sure we weren't Enemy, and spat out into space again, to make our way back home. I hoped they'd repaired the Dustpipe for us . . .

Then I *saw* the control board I'd been reaching for.

And almost gasped.

It wasn't the one that had been hanging over my tank when I passed out.

I said, "Shreekor? You awake yet?"

*=*Yes.*

"Look at your control rig."

*=*I have. I was wondering if you would notice. What are your conclusions?*

I took my eyes from the control board and looked around.

Second shock.

The entire compartment had been altered; my tank was opposite Shreekor's; between us, a large open space. To my left was Nikoi L'aan, looking puzzled, and the princess next to her, even more puzzled; then Shreekor, and finally the Jeweler, and a hatchway.

I said, still looking around, "No conclusions. Statements. We've been rebuilt by the Builders."

*=*Indeed we have. Our physical forms are unaltered. But we have undergone retraining.*

There was a knot of surprise in my stomach. It wasn't pleasant to wake up to something like this, without any warning, or reasons.

*=*Incidentally, the ship is nowhere to be seen. And our location has been changed. It might interest you to know that we are presently hiding in a cluster of boloids. Or meteors, if you prefer—although fairly smooth and rotund.*

"Hiding?" I said, stupidly. I could have checked. "What from?"

*=*Why not have a look?*

Well, if Shreekor could operate this rig, so could I.

And I did.

Linkscreen lit, radar tracks lit; both three-dimensional instead of the usual two dimensional layouts. Sensor reads flicked on, read out distance and mass. A lot of other stuff that I ignored; I wasn't piloting right now.

There was an anti-detection field; that was a new one on me.

Seven fully operational diamond-style ships; one disabled one hanging at a slant to the rest of the squadron; it looked as if it had been hit by an enormous foot. One side was chewed up.

There was another ship; an enormous cylinder, with one rounded end, one flat end; what appeared to be a control section jutted from the rounded end, a long thin finger exploding into a bubble. The flattened end had three thin angled rods jutting from it; they were spaced at points a hundred twenty degrees apart. Two of them had squat cylinders attached, flat black with protruding shields. Drive units.

The third angle rod was missing the drive unit and about half the top section. One of the remaining two drive units had a chunk chewed out of it.

I said, "Weird. Enemy attacks don't usually fail like that."

**=I believe I told you a good while ago that we might have some new information to take back with us.*

"There are still some ships to finish the job," I pointed out.

**=And we must therefore take care of* them.

It sounded right, but my mind rebelled against the idea.

My hands touched controls.

We hadn't the firepower. . . .

My fingers moved, touched switches.

The radar and linkscreens became target screens.

I felt a smile creasing my face; I'd previously only used poor weapons.

I said, "Princess? You coming duck shooting too?"

The princess said, "I . . . know."

**=We all know.*

The lifeboat was gone; we were in a warship, a potent little spacer with the kill-power to match the Enemy, and to beat the crap out of them.

We were being tested.

I said, "What the hell are we waiting for?"

And Shreekor kicked us into the attack; revamped jumpshift machinery and supercharged impulse drive—

We pounced like a hawk sighting a rat.

The Enemy ships scattered as we flipped head over heels and slowed.

First kill:

I let the computer pick up a charging Enemy fighter, let him fire once, and fired back.

The fighter seemed to slam into a wall; shattered into a starburst of light and died to black.

Two more ships vanished from the radar plot as Nikoi and the princess fired.

Shreekor bent the ship through as tight a turn as he could; kilometers at high speed involved. It could have been a fighter plane, only the scales were different.

Two Enemy came at us.

We fired.

One shattered like a plastic kit with the glue deteriorated, splintered, became glitterdust, and blanked out. The other vanished in a white explosion.

The Jeweler watched with interest.

We passed by the disabled ship; left sparkling dust to die.

Overtook a seventh ship, plunging at it like a hawk; snapped the mouse brutally, killed without compunction.

Shattered it.

The remaining ship attacked; over the top and into the jaws of death, last stand at the Alamo.

Our dragon spat fire—

Torched it—

A funeral pyre—

A victory torch held high on the wind and plunged into the soaked coals; a flame to the future.

Silent explosion.

The fight was over; a massacre.

I let my hands fall away from the board, and slumped back into the tank, staring at the studded blank space in the screen.

And thought: *why?*

Shreekor started to turn the ship back to the stricken freighter.

The freighter was en route to something the ship's commander called Soru Warbase, and was carrying a cargo of exceptionally powerful disruptors, plus the team of scientists that had developed them.

For use against the Enemy.

The ship had originally had a fighter escort; the Enemy squadron had destroyed it in their first attack, suffering a loss of at least fifty percent. The second attack lost them another twenty-five percent, and left the freighter with an inoperative main drive.

They probably wouldn't have survived a third attack; neither would the Enemy.

We'd come along just in time to help them out. So the Builders weren't beyond hitting back a little now and then, using the little people to do the job.

Well, stuff 'em. This was what I wanted: a chance to do to the Enemy what the Enemy did to us. I wanted to go play cowboy around the universe. We could help this freighter get to where they were going, and then go hunt up some more warships . . .

After all, that was what we'd been overhauled for.

The Builders apparently had other ideas.

Once we'd settled relations with the freighter—they'd been

keeping us under their guns all the while, although they didn't know our shields could probably take the brunt of their disruption effects—the Jeweler took off to have a look at our jump-drive, so he could build an edition for the other ship.

The rest of us were visited by an apparition.

It was at least three meters tall, although that could have been part of the illusion, and consisted of a hooded cloak, with only dark space beneath the hood; the sleeves were joined, no sign of hands.

It spooked me. I didn't believe in ghosts, but I couldn't avoid this. It was unreal. A projection, sure, but a damned good projection.

It said, *=*You are primed to carry out a task, that being the location and termination of the central base of the T'sooli within this universe. You have survived the first test-in-battle. There will be many more before you are finished.*

The voice was cool, feminine.

*=*You are to continue to Warbase Prime at Soru. You will be accepted and trained by our agents, and will use the means given to carry out your task. You must succeed. The T'sooli are an uncontrollable disease, a cancer. We will assist you where possible.*

*=*But for us to act by ourselves would be to court your destruction entire.*

*=*And we Build. The T'sooli destroy. For rule.*

And the projection was gone, if a projection it was. For all I knew, I'd been programmed to hallucinate this. I didn't even know if the drive to fight the Enemy was my own.

Shreekor said, *=*Look at it this way: it's your greatest chance in life.*

He sounded amused. As usual.

I said irritably, "Shut up, Shreekor. All it's gonna do is get my goddamn *ass* shot off."

The work on the damaged ship was tedious; the Jeweler and Shreekor first had to adapt the schematics of the drive of our ship so we could build something similar for the crippled ship. Then they had to do further work to alter the components needed to fit what the other ship had on board, which meant that most of their weaponry had to be broken down and the bits used as basic materials for the components we needed. It didn't have to be anything spectacular, just as long as the ship moved the five hundred or so lightyears before the makeshift rig clapped out.

Once the adapted drive had been laid out in schematic form, and all substitutions made as far as components went, the hard part started—building and installing it. That required stripping down a compartment big enough, and putting it together inside. Which meant that I had to handle a great deal of the heavy work, with whatever weight-lifter type aliens I could find aboard. The Jeweler and Nikoi handled the more delicate work, with three or four alien scientists for company.

For that part of the work Shreekor and the Jeweler split shifts, resting twelve hours and working twelve; I was assigned to an eight-hour shift, second in rotation, with eight hours free, and eight hours to sleep.

The end result was a collection of wires and gidgets neatly strewn around the compartment. Amazingly, it worked, and worked well.

Shreekor had mentioned that the commander of the ship was a hominid female; I'd half-expected another humanoid such as the princess, or Nikoi L'aan. Instead, when I went to see her, I found myself looking upward at an angle my neck wasn't used to being bent at.

She was at least as tall as a Krr'Hrshraa female, a deep lilac in color, and naked but for a wide-mesh net strung around her thin frame. Various objects, mostly unfamiliar, were hung on the mesh; one or two weapons included. Convenient and sensible on board a ship.

Her eyes were multi-faceted and metallic-looking, glinting from all angles, side-mounted to afford her a good view, and her skin was smooth, all the way down to swivel-jointed hips, almost in a direct line from the shoulders. There wasn't a neck; the head was mounted on a swivel-joint that allowed her to turn her head in a hundred-eighty-degree pan; with the side-mounted eyes, that gave her a full-circle viewing capability.

The mouth was a wide slash across the lower part of the face; no sign of any smelling organs, but I assumed there would be something to handle that. The mouth was flanked by twin mandibles, and twin anteanae, thick and flexible, sprang from either side of the head, curving out to face forward.

The arms and legs were multi-jointed, with three multi-jointed digits ending each limb; for general flexibility, she could easily match the Jeweler. All joints, and deadly effective because of the speed and power they afforded her. In fighting practice, she was tremendous to watch, all grace and speed.

That was what she'd been trained for, after all.

The rest of the frighter's crew and passenger complement was a mixed bag—Shreekor hadn't spoken up again about the unlikeliness of more than one species aboard an interstellar ship—with some from within a few hundred light-years of Soru Warbase, others from systems way out on the edge of this particular galaxy, and a scattered few from galaxies nearby. No doubt, the Builders' doing . . .

Trios of creatures like giant bean-bags wandered through the ship, legs hidden beneath overhanging sides, if legs they were; they operated various systems as they went, ignoring me. Flying pincushions missed my head every so often, chittering as they went by; oversized, skittering rabbit-like creatures dodged past wherever I went, sometimes in life-fields like mine; I had to wear one constantly, as the ship was a mixture of environments.

Purple and green rages. Vying for attention with the four-legged ottoman, on top of which rode a large avian dressed in orange and yellow feathers, and odd-looking glasses. The avian was carrying a small white card, on which it was making notations; a little later, I discovered that the pad was a miniature computer stage, the glasses serving to supply readouts.

I was beginning to feel as if I'd walked into a Lewis Carroll fantasy.

And the feeling was strengthened on the last day of the work on board the freighter; we'd finished work on the drive unit, and the Jeweler was making final adjustments and tests on the circuitry. As usual, once I'd finished my work, I went off nosing through the ship. There was almost a thousand yards of it, and I hadn't covered all that much.

There was a central corridor that ran the length of the ship; the rest was linked up to that main corridor by other corridors, and lifts.

I was about three-quarters of the way along the main corridor when I heard a noise akin to a flatulent dinosaur creating the basis of coprolites. It had come from behind me, from an adjoining corridor.

I was too curious for my own good; I turned and started back to see what was causing it. I had a feeling that I was going to regret it, but that didn't stop me.

FwooooorrrrrrrrTZZ!

plud

A definite sound of something impacting with the deckplates this time; possibly some kind of machine, or something that leaped around a lot. I stopped and listened; it came again, then once more. It wasn't far ahead, just about fifteen yards, and into the branch corridor.

I started walking again, turned down the corridor, and listened. Another flatulent emission, and a report, louder, on the deckplates.

I turned down another corridor. And stopped dead.

FWOOOOORRRRRRRRRRRRRRRRRRTZZZZZZ!!

And a rubbery *THWOOMPH!*

I started in disbelief. It was obviously sentient, and it obviously had a reason for thumping around—possibly it had seen me going by. But I wasn't sure whether it wanted to be friends, or to see whether I tasted right for supper.

It looked like a giant, hairy beach ball, in gray, standing on two huge, thick legs, both short and muscle-packed. Two thin, wriggling arms, with thin, wriggling fingers. No eyes; just a pair of wide orange stripes running from top to bottom on the globular body.

A heavy-planet sentient who found the low gravity to its liking, was my guess.

As I stood watching *Beachballius Maximus*—who was watching me—his mouth opened, a great horizontal slit in the lower part of his body that suddenly became a gaping cavity.

Ten yards down the corridor there was a rush of air being sucked in, and the beach ball shape inflated. He sank down, his legs compressing, then suddenly uncoiled and decompressed with the flatulent sound that had brought me here.

He sailed up, mouth closing, body twisting.

Coming at me . . .

I turned and fled, Beachballius right behind me, thumping and farting. It might all be a friendly game, but I didn't want to play—not if it meant getting jumped on by five hundred pounds of alien.

I went hurtling back out into the main corridor, checked each way and decided on one, and dashed down it.

Beachballius thumped along after me.

I got lost pretty quickly, trying to get out of sight of that thing.

About a half mile after starting, I found a doorway Beachballius couldn't follow me through, and took my chance while he was out of sight. I whipped it open and dived inside, slamming it back into position; it didn't slide fast enough for me.

I put my ear against the metal.

thump thump THUMP THUMP THUMP THUMP THUMP THUMP THUMP THUMP THUMP thump thump

And silence.

I relaxed. I didn't want to go through that again.

I turned around, to see where I'd wound up. I'd known I'd be entering a cabin, but I hadn't had much choice about it. I was sweating and still gasping from my run. If I hadn't come in here, the chances were that I'd have been flattened within another couple of hundred yards.

The occupant of the cabin wasn't happy at the instrusion.

She—and there was no doubting that—was mostly hidden by the sheets of her bed, and very annoyed—no doubting that either—at me for having barged in while she was bare naked. Not that I'd noticed. Sometimes the mind refuses to acknowledge additional dangers. . . .

I held up my hands, and said, *''No comprende.''* I hadn't got my translator switched on.

She wound up and let fly with a new set of squeals and squeaks, ten to the dozen. I didn't bother switching on the translator; I preferred to have her insult me incomprehensibly.

I listened for a few moments more, as the lady in the bed shut up, and heard nothing. I looked back at my new friend, who was watching me with puzzlement—saw she had triangular eyes, plus other features I'd have to enumerate later—and cracked the door enough to stick my head outside.

There was neither sight nor sound of friend *Beachballius Maximus*.

The lady in the bed let off a few more squeals and squeaks.

Well, that damned oversized rubber ball was out of sight and out of mind. And definitely out of my hair.

I slid the door open, and turned to wave goodbye to my savior.

She dropped modesty with the sheets, picked up something heavy and square, and threw it overhand at me.

I ducked out and slammed the door; whatever she'd thrown hit the other side of the door with a dull thud.

I shook my head. It wasn't my day for great friendships.

I wasn't happy. I couldn't be. I'd expected to complete the trip on board our own ship—which was linked to the freighter via astrogational computers, to make sure we both jumped and arrived together—which would make me feel much safer.

But while I'd been off getting chased by Beachballius, Shreekor had arranged with the commander of the freighter that I'd complete the trip on board the bloody rattletrap boat. As would the Jeweler.

So I would be sharing a cabin for a while with one of the passengers on the ship. Maybe we could stare morosely at each other.

But that all changed when I went through the door of the cabin I was supposed to be sharing.

I stopped as I closed door, and said, "Oh Christ. Wonderful."

Deja vu, or what the Christian felt on being passed down the line to the lion; it eats at you . . .

I'd thought the corridor had seemed familiar.

And this time my comkey was all set to translate everything she wanted to toss at me.

She said, "You." And got out of her position on the long couch at the far side of the cabin. It defied me to work out how she'd gotten into it in the first place.

"Me," I said, weakly, and checked my line of retreat. Which I'd just blocked off.

She didn't pick up anything heavy to bludgeon me with, or anything to shoot me with, knife me with, or otherwise harm me.

In fact, she looked positively pleased to see me, even a little coy about it. Well, there was an advantage—she was wearing a throat-to-ankles gown that would impede any attack she decided to make.

She stopped a short distance away from me, and said, "I was warned that I would have to bear with a guest for a space, but I was not told that it would be my breathless black invader."

I tried to look shamefaced, and said, "Well, we all have to bear with things we dislike. . . ."

In the face of death . . .

"I do not mind the intrusion. I am of understanding." She made a complex gesture in the air with one hand, and smiled, showing off a nice line in shark-style orthodontia. Pointed little teeth. "The—" the translator didn't bother with the multiple grunting noises she made—"have a tendency to forget the frailties of others. You were correct in attempting escape. But he would have avoided hurting you."

Some hope.

She tilted her head to one side, and I started taking in details; her hair was silver, metallic, and it rustled as she turned her head. The motion exposed one gracefully pointed ear that was accented by an earring shaped like a Möbius spiral. Her eyes were definitely triangular, obtuse, wide and flat, with irises shaped like a cat's. With the angular shape of her face, and her widow's peak hairstyle, the result was decidedly satanic, long silver hair or no. Adding to the image was the color of her skin—a deep, dusty red.

She stepped toward me, and my mouth went dry. I stepped back instinctively and hit the bulkhead.

That was it; no further to go.

I wasn't entirely sure about it, but it felt warm in here as well; it was a twenty-five percent oxygen atmosphere. The heat *wasn't* imagination. I hadn't got my life-field on, and the temperature in the cabin was above that in the corridor.

She shook her hair back, and blinked. "Why are you so frightened? Does my nearness cross a tribal taboo?"

I almost laughed; I just wasn't hysterical yet.

I took a deep breath and forced myself back to normality; this was a stupid way to wind up, especially for someone like me.

I said, "I was set off by your resemblance to a creature of myth on my home planet."

She looked surprised, which surprised me a little. Too easy to read expression. Or perhaps she was annoyed.

She sighed and shook her head. "I was not aware that spacefarers were prone to being frightened of mere superstition." She hadn't met the Chakta yet. They run their entire system by superstition. "Perhaps you would be less frightened to know I am a truly gentle one?"

It was my turn to be puzzled. "I don't understand."

She spread her arms in a gesture of frustration, curving her body as she did so; the only time I'd ever seen that collection of curves before was in a Will Eisner comic strip, *The Spirit*. Eisner's women always manage to get that curve, torso out one way, butt another, legs curving back; I think they call it languorous. The pose seemed out of place.

"What is there to understand?" she asked.

I sighed and tried to untense—the body taking command again, dammit—and said, "For one thing, 'gentle' ones do not throw heavy objects at escapees from oversized playful medicine balls. Secondly, they don't, in my prejudiced view, look like the Devil come to life."

She seemed amused by that. "I am not one who—" she leaned forward, jabbing me in the chest with a long finger, her other hand on her hip, palm outward, mock-scolding tone to her voice—"has her quarters invaded regularly while attempting to sleep. Especially not while the priestess is naked, as a priestess should not be on visitation."

And she winked.

Slowly.

And smiled.

I sighed and thought, *why does it have to happen to me?* I get all the crazy situations; the lifeboat was bad enough at times, but this was even worse.

I said, "Okay, I'm sorry it happened. But I was under the impression that your friend was going to put a permanent crease in me."

She gave me a lazy grin; it didn't help the devilish aura—and it made me regret my upbringing.

She stretched herself, reaching towards the ceiling, relaxing. "Do not upset yourself. It is duty to a priestess of Lachalla to give sanctuary—and comfort—to those who require it."

She was one hell of a ship's chaplain.

"I suppose I'll get over it in a moment," I said.

She grinned again, giving me another uncomfortable look at her teeth. Not quite as many as a great white. . . .

She said, "Discomfort will cease very soon," in a murmur; she seemed to be of the opinion that I was ready for Number Three Furnace. It was definitely hot in the cabin. Probably because she had a higher body temperature than myself. "However, we must be familiar."

Not bloody likely, I thought.

I said, "In what way? I seem to have some difficulty in understanding you . . . my translator is—"

"I see," she interrupted. She thought for a moment, almost rivaling the Jeweler for depth of concentration; working out how to slip it past the dumb translator—which couldn't handle concepts that are supposed to be implied—in a way I could understand.

She looked up and said, "The familiarising with each other of . . . titles. What do you say?" She tilted her head to the other side, resting one finger, complete with sharp fingernail, on one cheek. The fall of hair revealed the other pointed ear, complete with hexagonal earring. Anti-symmetry, the art of altering slight details to affect the whole picture.

I said, "Names."

I felt relieved; some sentients have weird methods of greeting people, at least from my point of view. The Shinshi, for example, greet their friends by attempting to knock them on their butts, if it's possible. The friendlier it is, the more business for the plastic surgeon—I've seen two female Shinshi kick each other around the room after being apart for some time.

Life for the average Tomari is dangerous.

The priestess said, "Names, yes." She thought about it for a moment, then nodded, sharply. "This naming is a pleasure."

I grinned; I had to. I said, "One of my people, the Jeweler, has a saying that goes something like that."

She stared at my face for a moment, apparently out of scientific interest, complete with studied detachment. "Your teeth . . . flat-edged. It is unusual. Are all your people the same?"

I raised an eyebrow. "I think so."

"Interesting. But not for the study of my temple, however." She sighed, apparently resigning herself to the fact. "We merely deal with gentlenesses and comforts."

"Well," I said, "that's a lot there." She nodded and shook her hair back into place; it made a metallic rustling sound as it shifted around, and fell back neatly. "Besides, I thought we were supposed to be finding out who we are."

Her eyebrows arched, briefly, and she blinked. "I know who I am. Do you know who you are?"

I laughed out loud this time; which may have been her intention, although I suspected the squawk box was behind it.

I said, "I think so. I meant names. Titles."

She nodded again, reminding me of the Japanese and their air of ceremony. "I see. The familiarizing." She ran a hand through her hair, making it rustle from side to side, like a bead curtain. It seemed to be made up of millions of tiny strands of silver.

She bowed slightly, then straightened. "I am Chamzeen, Priestess of the Temple of Stars, dedicated to ship and duty, therefore honor-bound."

I raised both eyebrows; quite a mouthful.

She waited.

I repeated the tiny bow, and said, "I am Agent Commander Kevven Tomari of Area Fourteen of the Builders network, serving special duty, personal title of Chieftain of the Mala, of the Bantu peoples of the nation of Africa, Earth, and generally incoherent any way you find me."

Bluster covering bull; my relatives call me the Chieftain of empty air. I don't have a tribe to lord it over. At least I'd managed to outdo her with my mouthful.

She stepped back a pace and bowed again, deeply this time. I bowed in return, feeling naughty for not having removed my boots—she was barefoot. I marveled at the way her hair fell; like a silver waterfall.

Then, as smoothly as a lynx, she flowed up against me, wrapped herself around me, and kissed me the hottest way I've ever been kissed.

Her normal body temperature was 129.77 degrees Fahrenheit; she was a fever dream.

No wonder the cabin temperature was so high.

She unwrapped herself just as the cabin wall nearest me turned opalescent; the face of the ship's commander appeared, and Chamzeen turned to face it.

She glanced at me while waiting for the commander to say something, and said, "You are cool."

I didn't have an answer for that line.

There was a mental chuckle, and Shreekor said, *=*Such confusion. Prepare for jump.*

I almost managed to repress a smile. I said, "How long do I have, you sneak?"

Chamzeen looked at me; but I'd turned the comkey off.

*=*What, mad at me? You have two minutes.*

There was a short pause, and I could feel a question building.

Shreekor was trying to find a funny way to phrase it, and failing; but he couldn't resist it.

*=*How are you finding your company?*

"Oh," I said, offhandedly, "friendly, warm . . . it might be a hot prospect, though."

*=*Do you realize that your puns are getting worse?*

"Yeah," I said.

The commander was speaking rapidly

*=*Better strap down. The next stop is the warbase.*

Chamzeen started setting up flight rigs, and I said, "Don't forget to punch the tickets, now."

*=*Feh. The Jeweler is building a machine to do such menial tasks . . .*

9 The Warbase

Soru: Reduced to simple notes on a simple scale, an earthlike planet in orbit around a G3 sun, oxygen-nitrogen atmosphere with trace elements similar to Earth's, 23% oxygen. Larger diameter than Earth, but less mass due to partial hollowing and removal of heavy metals, a gravity of 0.93g.

The planet is a pleasant place on the surface.

Underneath, it's a war machine.

The natives are an average of seven feet in height, humanoid, and built like mobile blue brick walls. Scattered in between them: a variety of aliens much like the scatterings found on Builders' bases.

But this base was built to destroy, not to observe.

The Enforcer ship stayed in orbit; it took two days for the weapons and people aboard to be offloaded to the planet beneath, giving me time to absorb the neccessary information. I hadn't heard of the place before; an example of a well-kept secret on the part of the Builders.

But Nikky had heard rumors. Soru Warbase was part of the "force" that she'd been telling me about on board the hulk of 908.

Once the ship had been unloaded, it was invaded by assorted relations of the crew members, including a dozen members of Chamzeen's temple, all with similar names and similar dispositions. After being introduced to each in turn, I was beginning to find out about the warmth in relationships.

I made a swift exit when Beachballius was greeted by a large group of highly active miniature basketballs, and one slightly more docile—but far noisier—fully-grown beachballius; I was still recovering from Beachballius' "game," and wasn't in any mood to greet an entire family of the things.

At least it gave me a cue to go back to my own ship, which was linked to the freighter by a broading tube.

Shreekor was smirking all over the telepathic lines when I went through the lock; he was floating over the Jeweler, who was engaged in putting something together with tools and components borrowed from the freighter. If nothing else, he was creative.

Shreekor followed me as I went through the hatchway to the control section. I wasn't too sure what sort of reaction I was going to get—both Nikoi and the princess had been present at my meeting with the priestesses, and both had left well before I had.

As I stepped into the control area the princess took one look at me, sniffed loudly, and brushed by me, ignoring me entirely.

I watched her until the closing door cut her off, my eyebrows raised. Then I looked at Shreekor, who looked back at me, two eyes on the door, two on my face.

He didn't say anything.

I looked around at Nikoi.

She was watching me in silence, with the Great Stone Face set well in place, her eyes glowing lightly. She wasn't going to say anything; that much was obvious.

What wasn't obvious was what I was supposed to have done—I'd been following a ritual; I'd expected joking, and gotten amusement from Shreekor,

But this?

I walked across the control area, watching Nikoi, and climbed into my crash tank.

She watched me all the way—*staring*.

Those eyes were killers.

Shreekor settled into the air next to my tank, folding himself up, comfortably.

"And *you* shut up," I said, testily.

*=*Such temperament.*

"Shut up."

*=*Two jealous females and you're upset?*

Jealous? That didn't look like jealousy. More like disgust.

"Shut up," I said.

*=*Poor Kevven. He doesn't know what to do.*

"Shut *up*."

*=*Would you prefer the warmth of the priestesses to the cold in here?*

''*Shut* up.''

*=*You are an inspired conversationalist today.*

Shut up.''

*=*Whatever happened to that glib tongue, that incredible wit—*

''Shut up.''

=—that marvelous sense of humor, and that great sense of ethnic wonder that you used to present us all with?*

''*Shut up.*''

*=*And so vanishes another of the great lovers of our time—in a haze of—*

''*Shreekor—*''

—shut-ups. Ahhhhh . . .

And he chattered on. Trust him to have a good time at my expense.

I gave up and pushed the sleepstim switch; the hell with him. I had to go down to Soru.

And I might as well sleep until then.

An oversized walking ottoman started across the street in front of me, and I tilted the steering bar of my floating truck to go around it.

Behind me, the Jeweler chittered something; as I looked over my shoulder, he went back to adjusting his toy—he had finished playing with the components he'd appropriated, and the resulting gadget turned out to be a neat and effective sonic cutter.

My destination was the center of the city; the entire central area consisted of one large park and a plaza, in the middle of which was the main surface building of the Warbase. The rest was almost all beneath the surface. Some segments were out in space, scattered around the system.

It made a neat defense against attack.

I slowed down and stopped at an intersection, to let a massive floater truck, carrying a blobby mass of protoplasm, cross in front of me; I'd seen the signal change well before.

I looked over my shoulder at the Jeweler. He was standing up.

Worse: he was aiming his Tinker Toy at a spire some way distant.

Even worse than that: he triggered the cutter before I could stop him.

As I watched, the tip of the spire wobbled, tilted, and fell; the Jeweler made a sound of satisfaction as it dropped.

It was caught by a tractor beam in mid-fall, and slowly lowered.

I opened the throttle all the way the second the signal changed; the other floater had vanished down the street it had been aimed at. The Jeweler stumbled behind me, and I looked around; his toy had cut a neat, thin line into the roadway.

I didn't have to stop after that; I suspected someone preferred that we didn't.

A short while later, I slowed the floater through an ornate archway, into the park grounds, and followed the roadway through to the main plaza; I had to lean sharply on the steering bar to avoid a massive square creature that was bulldozing toward the road.

I'd been given directions to find the entranceway that was suitable for the Jeweler and myself; it didn't take long to find it. I cut the power as I stopped next to it, and stepped off the floater as it settled onto its stop-field; the Jeweler stepped off behind me, and followed me inside. I hoped he wasn't pointing the cutter at anything vulnerable. Like me.

There was a click behind me, and the light vanished, replaced swiftly by artificial lighting. I turned around.

A door had appeared, shutting us in.

Well, I'd expected something like that.

A moment later, the floor gave a jerk, almost overbalancing me, and started moving smoothly forward. That was a new one on me; the bases used floaters for most heavy work, and everybody walked where they were going, unless they were in a hurry—the bases were small enough, and lifts connected the various levels.

The air smelled conditioned; on the outside, it had had the smell of a summer's day, an equatorial smell.

Two minutes later, the floor slid to a stop, almost throwing me forward. I felt the Jeweler bump into the back of my legs; he hadn't been expecting it either.

*=*Hold your positions, visitors.*

The voice sounded feminine; female tones seemed to be common.

"Pretty," the Jeweler said. He hadn't spoken any sentences longer than a half-dozen words since investigating our jump units.

We dropped.

I thought it was a tube elevator, with a floorplate for standing on. Until I made the mistake of looking down.

It was one hell of a long way to the bottom, and the only thing stopping us from attempting to keep on falling once we hit it was a slider field.

I looked up, almost too quickly; my stomach wasn't going to forgive me for that very easily. It was difficult to ignore the sensation of falling.

It took a minute and a half to complete the drop; as we slowed, the field folded under us, folding us into shapes suitable for sitting in the cushioned seats that we landed in. Neat.

I looked at the seat; basically a comfortable easy chair on a floater platform, with a control bank set into one arm. About half the function lights were lit; preprogrammed.

The chair moved out of the elevator siding, and into a wide, glimmering track; to all sides, I could see other chairs, both with passengers and without, among assorted couches—one of them with three chatting priestesses lined up on it, of apparently different temples—flatbeds, and others, all moving at fairly high speeds. There seemed to be some sort of force field in front of the chair; there was no trace of aircurrents.

Overhead was a curving black ceiling; it was at least a hundred yards up, and against it, I could make out one or two fliers. Whatever else the warbase on Soru did, they obviously didn't believe in economy in building.

I looked back at the Jeweler; he had the top of the control panel off his chair, and was fiddling inside, flicking his fingers across it.

His chair started a side-to-side dance; he flicked his fingers across the panel again, and it turned in a three-hundred-sixty-degree whirl, and stopped, still moving forward, while he fiddled with the exposed circuitry.

A few seconds later, it accelerated, ducked to one side of my chair as I ducked down, overtook me, and moved back into my lane in front of me, still accelerating. The last I saw of it for a few moments was when it ducked to one side of a huge flatbed carrying what looked like a pile of cold, dry porridge, and vanished on the other side.

I sighed, shaking my head. The Jeweler might be a genius, but he had all the sense of an eight-year-old kid. One of these days, he was going to do something silly and get himself killed.

As that thought trailed away, my chair did a fandango, and my stomach and brain went into a whirl, in opposite directions.

With a rush of mild g-force, it accelerated towards the flatbed.

I opened my mouth to yell, and got ready to jump.

My chair lurched to the side and missed the flatbed by a matter of inches; I watched in horrified fascination as the gray-green side zipped by. The alien on board didn't give any visible reaction to my passage.

I sank back into the seat and almost turned to jelly, as my chair caught up to the Jeweler and slowed to match his speed. Accident avoidance system, of course. Sensors on the chair linked to computer control. You can't hit anything. Not that thinking about it made me feel any better.

I looked at the Jeweler and used some fascinating words, with roots in anglo and non-anglo languages; some aliens know how to cuss.

The Jeweler grinned and bobbed his antennae at me.

I couldn't check off the miles we covered over the shining roadway, or how many turns we took—we branched off in other directions four or five times, the roads often changed course suddenly—but I'd guess we covered at least thirty miles, all at high speed.

And all the while, we were dropping further into Soru itself.

Finally, the chairs started to slow down, moving swiftly onto a side track, and down a long corridor, to stop in front of a blank wall.

We sank into the floor, dropping perhaps thirty yards, coming out facing down another long corridor.

The chair moved leisurely halfway down the corridor, then stopped and turned ninety degrees.

The wall in front split into two large sections, folding away, leaving a large space; we moved inside, and stopped.

We were facing at least five dozen assorted types of sentients, from humanoid to blob type; every one of them different. They were lined up on everything from chairs to flatbeds, many of them protected by the pale luminescence of life-support fields.

I opened my mouth to say hello, and was interrupted by a voice saying, *=*State your title/name and your origin/planet of birth.*

Female again.

I obeyed automatically, giving name, number, details of hereditary titles, rank, original assignment, present assignment, planet, and base. It surprised me; I wouldn't normally have bothered with everything.

That meant programming.

At my side, the Jeweler was reeling off things as well; short style, thank God. He seemed mildly surprised.

*=*Location of Terra/Área Fourteen noted. Explanation of hereditary title requested. Purpose: records.*

That one was easy; the original destruction of the Mala by slave traders, the rescue and training of my ancestors, and the direct line from there to me, the Chieftain Of Empty Air, as my relatives *enjoy* calling me.

*=*Noted. Present assignment?*

I wasn't so sure about that.

But response was automatic.

I said, "To cooperate with the personel of Soru Warbase in a search and destroy operation directed at the T'sooli. I am to operate with the objectives of the Builders as my guidelines, and will be trained as part of the complement of the warbase, as will my present crew."

No wonder Shreekor had been smirking. I sounded like a pamphlet for the Italian Communist Party.

I glanced at the Jeweler. He was still talking away. Either he'd been asked for different details, or he'd dropped back into his relaxed mode, which would bore everyone half to death.

The voice said, *=*Noted. Your other crewmembers?*

I listed them. It surprised me to find myself accepting Nikoi L'aan and the Princess Meheilahn M'jura ka Opul as part of my 'crew' . . . but the Builders had arranged that. And that, I guessed, was that.

The other thing that surprised me was that I'd been given a few extra details as far as Nikoi was concerned; I simply hadn't been aware of the details until the right stimulus had been provided.

*=*Noted.*

And my mind was suddenly near overloading with immediate details of other involved independent team leaders, names, origins—plants and bases—and dozens of other points of interest.

The pile of information faded into memory quickly, but left me with a dull ache behind my eyes; telepathic training can be painful.

*=*I hope,* Shreekor said, from where he was, still in orbit, *=*that you know you're considered our commander/leader.*

I raised an eyebrow.

"Does that mean you're my underling?"

*=*No.*

I grinned, and settled back into my chair, watching the cluster of sentients. None of them made any sign of recognition; but all of them were my colleagues in this. Only a few of them, true. But quite enough.

The other voice said, *=*Do you have a preference as to the type of director of training who will be personally responsible for you?*

I straightened up a little, easing kinks out of my back. "Do I have to choose among sentients? I should imagine any director would be as capable as one I might choose." The voice waited for a moment. "Any humanoid would work well—considering my species type."

*=*There is no need for specific choice.*

There was A Pause That Refreshed, and I cleared my throat.

*=*You are hereby assigned to Chamquee.*

Uh-oh.

I said, "Chamquee? A Lachallan?"

It was like having a computer display in my head; on saying that, I was presented with all the details: Chamquee, Priestess Of The Temple Of Lovers, originally assigned to Starwarrior Seven —a Soru ship—that patrolled a route between Soru, and a planet called Bara, presently assigned as a director of training.

Her temple sounded slightly more heady than Chamzeen's.

Well, if nothing else, it might be fun.

I said wryly, "The information is noted."

*=*The remainder of your crew will be brought down and assigned. You are relieved of responsibility until training is complete.*

Great stuff.

My chair turned a hundred eighty degrees and started back the way it had come.

I stepped inside and the doors closed with a chime, leaving me standing before a bead curtain.

It shimmered softly in diffused light, jangling in a minor key, soft as the winds; this seemed to be a temple, rather than the quarters of an agent of an organization designed to destroy.

The curtains rang softly as they parted; a short, satanic figure stepped through, one hand holding the curtains apart. She had shimmering green hair, long ears that protruded through the fall of hair, and eyebrows that had a more Grecian curve to them; her eyes were larger, flared by expert traces of unusual cosmetics.

But otherwise, she wasn't much different from Chamzeen.

In English—surprising me—she said, ''Greetings. I am Chamquee.'' She bowed slightly.

I returned the bow and announced myself.

She surprised me again by acknowledging me with a nod and turning away to go back through the curtain. It didn't faze me too much: I wasn't desperate for the usual cuddle and kiss treatment.

But I'd have to start learning something about Lachallan customs; I was probably going to run into other temples before long.

I followed her through the jangling curtain, feeling metallic cold as my hand touched it, and into the room behind it. It wasn't very colorful; the main decor was black and white, sparsely furnished—black and white cushions spread around, plus what appeared to be the Lachallan equivalent of bean-bags.

Chamquee sat down on one of the bean-bags, and curled herself up gracefully. She didn't invite me to sit down; instead, she looked me over with the air of a cook in an Art Deco delicatessen inspecting the offerings.

I stared back at her.

After a few moments, she said, ''I am here to teach you, Kevven Tomari. And I shall expect you to learn, rather than standing and looking like a particularly stupid black sculpture. Take heed.''

I raised my eyebrows, surprised. Chamzeen and her sister priestesses had given me the wrong idea about her people.

"I'll learn," I said.

"Good."

She uncurled herself again, and stood, stepping up to me.

"Your first lesson," she said, "involves trust."

Her arms went around my neck, and I resigned myself to custom and Lachalla. And got surprise number three.

In four seconds, I was writhing on the floor, convulsing in pure agony, struggling to breathe. She'd done something to the back of my neck, hit me twice with light, excruciating blows to the stomach, kicked my ankles to either side, and thrown me among the bean-bags.

She came and stood over me, bending and touching pressure points along my body; most of the pain went away, leaving me breathless and weak.

She stepped back as I rolled over and sat up, groaning and rubbing the back of my neck; I could feel the nerves still reacting.

She said, "That is your frist lesson. There is *no* trust." She smiled, bitterly, and held out a hand. "Now take my hand. I will not hit you again."

Suckers never learn.

I took her hand and she hauled me to my feet with surprising strength.

Then whirled in a circle after releasing me, and launched a vicious sidekick that impacted in my stomach, driving me backwards, pain exploding from groin to throat, mind exploding in agony again; something had been crushed inside, probably assorted torn muscles—

I hit a bean-bag and toppled backwards, striking a wall; I couldn't breathe again.

I struggled to get the hell out of the way as she jumped the bean-bag. Her shoulder caught me in the chest, slamming me back against the wall; I felt something snap, more pain.

I started to slump, sliding down the wall, struggling to get up, starting to black out, as she whirled away, dropping into a crouch.

She kicked from the crouch, lazy and elegant; her foot hit my jaw, and I felt bones shatter as my head smashed back into the wall.

The pain went away.

Light.

I tensed for pain, didn't believe it when it didn't appear, thought it over and considered what had happened in the space of seconds; *I should be dead*. Fractured skull, shattered jaw, various fragments in the brain, massive hemorrhaging in stomach and lungs . . .

All considered and rejected; I was alive, and I was in good physical condition.

I opened my eyes and looked around; seemed to be the same room, with the addition of the table or bed that I was laid out on, and the subtraction of a number of cushions and one or two bean-bags.

Chamquee was sat on a bean-bag nearby, watching me and smoking something that looked suspiciously like a cigarette; it was more fragrant. But probably no more narcotic than tobacco.

"I see that the student has wakened at last," she said. "How do you feel?"

I didn't say anything for a moment, looking at her. I couldn't easily see the Lachallans as being violent, at least in the way she'd struck out. You live and learn.

I said, "Stupid."

She nodded. "At least you have some semblance of honesty." She stood and went to the wall, dropping the cigarette into a slot, then crossed to stand by the table I was lying on. I was shirtless. "I suppose you have taken your first lesson to heart."

I said, "Sure." Wrong again, Tomari. But I wasn't going to find that out for a while. "I'm surprised I feel so well, though."

I swung my feet from the table and sat up, staying still.

She gave me a dark look and said, "Our medical techniques are somewhat less than primitive."

I shook my head. "That wasn't what I meant. I'd have thought you'd have let me ache a while to get the point across."

"The inflicted pain is sufficient."

"Yeah?" I started sliding from the table, relaxed. "Well, I guess you're right. I learned the first lesson al—"

Dropped, tensed, screamed as I kicked out, hitting her in the stomach, pulling it to prevent hurting her too much; I wanted to shake her up, not damage her—my chauvinistic tendencies wouldn't allow doing so much damage to a female, no matter what had been done to me.

She rolled in mid-fall, turned the momentum into a semi-somersault and twisted lynx-like to end up holding a mantis-like fighting position, broken-wristed, finger-twisted, eyes intent.

I slid back, foot-slide-shuffle, defensive, hands protecting groin and face, moving easily and watchfully, a pugilistic ballet.

I said, "First lesson learned, see? No trust, right?"

There was the flicker of a smile; I felt a misplaced dart of love for her—she wasn't in the right place, and I knew it. She *had* to do it, *didn't* want to. . . .

Anger roared from the back of my mind and gripped my stomach and throat, made me snarl.

Her hand snapped away the decorative clasp at her throat, and she unraveled her robe with ocelot/minx motions.

I'd been set up.

She was wearing a combat costume that left her arms and legs free; not flex-armor, just cloth. But effective.

I risked a glance back; the table was gone.

The bitch had been expecting it all the time.

Light on her feet; she came at me in a gentle dance, gliding. I retreated, circled away from her, and around, then attacked, fast, going for a throw and lock.

She twirled away from me, slid into my side and pulled me through as she turned again, using momentum, slammed her right hand, heel of the palm, into the back of my afro; the mass of hair stole some force, but the blow still staggered me.

I fought gravity, caught balance, twisted swiftly on the heel of one foot, slammed the other foot down at ninety degrees; she struck with a fist blow and I plucked it and diverted it with a cross-arm parry, turned and stiffened the arm, slammed my free elbow down onto it, with no effect.

Using her arm as leverage, she twisted and arced her foot around, into my stomach, drawing pain and knocking some of the wind out of me as I tried to spin away from her. I winced and struck with a whipping branch forearm blow that impacted on her shoulder, kicked out with a roundhouse foot, caught her on the thigh, sent her sprawling.

(Wonder if Tarzan ever beat up on Jane—?

I closed in to end it.

She kicked up with both legs, back arching, hands used as base and propulsion, hit me in the chest with both feet, sending me reeling back and over; I landed on my butt, cursing under my breath.

We both got back to our feet together.

(Beatin' up on the preacher again.)

Dropped into a temporary defense and stood to the side, changed the stance to attack, struck first with fast punch, twisting hand, automatically followed up with a kick.

Crossed wrists blocking the punch and holding my arm for a space as her hands snapped open and around, unbalancing the kick, curving her body around the blow; she broke the lock and struck, a chop at the side of my neck as I twisted to avoid it; I took it on my shoulder, winced as a snark ripped into nerves, cramping.

I struck from semi-crouch, before she could effectively dodge, hit her with a cupped-hand slap over her high cheekbone; would have laid any human out, writhing in blind agony; it dazed her, that was all.

(Scratch the KGB methods.)

She whirled away, pivoted, pirouetted back, hands floating gracefully, killer motions, suddenly twisted and flew into a faeriedance flying kick, leg shooting from beneath her, pinning into my chest, staggering me before I could slip out of range.

She landed, swung three hundred sixty as a ballet dancer, kicked roundhouse, eyes deadly, expression stone; sent me into the floor, pain arching from stomach and chest and back.

(No time for rules, fightin' dirty, m' man.)

I lifted an arm, trying to get up, saw it blurred in front of my face; give me ten seconds, I'll have it; I waited for the *coup de grace,* this means another shattered jaw; *goddamn monotony!* because she was whipping me easy, and I was fool enough to walk in wide open. *Don't trust.*

She didn't finish me off.

I watched as my head cleared; she circled me, watching me coming back to some sort of shape, hands flickering, waiting to strike.

I rose, circled, closed, twisted, kicked leftside, balance not perfect. She blocked it, dumped me back on the floor, dazing me again.

She waited for me to get up again, triangular eyes intent.

I shook my head, bullish, trying to get rid of recalcitrant cobwebs, got to hands and knees, watching her, pushed myself up and circled away, defensive, hands float-dancing.

She dodged in at me, evaded my poor attempt at blocking her, whirled around me; I felt her elbows strike either side, like lightning, and pain jarring, not bad, but not good either.

(She's playing with me.)

She whirled away as I staggered; I turned and then dodged as she came back at me; she whirled, mouth half-open, shark teeth showing, ducked inward, slammed out with a punch to my waist; I yelped, staggered, regained my balance as she came back at me; her hands flashed, twisting from her waist to my stomach, folding me as calmly as if she'd struck a playing card.

I fought an urge to vomit, grunting and gritting my teeth like a good ol' boy, battling cramped guts.

She snatched my hair, yanked my head back—felt like roots tearing out—heaved me into a standing position, still feeling the pain in my guts, sweat starting to pour down my face, teeth aching from gritting them.

(Enough! Goddamnit! enough enough enough enough!)

Stopped trying not to hurt her, screamed and slammed both elbows around into her sides, dug in, raised my hands back and over, grabbed her hair and twisted it into my hands, feeling warmly metallic, yanked and kept on yanking, heard her gasp, felt her release my hair, felt her slam the heel of one bare foot into my calf and scrape down, cramping muscle as I fought to uncramp.

I heaved harder, pulling her head back to mine.

(Don't give a damn whether you don't like it baby—)

She ramed an elbow into my side, drawing pain and a grunt.

I pulled, gritting teeth harder. She gasped again.

(—'cause I just had all I can take, that's it.)

Felt her tense; bitch was tough as hell, strong as me, maybe stronger, better trained, probably; took effort, but her arms came back, hands locked under my chin, pulled, felt my teeth grind together, pain shooting into my mouth, tensing my neck muscles as she bent my head back; she levered me over her back, despite the pain obviously half-killing her, threw me, letting go of me; had to have a crick in my neck; kept my grip on her hair, so we both went together.

We hit the floor with a crash, she twisting to avoid smashing her face.

She slammed hands into the back of my head, mashing my face into the floor. I felt blood running from my nose, hardly any more pain, system overloaded and killing impulses now, not much further to go, almost done the distance and winded, second wind wasn't going to last long.

(. . .)

Past the point of thinking straight; I clung on to her hair, twisting it around my hands, much longer and I'd rip it out

She slammed her fists into the sides of my face; felt like a cheekbone gone there, blood filling my mouth, probably broken teeth, lacerated gums and cheeks, and more.

I spat a tooth out, with blood.

Let go of her hair with my right hand, slammed it knife-edge into the side of her face, slammed again, slammed again, felt something break.

She hit back, slapped lights out of my face, black eye probably, pretty vicious.

Struck with a knuckle blow into the side of her face again; pulpy; she wasn't gone yet.

She smacked my head twice with open hands, changed her tactic and went for my carotids; I heaved with the hand holding her hair, rolled and let her loose, came to my feet, feeling blood dripping from my chin to my chest, rivuleting down, wiped it and saw red gleams on the back off my hand. Light-headed and dizzy, pain distant. Running with sweat and blood, temperature in here up high and humid.

She came up, circled away. defensive; cut and bruised, costume torn in a couple of places; her blood darker than mine; her hair was all over, and she shook her head, shaking it back; one eye was swollen almost shut.

We circled for a minute, watching for openings and attacks.

Then I charged her, screaming in attack, striking hard, fast, often. She went down under the attack; no warning, just a snap decision. The body acting in place of the mind; to end pain, attack.

I swung as she rolled away, intended to slam her down again; she came up instead, moved like scared lightning, butted me in the stomach as I was moving forward, sending me backwards, clawing at her; we went down together, fighting and scratching like wildcats.

She threw me backwards, hurled herself at me as I snapped my legs back to my chest; I brought my feet up into her stomach as she came down on me, flipped her up and over, straining to get the neccessary power, getting it and feeling worse for it. She hit the far wall upside-down, thudding, twisted as she dropped, almost managed to land easy, but felt it through her, wincing.

I'd already rolled and come up again; as she landed, I charged again, saw her flip herself over, a sylph in kinetic body; she twisted, trying to dodge before I hit, didn't make it, was driven back into the wall by my shoulder, driven back again as I whirled and hammered my elbows into her, slipped and fell as I ducked away, caught herself as I slipped and went to one knee; I got up again, shaking my head, hands out and broken-wristed, ready for attack, mantis stance and murder.

She went into defensive, spat out a spike passing for tooth in a coagulation of blood, blood trickling from her mouth and down her chin, staining the costume.

She circled away, around as I backed away, watching. I wiped a hand across my mouth, spat blood and saliva, shook sweat away, and tried to dodge as she attacked; didn't make it; felt skin shred and blood flow as her fingernails raked my forehead and cheek; my heart like a drum, running counterpoint in a 78 rpm march.

Blood blinded me; I wiped my hand across my eyes, kicked her as she spun away, turning to do it; my foot connected with her backside, sent her sprawling onto the floor, sliding shortly.

She rolled, came up in a turn, pushing herself into the air, somersaulting with the sensuous litheness of a dancer, landed before me, elegantly high-kicked to my jaw as I tried to ride the blow out, pushing myself up and over and back, trying for a back somersault, landing on my hands and cartwheeling back, straining not to fall and crack anything, landing awkwardly, the grace of a penguin, twisting and balancing out.

(—fury I'm mad and gotta end it—)

Delirious.

Closed on her, left fist to the stomach, right fist up under her jaw as she tried to butt me and I ducked, taking the strike with the afro and cushioning it, felt and heard the fist connecting with a cracking sound and feeling as her head started back; lifted her from her feet, snapping her head back.

Stood swaying as she fell back full-length and hit the floor, left fist back at the waist, palm up, right arm out at an angle, stiff, last blow.

She didn't move.

(—beat—)

I checked, careful.

(—said no trust—)

Alive, but out cold.

I sank to my knees next to her, shook my head.

"You sorry little bitch," I said, painfully whispering.

Felt blood coursing, mind swimming through a lake of hazy pain.

Muscles giving up.

I collapsed across her prone form.

And passed out.

10 The Attackers

Champquee was waiting again when I woke up. I didn't do anything stupid this time; I was learning.

She said, ''you have learned another lesson. Never pursue a course of action without first considering your position and assessing the background information. You must also consider what action you are to take, and *think* while you are in motion. You can never be perfect, and this means you may be defeated by an enemy who is your equal, or your superior in some way. And it is possible that if the foe is determined, that the foe may destroy you even while your inferior, and even more possible that the foe will achieve his aim if well-trained.''

I had no arguments; Chamquee had known a little about human anatomy, but she hadn't known what sort of reactions I'd have, or what sort of abilities. But she'd still whipped the hell out of me; I'd sent her down in the second round, but she'd taken me down with her, and made me look like a fool in the process.

I listened and acted carefully from then on.

Training on Soru wasn't easy; each day exhausted me. But I was being made over into an effective fighter, without rebuilding me physically with mechanical and electronic components. We'd been sloppy; we had nothing to compare with Soru, and had never bothered to develop worthwhile defensive skills.

If and when I got back to Area Fourteen, somebody was going to be hit by one hell of a shakeup; my rank would see to it. And I had the Builders' sanction to work with.

Chamquee supervised my training program, working with me to develop me as a fighter—and as a thinker.

''Brute force is futile without consideration, application and planning; strategy is the application of force in the required place in the necessary degree."

I knew that by heart in sixteen languages; if I heard it, it meant I'd screwed up in something.

I started easy, with sleepstim sessions during which I was given subconscious programming that I could use when needed; recall wasn't conscious. If a certain piece of information was triggered by input, I'd know it. If the information wasn't there, an impulse to check certain things would appear in place. To save time and energy, there was an implant behind my left ear that could be utilised to patch into assorted library computers. I was loaded up with material I'd probably never have a chance to use; having it well below conscious level allowed me to keep a clear mind.

Otherwise, the languages: I could read in all of them, understand them, and handle most of them. The Beachballius language was a throat-ripper, and I didn't have the low vocal range to handle the various growls, grunts, snarls and belches. The Lachallan language was easier to master: it was simply a matter of hitting the correct intonations, a form of singing, but slightly harsher. The main problems lay in *knowing* languages, but not being able to speak them at first, getting used to them; it frustrated me at first, until I started to get used to the idea.

But I had a sore throat for at least a month, from practicing languages that consisted of screams and yelps, and languages in which normal conversation consisted of bellowing at the other party.

After a while, the sleepstim sessions started to include programs of combat; first I had to unlearn the methods I'd previously been using, then practice like a demon to get into the habit of using the methods I'd been given. Some of it was easy; I'd already been fed one bunch of combat methods by the Builders. But most of it was hard work, whether fighting with simulacra of various aliens, or piloting a simulator to ram a spacecraft in motion—and running with a computer playing random patterns.

Flunking simulator tests usually got me chewed out at length by Chamquee, who didn't hesitate to make me feel small. Screwing up with the simulacra was another matter entirely.

If I flunked out on those tests, I got hurt. Often, and badly. I wound up being sent for assorted repairs quite a lot at first. The repair sessions decreased fairly rapidly.

Pain has a disciplining effect on the mind.

If I had any spare time, I used it to practice and study. It gets to you after you've been battered to a pulp three or four times.

By the time the war machine spat me out at the end, I could catch and kill a Jet Jumper, on foot and without weapons; I could also do some interesting things with spacecraft, fight in space against a suited alien with only a life-support field to assist me, and more. Maybe not as effectively as some—a Beachballius could do the spaceside stunt with one lazy kick—but effectively enough.

When they'd finished with me, I was an Enforcer, an Enemy-slayer with lightning in one hand and a gun in the other, efficient, deadly, careful.

A human killing machine.

It was a thought that plagued me now and then.

It was Chamzeen who finally disabused me of the notion, on one of her occasional visits, after the training was over; I hadn't been sent out on any missions yet, but I'd picked up rumors here and there around the base—usually from the homo sap Enforcers who were either friends or liaisons—that I was slated for something soon.

It wasn't just Chamzeen who cured me of the worries that I might have been made inhuman by the training process. But she kicked it off.

She pointed out that she had been through the training, as had Beachballius Maximus, and neither of them had lost their personal qualities. Beachballius Max had always liked to play stomp-the-being, and Chamzeen still continued as a priestess, with her duties still the same as before, only now applied to the needs of Warbase Prime. And, she noted, with one eyebrow raised and an arch tone to her voice, I'd still got a conscience—I worried about the effects on me, didn't I?—a weird sense of humor, and bad taste in puns.

I pointed out the case of Chamquee.

Chamzeen pointed out that Chamquee hadn't harmed me herself since she'd kicked my teeth halfway down to my ass; in fact, Chamquee had been closer to me than most of the other sentients on Warbase Prime. Even my second sense of humor, Shreekor, hadn't been around me much, and I'd hardly seen the others at all. And the priestess had—Chamzeen said—been watching out for me, just in case I came near getting my skin stripped off for use as a hearthrug.

She finished up with, "It pains her most brutally to see you hurt."

She gave me a look of triumph; so there, Tomari, what do you say now?

I said, "How the hell do you know?"

Chamzeen was sat on a bean-bag in my quarters—they'd turned out to be almost standard furniture in the Warbase; you could get an alien visitor who wouldn't fit your type of chair. She was smoking one of the odd Lachallan cigarets.

She said, "I am a sister priestess to Chamquee, in all honor. We hold no secrets from each other." She smiled, showing off her teeth, and curled up more, slouchily, on the bean-bag. "It is cold in here."

I shrugged; the temperature was up at ninety degrees, and if I hadn't been wearing a thin foil uniform, I'd have been sweating like a pig after a hundred-meter dash.

"I happen," I said, "to find it a little warm. I bear with your preferences, Chamzeen. But only so far."

She seemed amused by that. "Very well . . . but of Chamquee?"

"What about Chamquee?" I looked up from the panel set into my chair, tapping out an order for water without watching—I was used to doing it.

The delivery tray produced a plastic glass, condensation showing on the sides.

Surely you have feelings toward my sister priestess?"

I picked up the glass and sipped some water, swirling it around in my mouth for a moment; I set it back on the tray, carefully.

I said, "Certainly I have feelings toward Chamquee."

Chamzeen clapped her hands. "Good. Explain." She leaned forward, intent on what I had to say.

I leaned back in the chair, clasped my hands over my stomach—I'd lost pounds and gained muscles that surprised me—and took a deep breath.

"I," I started evenly, "could not bear with her for anything other than the period of training, because she's annoying, pushy, violent, bitchy, self-assertive, self-righteous, bitter, bad-tempered, and generally downright degrading. Also, her normal blood temperature is around twenty-two degrees higher than mine would be if I'd just died from fever.''

I picked up the glass and drained it, ordered another round.

Chamzeen blinked and took a few seconds to digest my attack; she seemd slightly offended, not surprisingly. Then she leaned back, looking at me.

''Those are feelings of dislike,'' she said. ''Have you nothing positive to say about her?''

Her tone seemd to include hints that I was being exceptionally nasty, without needing to be. The Lachallan language was quite capable of that.

''Yeah.'' I grinned. ''She's cute. And a little pretty as well.''

''Well, that is but the beginning!'' Chamzeen shook her head and jabbed a long finger at me. ''You should attempt to see beneath the surface!''

I sighed; this looked like being a Lachallan lecture, and it could get exceptionally convoluted before long—Chamzeen could outyatter me on anything I cared to choose.

I said, ''When you're greeted by having your teeth rammed down your throat, you do tend toward making severely negative judgments as per the person who's doing the ramming.''

Chamzeen slapped a knee, with a loud crack. ''Those were *lessons!* They are given to any chosen to become Enforcers—consider your friends, and how they might feel!'' She stopped the diatribe suddenly, sighed, and ran a hand through her hair, causing the light to ripple away from the metallic silver strands. She looked a little . . . *guilty.* ''I admit, though, that I once thought of her in a negative way.''

I stopped in the middle of picking up the new water glass, and half-stared at Chamzeen. ''She banged you around, as well?''

The phrasing amused her a little; she lit up with a rueful smile.

''Indeed she did, and she was very methodical in *banging* me around. She works effectively with the teaching—she broke many bones. One should never attempt to teach the teacher.''

Oh man, this was worse than being in the audience at a kung fu flick in Kingston, Jamaica. If I'd noted that, Chamzeen would probably have listed each bone broken, and how.

''Fascinating,'' I said. ''We just kindly beat each other up in the name of education. Great way to spend a day.''

Chamzeen laughed, a sound like a hyena with a splinter in its paw.

"You make a joke, of course," she said.

I sipped some water and said, "Of course. Look, I don't like being pounded on, and I particularly hate being told I'm useless after a *machine* has just done the pounding." I put the glass aside.

"But it happens to all Enforcers," Chamzeen insisted. "There is no reason to be bitter about it—you are only one among thousands." She flicked at her hair with one long finger. "You should take some comfort from the fact that even priestesses have to feel some pain once in a while."

She paused and aimed a sly smile to one side of me; in her position, she looked like an offbeat Cleopatra. "Besides, Chamquee dislikes having to do such things, neccessary as they are."

"Chamzeen—" I said, as I realized what she'd done. "I ought to pick you up and use a switch on your tail."

She made an eloquent gesture in the air, and looked immoderately proud of herself, holding back laughter.

From behind me, Chamquee said, "But it is true, Kevven."

Chamzeen was having a problem containing the giggles; every now and then a yip escaped her.

I looked around; Chamquee was looking down at me from behind my chair, looking distraught. And slightly amused.

She moved around the side of the chair, gliding, and said, "It causes me grief to cause pain to others."

It fitted; her Lachallan training was conflicting with the training she'd had on Soru. Result: one slightly screwed up priestess.

I spared a glare for Chamzeen, who'd settled for a smug look, and said, "Sit down, Chamquee."

"I thank you," she said, formally.

And she sank to the floor at my feet, her head bowed.

"You have lost none of your grace," she added.

I stared in amazement; the hell with grace—I'm graceless; and I'm polite because that was the way my Daddy taught me to be. The old man is one hell of a hypocrite at least half the time. The other half of the time, he manages to cover his trail better.

I said, "Okay. Why are you sitting at my feet?"

"It is my place." She sighed and traced a complex design on the floor, absently. "I have done you harm."

"So what?" I glared at her, then at Chamzeen because I couldn't glare into Chamquee's eyes. I'd been neatly bound by Chamzeen. "Chamzeen says it's your job."

Chamzeen herself was struggling still not to laugh. ''It is, Kevven, Chamquee's way. She must, after having done her job, atone for having done it.'' Chamzeen slouched back again, having scented her victory already. Never trust a Lachallan with an intention—they get devious. ''It must prove to you that Chamquee is not bad at the center of the soul.''

I sighed, exasperated.

''Also,'' Chamzeen went on, ''you should have seen your expression when you realized . . . it was wonderful.''

I shook my head and looked at Chamquee, then at Chamzeen. ''Okay, I agree, she's not bad. Much. I also agree that you've made your point. Now, I would be happier if Chamquee would quit acting like a stupid slavegirl, which means I do *not* wish her to continue sitting on the floor, curled up around my feet.''

Chamquee nodded, and got up, still looking disconsolate.

A moment later, she dropped into my lap and curled up comfortably.

Chamzeen couldn't help herself anymore; the wounded hyena sounds started up again.

''Do you forgive me, Kevven?'' Chamquee said, looking at me.

I raised my eyes to give a sad look to the ceiling; Chamzeen was really getting some amusement out of this. Well, maybe a positive answer would get Chamquee to leave me alone—the ninety degree atmosphere was bad enough, but having nearly a hundred thirty degrees sitting in my lap in a hundred-pound bundle was torture, not to say uncomfortable. I was being boiled where I sat.

Besides which, I didn't hold a grudge against Chamquee—I'd just had a case of the macho sulks from having been bullied into shape. And Chamzeen had cured those effectively.

So I said, ''I forgive you, so don't worry about it.''

Chamzeen looked pleased, and winked at me.

Then Chamquee kissed me; customs weren't varying—they'd just been delayed for a while.

But I didn't start thinking about that.

The implant behind my ear started roaring out the scramble signal, and the wall alarms started flashing frantically.

I shot out of my chair automatically, dumping Chamquee; she caught herself in mid-tumble, righted before she hit, landed in a crouch, and came back up, following me as the door snapped open.

The implant was giving instructions already. Both priestesses were on my team for the time being; immediate crewing of ships, all weapons to be used in defense, other crew data, and the reason behind the alert.

I didn't stop moving while I listened, but I did start swearing under my breath. We'd been tumbled and rumbled.

By the Enemy.

And they'd sent an armada to wipe us out.

I turned the last corner and almost dived into the shifter, Chamzeen and Chamquee right behind me.

It was going to be hard.

I hate sudden-death playoffs.

"Systems confirmation call. Fourteen zero nine."

I was automatically checking systems on my flight board; the ship was being slotted into place on the launch rack already.

I said, "Fourteen zero nine to control dispatcher, Pilot Tomari, all check."

Chamzeen, buried beneath a control and computer fire control helmet, finished running her second-and-third systems checks, and said, "Co-pilot Chamzeen, all check."

Ablative heat shields snapped into place around the ship, and I watched compensator lights carefully. If the compensators went, the acceleration placed on us would destroy the ship, immediately after crushing the five of us into something resembling jelly.

Chamquee said, "Drone controller Chamquee, all check."

"Weaponsmaster *Haahrrraagh!* all check."

That was a Beachballius; the grunting sounds plucked at my ears from the headset.

One more.

We snicked into the final track and my board lit up with series of new reads; we were now under mass driver control.

"Navigator Bia, all computer systems and sensor segments check."

Bia was one of the giant blue Soru.

The three of them would feed Chamzeen and me information during the fight, and target attacking ships so we could pick them off. Not a dogfight: we'd be moving far too fast for that. We'd be hitting as we went by; a turn would require fast work from the computers, and by the time we got back, the other ship wouldn't be there.

Hit and run.

Control said, "You are ready for launch, fourteen zero nine."

Chamquee said, "Drones in place and activated."

I said, "Confirmed, Control."

The activation lights in my headset altered color.

Control sent us hurtling along the mass driver after the fighter that had gone two seconds previously; the various mass drivers and launch systems scattered around the Soru solar system were capable of spitting out over three thousand fighters in a minute. Other systems handled destroyers, which were less effective in a hit and run situation; more mass meant more inertia to combat, so destroyers sat and shot at each other.

The flight board registered entry into atmosphere; that meant a Soru launch, from a desert blow hole, or a sea tube; the sonic boom would be heard for miles.

Seconds later we were in space and under power, arcing away from Soru.

My implant spat a string of figures, and my hands automatically fed the board instructions; the remains of the heatshield spat away, exposing space and stars.

More lights on my headset; all shields up and operating perfectly, fire control waiting for instructions.

I triggered the jumpdrive and space folded up, placing us in another sector.

No Enemy.

My implant spat more figures, and my hands worked over the board again, hit the activation switch.

We came out of the folded space into a squadron of Enemy fighters; they weren't the only ones present, but they were the nearest.

Chamquee launched two drones as Chamzeen took control from me; I watched the board as the computers targeted an Enemy ship—the jewels looked like bugs, the instinct was to *squash*—and our course altered to take it in. The fighter fired; our shields absorbed the energy, glowing red.

I triggered the disruptors; the fighter exploded in a burst of blue. Two other fighters vanished from the screens as Chamquee's drones fired. Then we were shooting out of range, drones following.

The Enemy ships broke formation, altered course, and lit out after us. Chamzeen let them gain on us, and Chamquee's drones looped over them and in amongst them, firing.

Chamzeen bent our fighter through a turn, the computers watching the angle, and we attacked again, ships in two directions.

There had been ten or eleven ships. Two left.

The drones swept around again, firing.

And there were none.

The other ships were too far out of range now.

The implant spoke up again, and my hands touched the board a third time, programming.

Folded space and we dropped onto a target like a spider; our weaponsmaster dropped a torpedo in its direction and we shot away.

The screens registered the detonation; that had been a troopship.

The implant chattered.

Our next target was an overgrown jewel, a bomber/carrier, a nice juicy target filled with fighters and other goodies.

Chamquee directed her two drones at it, let them blast through the hull and well into the interior before detonating them.

The gigantic jewel was rent by the twin explosions, thrown into a shattering spin, snapped apart, and went spinning away into darkness, space-junk.

Registering noise behind my ear, operating, maximum pitch, *go!*

A pitched battle; one of the main forces, clumped for good defense; swarms of our ships were tearing through the clump, destroying as they went.

One of our ships went up under massed fire, vanished.

Another of our fighters tore through the cluster of fighters, burned and ravaged, left hulks and dust.

The implant told me all I needed to know; this was an attack designed to destroy Warbase Prime. But they had it wrong. Warbase Prime wasn't in one place; the whole bloody system was the Warbase.

Chamquee launched two more drones, leaving them to fight by themselves, onboard computer systems doing all the work.

We looped around a back and forth fight between an Enemy destroyer and one of our more compact tubs; as we shot away, the Soru ship unleashed a vicious broadside, stripping away the Enemy's screens along with half of the ship.

We cut a line through a cluster of Enemy fighters; grouping

was bad for them, because we got more of them that way. Before we lost them, Chamquee dropped a drone on them, programmed it to follow us when it was finished.

We sighted on an Enemy destroyer lumbering on its way to Soru, ripped over the top of him, firing along his line, punching holes through his screens and into his hull, slamming torpedoes straight through the holes, the bangs following our line.

The destroyer tore itself apart as we swept away and onto the next.

It fired as soon as we were in range; we held the course as the screens went up through the colors to almost-white, almost overloaded; he'd turned everything he had on us.

I hit fire controls, held the power up, poured everything into the ship as we went by; my headset registered the weaponsmaster dropping things in with the beams.

The screens shot back to normal; there was a careening clutter of debris where the ship had been.

Chamzeen damn near played a symphony on her side of the flight board; her implant would be spitting everything from delta-vee to optimum attack velocities for any of a dozen Enemy ships. Mine was silent for the moment; I wasn't flying the ship, just watching where the computer said I was supposed to be shooting, and occasionaly programming the jumpboard with figures given.

We came down on top of another destroyer; it had seen us coming from long range and had started to come around. Not the cleverest of tactics, but he could have had a chance if he'd made it.

We hit him in the middle of his course change and broke his back, thumped torpedoes into the two broken sections, and broke him into very small pieces.

Chamzeen brought us around again as Chamquee called her drones in; seventy-five percent of the Enemy division had been wiped out already. Our losses—I called up the required information, almost whistled—around ten percent so far. Overall Enemy casualties, around fifty percent. The Builders had put something into the Soru ships all right.

A cluster of a half-dozen Enemy ships chasing one of ours; Chamzeen poured power into a course change, and we lit out after them. Not fast enough.

The fighter had used up all its drones; it only had onboard

weaponry to defend itself; it vanished under the massed firepower of the Enemy ships.

Then we were on top of them and firing: Chamquee punched a drone amongst them, detonated it before they could scatter. Two of the ships vanished in the blaze, another spun away, turning, disabled. She loosed another drone as they came after us, finished two more.

Chamzeen let the last one catch up, and I fired again.

Glitterburst and dead space.

Six for one: good odds.

And a far cry from the days when men used to fly wood and paper machines through the skies over the poppy fields of France, shooting at the enemy fighters with revolvers.

We hit another Enemy fighter in the middle of his course change, dusted him.

Implant spat, hands moved; I hit the jumpboard activator and space folded like paper.

We came out on top of a fighter, cashed his chips in automatically, before he had chance to fire.

Chamzeen threw power into helping us avoid the black shape that suddenly registered on the screens; it hadn't been radar-visible until almost too late. The blasted thing was fitted with repeaters and totally blacked out. The edge of our shields flared as we scraped the Enemy's screens.

Chamzeen cursed in Lachallan and fought the ship's sudden yawing motion as we left the big ship behind, poured more power into bringing us back around. My screens registered a swarm of at least a dozen Enemy fighters, acting as fighter cover for the ship.

My implant started calling information up, pouring it out; robot ship, computer-controlled—

We passed two Enemy fighters, fired, left glitterdust dying.

—with a good escort. What use was it? No passengers or crew; not much sign of weaponry. It hadn't blasted us yet.

Chamzeen matched speed with the ship, took us along its line at a fighter, and I got ready to fire as we headed at his nose. He fired.

Our screens immediately went white, and danger telltales lit in my headset.

Chamzeen risked blowing equipment, smacked us into overdrive and away; too close. We'd been decoyed; the other ships hadn't been fitted with that kind of weaponry—it had been easy up until now.

And I knew what that ship was.

A planet-killer.

One big mother of a bomb; all they had to do was make sure it got in, slam it down on the planet, and activate it. With a bomb that big, there'd be one hell of a Dresden effect; big enough, or enough bombs, and the entire crust of the planet would be ripped away, along with the atmosphere.

They weren't bothered about the outlying sections of Warbase Prime; all they wanted was the nerve center. They'd hammer it into dust and leave. The rest of the fleet was running interference; by tying us up, they could get the planet-killers in close enough, and then it would be too late to stop them.

Chamquee rammed a drone through the fighter's screens, dusted him.

I blew air out, shivering. We'd tumbled to them, but if the rest of them were so powerful . . .

I said, "Chamquee, hit that monster with every drone you've got, and blow them. Chamzeen, get us the hell out of here, we're in trouble."

They didn't question it; Chamzeen swung us away from the ship, the fighters lighting out after us, while Chamquee sent every drone at the bomb, punching them through its screens and ducking them around the scattered fire.

She slammed the drones into the bomb's hull, firing, let them punch through, and activated the lot.

The blast was glorious, a small sun in the space of silent seconds. Some of the fighters vanished with the blast, the others came after us.

I was too scared to do much thinking about those things.

And—

Just where the hell were the others hiding?

11 The Stormriders

Fifteen thousand subsectors, and any amount of planet killers.

We had four main segments of patrol space in the system, divided into a total of a hundred patrol and defense sectors; inside that, each sector was divided into a hundred fifty defense and attack subsectors, into which ships could be sent on a random basis. It made defense a terror for any attackers.

For us, the fifteen thousand subsectors made search pure hell.

It didn't take long to explain what was going on, and to get that information to Control. But it meant we had to abandon the battle with the decoy fleet and go look for planet killers, scouting subsectors one by one, looking for the faint emission trail of the bomb ships. It was the only way to find them; they were well-hidden, generally well away from the decoy fleet.

When the ships were found—hidden in maybe five percent of the subsectors—they had to be destroyed; against the decoys, our fighters had next to no trouble. But against the escorts to the bombs they were almost evenly matched. Ships had to be pulled away from other places to tie up the fighters as soon as a bomb was discovered, to allow enough time for another ship to destroy the bomb.

What had been an orderly mopping-up action swiftly became chaos; maybe eight hundred of those mothers, and six or seven thousand of our ships. We were tied up with the search and destroy.

We could have lost the fight, with our chances of survival then set at mediocre to nonexistent.

I had to fight to stop my body from panicking; the mind was

cold as ice, intent on the war. But the body knew the odds and tried to betray me.

We couldn't help out with bombing the bombs; Chamquee had used all her drones on the first bombship. But we stuck around for the fighting; we had to help tie up the fighters until Control recalled us. And that wouldn't happen until we ran out of everything but energy weapons that couldn't help enough.

The defense fleet had knocked out a couple of dozen bombships by the time that happened; our casualties had risen to fifteen percent, and probably wouldn't stop climbing for a good while yet.

My implant chattered at me, and my hands flew over my board, absently firing on a fighter, and we leapt through folded space, coming out over a moon of the system's eighth planet, coasting into the landing rack behind another ship as we started cutting systems and geting ready to debark. The ship would be checked, resupplied with weaponry, and sent back out with a new crew before it had even had time to cool off.

The rack moved forward as I read off status from the string of reads in my headset and along my board; seconds later, the ship was lifted again and slotted into a float field on the maintenance deck; the crews were swarming over the outside as soon as we were in place, machinery zipping around and settling into the required positions, sprouting tools and sensors.

Chamzeen and I stripped our control rigs off, stood, and stretched, easing strain and tiredness, exercising as we'd been trained; sitting and flying a ship for hours gets to you.

We went for the shifter, grouped inside, and waited; Control shifted us. There would be a new crew inside the ship immediately after we left.

I got a surprise when I materialized.

Shreekor was floating just a few feet away from my group, curled up comfortably, watching me.

He said, *=*Why don't they warn me? It's not enough to thrash me regularly? No. They have to send you.*

I grinned. "If you don't want me, I can always abandon you, Shreekor."

His eyes rolled to look up.

*=*Fates forbid! I am happy to see you. It seems we are to be sent on a mission—you recall that there was mention of an Enemy base?*

"Yeah," I said.

*=*You've been selected to attack it.*

"Jesus Christ."

*=*Commander Tomari. We are Builders.*

Three of them, cloaks with no figure visible, just black space under the hood; the effect chilled me. But I doubted what I was seeing; probably only images—Chamquee had trained me well.

*=*Please remain silent.*

Both of my crews—the original one, and the new one—had been combined, with additions.

*=*You have been given means and an objective. You will make your own plans.*

There was only one voice, but it belonged to the three of them; ideas wandered: family unit, or communal mind?

*=*This T'sooli attack is the most vicious ever recorded. The central source of these attacks* must *be located and destroyed swiftly, before the T'sooli destroy all that we have struggled to build and maintain within your universe. The T'sooli are murderers without justification, and must be treated as such.*

*=*Our aim has always been the peaceful development and observation of your universe. We have attempted to defend, poorly, our failing. We have tarried too long. We can no longer rely upon blind fortune and the efforts of our few Enforcers.*

*=*Previously, the encounters with the T'sooli have been skirmishes. Those skirmishes have escalated into a war. The prize: your universe, and possibly its life.*

I didn't like the sound of it; they seemed to making out that the whole mess was bigger than it had seemed—"*your universe*"? It made them sound like gods.

And maybe they were.

*=*A T'sooli base has been located. Your mission is to raid this base and retrieve information. You will need to know the locations of other T'sooli bases to end the War. You must strike at the center.*

*=*Search and destroy remains your objective. You have the neccessary forces to complete your present assignment. When they are needed, other forces will be made available.*

*=*We wish you much fortune, Commander.*

*=*Do not place your trust in it.*

And then—

They vanished.

Shreekor said, *=*Welcome back, hero.*

Annoyed, I said, "Shut up."

*=*Times don't change you much, do they?*

I grinned at him. "Sorry, Shreekor. I'm just feeling pretty weird. I've got a feeling that there's something the Builders are avoiding telling us."

I didn't know how right I was.

Chammekk, Priestess of the Temple Of The Seasons, yellow-haired, with delicate features, almost pixie-like to the point of cuteness; a larger leprechaun, *begorrah!*

Shreekor's telepathic voice said, *=*You're certainly picking up the ladies.*

I looked up from my musings on the crew list. "*Hmm?*"

He repeated what he'd said.

"Yeah."

The green lady with the ears and a lot of exposed skin was Swa; both ears and antennae. She could see in a good light, but in near-darkness, she was almost completely blind. The antennae gave her a radar sense.

*=*Do you think the princess and Nikoi L'aan have forgiven you?*

"Huh? How the hell should I know? What did I do?"

*=*Look.*

One of Shreekor's tentacles flicked around to point at the princess and Nikoi, who were sat well apart from each other, staring at me. As I looked at them, the princess turned away and Nikoi made a point of studiously inspecting a screen. I hadn't noticed the tension in the lounge before, but I became suddenly aware of it.

"What the hell are they mad at me for?"

*=*I've no idea. Do you want me to pry?*

He made it sound as if it were a disgusting idea; no doubt it was, to him.

I said, "Don't bother. I'll find out later."

Another Beachballius, whose name I couldn't pronounce; I designated the Beachballii as A and B for easy reference. They looked different: the smaller one was A, with a gray pelt, and the other was larger, with an almost black pelt.

Shreekor interrupted again with:

*=*All females should be like Shimo-sh'sasai females. Brainless.*

"Hell, octopus, they're still people. Good fun sometimes."

*=*Hmph.*

"Go discuss tentacle care with Shtolaquer or something." I looked up at him. He was looking remarkably fedup, for an octopus-type. "I'm trying to sort out who's who."

*=*Shtolaquer has no sense of humor.*

Shtolaquer wouldn't; he was logic from end to end, and an exceptionally powerful telepath to boot. He was also about five times as large as Shreekor and could cut him up something awful with a couple of words.

I said, "Then go bother the Jeweler."

*=*He's busy.*

"Doing what?"

*=*Constructing a computer tap.*

"Moo helping him?"

Moo was another Soru; built just as big as Bia, but with almost as much IQ as the Jeweler. The two seemed to get along well enough; the Jeweler needed an outlet for his brains, and Moo suited fine.

*=*Yes.*

Chamzeen and Chamquee were flying the ship, so that left them out; Chammekk was acting as navigator for the moment. Swa would be busy playing war games with the tactical computers.

I said, "Well, go talk to M'Goy then."

*=*He doesn't like me. He thinks I'm nasty.*

"He's right."

M'Goy 17654—I left the number out because I hadn't seen any sign of the other 17,653 M'Goys—looked like an oversized eyeball balanced on a popsicle stick; he looked permanantly sad and surprised at he same time, and did a good job of seeming effeminate without even being human.

Well, that settled my crew out, anyway, if I could keep them in order in my mind.

I looked over at Nikoi and the princess again; they were both ignoring me still, and they'd both been a touch sullen about taking orders from me. I didn't like it; it could screw up the entire mission if it kept up.

I said, "Shreekor, never mind. I want to talk to you anyway."

*=*What about?*

He sounded surprised.

I looked at him. "Females," I said.

*=*My favorite subject next to food.*

"Lucky you. I'm not exchanging notes, I'm looking to hash out a problem."

*=*Don't tell me—your sex drive is beginning to overpower your reasoning powers? Which one is it?*

I got up and shook my head. "Man, have you got the wrong end of the subject."

*=*That simply shows my knowledge of your species—how should I know how you mate?*

"Oh, shut up."

*=*Here we go again.*

I started for the doorway. "Just quit trying to be funny—" I went through, and turned around to see Shreekor floating towards me, one pair of eyes on the women as he moved, "and come on somewhere else. I really do need to talk this out."

*=*Oh no. You're queer for me.*

In exasperation, I raised my eyes to look at the ceiling. "In a minute, Shreekor, I'm going to tie you up and let the Beachballii play ball with you. I'm serious. Those two ugly-minded bitches in there are gonna kill us all if we don't do something about them."

*=*Why didn't you say? I thought you were sexually involved—if you aren't interested, then simply eject them from an airlock—*

I growled and started for him, ready to do some damage.

There was a flutter of apology.

*=*I am trying to relieve the tension—you are correct, and it is very serious. And I was not quite joking. We may have to resort to such harsh tactics.*

I nodded. "Yeah. So don't get funny. I want to solve this without killing anybody."

*=*But if you have to?*

I shrugged. I didn't want to think about it.

*=*Let's discuss it.*

He floated past me, and towards my quarters, and I trailed after him. Doing my best to avoid a serious question.

*=*Hsst!*

"Cut the gags, octopus."

*=*Well, what's wrong with humor? Lounge three, all alone.*

I looked up from the screen I was using; it had a cross-section of the Enemy base on it—the thing had been scouted out pretty well.

"Which one?"

*=*The girl with the x-ray eyes, who else?*

Trust Shreekor to drag that one out; that was what I'd called Nikoi some time before. Once.

I said, "Lounge three, huh? Where are you?"

*=*Next to an override board. Interesting what can be done with locks. Hint hint.*

I grinned. "Isn't it, though."

I switched the screen off and pushed my notes aside, standing up.

*=*Do you require any instruments of torture?*

"No, I don't think so."

I went to the door, keyed it open, and went through, turning for the lounge.

I stopped outside the lounge door, and just before I opened it, said, "Do your stuff and then don't peek—this might get too nasty for your delicate sensibilities."

*=*Me, delicate?*

"You will be if I kick you around some."

Keyed the door open, stepped through, keyed it shut again with my back against it, scanning the lounge. Nikoi was sat in a corner, working over a screen, making notes; from where I was standing, it looked like she was getting Swa's habit—playing war games with a simulation model of our present dreadnought and a target simulation of the base.

I said, "Nikoi L'aan."

She didn't look up. "Yes, Commander?"

I leaned back against the door, folded my arms and slouched. "That's no way to speak to the feller who helped you out when you got yourself marooned."

She didn't answer me; the simulation model on the screen suddenly burst into attack, firing.

I said, "If you want it that way, Nikky, you can have it that way. But one wrong step, and I'm going to have you dumped through a lock."

She looked up and around at me, eyes flashing. "You would do that?"

How the hell do I know?

"Yep. It's in the name of the mission—I'm responsible for this crew, and if I have to dump you to save the rest of the crew, then I will."

*=*Such tough talk.*

Oh, shut up.

He did.

I crossed the lounge and gave her seat a heavy enough whack to spin it around, and leaned forward over her.

"I want," I said, "to know what you're acting so self-righteous and upset about. I *don't* want to have to dump you. So you'd better tell me. If it's anything important, we can settle it right here without any fuss."

Her skin darkened by a couple of shades of gold, and she said, "You have the morals of a—" and paused to think of something bad enough. "A gutharl."

Which ate, slept, rutted and rolled in mud when available, and had no concern with morals; it was a native beastie of Soru, something like a hairy rhino with the cute face of a Pekingese puppy.

I said, "So? Why?"

"You are worse even than that."

Obviously she wasn't impressed with the conduct of gutharls.

"Nikky, maybe I don't have any damn moral sense, but if so, I'd like to know why you think of me that way." I paused. "Okay?"

She didn't say anything; might as well take a long shot. All this had started immediately after the session with—

"The priestesses? Is that what's got you so snarled up?"

She didn't say anything to that, but her chin lifted; her skin darkened another shade, and her eyes spat stationary sparks. Dyn-o-mite, smack on target.

*=*Get out of that one.*

Piss off, Shreekor.

I said, "Nikky—"

"No shame," she growled.

"Okay, so that's your opinion of me." I paused, but she didn't growl anything else; she was settling for glaring at me. "Dammit, Nikky, they have customs and rituals. Now, I'm sorry that those rituals offend your convoluted sense of morals. But I've lived my entire life in contact with all kinds of aliens, and I take rituals as they come, because that's what I've been trained to do.

"Yours," I added, "come from being inside one big tin can. I understand that. You don't exactly have room for a population explosion. But get this: the priestesses' rituals have nothing to do with sex. So there's nothing shameful or shameless about it."

"Kal dathara!" she snapped, and pulled an ugly face; I got the sense. A pretty deadly *Sasha-Ra* insult.

I grinned. "You've got to insult me in a language I understand, Nikky. And you're also going to have to take orders. So damn well stop acting like a colonialist with an ulcer!"

That last line came out in a deadly monotone.

Whack!

I reeled from her slap, the side of my face stinging; I hadn't expected her to get violent.

I took a step back and shook my head, then leaned forward again. "You are a brainless idiot, Nikoi, and that surprises me. I expected you to see some sense." We glared at each other for a moment. "If it means anything to you, I don't happen to enjoy having to put up with being kissed by every goddamned priestess who happens to wander in my direction."

She held another belt, surprised. "What?"

"You heard. I don't enjoy it." I took her hand and pushed it down. "I happen to find it very uncomfortable because they have normal body temperatures 'way higher than mine."

"You—"

I shook my head and sighed. "I put up with it because I've been trained that way." Nikky's eyes started losing some of their glow. "To put it plainly, neither I nor they are being wanton. I'm a nice—"

"They are shameless!" she spat. She wasn't sure; she didn't handle it very convincingly. But she was trying to make a field day of it.

I said, "Nikky, that's only by your standards. You've got to do better—you aren't among *Sasha-Ra* any longer. The standards are totally different." I spun the idea around a bit more, while she chewed her lip. "Look, you've been the commander of a starship. You've been trained on Soru. You ought to have some idea of cultural differences. You may not like it, Nikky, but you're going to have to put up with it."

She sniffed. "It is disgusting."

Crisis over. Thank God for small mercies. She really wasn't

sure now; I'd shaken her up enough—and Shreekor had been right; he'd suggested my hammering the point home repeatedly.

I grinned and shook my head. "To you, sure it is. But think on this before you judge Chamzeen: she happened to be operating as that freighter's director of religion when we pulled their fat out of the fire. Also, before I was put into this thing, she acted as my co-pilot." I paused for effect. "I've never seen Chamzeen turn away from trying to help any sentient, even those with strange values."

"A . . . Child-seeker?" Nikoi seemed startled.

"If that refers to someone who handles *Sasha-Ra* religion, yep, that's what she is, more or less. Also psychologist, hand-holder, friend, nurse and general conspirator in sorting out relationships."

"But . . . but I thought that they were wantons. Sluts to . . . to . . ." She trailed off, confused.

"You learn something every day," I said, and leaned back again. "Now, you going to behave yourself and stop acting like a jealous female?"

Her eyes blazed up again. "I am *not* jealous!"

I laughed, and patted her shoulder. "Okay, you aren't jealous. Don't worry about it. I'm just trying to keep this ship running smoothly."

She nodded, looked at the floor, then back up at me. "How do you think of me after this?"

I shrugged. "No worse than any other time. I still like you."

I stepped away as she stood up, to allow her to get past me; I'd been blocking her path.

She said, "I am glad." She glanced at the screen she'd been playing with; I looked too. "Oh, no."

The computer had kept up the program after she'd left it to itself; the simulated ship had been blown apart.

Nikoi looked at me. "That is all your fault!"

I held up my hands, palm out. "Sorry, but I had to sort you out."

She glared at me for a moment.

Then broke out into a grin.

"I," she said, "should push *you* out of an airlock."

**=Or you could both go together.*

Oh, shut up, smartass.

"...full phase attack," Swa was saying, using a pointer to indicate a point on the base. "Ramming will provide sufficient disorientation on the part of the T'sooli defenders and preclude possibilities of an immediate counterattack."

I scanned the screen; she was right. It was her job, after all, to kick around strategy and pick the best possible attack plan.

I said, "Okay. What about boarding? Moo says the tap will have to be placed on a computer line of some kind to operate."

Swa didn't pause. "The entire force should attack, with only very minor backups. There is no need for a full plan of attack, as we will only need to keep the T'sooli off-balance enough for the tap to be placed. Once the work has been done, we will withdraw. The base can be dealt with by the ship."

"Uh-huh, fine. Work on that and let me know—"

*=*Corridor seven.*

I looked up from the screen. "Excuse me, Swa. Work on that basis, and when you've come up with a complete attack plan, give me a buzz."

I turned and crossed to the door. Swa, watching me, the pointer in her hand tapping her spare hand, said, "What is it?"

The door slid open. "Interpersonal relationships among members of the crew. I just got a call."

She seemed puzzled, but didn't say anything. I ducked out into the corridor and started walking as the door slid to.

I said, "Corridor seven? The princess?"

*=*Correct. I believe you have confused Nikoi L'aan sufficiently, so I suppose you will apply the same methodology here.*

"Wait and see." I went through another door, and into a connecting corridor; I wasn't far from corridor seven anyway.

A minute later I was there. The princess was walking away from me, intent on a portable computer stage; she didn't notice me stalking up behind her. As I came alongside her, I slipped one of my arms through hers and locked her hand, making sure she couldn't pull away from me.

"How does it go?" I asked, conversationally.

She glared ahead, and hissed, "Release me, you motherless, fatherless, fit-to-be-*kreya*-droppings!"

I raised an eyebrow and grinned; I've been called some names in my time, but never that, and never in *that* tone of voice. She'd used an Aureon insult; one long, syncopated word.

Shreekor, sounding amused, said, *=*Pleasantries between good friends?*

A hiss from the princess told me he'd directed it at her as well.

I said, "I suggest you stop eavesdropping while I'm trying to charm a beautiful lady." Another hiss from the princess, as I stopped next to a door. "Otherwise, you ugly son-of-a-whatever passes for a bitch on your planet, I'll dig you out and tie all your tentacles together and hang you from the nearest ceiling fixture."

*=*Hmph. Spoilfun.*

The princess kicked me on the ankle, grimly intent. Fortunately for me, she was barefoot, so it didn't hurt too much. In answer, I trod on her toes; she didn't yelp, but her sharp inrush of breath was enough to let me know I'd made my mark,

Simply, I said, "Don't."

I hit the door switch and pushed her inside as it opened; it was a library room. I followed her in, hit the switch on the inside, and took the computer stage out of her hand.

Shreekor said, *=*If she beats you up now, you can't get out. Your sense of humor stinks.*

*=*Thank you.*

Oh hell, go away and don't bother me.

His presence vanished from around my mind. At least I didn't have to vocalise to speak to him anymore; Warbase Prime's equivalent of Telepathy I had disciplined my mind beautifully in that direction, even if it didn't help me become a full telepath.

I swung the princess around and dumped her, indelicately, into a seat; it rocked as she hit, and settled into place. She glared at me, then started getting up.

I gauged distance and force as her hand came up in a claw shape, going for my eyes, twisted, and kicked out, leisurely; my foot caught her in the midsection, folded her over, and threw her back into the chair, startled but unhurt.

Pleasantly, I told her, "I said, 'don't', and I damn well mean it, so you'd better listen to me." I paused, watching her to see if she made any kind of move at me; the princess was the one likely to cause a lot of trouble, and the top candidate for being dumped into vacuum if I didn't straighten her out. So I was going to have to think on her terms.

I went on. "Start acting like royalty, and I'll do my best to treat you that way. Act like a bad-tempered whore with a headache, and I'll treat you *that* way. Okay?'' She pulled a face, but stayed silent. And, more importantly, seated. She'd been trained by the same people who had trained me, and she was just as deadly. ''That's better.''

She looked away from me, pointedly. ''Black bastard.''

''So you had a bad day.'' I grinned again, but didn't feel it. ''So what's upsetting you? I want to know because I can't get along with a team member who scowls at everything I say, and who spends a lot of time trying to avoid me.'' I paused to let her take that in, and then went on. ''It has a tendency to get team members killed, and, as your commander, it's my job to prevent that as much as possible.''

And the hell with alien relations; it might be me who's doing the dying. The last thing I wanted was to get slaughtered due to a minor problem that could be solved. Nor did I want to have to sacrifice anybody; I didn't like the job I had because it meant I might have to do just that.

But I wanted to face the problem only if I had to. Murder isn't my style—it leaves bloody handprints all over the conscience.

The princess snapped, ''You annoy me!''

I frowned at her. ''I sort of had that idea. In what way?''

''You are fit for the gallows only!'' She sniffed and then spat at me.

Okay. Enough. No more pleasant Kevven.

I bent down, smiling, drew my hand back, and landed my palm upside her cheek with a loud crack, jerking her head around; the blow left a dark imprint on her face.

She looked back at me for a moment, shocked that I'd dared to hit her, then fury took hold; she struck at me. I caught her wrist easily and applied pressure on nerve points. She yelped this time, then went for my arm with her teeth, training beginning to assert itself. But not quite enough. She should have kicked.

I grabbed her waist-length hair, rapidly twisted a mass of it around my left hand and wrist, and pulled back, sharply; her head went back, her mouth half open, as I moved around for defense. She couldn't strike at me now without leaving herself wide open for retaliation.

I said, ''Behave yourself,'' and accented it with a twist on her hair; she struggled briefly, then stopped, watching me uncomfortably. ''Thank you. Now listen: if you don't stay put and listen to what

I'm going to say—and I don't mind objective, or even subjective, interruptions, just so long as you use your mouth and nothing else—I'm going to belt your backside so damned hard you'll be working on your stomach for the next month and wearing the scars for the rest of your life." It didn't come out as the sustained growl I wanted it to be; on the other hand, it was enough of a menacing monotone to make an impact.

For some reason, she started grinning; then she stifled it and scowled like a goddess with heartburn. "I hate you."

"The hell you do. All you've got is a mild sense of miff." I let go of her, and moved back, watchful; if she tried anything, I could counter it easily enough. Seated, she was vulnerable enough. "Now, you'd better tell me what's upsetting you before I get impatient."

She was silent for a few moments, probably puzzling that one out; she'd been expecting a talking-to. Then she said, "You first consort with me, then ignore me to chase common sluts."

I raised my eyes, stared at the blank ceiling. I was having trouble believing this. Royal jealousy? I said, "I don't recall seeing any of those types around here."

"Then you are both blind and stupid." She sniffed again, and her chin lifted as she gave me the royal evil eye. "What of the *creature*—" implying something spectacularly disgusting—"with the red and white hair? She first invades our craft, attempts to kill you, almost kills us all later, and yet you treat her as something special."

"I kind of think of people that way," I said.

She sneered at me. "She is common dirt."

I fought my temper to a standstill; Shreekor, typically, wasn't any help. Instead of helping to lighten the tension, he was totally silent. For once, he'd taken me to heart and kept out of it. Just when I needed him to be funny.

I said, "I don't think so. It's just that you're a spoiled brat. What else?"

She looked at me contemptuously; the Aureons sure as hell breed a fine line of sneering royalty. "Black pig."

"Pig or not—and you can switch to English all you like, it doesn't impress me—I still want to know what else."

Her voice dripped acid as she said, "Those pointy-eared red sluts with the silver hair are as bad as you and that other bitch."

Uh-huh, she hadn't met too many priestesses; nobody seemed

to like them—Shreekor, naturally, was indifferent. All they meant to him was a chance for some offbeat humor.

I said, "You're too snide, Meheilahn." She started; she wasn't used to being addressed with anything but assorted titles and polite forms. Well, she was going to have to get used to it, providing she wasn't dumped first.

I bent over towards her, teeth gritted. "I'll tell you this: you're going to have to start thinking about what you've been taught. First, you were brought up as a pampered little female in a royal society that is, to say the least, backward, in comparison to any of a dozen societies I can name, including the Lachallan one. Secondly, you decided that you wanted to get your pretty tail out of your tinsel and gilt palace and see some of the universe when somebody turned up to ask. As that doesn't make you special *at all,* and you got more than you bargained for in the first place, I suggest you down and make the best of it and damn well *listen* and *obey.* If you don't, I'm going to have you spaced. I don't need fights on board this boat, and I want to get the job over and done with as fast as possible, and with as few casualties as possible. And if it will help me achieve that objective, I'll stuff you out of the nearest airlock, *personally,* without a second thought. Got that?"

That was it: right out in the open, and sounding like I meant it. And I did; if I had to do it, I had to do it, and I'd also have to suffer the troubled conscience afterwards.

The princess didn't say anything; she just stared at me.

I nodded, sharply. "Okay, now you understand me. So you'd better start acting less like a princess and more like a normal person of no consequence, because that's what you are just at this moment, and all you'll achieve by getting haughty at anyone, whether it happens to be me, or Nikoi L'aan, or the Priestesses is the destruction of this mission, or your own death. And, if you'll try and get to know them, rather than just trying to be as bitchy as possible, you'll find that they're no worse than you are. Okay?"

I waited; after letting the diatribe sink in, she nodded, curtly, then stood up. I automatically went onto the defensive, just in case, but she didn't try anything—she was acting very wary.

She said, "Very well—" her hands a little nervous—"if it will help me to return to where I belong, I will do as you say."

I looked at her. surprised. "You're homesick?"

"And should I not be?" she exploded. "This is so far beyond those things I have been used to—I wish to return to simple things!"

I clapped a hand to my forehand. Culture shock. She'd been off-balance from the start, of course. And she hadn't been helped any along the way with one culture and another blazing to the fore. Probably nobody had thought about it until now; we were all used to the diversity of sentients and the extravagance as far as material things went. Before she'd run into us she'd never seen an alien, and all she knew about spacecraft was that they came out the sky with loud noises and did terrible things to her planet. Culture shock, for sure, and a pretty bad dose of it—and damn the Soru Warbase trainers for not catching it.

I shook my head and patted her shoulder. "Yeah, we'll get you back as soon as this is over, Princess. Until then, you're going to have to get used to it—and if you put your mind to it, you'll do all right."

She seemed puzzled by my sudden affability. Shreekor had it right: confuse 'em and keep 'em confused, and that's the problem over. Except I manged to do it by accident; and thinking of that, where was Shreekor?

The princess said, "I was told . . . there is no trust."

"Yeah, I was told that, too." I paused, found myself feeling a slightly rueful expression. "I'd say it was bullshit, Princess. We're going to have to trust each other quite a bit for a good while yet."

She nodded, slowly. "Very well. My life . . . is in your hands." So she believed my threat; good enough. The last thing I wanted was to go through with it, but I wasn't going to let her know that.

I said, "All our lives are in each other's hands. That's why I'm doing this." I put my arms around her and hugged her. "So don't worry too much about it. Just behave yourself and I'll forgive you, if it means anything." And, I thought, fingers crossed that I didn't screw up being spaceboss to this bunch of nuts.

She seemed to regain some of her royal pride, showing it in her stance. But she wasn't looking down on me; more as if she was looking across at me. Equals, at least, and she wasn't too proud to admit that—Soru had done something for her. She was also relaxed enough for the impression of one big feline—with claws—to return. It kept me wary.

She said, "Despite all the angry words, you are gentle enough."

"Yeah," I said, "I know. I learned to be nice to the ladies when I ought to be while I was growing up."

She smiled. "You had a good tutor?"

I nodded. "You might say that. A lot of 'em. Learning on the job, when I think about it." I paused. "Never stopped amazing me how some of those women could beat the hell out of me one minute and go all mushy the next. I never thought much about it, 'cause when *they* went mushy, *I* got all mushy too."

She laughed. "Then . . . there is nothing between you and those others?"

I raised both eyebrows, mystified. "Huh? No, there isn't. Why?"

"Oh . . . nothing. Just a thought to clarify." I wasn't sure I got the meaning right, but I didn't question it and her next line changed the tack rapidly. "As I am no longer a princess—" surprising me—"at least out here, I would suggest that you find some other title or name for me."

I shrugged, difficult while holding her. "Your name's fine."

Her smile twinkled in and out, and her eyes showed more experience than her age would have let me guess. "Very well, but be sure that you pronounce it correctly, and never use anything but that—I would not wish to be referred to by my father's name or my birth-area." She paused. "You do understand?"

"I get the sense, but not the name," I said.

She pursed her lips. "Well, how would you feel if I called you Tomari?"

"About the same as if Area Fourteen or any of my friends called me Tomari." I watched her for a moment. "But don't worry about it. It's Meheilahn, and that's that."

She smiled again. "And do not succumb to temptation. Or else."

"Temp—" But I didn't get any further, because she kissed me; so much for that sideline, and so long problems. I wasn't objecting.

Shreekor finally returned with, *=*I knew you had charm somewhere. Typical. Seducing every female in sight.*

That's it, octopus, which way you want your knots tying?

*=*I like my knots not at all.*

Just go away and leave me in peace. huh?

*=*Don't make too much noise—someone might become suspicious. You* are *supposed to use a library for reading, after all.*

Shtolaquer, handling special communications, said *=*Special report received recently from Warbase Prime. Reading that you are thanked for your response to the planetary weapons, the last of which has been located and destroyed. It has been noted that a number of these weapons were also decoys. Twenty-five percent of the weapons were anti-matter constructions.*

I whistled, softly; that was a beautiful panic move. That meant they wouldn't be giving up in the near future. And even Shtolaquer's totally emotionless telepathic monotone didn't remove the impact of the report. If we'd moved just a little later, bye-bye Soru.

Shreekor took it up with *=*The Builders also mentioned that a number of our ships were destroyed by negative matter; fighter screens cannot reflect the material, and many segments were flying around at the time. A situation admittedly much like the Terran sexual sense—once in flight—*

"It isn't a sense," I said, deadpan, "nor does it fly. Also, it's none of your business whether as per speculation or as per fact. On with the report."

Shreekor, typically, was floating just in front of my work table, folded up like a frightened octopus, his eyes—which provided a lot of expression if I watched for it—on me.

*=*I thought we were friends.*

"We are, but I like to think of some things myself—and this is supposed to be a mission, so before I demote you to lavatory cleaning or something, get on with it."

*=*Hmph. Very well. They also note that due to the necessity of locating and destroying the planetary bombs, a number of Enemy ships were able to come through the main defense. To wit, some two hundred seventeen fighters, eleven light destroyers, seventeen heavy destroyers, and seventy-nine troop carriers*

took on Soru. Warbase notes minor surface damage, no surviving Enemy craft.

I nodded and laid down my computer stylus, automatically keying the computer out of the table circuit. "So we beat 'em good and proper this time."

Shtolaquer's icy telepathic voice: *=*Once, and once only. Warbase notes that our mission is now scaled as priority most high. If another attack is launched at Warbase Prime, it may well be the last—if it comes before Warbase Prime's fighting strength is built up again. If that occurs—*

"We're through," I finished. It was straight data. It had taken a lot of time to build up something like Warbase Prime; if Prime was knocked out, the secondary bases would simply tumble like dynamited smokestacks. There wasn't enough capability within the secondaries for them to regroup around a new point.

Shreekor, wryly, said, *=*How does it feel to be the last hope for the universe?*

I picked up the stylus, looked at it, let it drop back again. It clattered on the worktop, bounced, and stopped. I looked up at Shreekor's floating form, slowly shaking my head.

I said, "M' man, it feels goddamned magnanimous."

12 Sortie Factor

We went into jump still accelerating, our velocity shading close to thirty percent of the speed of light, We were traveling fast enough to feel a few relativisitic effects. Our attack program, supervised by Swa, was under computer control.

We flashed out of jump approximately a second distant from the Enemy base, switching immediately into deceleration mode. I watched, my mouth dry, as my linkscreens ticked off attack steps. Decelerating as hard as possible, we looped around the base and started back. Drones vomited from the ship's launchers, went for their ships. We looped around again, still shedding speed, firing nonstop into the base's screens. Fire erupted around the base, electronic and brilliant, as the screens tried to dissipate the energy from the barrage.

The ship oriented itself and rammed into the screens. There was a silver and gold electronic explosion, a grinding shudder as the ship tore through, and a fortunately unfelt crash as the ship, its occupants protected by stasis fields, rammed the base. The base's gunners had no time to start firing before we hit.

The ship ripped through one of the base's triple rings, smashed into the one above it, and halted, vibrating, the false ramming nose smashed to a molten pulp.

There was no time to feel good about surviving the attack. The boarding party was already up and moving, assembling at the expansive attack locks with weapons at the ready. Shreekor and Shtolaquer were to stay aboard the ship to lay down a covering barrage. The princess would remain on board as medical co-ordinator, waiting with emergency equipment in one of the ship's locks. It wasn't a move I was particularly happy with, due to the danger it presented to Meheilahn.

The locks snapped open. We poured out into the base, moving as a unit, weapons laying down fire as we moved. Even so, I noted that the only things moving where we emerged were machines. Anything alive had been killed either by the impact of the ship or by decompression from the ram-and-board. Wreckage and bodies lay scatterd around, where they hadn't gone whistling out through the gashes in the base's hide.

The Jeweler skittered along by the wall, fast and effective, using a tiny disruptor of his own design, picking off machines that came at us. Moo followed him, a huge weapon balanced in his great blue hands, green fire crossing the corridor to touch machines, leaving wreckage each time.

I was carrying a compact tubular weapon that was linked to a backpack. I halted before the next bulkhead in line, raised it, and pressed the trigger. It bucked in my hands. With a bright flash, the wall ahead of me collapsed.

One of the Beachballii hurtled through the hole, bouncing and kicking, careening into a small squad of Jet Jumper suits. There was a brief flurry as bronze suits were slammed in all directions, and a blaze of fire as my squad finished the job. The Jumpers didn't take it very well—no sensayuma, that's what I say.

We crossed into the next section of the base. I swung my blastpack, firing, segmenting attackers. At my side, M'Goy was firing a disruptor rifle, picking off machines and minor attackers that I missed. I watched the Jeweler skittering along the wall, Moo following, as he looked for a place to patch our computer tap into the Enemy's cybernetic system. I couldn't take time out to hope to hell or pray to heaven; I had to keep my attention on the firefight. The faster the job was done, the less casualties we would have.

Bia passed me, his legs pumping up and down like big blue pistons. He left the floor in a leap, lit into a mass of Jumpers, crunching them against each other as though they were dolls, using the remains to splinter other Jumpers.

I lined up the blastpack, blew out the next bulkhead. Chamzeen, using a floater and traveling against the ceiling, went through, firing her disruptor rifle non-stop, laying down fire in an arc. The Enemy squads waiting on the other side of the demolished bulkhead, greeted by massed fire and a hand attack, tried to back off. It didn't do them any good; they were cut off.

A Beachballius landed among the Enemy troops, kicking and stomping. I sighted what appeared to be a computer terminal, got my head down, and went for it. M'Goy, seeing where I was headed, followed me, laying down covering fire while I spliced one of the Jeweler's bugs into the line. Finished, I turned, used the cannon to open a path through the battle, and moved again. Chammekk was already dealing with the next bulkhead, and the troops beyond it. I turned the cannon, fired, ripped a broad hole in the ceiling, fired again, saw the glimmer of the bolt against the darkness of space. I activated my flight pack, chased it. Chamzeen and a Beachballius followed me as I headed for the next ring up. The first bolt had dented the base's hide; I fired a second as I flew, saw the metal splinter and flash. Debris and bodies poured out into space. I fired again, for the sake of causing havoc, fired a third time, and a fourth, and a fifth, not caring where I hit.

I let my mind murmur. *Elapsed time: one minute, forty-seven seconds.*

We went in firing. Enemy units seemed almost to froth out of the walls, waves of them, oceans and storms of bronze and blue and red and answering fire as we opened up into them. The blastpack kicked in my hands, weight and reaction. An answering shot slashed a blistering black line across the Beachballius's hairy hide, even as he hurled himself at the marksman. He landed, kicked once, and the Enemy was well and truly broken up by his latest friendship.

We blasted out of the ring, crossed space. As we crossed space, the ship shuddered, then, ponderously, moved backwards, pulling out of the huge hole it had made in the base's skin. The nose would have been blown off by now, permanently jammed in the base.

I saw Meheilahn's silhouette in an open lock, behind the thin safety of a force screen.

The ship opened fire. Pieces of the multiple rings began to disintegrate.

I opened fire on blank metal and we dove.

Suddenly, Shreekor's telepathic voice: *=*We have the information that we need. I suggest that we finish the job as quickly as possible.*

Okay, I thought. *Order the retreat.*

I dove into the opened corridor, waved the cannon around for a few moments, without any particular purpose unless it was a juvenile urge to make a mess of things, and got back out again, fast, as Shreekor relayed the retreat order. Chamzeen and the Beachballius followed me.

We went straight back to our starting point. The team I'd left behind was still at work; holes and tears were appearing with rhythmic regularity. I barged in through the nearest large hole. One shot from the cannon cleared my path. Signals were exchanged, and we started backing up to where we'd started, firing simply to destroy.

I checked the group I'd pulled back together, checked the computer link on my wrist. We were missing the Jeweler, Moo, Bia, Chamquee, and one of the Beachballii.

Shtolaquer's icy voice echoed in my head. *=*A squadron of ships is approaching the base.*

He sounded like something from an old-time radio serial.

From Shreekor: *=*Move it, Kevven. We can't do anything more until you get out.*

"Coming, I'm coming," I said, and signaled my group to move out. "Jesus Christ Almighty."

I went searching, turned a sharp corner, and went through a ragged tear in a bulkhead, and answered the mystery of the Beachballius. He was floating against a bulkhead, black, blistered lines crosshatching his hide. His rotund form was slack and flabby-looking, torn, exuding blood and pulp. He was dead.

I made a quick check, saw the reason immediately. A fighter had gotten in close, through shields and life-support. Before the Beachballius's final kick had splintered it, the fighter had managed to close its claws on the Beachballius's life-support unit, crushing it and ripping it away. Simple explosive decompression.

I left the body, hurtled on, passed through another torn bulkhead; this one had been neatly cut by a cannon similar to mine. A short distance past it, I found three more of the missing. The Jeweler, Bia, and Moo.

Moo was slumped across the floor, among piles of dead Enemy. Across his back there was an ugly black line, the burn from a beamer. It had killed him.

The Jeweler didn't seem to be able to understand it. His eyes were wide, and his mouth moved softly, although no sound came out. He had a hand on Moo's lifeless shoulder. After a moment, he drew the hand away, looked at it.

"I grieve for my brother," Bia said. His voice was stern.

I nodded. "I'm sorry, Bia. War." Glib. Doesn't hurt. *Ha*. The hell.

"It is bad, but necessary," Bia said. He sighed. "Grief and tears. At least he died in honor, and with much courage."

"Yeah." I looked at the Jeweler, and my heart nearly broke at the sight. "It hits some of us harder than others." I looked back, swung and fired as I saw a Jumper shuffling towards us. "Better get back to the ship. We can't do anything more here."

"Very well." Bia turned away, then turned back. "The little one . . .?"

"Hold on for a moment." I hunkered down, facing the Jeweler across the body. "There's no time for grief here. There'll be time for it later, aboard the ship, okay, friend?"

The Aldebaranian nodded, slowly. "He died well." It was the shortest normal statement the Jeweler ever made. "I go." He stood, turned, stopped, turned back, taking a tiny device from a pouch, laying it beside the body. I managed a sad smile, recognizing it. It was a compact light and sound show, designed and made by the Jeweler and Moo, one of their first collaborations. They had made one for each of us.

With an abrupt nod, Bia turned away. I lifted the cannon, fired, took out part of the wall. Bia and the Jeweler stepped out into space, their life-support fields glowing against the dark background.

I found Chamquee a few moments later.

She was slumped against a bulkhead, grimacing, an expression I recognized as agony, clutching her left side just below her breasts. In her left hand, she held her disruptor rifle, ready to fire at approaching Enemy. I crouched by her and checked her. A beamer shot had taken a piece out of her side, about the size of a half-dollar coin. It was repairable, not fatal, but still very bad.

I hailed Meheilahn, blew out the wall, then bent to see what I could do. The beamer had cauterized the wound immediately, but Chamquee's subsequent fall had opened it slightly. There was a trickle of blood, making a gummy mess of the wound and its edges.

As our life-support fields came together, Chamquee whispered something that I didn't catch. I leaned closer.

"Get out of here and leave me," she hissed.

"I can't do that, I won't do that," I said. "Like hell am I gonna throw your life away."

"Do it. You must. You have heard what Shtolaquer has said. Ships will be here soon." She moved slightly, groaning, coughed. She was hurting too bad to glare at me. "You might kill everybody if you don't leave me."

*=*She might be right,* Shreekor said.

Shtolaquer was more definite about it *=*Enemy vessels now one lightyear distant, on approach course preceding final jump.*

"You see?" Chamquee whispered. Her eyes started to close, then snapped open again. "Go! Forget me! Hate me for all I did to you."

I ignored that. "They always used to play this out in the movies on Earth," I said, softly. I stroked her face. She was in a fever, hotter than ever. "Most of them had the same thing happening. The other person gets stubborn. Like me."

*=*The princess is on her way,* Shreekor said. *=*She'll be there in a moment.*

"Okay, great." I let thoughts cross my mind for a moment. "You think we'll cut it close?"

*=*Not really.We might escape.*

"Singe the beard of the King of Spain," I said, grinning.

"You are stupid, obstinate, idiotic, and worthless," Chamquee said. Her eyes closed and she slumped, letting go of the disruptor rifle. She was out cold. That suited me fine.

Meheilahn was with me a moment later, already unhitching her pack as she landed by my side. She blinked once as she saw her patient.

"No foolishness now," I said, as she crouched.

"Be silent and let me work," she said. I grinned, then backed away to give her more room.

She went to work quickly, pulling Chamquee's hand away from the wound, quickly trimming away a large burned and bloody area of Chamquee's combat costume, showing up surrounding damage. She picked out a large medipak, activated it, stretched it efficiently, and clamped it into place over the wound. A telltale flashed on as the pack went to work.

Quickly, Meheilahn fished something else out of her pack, fingers flicking. The new object unfolded itself, inflated, revealing itself to be a blow-up stretcher boat. A unit on the end was an inactive stasis generator.

"Enlarge the opening in the wall," Meheilahn said, as she set up the stretcher. I nodded, turned the cannon on the wall, and fired. The wall collapsed outwards. I helped get Chamquee into the boat, my mind on the problem of watching for attack.

We got the hell out of there. As we crossed open space, with the stretcher boat between us. The ship's weapons made space blaze as we fled, covering us, taking the base to pieces behind us. The after-images were brilliant and shifting, a peculiar flickering tracery before my eyes. I looked back, saw great chunks missing from the base.

We hurtled into the open attack lock, coming to rest as it closed behind us. The lock cycled quickly. We pulled the stretcher through the door as it opened, ran with it all the way to sick bay.

*=*Enemy ships have jumped.*

From Shtolaquer.

*=*The station has been finished.* That from Shreekor, He went on *=*You don't have time to get to your shipboard stations. You had better prepare for acceleration where you are.*

He didn't have to tell us. We were already at work. Chamquee, in the stretcher boat, was safe enough once the boat was clamped in place. The princess was setting up two beds while I activated linkscreens. Some way to fight a war. Sitting in sick bay because you just happened to save a life in time. It was worth it, and I felt like resting.

I watched. The station was finished first, totally disintegrated by massed fire from ship and drones. The Enemy ships arrived a few moments later, by which time the drones were already being redeployed and the ship put through some very complicated evasive maneuvers. While the ship's normal space drive field acted on the ship's components equally, stopping the craft from ripping itself apart every time it changed course fast, said field didn't work on sentient organisms—the electronics involved were somewhat different. Hence stasis fields.

The Enemy ships gave chase. We let them have a fair chase, Chamzeen opening the throttles all the way. A few minutes was all the time we needed to judge their capabilities, just for the record.

When they were moving too fast to evade, intercept, or get the hell out in time, our weaponsmasters started deploying our drones and torpedoes, slotting units into the gaps between Enemy ships. Space lit with the brilliance of a series of novas, flickering and sparking, colorful and deadly, hard radiation and smashing force ripping through the pack. One ship out of twenty-five was left operative; another half-dozen were damaged to various degrees.

We looped back, firing, took the operative one, smashed him to gas, went for the ruined stragglers, firing. Benevolence was a past dream by then. Genocide is a sick, dirty game, but if it was necessary, we could play it as well as the Enemy.

But only if we had to.

And, if I could help it, we would avoid it.

13 Ground Run

We ran headlong into the vacuum-spangled night, moving more swiftly than any arrow ever conceived and built, more deadly, moving with yet more purpose, striking again, striking again, striking again, hitting *zap*, kicking ass and breaking necks, coming on like gangbusters in a hit-and-run hell.

Chamquee recovered quickly, although she was angry at me for a few days, thanks to my "foolhardy" decision to save her life, which had, she kept pointing out, placed the lives of everyone else in danger. The fact that no one had been hurt, or that there hadn't been that great an element of danger until the ships had arrived, didn't impress her in the slightest. Nor did the common knowledge that she would have done exactly what I'd done, with less explanation, had the roles been reversed.

Suddenly, one day, she forgave me, hugging and kissing me with far more passion than usual. The heat I felt wasn't entirely due to her fifty-five degrees Celsius bodyheat. I raised an eyebrow as Chamzeen, in the course of duty, passed us; I grinned as she winked slyly at me.

Fuzz, the other Beachballius, showed no apparent upset over the death of his fellow sentient, which was fair enough. Being non-humanoid, I was at a loss to understand what motivated him. The ability to understand a sentient decreases the further its shape gets away from your own, in the main. It seems to be a kind of mental inverse square law.

The Jeweler took a while to get over Moo's death. He managed to counter his grief eventually by planting himself in the middle of a heap of electronics. I gathered that Chammekk was responsible for that—she was with the Jeweler a good deal of the time.

Chamzeen attended to Bia; she somehow managed to penetrate the stony facade that all Soru raise on the death of a friend.

Shtolaquer was our relay. Our ship computers had a severe case of data indigestion; the tap hadn't just been good, it had been brilliant. Every scrap of data in the Enemy machines had been pulled out. We got to the meat of it immediately; the first thing that Shtolaquer relayed was the seemingly endless list of Enemy bases. We were having to use Shtolaquer's telepathic abilities to prevent Enemy taps; even so, as information was fed directly to Shtolaquer's mind through an interface unit, we were phasing it. Without the angle of phase, any hostile telepathic tap would only get mush. We couldn't guarantee that with hypercom transmission. Shtolaquer was willing to undergo the tremendous strain until we put in at a base.

So we raided again, hit and run, in and out, torch and flit, not even waiting for ships, leaving shards behind, checking, verifying.

Then we lit for home; in this case, the dark beach ball of a field-hidden base that hung like a dark blob among masses of glimmering stars at the center of a galaxy.

I hadn't thought about Earth in days.

The Builders' ship was sitting by the base. Although the gargantuan ship still dwarfed the base, the base itself wasn't exactly tiny; it was more of a small moon, a planetoid. Something like that in orbit around a planet would have tidal effects. We parked our ship next to it, feeling pretty damn insignificant, which couldn't be helped, and transferred to the Base. The ship was promptly swallowed up by the Builders' ship; some while later, approximately a kilometer and a half diameter of disk was booted out. Said disk was matte black, came fitted with all manner of propulsion units, and not only had wall-to-wall carpets, but also wall-to-wall weaponry. Looking it over, I was certain only of one thing: it sure wasn't any damn Kenosha Cadillac.

R&R was a brief, colorful flash; only echoes remained of the events I was involved in. Meheilahn trying to fit my preconception of a female, and still finishing up being Meheilahn. The Jeweler and Chammekk always together. Nikoi L'aan's infatuation with holoart, and the resultant mild disasters as she tried new creations out on people at three in the morning. Swa's dancing and tendency towards solitude. Debriefing by the base Mastercomputer. Talking philosophy with the priestesses until early morning. Shreekor sleeping a lot, and when not sleeping, gassing, and having me help him with further research for his hobbies.

The Builders' ship vanished for a few days; I was told the Builders themselves intended to deal a few minor blows. When it returned, the word was that we didn't have to worry overmuch about the eight hundred plus Enemy bases in this galaxy: the Builders had seen to them. They seemed to consider it a minor campaign.

God help the universe if they ever decide it isn't worth letting it go on.

Eventually, someone decided we'd rested enough. Orders came down the line, and movement started throughout the Base, as fighters were selected, briefed, and shifted toward the ship.

The problem we had was an interesting one. We were to attack an Enemy base built into a planet. Normally, it would be a matter of just moving and mopping up. This time we had to exercise caution.

One of the members of the solar system we were going for was a neutron star. Collapsed from normal stellar size, but not having had mass enough to become a black hole, the thing was a cosmic vacuum cleaner, a roving gravity well. Coming out of a jump near that thing would result in a dandy little phenomenon called field inversion, peculiar to jumpfield units. Two things can happen. One is that everything becomes inverted. This results in a contra-terrene matter effect, which ends in complete conversion of mass to energy. A mother of an explosion—and that's the end of ship, crew, and Kevven Tomari. The second thing that can happen, thanks to the wonders of field inversion, is that everything within the inverted field simply collapses. Ship, crew, and K. Tomari thus achieve atomic collapse, wave to the collapsed atoms of the neutron star on the way past, and shrink into that semi-electromagnetic phenomenon, the black hole. I'm happy as a human bean. If God had intended me to become a singularity, He would presumably have given me pre-collapsed atomic structure.

I had faith in my pilots and planners to avoid field inversion. The secondary problem, that of placing fighters on the surface of the planet, was a little more sticky. Using landing gigs was out; they could be picked off one by one by a halfwit, never mind properly trained gunners. Our only choice was to teleport down.

The neutron star posed problems there. Shifter use requires fine control; landing fighters would have to be handled piece by piece, group by group, and God help those who touched ground first. No problem for a Jetson, of course.

The planning sessions lasted a lot longer than usual, and we solved most of the problems before we left. Not all. Just the easy ones.

The ship we were using was built for a big crew. Most of our fighting strength for the surface consisted of mechanoids and three hundred sentient types that I termed Square Meanies. They were cube-shaped, appeared to be built mainly of muscle, bristled with weaponry, and literally had eyes in the back of their heads, not to mention the sides. They were genetic constructs, designed for effectiveness in battle, cloned, I guessed, by the tonne-load. In addition to those, we had an assortment of Beachballii; Fuzz was still with us, along with his new mate, who, for want of anything better, I termed Fizz, plus the Fruit Twins.

In charge of planning was a tall, reedy alien named Ru. He was blind, possessing four antennae and an effective radar sense. My original planning team was absorbed into his.

Riorge, another Soru, was in charge of the Square Meanies and the mechanoids. His lieutenants were a pair of humanoids similar to the slightly insectoid transport commander whose ship we'd rescued way back when. They were of a mind to do a bit of worthwhile slaughtering.

Plus: a dozen of the walking ottomans; an avian scientist, complete with colorful plumage and computer pad, who quickly found his place with the Jeweler and Chammekk; a waddling cube that squeaked when spoken to, whose name was a code-reference; another half-dozen priestesses (*burn, baby, burn*) of different temples; and, last to board, five cephalopod types, including Mwork, who was the most colorful being I've ever seen, whose fifty tentacles were each of different colors. Said tentacles could perform entrancing and complex dances; Mwork modestly claimed they were simple—you know, anybody could do them, really, if they had fifty or so tentacles. . . . She also had the biggest eyes I've ever seen. A humorous twinkle shone like a nova.

Medical section had boarded earlier, setting up for work immediately. It made me uneasy, seeing exactly how large Medical section was—a dozen extremely limber, long-fingered iens were ready for work at any time. I hoped I wasn't one of e people about to end up requiring their help.

In, survey, out. In, survey, out.

It was tiring, frustrating, boring work. The system had barely een surveyed, so we were having to do a preliminary survey ırselves, being forced to duck the damn neutron star periodical-.

Eventually, however, we had some idea of where to place the ırious groups, for maximum efect; we had to hit the central ea, to immobilize the Enemy and to do the most damage.

We closed in, started putting the teams down, knocking out aceside defenses as we went in. I was in the second group own.

I came back to full awareness in the middle of a pitched battle, flickering tracery of groundfire around me. The scene was pidly punctuated by brief, effective explosions. I consulted the splays afforded by my exoskeleton, sifting through an assortent of tactical ideas, getting ready to move.

A blast rocked the suit, and beams splashed across the forward ields. I adjusted the mirror fields of my suit weaponry and nleashed high-power bursts in return. I think I hit my attacker; e didn't fire back at me.

I made a quick scan of the area, saw a trio of Square Meanies urtling across the plaza I was standing in. They were firing on e run, bathing a squat building in a green-blue aurora. They anished behind the building; a moment later, the entire conruction exploded.

I started forward. Behind me, the ground erupted. I ignored it, ınning, grabbing, priming, and tossing one of the things that e Jeweler had come up with back at the Base. He'd had them ın off in quantity; my exo was festooned with dozens of the ings. The tiny bomb removed half the wall of a building in a oundless—amidst the noise—explosion.

The ground erupted around me, and I ran on, came to a fence, ımped, sailed spread-legged over it, firing all the way, flicking e mirror fields of my beam weapons, picking off targets as my ırget computer indicated. Fighters and Jumpers fell. I pulled oose a grenade, primed it with a click, flipped it ahead of me, nd ducked back.

The ground vibrated and debris rained down around me
Something heavy thudded into the back of the exo. I straightene
out and looked, and got one of the three worst shocks of my life
I saw a head. Nothing terrible in itself. That's war. Blood
and sick. A head is easy to sever.

This head grinned up at me. Smoke trickled from it. The fles
was stripped in places, stained with black in others.

Metal glinted.

I reached out, picked it up, held it. Dazed, I touched th
twisted wires, bent component units, the articulating device tha
had led into the neck. The tactile sensors in the exoskeleton'
fingers registered the rough metal edges.

Years caught me a sledgehammer blow.

Robots.

Why?

Traces flickered across the exo's battle displays. I dropped th
head, whirling, firing, firing, firing as Fighters and Jumper
popped out of whatever they used for woodwork. I grabbed
bangum breakum, primed and threw it in one fast motion
moving on a course that would take me around their flank. I wa
past, still firing, as the orange-red-black flower of the explosion
caught them and threw them.

A building ahead of me. I saw a door, closing.

I charged, pounding concrete like a mad bull, head down and
fists clenched, moving like a rocket on roller skates, firing
continuously at the door. The exo's screens sparkled as I smashed
on through. I hit the floor with what was left of the door, rolling
and firing as I came up, hurtling forward, laying an arc of fire
ahead and around me, leaving a trail of shattered bodies, registering
that what I was seeing was metallic wreckage, robots, nothing
living.

I fled through the building, throwing bombs, two and three a
a time, just wrecking. Sections of the roof plunged down, and
dust, hot and thick, showered around me.

Stairs, going down, and an open well. I vaulted a rail and
dropped straight down. A Jumper, coming up, crunched beneath
the exo, not taking it very well. Shoddy workmanship.

I checked the first level, found nothing, worked my way
further down, shooting, but not bombing. I wanted a way out in
case I had to go fast.

Four levels down, I found machinery. It stretched away from

me, miles of it, enough so that it had its own horizon. There was a deep thrumming in the air, like the beating of an electronic heart.

I went down another level, and another, and another, looking, gauging, recording, thinking, shuddering each time the meaning of this discovery penetrated.

I saw Jumpers, freshly created, complete with Jet Jumping equipment. I touched one, felt it cold and dead—or unactivated?—under the tactile sensors of the exo.

Another area held Fighters, their claws glinting in the diffused light. I jumped up, landed on one, absently crushing it, looked beyond, saw a third type, a fourth, a fifth.

Going on, I found Earth models, touched the skin, found it cold, waxy. I prodded. The exo's finger split skin, crushed something pulpy. Thick red liquid oozed forth. Not a robot, this type. Android. Easier to pass in a living society, easier to use as spies, as infiltrators, as watchdogs, whatever you want.

I went to another type, prodded, ripped. More liquid oozed. More androids.

I stepped back, feeling cold, feeling more than a little sick.

Something swung, slid, dropped. I whirled, saw a grappler coming at me, aware suddenly that someone was now aware of my presence, aware that I was lost in myself. I ducked the first pass, the twisting hooks sliding past me only centimeters away, turned, fired as it came back, slicing through the main beam. The grappler jerked, spasmodic, plunged down, smashed into machinery, ricocheted, crashed through rows of androids, spraying pieces of synthetic flesh and gobs of synthetic blood.

I turned and ran, loping across rows of android bodies, across machines I couldn't assign functions to, priming and throwing bombs, trailing orange and black blooms of thunder as I hurtled. The walls and the ceiling jerked, buckled. Machines collapsed in on themselves. Androids became shapeless, ruined masses. Fire belched at me and was warded off by my screens.

I careered up the stairway, flailing, smashing Enemy attackers down into the open stairwell, looked into the next level up, saw the floor buckling, shivering, threw in a bomb to help it go, and started up again, then on to the next level, and the next, and the next after that, bombing and forcing the factory into total collapse, making it rubble. The stairs shuddered as I moved on up, the collapse following my climb to the surface.

Wreckage stopped me at the exit to the surface. I flipped a couple of bangum breakums back in case anything had a mind to follow me, got a shoulder under the rubble, and heaved. It moved. I kept pushing. There was a helluva lot of junk blocking the way.

My mind went on working while I strained my back via the exo:

One: If this was a robot/android factory, who supervised?

Two: If robots ran the place without organic sentient guidance around, producing robots and androids in berserker fashion, then who/what made the rounds every so often to check that everything *was* working? *Precedent:* the Builders and their long-range "repair" ship.

Three: If there was *no* overseer at all, anywhere, then what the hell were we fighting? Berserker machines programmed to destroy for no purpose?

Four: If we were fighting robots, who and where was the original Enemy?

I kept pushing, pulling, ripping, trying to break out. A Jumper bumped up through the stairwell, and I swung an exoskeleton arm, hand fisted into a club. Metal crunched. The machine dropped. I heaved again.

Five: How had it started in the first place?

Six: Were the Builders hiding something from us, and if so, *what?*

Seven: What was behind the folderol? There was far too much needless cloak and dagger, too many cute coincidences—the appearance of the Builders' ship, for one, and our encountering Enemy everywhere we turned, no matter what we were doing.

I stopped for a moment, staring into darkness. This whole thing seemed to have been coldly deliberated beforehand, as though we were being used, or manipulated. We weren't needed. We were just small, inconsequential beings, caught up in a weird war. Being used like trained dogs. *Go, Mutt, fetch!* With the cloak and dagger to entertain us, maybe.

Angry, and unable to fathom why I was angry, I heaved at the rubble.

I couldn't make sense of it. They could easily fight their own war, handling their own way, instead of making us do it this way, this slow, painful, murderous way. Christ Almighty, what was the *point?* We weren't *learning* anything. We were just dying!

I grunted and heaved. The wreckage finally gave way, exploded out, taking me with it, awkward. I saw open space on the battle displays; there was very little left of the building. I checked visual, saw smoke and dimmed flame and a storm of hot dust.

I came out of cover and crossed the open area at a fast run. I saw an explosion, distant, something in it, went to long-range visual, and saw an exo midway in the air, its shields gone. It seemed almost to float up. It stopped. Fell. Hit, tried to keep going, finished as a twisted heap, suddenly vanished, an emergency pickup.

The exo-rider was Nikoi L'aan. My heart pulsed.

I didn't allow myself the luxury of worry, swinging and looking for something to bull through. I saw Meheilahn's exo dodging Enemy groundfire, barely avoiding explosions. I wanted to tell her to take it easy, but couldn't, wouldn't.

She dodged a floating mine. The mine exploded just behind her, and the shock just caught her, kocking her exo off-balance. I started towards her, the hell with war, was relieved as she got up, flinging bombs at hidden Enemy gunners.

Two Meanies passed me, heading at a fast trot for an emplacement; it was a *kamikaze* run. An explosion beneath one Meanie lifted it into the air, shredding flesh from bone. The shattered form landed limply, didn't vanish. It was dead. The second Meanie vanished into the emplacement and didn't come back out.

A mechanoid skittered across the open air, moving in a randomised evasive pattern, laying a pattern of fire down as it moved. I went after it, in case it turned up something I could take a look at, or hit myself. I didn't see anything. Enemy fire caught the machine, damaged it. It struck the ground, rolled, found an emplacement, dropped into it, and exploded, making metallic shambles of the emplacement and its crew. Another mech cut across the area; I left it alone.

I loped-jumped-ran-scuttled for a few kilometers, and saw Mwork, her great body comfortable on a floater unit. She was skimming easily around groundfire and explosions, her shields shifting to protect her, crunching a bunch of Enemy in her tentacles as though they were no more than a bunch of gray flowers.

I kept moving. I saw the Fruit Twins hopping about among a

group of Enemy, firing and stomping. A series of heavy explosions strung like jewels across the horizon. Bright lines criss-crossed the sky. The ship was at work.

A squad of Enemy made for the rampaging Fruit Twins, I went for them, bounce-bounce-bounce, kicked as I landed, kicked again, flailed with my metal fists, felt and saw them breaking, bits and pieces flying in all directions, such *shoddy* workmanship.

I ran on, slammed into an Enemy mechanoid, went ass-over-teakettle as is shattered, ended up skidding into more Enemy. They tried pinning me down as I flailed, fired into my shields, close range, giving me a brilliant aura. I bucked, fired back, bucked again, hit and kicked, sent pieces flying, got up and whirled like a carousel, spraying Enemy from me. I jumped, priming and dropping a bangum breakum into the middle of what was left of the Enemy squad.

I landed again, looked around, grinned as I saw Meheilahn's exo, and right about then stopped bothering about the battle.

The explosion was directly under my tail, a thudding concussion that rattled every part of me, lifting me into the air as it did so. My shielding and power units, overloaded, packed up. Flailing under 0.5g, me and about eight hundred kilos of exo sailed up for what was probably fifty feet and felt like fifty kilometers and stopped. Hung.

Like a pile of lead bricks, exo and me, frozen, dropped all the way back down again. I heard a lot of cracking and popping noises when I hit, felt and heard the exo buckling, felt what I assumed was me *also* buckling, then got lost in pain, rushing noises, the taste and feel of blood, white light-white noise-white heat, and—

—darkness.

14 Gathering

I managed about a sentence and a half of rapid swearing, all of it highly detailed, before my mind caught up with facts. I was still thinking in terms of something going bang under my ass. Situation No Longer Extant. *Click.* I meshed with local reality again, and, as trained, scanned for clues, finding them, spinning a real-time frame and hanging in it.

Meheilahn sat watching me, grinning. Subtle, like a she-wolf. The couch she was sprawling on had a lot in common with Lachallan furniture, being soft and hugging. It suited her.

Meheilahn finally said, ''Hero.''

''Oh, shut up,'' I said, irritated. I looked for Shreekor, but he wasn't around. Lucky me. I checked myself, found I hadn't lost anything apart from a few treasured scars that I could live without. ''What happened?''

''To you: a mobile mine. Up, down, and *poof!* Vanished. Worrying me terribly, swine. But they put you back together, each piece in the proper place—fortunate, I would say, for myself. It might, though, have been a useless venture to undertake the repairs.'' She grinned again. I winced.

I sat up, got my back straight. There was a trace of perfume in the air, a Lachallan scent. I said, ''I noticed the part about getting blown up. What about the rest?''

Meheilahn unfolded herself from the couch and made herself comfortable on the bed, making me paradoxically comfortable and uncomfortable. I didn't mind Lachallans; they were pussycats for all their teeth. Meheilahn was a pussycat too. One of the big huge types, all jungle grace. I was tempted to play Tarzan, myself, but would probably only finish up falling on my ass. Meheilahn frightened me, and enjoyed frightening me.

She said, "Do you really want to talk of war so soon after being a casualty of it?" She said that with her lips so close to my mouth that I was tempted to malinger for three or four hours, with expert nursing from Meheilahn.

I resisted. Damn me. It was one of the most difficult things I've ever done. I said, "The details, Princess Meheilahn." I croaked most of it.

She made one last shot at pleasure in favor of pain. "You must not. Please. For my—" She kissed me. She was putting a lot of effort into this. I was putting a lot of effort into resisting it, more fool me. I was infused with job worship. When Meheilahn released me, she said, "You must rest, for my sake."

"I've been resting," I said. I smiled. "Work won't wait and all that. I've got to—"

She pouted. "Do nothing! Damn you, you black fool. I am trying to do what is *best* for you. There is a time for fighting and a time for—"

"Making love," I said.

She took that as a cue. "Yes. Now." She started fiddling with some complex clamps. I was impressed. I realized suddenly that she was wearing a Lachallan informal gown and cloak unit. Conspiracy to seduce. That made it much easier.

I said, "There's also a time for updating your commander, Meheilahn." She glared at me and did something distressing with a clamp. "Slink back into your robes and brief me. You can't win now. I've got American sexual neuroses on my side."

She made an offended sound. Her long fingers fiddled again, and the clamps were expertly fastened. "You can get the list of dead and wounded from the computers. The planet was taken. The Builders came and took away the deadly star."

That one stung. They'd said they wanted it for their own purposes. But why collect it later? It would have helped us more if they'd taken the damn thing first. I don't like games.

I said, "The dead and wounded. Anybody I know personally?"

Meheilahn eased herself around on the bed and got comfortable, following every bend, jutting bone and whatnot like a second skin, speaking into my ear, making the side of my face uncomfortably warm and damp. She said, "Bia is dead. He was not so fortunate as you."

Damn. "Yeah, thanks. Don't remind me."

"I had no intention." She kissed my ear. "You see, I know what is best for you. Stubborn male. Even your friends, the—" she made a noise that approximated Beachballius for Beachballius—"know this. Two of them have mated." She grimaced. "Fizz and Fuzz." She didn't like my casual nicknames.

I said, "Good for them." I connected Fizz and Fuzz in my mind, and ended up with medicine balls. "But I won't be tempted *now*."

She kept trying, kissing and touching. "I am evil, Kevven. I am a fool. Be silent."

"Come on, damnit," I said. "This is *my* ship. I'll have you keelhauled unless you stop messing about. Make you walk the plank. Hang you from the yardarm."

She told me. She'd briefed herself before coming to my room, but she intended to brief me her own way. I let her. The information wasn't all that inspiring. Nobody I knew had been killed, other than Bia. Most of the Square Meanies had gone *kamikaze*. Mwork and a couple of priestesses, Chamlah and Chamsara, had been injured, and so on and so forth. A drizzle of very minor details.

I remembered an exoskeleton going up and coming down, vanishing, and said, "Nikoi L'aan?" Wrong question. Meheilahn tensed. I scratched at my afro, puzzled. "What's wrong?"

"Nikoi . . ." She stopped. Her voice sounded hollow, echoic. "Nikky. She lost an arm and an eye."

It was like frogs out of a clear sky. Meheilahn started crying, bawling like a jilted bride. I was suspicious for a few moments, then surprised, and then I was aware that I was out of my depth. The only thing I know to do when a woman turns on the taps is to kiss and cuddle. That seemed wrong for this particular situation, as Meheilahn wasn't exactly clinging to me. I copped out. I reached out and laid my hand on the plate by the side of the bed, calling for a nurse.

The door opened, and a lilac-haired priestess stepped inside. I dug around in memory, found a name: Chamwheer. The door closed behind her.

She took one look, smiled, and almost had me trying to

explain. She seemed to catch on pretty fast, though. In a few motions, she was comforting Meheilahn on the couch. Within a few moments, Meheilahn was fast asleep.

Chamwheer said, "She will sleep for a short time. I understand her grief."

"Empathy?" I said.

Chamwheer inclined her head in agreement. "That, and a tinge of telepathy. The Temple Of Understanding cultivates such qualities. Genetic guidance over a period of time has developed empathic abilities to near perfection."

I raised an eyebrow. "Well, glad to have your help. I was lost, just there."

Making Meheilahn more comfortable, Chamwheer said, "I am honor-bound to do my duty." She smiled. "And I enjoy what I do. Should it not be so? Harmony among diverse beings is a prime function of Lachalla." She came and sat by me. "You know very little of us."

I shrugged. "Hell, that's confusing enough."

She placed hot fingers on my throat, feeling for my pulse. "Ah, but all races are confusing. We are an ordered society, the product of many millennia of organization and ritual and planning. We . . . we are not so far from you, spatially. Your homeworld is in the same galactic arm as ours, did you know?"

I shook my head. "No."

"But within a different sector. If your race achieves starflight, they will eventually find us." She winked. "Our races will commingle well. And will harmonize with other races. But—" She touched my forehead—"you teem with questions and thoughts and I alone would grow old and weary answering everything. Let us have mystery."

"Why?" I said.

She smiled. "It is entertaining, enjoyable. We are playful."

"You're a tease," I said. "You're making fun of me."

"Oh, no. Teasing, yes, mocking, no. There *is* more you have to learn, but *I* am not one to teach you. I apologise." She kissed me, and I thought I recognized her style. When she released me, she giggled and said, "I hear your mind. Yes, I am teasing again. We of this Temple can mimic the outward display of personality too. I do this to you simply to lighten your spirit. We of Lachalla like you."

I smiled. Yeah. So now, not only Meheilahn wants to seduce me, but you too.''

She pursed her lips and managed to look affectionately cute. ''You object to being found desirable? But your world, your specific *country,* has social rules requiring females to be desirable. Why not men also? Must women be the target of male aggression, passive? A male may be wanted by a female, and may be the target for female passion and aggression without psychological damage. Speaking sexually, of course. Should a woman not seek you out, for the sole purpose of sex?''

''Chamwheer—'' I started, but she was ahead of me already.

''Yes, it was I who loaned her clothing. And more—it was I who taught her certain . . . approaches.'' She smiled. ''I experienced what she felt, you see? I, of course, sublimate such feelings as false memory and the like. But—'' She kissed me again. ''But you put duty before love. Be careful; there are times for all things. Humanity should be less war-oriented. Healing is first in importance. Returning to the battle comes after. Be healed.''

''I have a job to do,'' I said. ''I'm fighting a war.''

''But you forget. There is the war of the mind as well as the war within the universe. If you lose the war of the mind, you become animalistic, no better than the Enemy you are fighting.''

''You're moralising.''

''No; simply attempting to practice understanding. Physical violence is simply futile without careful thought.''

''Yeah, so—''

''My physical contact with you is carefully considered. However, it is motivated by emotion. I enjoy it.''

''Yeah. Just remember you're red hot compared to me. I'm broiling.''

''Merely uncomfortable. My nearness is more than half of the problem.''

''Right.''

''Would you be offended to find I desire you?''

''Me, probably not. Meheilahn would probably beat you up.''

Chamwheer chuckled. ''Theft. She is impulsive and violent. A very entertaining companion, not at all bland and boring.''

''Yeah, if you say so.''

She kissed me again, taking her time about it. Presumably

getting an empathic kick out of it. Eventually, she said, "Enough. I sense a specific problem. Nikoi L'aan."

I nodded. "Thanks, at last. It's about time."

"I am tempted to continue teasing . . . but you suffer enough. You will find her in room nine." She gave me instructions for getting there. On my own ship. "I will attend to your princess."

She kissed me again, then unraveled herself from me—I hadn't been aware that she was so tangled up with me—and slid from the bed, elegantly managing to bare a long, dusty red leg. She winked. A real terror.

I made it out the door without being brought down by flying tackles, and scooted down the corridor. I felt like a terminal case, white gown fluttering around me.

Nikki was in bed, the lights down and suitable music playing: wind-bells, what sounded like a couple of thousand of them, chimed, while what seemed to be a gentle wood-flute wove careful patterns on an unfamiliar harmonic scale.

Nikki's left side was half-hidden, from shoulder to hip, by a regenerator unit. The lost arm wouldn't take too much time to regrow; the regenerator not only triggered regrowth, but induced metabolic acceleration, reducing the time taken. She would be up and around in a few days; retraining would take place after that. There was a smaller, thinline unit across her forehead; it came down over her right eye, covering it. The rest of her was in normal shape.

As I walked over to her bed, she said, "Kevven Tomari, our big black commander, visiting his underlings in their deathbeds. I see you finally decided to get up, you lazy bastard." She sounded happy.

I sat on the edge of the bed, on the unregenerated side, grinned at her. "You're lucky. You only lost and arm and an eye, and they're growing back."

"What did you lose?" she said.

"Well, the explosion I set off to take out my bad tooth, they tell me, has taken my brains out my ears." I managed to stay deadpan. "I'm also told I won't miss it."

"True. I never noticed that you had a brain in the first place." She made a rueful face, watching me with her one good, glowing eye. "This is not good at all, making jokes about almost getting killed."

"I'm glad it was only nearly," I said. "How do you feel?"

"Uncomfortable." She pouted. "I am forced to lie here like a potted plant while my missing parts grow back."

"It's a rest from all the hard work us healthy ones have to do," I said. "You've done pretty well up to now, anyway. Bet you didn't think that would happen when you first got into this mess."

She laughed. "I thought I would be shot." There was a nervous vibrato to her voice, and she sounded a little breathy. "I almost *was*."

I grinned. "I had no intention of doing any such thing. Besides, *you* almost shot *me*, so we're even."

"I suppose we are, at that." She wriggled and shifted slightly and settled down again with a breathy curse. "I think it has been good. I was fortunate in my exile. This has been exciting, different."

"It sure as hell has," I said. I looked towards the ceiling. "And it was bad of you not to let the princess know that your injuries are far from permanent. When I left her, she was sobbing as if her sister had been hung, drawn, and quartered before her eyes."

Nikki was unrepentant. "She should know it is not permanent."

"She doesn't." I frowned at her, because I didn't know whether Meheilahn knew or not. Sometimes, knowledge doesn't matter. I wasn't going to admit that just now, though. "She thinks you're a basket case."

"Well," Nikki said, huffily, "I had my mind on other things. I wasn't aware that she cared. She could always have asked a priestess, anyway."

"Okay, okay, don't pitch a bitch at me. Let her know, huh, Streaky?"

"Streaky?"

I reached out and curled a lock of her hair around my fingers. "Your hair, pretty baby."

"Oh. I see." She grinned, wrinkling her nose. "Curly-head."

I stood, chuckling. "God, recognition at last. Have you fighting tigers before long."

"What is a tiger?"

"Nasty kind of pussycat. Like Meheilahn or you in a snit. All teeth, claws, stripes, and tail." I touched her shoulder. "Okay, now for a redundancy. You try and get some rest, huh?"

She made a rude, disdainful sound. "You shall have me in my grave with your comfort, you mushbag."

I shook my head. "That's no way to speak to your commander."

"I shall speak to you how I please, you fake."

"Then you shall," I said. "And I'm about to leave. You're so sick you can't have me hanging around you like this."

She made a distressed face. "I am unloved. I am unwanted. I am unneeded. All because of the loss of two mere pieces of me."

"You're also trying too hard," I said. "If you aren't careful, you'll wind up with scars on your backside as well."

"You are *evil,* picking on weak and wounded females for your terrible amusement." She waited for a moment. "Boo-hoo."

"Stop laughing. It only makes it hurt more." I folded my arms. "I know.'

"So you claim." She snorted.

"I'm not saying anything."

"Then keep quiet, because you lie even as you speak." She waved her remaining hand in the air, her single eye fixed on me. "*Away* with fools. Away, *away!*"

"You're getting like Shreekor. When *he* gets the funnies, he starts waving arms around like that."

"*Ptui*. You'll talk about *any*thing. *Out* of here with your mouth. Go chatter to the Jeweler."

I started for the door. "Well, if you feel that way about all this jive stuff—"

"Kiss me before you leave, wanton pig. I am curious about the custom."

That one stopped me. I managed to about-face smoothly and start back. "If *that's* the way you feel, I'll delay my return to my bed of sickness and return to yours instead."

She managed half a glare at me. "I wish to see whether you cease talking, too."

"Dirty pool, dirty pool," I brayed. "Not cricket and all. I do."

"*Ha!* You are silent only if someone blows you up."

"I'm henpecked! First Meheilahn starts trying to make my love come on down, then Chamwheer starts juggling riddles and jiving me so much I end up with a head like a vibrator—and now you. You'd make a good American wife, you red-headed, sharp-tongued, greenskin banana.'' I didn't give her time to point out her skin was gold, not green; it didn't matter. I kissed her, delicate and gentle. And: ''There, you see. I stopped talking.''

She wrinkled her nose again. ''Not for long. Must I do this all the time, just to preserve peace and quiet?''

I went out the door, yowling quietly like a wounded puppy. It wasn't unpleasant. Just discouraging. Either the universe was crazy, or *I* was.

Guess which.

It was the biggest goddamned fleet of ships I'd ever seen. Judging by reactions observed, it was the biggest fleet *anybody* aboard had seen. I'd thought the Enemy fleet attacking Soru had been big. But this fleet took a combination of both Enemy and Soru fleets and tucked it away into a corner.

Big ships.

Little ships.

Warships.

Scoutships.

Fighters.

Bombers.

There were ships made like solid slabs of metal, ships that seemed to be made of fragile webs, ships that had been added to piece by piece until it was impossible to tell what did what or went where. Ships shaped like cigars and ships shaped like plates, ships shaped like silver teardrops and ships shaped like crosses. Gold ships, red ships, black ships, blue ships, white ships, and transparent.

I guessed at half a million ships and was too frightened to check. I never did know how many ships were in that fleet.

Fireships.

I played awhile with the puzzle of the war, and came to no solution. The pieces were still scattered, pieces missing. This looked like the final blow, the final part of the game. Perhaps. Perhaps not.

I was shocked out of frustrated thought by the announcement that our ship would be flagship. After I'd managed to assimilate the fact, I came to the dreary conclusion that it maybe didn't matter. *Any* ship could be flagship.

Organizational formats rose and fell like houses of cards as we looked for strategy. Attack groups were put together, considered, discarded. We tested the effectiveness of small groups, then large groups, sweated, slaved, and eventually came up with what seemed to be a good attack plan. It wasn't perfect. Still, it covered contingencies, allowed for shifting organization, incorporated a shifting apex system in case the flagship was destroyed, instituting a line of succession. The only instructions we had: *destroy.* We didn't know what the target looked like, wouldn't know until we reached it. Scoutships sent to observe never returned.

Communications had a hard job while we were planning. We used our ship as a central base for strategy; we had the input of the entire fleet. The computers were at work nonstop for days that became weeks that became months. If you were a tactician, you were exhausted. It was necessary; with an armada this size, we could end up shooting at our own ships. In between, there was the problem of Enemy defense.

Things grew quiet in the universe. The Enemy *knew*. This was the final battle, winner-take-all. The waiting was the hardest part. We were scared.

Go-ready.

Ships moved, drifting, gathering speed. The armada's shape altered, slimmed, becoming arrow-shaped. Positions were taken, checked against the plan by the computers. The flagship's bridge was fully active, all the walls relaying information, displaying charts, showing the various ships of the fleet. The command station was a bubble suspended in the center of the bridge. I watched orderly confusion and didn't try to keep track. Much of what was happening was beyond my control; we were forced by dimension to let the computers do most of the control work.

We kept gathering speed, changing formation. Ships were spaced a hundred kilometers apart, each with its contingent of fighters. The eventual formation was the shape of an arrowhead. We had considered surrounding the target and closing in, but had come to the conclusion that we would probably end up shooting at each other. We had also considered the possibility that the target might be a solar system. We had the technology on hand to detonate a sun. It was unlikely that there was a sun to detonate within lightyears of the target, though. It's easier to hide something in empty space.

We moved ship by ship to the selected velocity, held there by computer links between ships. There was a buzz of talk on the bridge as the last ships reached the target velocity. Warning signals flashed into life.

We went into jump together. I tensed.

The screens cleared, showing our target, clear and bright.

There was silence on the bridge as we stared at it.

15 Fireship Run

It was a lot like the graphic models of atomic structure that they have in museums and schools, the nucleus surrounded by multiple rings that represent the orbits of electrons. We scanned and found six rings, joining at the poles. The core was metallic, either solid or a sheath for something else. Core/nucleus and rings were connected by what might have been struts, or conduits for cables, or, most probably, some form of waveguide. I couldn't see any *structural* necessity for the struts. The entire assembly had the look of an incomplete Dyson sphere, or a peculiarly sectioned metal soccer ball.

Visual inspection brought the first references; electronic analysis began just after we came into the area. Most of the resulting data concerned the nucleus. The general assumption on my bridge was that it was a sun, harnessed to provide energy for the whole assembly. *How* it had been harnessed was another matter entirely.

And we were headed for this monster. Looking at it, I had my doubts about the coming battle. Destroying a small world was one thing. Taking on something like this, something the size of a solar system, was another matter.

I don't think I was the only one who felt like turning tail and finding a cozy hole to hide in.

A fleet of tiny Enemy fighters looped out from the cover of the Enemy base, diamond shapes catching the starlight and splintering it. They came straight at us, charging our combined front screens. Our own fighter cover started to shift, regrouping into proper defense formation. Fighters on the edge of the armada peeled away, waiting for the edges of the Enemy fleet.

Space grew bright as the fighters opened fire on each other. Tiny ships became small clouds of energy and debris, became nothing. The main part of the armada held its course, passing through the central part of the battle. Enemy fighters, pursued by our own ships, went for the edges of the fleet, were destroyed quickly by the defensive fire from the big ships.

It was fierce and brief. When it was over, the Enemy fleet was finished; half of our own small fighters had been destroyed in the process.

The rear section of the fleet formation broke away, ships taking new courses, spreading targets as far apart as possible, to break up the fire from the Enemy base. Fighters accompanied the spreading ships.

I watched, waiting, wondering how in the hell, even with a fleet this size, we were supposed to do any damage to the base.

A heavy fighter curved in on an attack course, tiny against the monster we were going up against. Defensive fire caught it in the midsection tracking it, turning its attack into a *kamikaze* run. The ship's false nose exploded away, splitting into a hundred sub-sections that each shot away on its own course. The doomed ship careered on for a few more seconds, firing back, and exploded. Most of the trick nose sections hit the base, but the explosions were almost undetectable against the surface of the base.

I had a sinking feeling that enthusiasm, dedication, and gimmickry weren't going to be enough to save us.

Our ship went into a short jump, came out again, went into a curving attack course, disruptors fully opened up, cutting metal. Our weaponsmasters ejected drones, guided them along our course. A suicide run is a hell of a way to run a show; sometimes it's the only thing left to try. And it can be effective.

Our shields lit as the base opened up at us. We hung on until the last millisecond, jumped to safety, jumped again, renewed the attack. In this situation, the flagship was as dispensable as any other ship; I still hadn't figured out why I'd been named the fleet commander by the Builders.

The shields brightened, whitened, and we jumped again, and ended up inside the rings. The ship shuddered and buffeted coming out of jump, and was quickly stabilized by the pilots. Our weaponsmasters loosed a small fleet of drones to help scout the inner surfaces of the rings.

Seeing the size of the thing close up, on visual, gave me spinal shivers. The pilots and weaponsmaster had no time to worry about it; I did. I was looking for solutions, which was supposed to be my job. The best I had to hand was active strategists and overworked computers, all testing simulations. We were about to take a licking, I didn't doubt *that*. I just wasn't sure whether I was going to get ulcers or get killed before they could develop.

A ship warped in nearby, opening fire as it appeared. I watched it on the screens for a moment, then we were being jumped out of the area. The ship had been one of the biggest of the heavy fighters.

We came out of jump in the middle of a full-scale space battle. The Enemy had run out of small fighters, using them all, it appeared, in the first phase of the attack. Now they were using big ships, driving them full tilt into the empty spaces between the thousands of ships of our attacking fleet. There was very little finesse called for; they were, from the number of collisions, content to hit and run. Our fighter fleet, what was left of it, wasn't much use against that sort of assault, except to strafe and run away; most of the fighters were assisting the big ships in the attack on the ring assembly. The major part of the battle away from the ring was ship-to-ship.

Our ship bore down on the fleeing tail end of an Enemy destroyer, firing, forcing his shields up through the range to shimmering whiteness. A drone was dropped to complete the job and we curved away on an escape vector as the ship opened fire on us. Another couple of seconds and the ship was gone, shields ripped and imploded by the drone's weapons.

One more down.

We warped.

We came out of jump near one of the mysterious struts. I started issuing the fire orders, but the weaponsmasters beat me to it. The strut's surface was shielded, but a sheer physical attack broke through; a drone impacted on the surface, exploded, fused part of the strut to slag. Additional fire almost broke the shields down, but the power involved in shielding that much surface countered our attack. Two, three, four ships would have done it; one alone couldn't. Another drone was smashed into the strut, into the damaged area, other drones brought in to aid the attack.

The strut broke so suddenly I flinched.

At the same time, one of the rings went dead over a large area. All fire and scanning stopped from that area.

Four of our biggest ships detected the change, warped closer, scanning. Then, one by one, they dropped towards the ring, strafing as they passed over the dead area. Boats dropped free, made a hurtling, destructive pass, landed, squatting for a minute and suddenly disgorging hundreds of efficient killers and tonnes of highly effective ground weaponry.

They didn't have to use it.

The place was *dead*.

I watched the screens as they searched. They found an emergency computer that was trying hard to return power to the area, and blew it up.

So much for that. I was thinking about it, and thinking hard. Trying to make a decision that would save our lives or lose them all.

The Enemy ships were making a serious dent in our fleet. Their tactics were next to non-existent, but when you're throwing ships away by ramming them into other ships, you don't *need* tactics. A kilometer and a half long ship can't just casually turn tail and get the hell out; too much inertia that even a really good drive field can't handle too easily. In some cases, ship screens would be enough to prevent serious damage to the ship being rammed, but in all too many cases, our ships were being wiped out. At any particular time, the Enemy were losing up to eight ships for one of ours. But they kept coming; our fleet kept shrinking. We were losing too many ships. A quarter of our big ships were gone, completely destroyed. Reports were coming in from others of damage ranging from minor hulling to wrecked drive units and inoperative shielding units. The worst cases could only be counted as losses.

It didn't stop us.

The main part of our fleet kept on pushing through the defending fleet, either jumping from area to area or simply using brute force. The Enemy fleet had to get close to do any damage; it put many of our ships into an advantageous position.

Even so, we hadn't done more than inflict minor damage to the base, the shut-down ring area aside. The landed force was managing to hold the area, but couldn't spread out from it. They were pinned down at the edges, and would have had far too much area to cover in any case. The defensive fire from the ring sections was still playing hell with those of our ships that entered the inner area of the assembly, forcing each one to dodge and duck as it attacked.

A big troopship warped into the empty space inside the ring assembly, moved onto a suicide vector, dropped a few thousand tonnes of fusion bombs and a couple of tonnes of persnickety antimatter bombs, warped away for a few moments to let the noise and confusion die away, and returned, diving down through the debris still hurtling away from the base, and dropped loads of troops where anything happened to be moving. Defenders erupted from the metalwork, some carrying energy weapons, some using little more than twisted steel bars with rough edges, some even using only bare hands. The battle that broke out was fierce and frantic, many of our fighters vanishing beneath swarms of bare-handed Enemy, only to reappear seconds later in a hail of electronic fire and metallic debris. Most of the Enemy defenders had no chance at all, but that couldn't have mattered to them; robots don't give a damn about dying. Somebody was guilty of poor planning; even if the throw-away tactics were meant to gain time, it was a waste of material.

While the central punch-up was raging along, two small teams slipped away, to locate and mine computer installations for the area. It took them a while to finish the job; the resulting explosions were small, but effective. Most of the ring defenses shut down immediately, although the hand-to-hand battle continued, slowly dying out. Two areas were now under our control; possibly a third, if the ground team in the second area could move into the next.

My attention was drawn from the tail-end of that battle to the plight of a ship that had been disabled going into jump. It had emerged shakily from its jump, inside the assembly, materializing near a strut. It managed some semblance of controlled flight for a few seconds, then went into a wild spin, its pulse drives out of control. It careered into the strut, crumpling the metal of both strut and ship, and detonated.

The strut broke.

Another ring area darkened.

I waited, tense, hardly breathing, trying not to look at anyone, even though Chamzeen was watching me intently. A fighter made a scouting run, low-level, over the ring area. Its report was the same as the report on the first ring section.

Dead.

Completely and utterly.

I took a deep breath and wondered how to use what we now knew. It had been obvious from the start precisely what the "struts" were; power channels, immense, stable waveguides. The *why* of them was possibly more difficult. Power transmission hardly required waveguides, after all, although they helped a little. It was possible that they handled matter transmission, of course, but we'd been doing that over far longer distances by simple use of geometrical techniques that didn't require total breakdown of matter into energy.

I was suddenly uncertain of myself, and of the situation. We'd been taking a beating up until now, still were, and suddenly I had *this* wide open to me. An easy way out. I was suspicious.

There is no trust.

Damn.

I was starting to see masks where others saw faces.

I'd started out in this playing a bit part, bumming around some alien worlds, a jetjump jiver. I'd been part of the base network all my life, accustomed to exotica, with only the occasional romantic scrape at home, and a couple of chance encounters with Enemy to singe my hair. Okay, so I'd been sent on the occasional mission where the chances of my getting back in one piece, still wearing a slightly lightened black skin, were something a pro gambler would cackle at.

Now I had the feeling I was here by accident. *This* all-or-nought hell wasn't my turf, man, I hadn't *dreamed* of kicking ass like this. Or of getting *my* ass kicked in turn. Area Fourteen had sent me to kidnap a princess on some backwater planet in M-31. I recalled, kind of dimly, playing the fool with Annabelle Freeman, even feeling sorry for myself over a couple of things connected. She probably thought I was dead by now. Be a surprise to get back to Area Fourteen. *Hey folks, we won the war!* Yeah.

I'd come through to here the way *all* of us had, by taking what was offered, and using it, turning to the attack, going up against the bastards who'd been killing us up until now, killing them. Finding—

—a *mask*

And behind that, what? Another mask?

What about the role of sentient beings in this shadow play? By now I was dead certain that there was *some* motivation behind this, some reason, intelligible to mere mortals or not. I can stand some pretty hairy coincidences. I can stand my being in the same place as the Enemy by accident a number of times, possibly even stomach appearing next to another spacecraft, cubic lightyears of empty space aside. But all of these things had come one after another, seemed too neatly ordered to be natural.

No trust.

Masks.

The Builders had come to see to their chosen children, had found them confused, and had given them new toys to try and make them happy. We were being made to grow up while they sat and watched and nudged to make sure we got the right idea. Maybe they were pleased with us, too. We seemed to be doing the right things.

Or maybe there had been a war, once, and they'd won it by genocide, or the Enemy had killed themselves off, or died out. Leaving behind their machines, their planet-wreckers, their factories, their berserker programs. And we were the cleanup squad.

I wasn't sure I liked either idea. I'd seen my friends dying, and I didn't like it. Living beings were being massacred all around me, and it made me feel bad.

Toys.

Children.

Masks, and trust. I couldn't trust what I saw, I wasn't supposed to trust my comrades, even myself. Confusion shaking me. Meheilahn, for example. I'd threatened to kill her, and perhaps I would have, if it had come to that. Was her sudden closeness false, a mask designed to save her life?

I sat and stared at the screens, almost panicking, scared of even placing trust in the Builders, those selfsame semi-mystical, semi-mythical beings I'd trusted implicitly from my childhood.

I was scared as hell. I didn't have all the pieces of the puzzle. Hell, I didn't have half of them. I didn't have a clue what the eventual picture might look like.

Groping.

And a darkness filled with diamonds that was being split and smashed by the colors of death and destruction, leaving afterimages that spread and changed color each time I closed my eyes.

I had my key and my decision by the time the third strut was roken through. Another wounded ship, miscalculating its course y just a fatal fraction.

There was a minor panic as tacticians started working out the est way to go at the thousands of struts that crossed the billions f cubic kilometers of space from assembly to nucleus. Our ilots were twice as confused as the tacticians, as flight plan after ight plan appeared on the big screens, only to be replaced gain, each new plan a subtle but complex refinement of the one efore.

Step forward.

We attacked, coherent and hopeful, knowing, knowing, know- ng, and still praying: *if only—*

If only we still had the time.

If only we still had the forces.

If only—

I watched the battle maps, fretting, watching the bright little lots of our ships, appearing, vanishing, moving in formation, in lanned attack, watched as they were chased, surrounded, attacked y Enemy ships. On the screens, ships were shown, most of hem webbed by Enemy fire as soon as they came out of their umps, watched as they dodged fire by the eyes and other seeing pparatus of my bridge crews. Chamzeen came and massaged ny neck and shoulders with her hot hands, while I watched, ense and uncomfortable.

"You must be careful of yourself, Kevven," she said.

I nodded. "I'm trying. Christ. I'm scared."

I felt her lips brush my ear. She whispered, "You are our commander. You are not permitted to fall prey to sickness, at least of the soul, until after the battle, after the war."

I shuddered, swallowed. "I never asked for this. Goddamn it, it's a mistake."

"Use it, then," she said.

I was already back at work, noting a slight tactical change. Some of the smaller ships were going in with the big destroyers, drawing defense fire while the big ships worked on the struts. Some of the cannier pilots were using the defense fire to help damage struts. I condoned the latter action, but advised caution; I didn't want to lose many more ships.

Havoc.

Outside my ship, inside the Enemy assembly, it had turned

into Armageddon, yet we were having more success with it than with better structured plans.

Suddenly, I said, "Too easy."

We were working on a ring section ourselves, defended by small ships that skipped around us like cleaner fish around a manta ray. Chamzeen was still in attendance.

She said, "What?"

I said, "It's too easy. Too goddamned easy. Like all the times before, we have hell and damnation at the start, then we find a weak point, and the whole thing starts falling apart so fast you miss it if you blink."

"Oh." I felt her hands on my shoulders. "It is an anticlimax."

I slumped suddenly. "Yeah, I guess you're right. Not what you think you're gonna get." I rubbed my eyes. "Christ on crutches, I'm starting to get tired. Staring at that screen for hours on end. It's getting to me. A clockwork Tomari."

"*Shhh*. You must sleep soon."

"Yeah."

I kept staring at the screen, all foul moods and blue feelings. We were shooting still, and sections of the base were darkening with boring regularity; we were literally unplugging the place, section by section. Another couple of days, and the job would be finished, the place would be ours.

Looking at it, I couldn't shake the bad feelings, the expectation. There just *had* to be something bigger to come after it.

We were chasing an Enemy destroyer along a broken conduit, toasting his ass for him, when an anomaly on one of my sensor boards caught my attention. Whatever it was, it was unexpected, and happening at the nucleus of the assembly. The core was giving off bursts of radiation in a deliberate, structured, pattern.

The destroyer fleeing ahead of us suddenly exploded, a dirty white cloud of energy and debris.

When the output from the cloud dropped to zero, I checked the core radiation again, correlating information from a number of displays automatically as I studied the central sensor picture. I couldn't help my worried feeling; anything out of place was a source of additional danger.

I signaled Shtolaquer, let him study the picture for a couple of inutes, in case he had anything to check it against in the icyclopedia he thought was his brain.

"Well?" I said, eventually.

*=*Mysterious*.

"You bet your tentacles it's mysterious," I said, feeling a ttle let down. I tapped out a comcode on my board, patching rough to our library co-ordination section. Data input on a ship is size, in a fleet like ours, fighting a battle of this sort was a ajor headache, eased only by the aspirin that was library o-ordination, which did nothing but compile ready-references. nstant availabiity of *all* information. Chamloy, a priestess, nswered the signal. I said, "I want a close look at the core, the ucleus. Can we do it? It's acting strange, and I'd like to get a ood look, close enough to really mean something."

"One moment." There was a brief pause while they checked ther data and got the computers to investigate. "It is possible to lose on the core."

"Good." I tapped out another comcode, linking this time with Chamzeen, who had taken over pilot control from another riestess. She could, in an emergency, take over from any of the ilots. Each pilot handled a separate function, and backups were eady in case one system was burned out. The general assump- ion was that backups were unnecessary; if anything hit us hard nough to damage control circuits, it would probably destroy nost of the life-forms aboard at the same time. Chamzeen's nain job was co-ordination, centrally of data. Like her, I could ake over all pilot functions, or any separate pilot function, at ny time.

I gave her the flight orders and let her do the rest. Our ship lid away from the strut, accelerating before entering jump stage. We emerged already set for a hyperbolic throw orbit that would ake us close to the nucleus, and then back out into the open pace between the struts.

I scanned my boards, concentration at peak, aware dimly of he signals that indicated that digital records were in operation. On ordinary visuals, the core was featureless, neutral, the only hings to be seen being the places where the struts joined it.

To the other sensors, the thing was a fireball, flashing in a epeating, rhythmic pattern. Converted to visual for me, the esult was coruscations of colored light on my screens. Judging by what we were picking up, that core was producing enough

energy to keep a couple of thousand assemblies the size of thi
one running for half of forever.

Nikki had joined me in the command area during the approac
run, and was watching the screens. Her new arm was sti
difficult to use, and her regrown eye was covered by a larg
patch for the moment; it was still sensitive. As soon as we wer
on the outward run, I widened the display screen's output rang
at both ends, into infra-red and ultra-violet. Nikki gasped slightl
which made me wish I could see in the ranges she'd been bor
seeing. To Swa, the visuals would be even more spectacular. He
eyesight extended all the way into x-ray.

As we hurtled away from the core, I made another decisio
and called Chamzeen again, requesting a stable monitor orbi
with a very high apogee in case we had to make a run for it. W
hadn't been able to make any sort of proper estimate of the mas
involved at the core, and I wanted to be as far away from it a
possible before doing any of those fancy geometrical trick
bunched together under "warp" and "jump."

I kept my displays running at peak, scowling at them an
trying to apply a layman's solution to what seemed to be
complex scientific problem. The radiation ripples and pulse
were definitely patterned, and definitely had a steady beat,
rhythm. I couldn't figure it out. The puzzle was extending itsel
each time we turned up a new piece.

Shreekor called. *=*What do you make of it?*

"I'm jammed up against it, and I haven't got an *inkling*
man," I said. "Only one pattern visible the way it is now, mayb
there's more involved, computer-separable. Warning, maybe?"
peered at the screen, hardly aware of Nikki at my side, purse
my lips, frowned. "Could be overloading."

*=*I have that idea myself. However, the effects shown ar
recent, and there seems to be no other evidence of overload; no
does the effect change, despite further damage to the assembly.*

I sucked my lower lip for a few seconds, thinking so hard
put a dull pain between my eyes, where the frown-lines were
"Ye-ah. But it could just be well-shielded, anything . . . think
about it. It could be an overload signal, or some kind of dange
signal. Sure as hell can't be missed, now can it?" I scratched a
my hair, felt how much it had grown in the past few months
damn near a full bush instead of a thick mat. I hadn't had it cu

for awhile. I didn't even know how long I'd been deeply involved with the war. The past was dreamlike.

*=*The assumption is good,* Shreekor finally said.

There was a fairly lengthy interval, which I used to consider the possibility of getting Meheilahn to mow my hair to a reasonable length. Trim for brushing, maybe.

Shreekor returned to my mind. *=*The Jeweler is puzzled by the core effect, too.* Shreekor's return caused me to reflect on the absurd things you think about in times of crisis. Hair. Oh well. *=*He says that an overload alarm is pointless. Excess energy can be bled off into space, or any one of a dozen safe areas—any of a choice of subspaces, for example.*

"Uh-huh, safety valve system. Don't think logic neccessarily applies thinking about whatever produced this setup. Maybe, I don't have a clue, m' man. Maybe all those goddamn machines *are* super-logical." I scowled, wanting to growl, and hit blank space on a display board, automatically avoiding busting anything I might regret later. "You think the Jeweler and his little old green banana can cook us up a doohickey that'll survive the trip to the core?" I glanced at Nikki, whom I'd forgotten for a few moments. She was watching me with a mixture of wariness and concern. I realized with a start that she probably wouldn't understand half of what I'd said. There was a slightly puzzled feeling from Shreekor, even. I said, "Jeweler and his pet priestess. I want a probe."

*=*I gathered. You were unspecific. You're tired.*

"*You*'re fired."

*=*Thank you.* He was silent for a fair interval. *=*The Jeweler says that it will take about two hours. They will be in constant communication with computers and assistants during that time. Please avoid disturbing them.*

"Will do," I said. "Get any help they need from other ships, if you can do it. If they need outside help."

*=*Already set up, oh Master Kevven.*

I smiled slightly. "I trust you're doing your job."

*=*And yours, too.*

"Yeah." I tapped a code out on the comboard, patching through to Swa, who was monitoring the battle's progress, as well as co-ordinating our onboard tactics section. Fleet Tactics were beginning to tighten up a little, organization shifting to accomodate losses during the battle. The latest news from Swa was that the radiation from the core was causing some slight difficulties with the Tactics links. Ru was whipping some technicians along, trying to find some way around it. Digital transmission and subspace phasing of same was supposed to get through anything, but that was only theory. The problem was that it was slowing down Tactics' cross-thought.

We'd lost twelve more ships for sixteen struts, the average rising by one point three ships per ten struts in the last hour alone; they were starting to get our number. Still, with ring defenses falling faster and faster, it wouldn't be too long before the average dropped to something more resonable. Main trouble was from Enemy ships, which were still prone to suicide attacks.

I acknowledged the report and cut the channel, sitting back in my command chair, letting it attempt to make me comfortable, and asked Nikki to get me a cup of coffee, or something reasonably similar to it. She hesitated before going, swaying back and forth, as though she wanted to say something. Finally, she went, silent. I put my feet up on a console, sighed what I hoped was a properly commander-like sigh, and tried to relax, which was impossible. I had too many thoughts to grapple with.

Nikki came back with my coffee, saw me trying my best to keep my eyes fully open and uncrossed, and propped herself on the edge of a console, staring at me, her eyes glowing. She said, "You are tired."

I snorted. "Can't be. Jeez, everybody's telling me I'm tired. So I can't be."

"Do they send commanders into battle on your world?" she asked.

I shrugged. "Kind of depends. Most of 'em, nope. They stay way back and let the common dogfaces get their asses shot off." I took the coffee as she held it out. "Kind of depends on the distance and a couple of other things, I guess. Can't exactly have commanders sitting back at home in this kind of punch-up."

She didn't have a chance to ask for explanations or to tell me I was tired again. My attention was taken by the sudden new appearances on the scanner plots. Three ships, large, moving like gangbusters. They were identified as Enemy inside a couple of seconds, and I ordered firepower into action. I was surprised we hadn't been attacked earlier; there didn't seem to be any core defenses.

The first ship came on at full tilt, on a collision course; the combined attack of main ship and drones turned the ship to gas in seconds. The second ship, which attacked at right angles to our orbit, went the same way a moment later, and the third, who was coming for our tail end, expecting to find us tied up with the others, got surprised by a full-scale defense.

That woke me up a little bit, with the help of the coffee. I picked a couple of dozen likely points around the core, where our orbital path threaded through the conduits, and ordered potshots, hoping to cut the struts, or whatever the hell they really were, close to the core, I wanted to see what happened. There was still no attempt at core defense.

Two hours later, the finished probe was mounted into a torpedo casing and fired from a forward tube unit. It turned ass-over-elbow as it arced away from the ship, and dropped in towards the core, retro-firing, its onboard computer correcting its course when necessary. It floated down nicely.

The casing cracked open, and the probe extruded instruments and sensors and fired its own small engines, relaying detailed information back to us while dropping toward the surface of the nucleus. It operated beautifully, and would have done a perfect job, except for one very minor point.

The sonofabitching thing never landed.

Transitions with which to develop ulcers: one instant, it was *there*, floating slowly towards the nucleus. Then, as though you'd blinked and somebody had changed channel while you had your eyes shut, no probe. Just space and nucleus and struts. Checking everything for traces proved only what visual indicated.

No goddamned probe.

Further to that point, no evidence that it had existed, barring the light traces that its retrodrive had left. There'd been no telemetered report that tolerances had been exceeded, no indication of attack, no sign of any wandering phenomena such as wormholes and warps and black holes, just a nice level nothing.

We ran the recordings over, and got the same thing every time. There, then gone. No destruction, no attack. Just *gone*.

Of course, that intrigued the Jeweler and Chammekk, who just had to go build another probe. This one was a damn sight more complicated than the first—the equipment on it could pick up the farting of the bugs on a fly, doing so in complete vacuum, and, in doing so, give spectroscopic analysis, duration, intensity, waveform, frequency, carbon-14 count, and the composition of the meal that gave it gas in the first place. Handy little item, that probe.

So, confident, we loaded it and lobbed it at the nucleus.

Goddamn if that one didn't up and vanish too.

Patient as the pyramids, and just about as silent, the Jeweler got right back to work. He upped the computer power tied into his probe systems, did a lot of nimble-fingered programming, and started running the recordings through some pretty unusual scan systems. Everything was done digitally; it kept the recordings clear and clean. He zeroed in on a particular set of points, upping magnification, and cranked the playback right down until the image was crawling.

He kept on slowing it down. And kept on.

It wasn't enough, from the look of it.

Eventually, he let out a little *umph* sound, bounced to his feet and grabbed Chammekk's arm. Chammekk didn't protest as he tugged her toward the workshop area, although she looked remarkably bedraggled for a Lachallan priestess. I didn't go chasing after them. The door shut off my sight of them.

I looked up at the flat screen that was displaying the superslow playback of the second probe's descent, felt my eyes getting sore, and looked down again. I went into the bathroom next to the R&D section, splashed some water on my face, and looked into a mirror. It shook me a little; it had been a while since anyone had mentioned I looked tired. My mind had been gummy enough as it was. My face was pale, muddy-grayish, with ultra-dark areas under my bloodshot eyes. Our science was good for a lot of things, but it couldn't keep an unaltered human being like me going for as long as I wished it could, not in the middle of a battle.

I clucked with my furry tongue, and quit trying for the battle fatigue record. I relayed a message to the bridge for one of my second-level command staff to take over; it was Nikoi L'aan in this case. After which I went totter-stagger-shuffle to my quarters, which I reached upright but with my head about level with my shoulders. Even so, when I collapsed onto my two by one meter bed, I didn't drop right off into Nodland. My subconscious kept sending rebellious signals, in the form of guilt feelings and threats that I'd forgotten something important. I tossed and turned for about fifteen minutes, wishing I could believe everything was all right, debated calling a priestess or Meheilahn for a minute or two, and, in the end, set up the sleepstim timer and got to sleep that way.

Five hours.

Gentle uphill slope into wakefulness. I still didn't feel all that brilliant, but it would have to do. The bedroom's linkscreen was lit, displaying a brief message from the Jeweler. I rolled out of bed, called the science section, and had them relay a note to him, after which I went into the bathroom, where I managed to carry out all the normal functions of a more-or-less waking human being, all without needing help. Wow. Showered, considered growing a beard for the usual ten seconds, then used depilatory, wiping it off after a moment, along with my whiskers, dried my face, cleaned my teeth with the fast-acting but lousy-tasting detergent swill provided for that function, spat out same, rinsed my mouth out with water, spat out same, drank a pint of water to get me moving better. I ran an afro pick through my hair, blinked at the bags under my eyes, scratched the back of my neck, dialed up a couple of energy-boosters, and downed both, which eventually made me feel just a little under subhuman. The bags didn't go away. Back in the bedroom, I dialed a big breakfast, activating the floater unit in the tray when it arrived. I drank my coffee on the way down to the science section, pushing the tray ahead of me with my spare hand. In the interval between dialing breakfast—which should have been dinner—and getting it, I'd dressed. It made me look like a Moorish spook.

Chammekk was having a meal when I got to the Jeweler's work area. As I sat down across from her, she flashed me a weary grin, all sharp little teeth. The Jeweler was perched on a chair, thankfully not hungry. While Chammekk and I ate, he gave me a rundown on what they'd been doing. Chammekk occasionally broke in to explain something in detail.

The Jeweler had, by working nonstop for hours, managed to patch together equipment that would make recordings to such fineness of detail that it almost defied reality. By constant magnification, via computer, and analysis of each point in the digital picture, he could scan subatomic particles. In addition, all this could be used to slow the action down as close to dead halt as could be possible without freezing the action completely.

And then there was the latest probe, put together rapidly, but with painstaking care. Individual segments had been assembled and tested on an assortment of ships, and shifted in to our ship. It was a fantastic little item, a space researcher's dream machine. It didn't need a torpedo casing; it had been designed as a single unit, with all the necessary doodads built in. It was launched by putting it into a cargo lock and opening the outer doors. It was far too big to be ejected as a torpedo.

It was launched as I fed my empty tray into a kitchen slot. The Jeweler sat at a control console, only his hands and eyes moving. The probe's onboard electronics would take care of any emergencies that came up, but the Jeweler intended to take the machine down himself. He did, building thrust, jogging it, slewing it slightly, pushing the machine to where he wanted it, using it as an extension of himself.

Most of the crew was asleep at the time, unconcerned in their lack of knowledge about the nucleus. When the present shift was over, some of the sleepers would take over. Others would have little or nothing to do. The ship was incredibly quiet, still, as if the pitched battle outside, the battle that was burning ship after ship, didn't exist. Unreality. That's the way space is. It can drive you crazy if you don't take care.

The wait while the probe drifted down to the nucleus was an ache, but we hung on all the same. Not one of us dared make a move to leave, just in case something unexpected happened.

Nothing surprised. The probe was, then wasn't.

The Jeweler rocketed from his chair, went bouncing around the room like a hyperactive tennis ball, and was set up for the search problem in seconds. He juggled the recordings to find the point he wanted—the instant when the probe blinked out of existence. And we *saw* . . .

The probe seemed frozen on the screen. A halo appeared, patterned, surprisingly, like the radiation pattern that had attracted us in the first place. The probe touched it, and appeared to sink into it, like a lead block into quicksand, slowly, ponderously. Information cut-off occurred as the probe was halfway gone, then, as the top of the probe sank into it, the halo was gone. Computer estimate of the time involved in the transition: under a billionth of a second. Even slowed this way, it seemed remarkably rapid.

The Jeweler programmed his equipment and sat watching the

display screen as the probe reappeared, vanished, reappeared, vanished.

It was a neat defense, but it looked like the probe was *not* destroyed. Just removed. The halo caused it to pass through the core, or into it, and from there, presumably, into some other spatial area, whether our own geometrical area, or some other.

The Jeweler checked that with a simple probe; this one consisted of a simple nuclear warhead, a casing, and a length of stiff wire that acted as a trigger. If any part of the trigger was destroyed, the circuit would be broken, and the probe would explode. We would only be able to detect the first stages of the detonation, but it would be enough to tell us what we wanted to know.

The probe was duly launched, and vanished on schedule. Information recorded as the probe vanished was immediately played back and sifted through. Four kilometers of trigger were swallowed whole by the halo; none of it, from the looks of it, had been destroyed. The probe sank just as quickly—or the halo rose to it, whatever. No trace of the beginning of an explosion.

I was quiet as the Jeweler worked, thinking about it. The halo didn't extend more than a couple of hundred kilometers above the nucleus when it was activated. We were orbiting a couple of hundred thousand klicks from the surfce. We *might* be safe.

Then again—

It promised some answers, and I needed some good answers to put the puzzle together the right way.

The nucleus was a gateway. There couldn't be any other answer to that question. It gave glimmerings of an answer to the *why* of the struts, or whatever we were cutting through.

But a gateway to where?

16 The Jackpot

Fighting still raged inside the ring assemblies.

By now, there was only minor trouble from Enemy ships, but the defenses built into the base itself were still operating in areas that hadn't been cut from the circuit. A heavy crossfire forced our ships to do a lot of fancy dodging, their tails periodically heated up. The problem was that a ship had to stay in place for a minimum of ten seconds to take out a strut, or fly a preset course for at least that long. The Enemy gunners were aware of this, and were programming accordingly

The only ship that was in anything of a reasonable position was ours, still in orbit around the nucleus. We could cut struts where they started, at our leisure. They couldn't fire at us from the ring surfaces, simply because, if we scooted, they'd hit the nucleus. We didn't have a clue what sort of damage attacking the core directly would do. The Enemy obviously didn't care to find out, and, being so close to the damn thing, neither did I.

Personally, I didn't even *attempt* to convince myself that that thing wasn't capable of making the combined firepower of Enemy and Builder fleets look like that sweet old cliche, the wet firecracker.

All of which didn't help my mental condition in the slightest. I kept dragging my mind back from the gulf outside the ship, only to have it up and run right back to the problem of the nucleus. Maybe it came under the heading of command duties, nebulous things that they were, but I wanted to keep my mind on the battle we were fighting. Waiting in vain for solutions, *of course,* and getting ragged again. It was the usual full-house mess, leaving me floundering like the guy you've all heard about. Up shit creek, *sans* paddle, in a leaking canoe. *Blub blub.* My demeanor was starting to make the Lachallans nervous.

So. Halo and core were two distinct parts of a gateway. What else was involved not even the Jeweler could guess. For all we knew, the things that went through there might be going into the heart of a sun, intergalactic space, a neutron star, even a black hole.

There was still the idea that it was the power source for the base. The gateway might be a feed-through mechanism, working in reverse to safeguard the source of power . . . but if that was so, why hadn't it yet reached for us? It could be a displaced sun, a tapped black hole, even a discrete generator. If it was the latter, a mechanism of some sort designed to produce power and other items for the base, then it could, eventually, be figured out. We had plenty of scientific and technological thinkum-power to do the figuring with.

My guess was a two-parter: one, that if it could be figured out, it would be birthday special for us; and two, it wasn't going to be figured out by us. Chances were an accident with it could demolish half this particular galaxy.

As for the theory that the shielding hid a black hole: well, if it *was* a collapsar, then we were in dandy trouble. We knew a hell of a lot about the things, but so far as I knew, nobody had yet successfully managed any kind of interior exploration or investigation. The collapsar effect came in useful for a goodly variety of applications, but the physical effect itself was more of a nuisance than anything else.

I checked, tapping the library direct, getting a condensation of available material on the investigation of actual black holes. It didn't take up much space. One or two exploratory vessels had been tried, but those that had tried to find out what went on *inside* a black hole hadn't come back. They'd either been crushed out of existence entirely, or they were still falling, prone to singularity. If the forever fall theory was correct, we could probably toss sugar cookies in after them to make sure they got fed.

So if that thing *was* a black hole under cover, our science boys were going to have a ball for a couple of thousand years. Providing we got through.

I itched for information, but the probes hadn't provided any useful data before vanishing. The damned radiation patterns were still present, making the displays light up like Christmas in the Crab. We hadn't even made a start on figuring out what they meant, or what had caused them to start. From the evidence present, the patterns were connected with the halo and the gateway effect. So far, we hadn't detected the slightest fluctuation in rhythm or intensity.

Specters in my pockets, silent and ungiving. I wanted to yell and rage, and couldn't do either because of my position. I didn't like being leader by default.

Cryptology: we considered the phenomenon as a deliberate signal, with a specific meaning, coded. We tried deciphering it. We ran it through forwards, backwards, frozen, scrambled, rescrambled, band-screened, wavelength-screened, using combinations of single and multiple wavelengths, screening at random, slowing it, speeding it. Solarized and amplified and compressed the signal output, flip-flopped the frequencies, more even than that, using techniques that hadn't existed until somebody aboard the ship thought of them.

Total bloody result: *nothing*.

Specters. I got *specters*.

I quit trying. *My* mouth was furry-feeling, and the fur tasted of coffee. I finished another cup as my command print terminal spewed out the solid copy of a progress report. With the folded printout in one hand—I was using the other hand to rub the back of my neck—I shuffled back to my quarters, where I threw the copy on the bed, stripped, stuffed my sweaty coveralls into a laundry slot, and went to shower off. That woke me enough to actually sit and read the progrep.

Progress was being made on the struts. Tactics, suddenly aware that we were ahead of the struts in numbers, had computer-designed new attack strategies. Now, instead of being wide open, a ship could make a randomized run at a strut, while a companion ship went in low and strafed defense installations that might be inclined to bring weapons to bear on the strut-cutting ship. Hard on the pulsating trail of the first ship would come a third, which would finish the cutting job started by the first ship, which would, by then, be off somewhere else, repeating the attack. It cut losses and speeded things up a little. Latest estimates of the time to completion ranged from two days to seven, depending on the complications involved.

So. Still a hell of a long way to go. I fed the report into the disposal, thinking that, if we could, we'd reduce the Enemy to throwing spitballs at us, instead of beams and bombs.

I got into bed, covered myself up, and pushed the sleepstim switch.

I slept for five hours again. When I woke up, the situation hadn't changed much. I ate breakfast in my quarters with the progress report by my tray, frowning now and then as I pretended to be a commander and a leader of men, women, and things. When I finished reading, I balled the sheets up and stuffed them into the disposal.

I took my coffee and my ragged-ended nervous system along to the Jeweler's work area. The Jeweler was out, but Chammekk was present, and she explained that they'd been hard at work while I was snoozing. They'd slowed the action down a hell of a lot more. The Jeweler was working on cutting the speed down even more. Something he'd picked up during the latest cut-down and analysis had caught his attention. He wanted to get at it, see it better.

I told Chammekk not to bother waiting for the Jeweler to finish, but to get some sleep first. Being Lachallan, she could go quite a long time without sleep, even without boosters, but she'd been on her feet far too long—she was showing signs of strain. Then I left, and went back to the bridge, to my dearly beloved command bubble.

Chamzeen was sitting in for me, keeping track of everything that needed to be kept track of. She stood up as I came up onto the commander's dais, to let me sit down in the big chair. It was pretty warm.

I wasn't too thrilled by the action. I had to sit and watch my screens, listening to the fairly routine reports that were coming in from various stations. I had to approve an occasional item so that action could be taken.

After a few hours of that, I handed control over to Nikki and wandered through the ship, making snap checks on various sections. My path led me eventually to science section and the Jeweler. He still hadn't finished working. By this time his equipment was starting to crowd out of his workshop, into the room Chammekk and I were in. I stopped for half an hour, chatting to Chammekk about mundaniac—such as the battle, the Jeweler, the battle, the nucleus, the battle, the Enemy, and all that, by which you can see our minds were light-years away from what was happening. During that time I managed to convince myself to have a meal.

Before I left, I looked through the open workshop doorway. The Jeweler was sitting on top of a video amplifier, looking patiently at a holoscreen rigged up in the middle of the place. A probe was displayed on it, in three-dimensional form. The probe's body was surrounded by a dim nimbus, and there was a shimmering effect and a burst of light where the end of the probe touched the halo at the nucleus.

The Jeweler seemed to be after something more. I left him to it; much as I'd have preferred it, I couldn't sit around just staring at a screen.

I jogged back to the bridge, chased Nikki out of the command chair, and whistled up a report. Business as usual, still shooting at struts. A good many ring segments were still operative, and shooting at our ships, but casualties had dropped again. It wouldn't be much longer before the job was completely finished; we were practically coasting now.

I was still nervous with anticipation. My specters refused to get the hell out.

I was just considering, for the *n*th time, that it was a hell of a distance from stereotyped badass spade dude, and bad at it—Area Fourteen hadn't exactly been intensive in teaching me proper slang and usage of same, being under the impression that it would be better for me to learn on the job, as it were—to supreme commander of a fleet that was slowly dropping in size while taking on a solar-system sized homebase belonging to an Enemy nobody was sure about. Some trip.

The buzz of my comboard brought me back to mundane reality. It was Chammekk, and she was grinning, showing off her rows of needle-teeth while still managing to look like a perverted pixie.

"The Jeweler wishes your company," she said. "For a few minutes only. Are you busy?"

I shook my head and my eyes got to feeling sore and gritty. "Not very. I'll be right down."

I cut the channel and stood up, managing only a stooped position. What I needed now was about three days of sleep. I handed control to Chamzeen, and went to my quarters, where I doused my face with cold water and took a couple more energy boosters. Looking in the mirror, I saw red eyes. Count Tomari, vampire. I checked, but my incisors hadn't grown any, so I was probably okay. Just sleepy-delirious. I knew that because of the occasional garbled voices I kept hearing.

I went on down to the Jeweler's work area.

The equipment had continued to crowd through the doorway and now occupied the outer room as well as the workshop. The holoscreen in the workshop was still alight, some prize for the barked shins and bruised thighs I got in getting there.

The definition of the image was fantastic, clear as vacuum. The probe the Jeweler had picked was motionless, at the edge of the halo, which was starting to flare. The dim nimbus I'd seen before now flared up, swirled around the probe. A burst of bright, colorful light appeared at the bottom of the probe, faded, was replaced by another burst, which faded. Then, with a violence that surprised me, light flared up and filled the area originally occupied by the dim nimbus. When the burst faded away, the nimbus remained.

The Jeweler made a slight motion with one hand, barely glancing at me to let me know he was aware of my presence.

The holoscreen's image adjusted, to allow space for an inset. The inset indicated flares of radiation, in a peculiar burst pattern. It didn't take any checking to recognize the pattern. I'd seen it too many times. Hell, it was the number-one hate of my life right now.

The flashing ripples kept coming and going. The original intervals and burst-lengths were so short as to be unnoticeable unless you really worked at digging them out. They were barely more powerful than the halo itself, in terms of radiation output.

The probe sank. Something went crawling along my spine as it was swallowed up. It went so quickly, even on this complex rig, that I was shaken. I was even more shaken when the goddamned probe reappeared, until I realized that it was simply the playback starting over again.

The Jeweler signaled, and Chammekk switched everything off. The picture faded.

I perched myself on something less uncomfortable than the usual, and stared at the blank screen. "So," I said. "We're certain we have a gateway." No one corrected me. "I'll bet that pattern means it's idling until something comes into preset pickup range. Which is, no doubt, the outer limit of that halo effect. When that pattern effect first appeared, it indicated the gateway was coming onstream.'' Something else occurred to me. ''Evacuation signal. Good Christ, so *that's* what it is. Gotta be what it is.''

Chammekk sat down across from me, watching me in silence for a moment, her triangular eyes half-closed. Finally, she said, ''Yes, that is what we believe too. The nucleus appears to shield surrounding space from the effect of transmission, presumably also holding and protecting a certain amount of equipment. The effect involved is possibly similar to that of a collapsar . . . . referring to certain theories. A closer comparison might be that of a wormhole. But instead of being from one spatial area to another, this would be from one geometrical plane to another—an alternate continuum, in fact. The conduits are possibly waveguides for impulses transmitted to this continuum. An energy-matter converter at either side of the pipeline would complete the process.'' She paused momentarily, regarding me, then added, ''Speculation indicates the possibility of this alternate contiuum being a contraterrene plane. More simply, antimatter. In this case, the devices we see are then comprehensible—they provide protection from terrene matter until a conversion unit is reached. This provides also an explanation for the utilization of antimatter bomb-ships.''

I shook my head. ''Wasn't after an explanation, Chammekk. Just avoidance of a repeat performance.''

She nodded slightly. ''I agree. However, further to this. From information available, the effect is operative in both directions. Presumably, if the alternate continuum is antimatter, all objects being transported, such as our probe, are then destroyed. It is, you see, defensive also. We cannot harm it by use of our weaponry—the halo, it would seem, shields it.''

But, I thought, we at least had a link to the Enemy, to the *where* of the *what* that was behind the war. Obstacles involved could be overcome by sheer fanaticism and plain hard work, if nothing else. Given a method of avoiding immediate destruction, we could take a fleet through and finish the job started here, if there was any job to finish.

I stopped there, mind occupied with hesitant thoughts. Robots were one thing—they were infinitely useful and supremely disposable. They were material, and could be destroyed without qualms. Sentient beings were another matter entirely.

Could I live with genocide on my conscience?

I didn't know. I knew the stories about the men involved with the Manhattan Project, and I knew about their feelings of guilt. Even the man who invented dynamite, who was moved by conscience to found the Nobel Peace Prize.

There'd be nothing for me to use as a safety blanket.

I was suddenly very scared by responsibility.

Chammekk postponed the thinking by speaking again. "View this." She activated the screen again, picking up a hand computer deck and tapping out instructions on it. A close view of a conduit appeared on the screen, where it joined the core.

Or, rather, *appeared* to join it.

Chammekk said, "This is a computer-resolved image from the last probe sent down. Magnified." The image grew until we were looking very closely at the point where conduit joined nucleus. "As you see, the end of the conduit is shrouded by the halo effect. The conduit does not enter the core, but, rather, enters the halo."

"Gateway field," the Jeweler corrected.

"I get the idea," I said. "Okay. Fact out of theory time. *Where* does it lead to?" Chammekk frowned slightly, and I added, "I haven't forgotten what you said. Go on."

Chammekk shook her head. "We do not *know,*" she admitted. "We have only the theories. That is, that it is a seperate continuum from our own."

I frowned, sucked my lower lip for a moment. "Not just an extra dimension of our own?"

She shook her head, making her metallic hair rustle. "No. It is a discrete continuum."

"An alternate universe." I raised an eyebrow, looked at the screen, at the image of the conduit. "Man, what a complexity. Masses of theoretical material and nothing solid. So we're blind unless we can find some way of sending something through and getting it back."

The Jeweler looked at me and nodded. His expression was smug, though pleased. He knew I understood it, even with my limited mentality. Thanks, pal.

I shrugged, and said, "Wonder how many more discrete universes we've got out there?"

Chammekk said, "An infinity. Some, possibly, with gateways such as this to link them." She glanced at the screen. "Speculation is a major part of life on my homeworld. We would by now be hearing such a racket from my people that worlds would quake." She grinned. "Discussion with amusement as well as seriousness, of course. We lack application, in the main. Theory is our greatest achievement."

"Yeah, well, this is bothering hell out of me." I stood up, blinked, shook my head. "Christ, I should talk. Everything to think about, and *all* I need is more troubles."

I could almost hear those goddamn spooks laughing behind my ears, or maybe it was the voices from lack of sleep.

I left.

I handled my duties for a few more hours, growing steadily more nasty and dull-witted as the hours passed. Either I passed out in the process, or somebody decided I ought to take a break, as there was a fuzzy memory of mild darkness, after which I found myself stretching and turning over in bed. I didn't raise hell over it. I felt pretty reasonable for the first time in ages.

Swa was in the command area when I reached it. I looked for Meheilahn, but didn't see her. She was on a different shift, from the look of it.

Swa said, "We have lost no more ships in the past two periods." That pleased me somewhat. "Destroyers are gathering to destroy the final strut."

That caught me by surprise. Things had been moving pretty fast while I was out of it. Then again, each strut that had been broken after a certain point simply let more ships gather together for later attacks.

I said, "That's great news." I looked at the figures on the board, as she called them up from the computers. "Situation on disabled ships?"

"Free ships have almost completed retrieval procedures. Survivors are berthed or under medical supervision."

"Fine." I dropped down into the command chair, and tried an imperious scan of the bridge area. No way. I wasn't haughty enough. Operations were proceeding smoothly enough. Chamquee was the pilot overseer for this shift, her attention fully on the consoles surrounding her.

The bridge was hexagonal, with four entrances and multiple emergency escape routes. Set around the bridge were display screens, some carrying information for general attention, others carrying visuals. If necessary, the multiple individual screens could be coalesced into one giant screen. One of the mini-screens had the visual of the group of ships moving into position to destroy the last strut. Tapping out the code to expand the screen size was an automatic gesture. The muted noise on the bridge showed it was appreciated.

The ships were avoiding sporadic fire from the ring segment they were about to kill. They weren't having much trouble.

I leaned forward, briefly looking over the bridge. It was moderately populated normally, with about two dozen sentients performing assorted functions. Now our spacious bridge seemed crowded. The news had gotten around. Chamzeen replaced Swa at my side. She looked at me for a moment, then perched herself on the arm of my command chair. She looked dainty.

I watched readouts and displays, then looked up at the giant screen surrounding the bridge. The last ship of the attack team was moving into position.

There was silence on the bridge.

A display flickered, changed, went blue, then red, then blanked.

One word, translated for me: FIRE.

Space filled with rainbow fire and fifteen kilometers of strut simply vanished.

In the final ring segment, energy systems died.

The base was dead, the battle was over. I stared in disbelief, and wasn't alone. Anticlimax.

I still didn't feel right. There was still the sense of foreboding, the feeling that there was something else, that this was nothing but one more mask, covering a mask, covering a mask, covering a blankness so long accustomed to a mask that the true face has vanished.

Suddenly, the bridge was noisy with cheers and equivalents, some of them pretty hair-curling. I shook, untensing, snorted, then chuckled, then laughed. Chamzeen twisted like a whip and went *kerplop* straight into my lap, where she proceeded to bounce and wriggle energetically. I kissed her, and she thereupon refused to let go of me for a minute or two; not that I minded all that much.

It was when she deigned to stop boiling my blood and I glanced at my command boards that I almost had a fit.

The radiation patterns had stopped pulsing from the nucleus, had frozen. I checked. Had frozen just a while ago. Now it was producing a constant output.

Pulse.

As I watched, the output shot up, then dropped, almost to zero. It stayed down for a moment, held, and then pulsed up again, output even higher than the previous level. It dropped again, almost died. It spooked me, even more so with the jubilation on the bridge. The nucleus was beating like a heart, pulsing its last. But I couldn't accept *that* as an explanation.

Pulse. Up, down, output level higher with each pulse.

I tapped out a code on my comboard and got Chammekk. She looked harried. I said, "The nucleus. What the hell's going on with it? Got any ideas?"

She shook her head. "No. We are working on it, but have no results as yet."

I cut the channel and checked on Chamquee, who was intent on keeping up with pilot information. The rotational speed of the core was forcing the pilots to keep a sharp eye on our orbit; we might just plough into something. I didn't say anything to her, nor she to me.

I was aware of it, though, when she stiffened, staring at a readout. Before I could check my own boards, she overrode pilot controls, slammed on ship-wide stasis fields, and programmed emergency-level normal space drive.

The ship broke orbit.

I scanned my boards quickly, swore. Instead of getting away from there like a bat out of hell, we were wavering between fully breaking away and plunging down toward the nucleus.

I looked up, watching the screens, changing the view to one of the nucleus. I could see an aura around it now, beyond the halo, an aura filled with scintillating colors.

I felt Chamzeen's hand on my shoulder, was suddenly aware that she had slid out of my lap.

So my sense of foreboding had been right. I hit the communications override, linking me with everybody on the ship, and all the other ships left in the armada.

I said, "This is the commander." I heard alarms starting.

"We've been caught by an unknown force, possibly emitted by the nucleus. Use of our normal drive is proving futile. We are going to make further attempts to break out of the capture field, but there may be some damage. Check all safety procedures and make sure you are wearing life-support equipment. All other ships: do not, repeat, do not approach the nucleus, not even to help us. Out."

The alarms continued for a few seconds, then died. I stood up and went over to Chamquee's pilot position, stood behind her. She cut the drive, slammed it in again, building the power level up to the danger point. I felt the whine of building overload with my feet.

Nothing.

I stood in silence for a moment, then said, "Jump vectors."

Chamquee glanced at me, said nothing despite the deathly silence of the bridge. She nodded, went to work, programming her boards. It was chancy, but it had to be done. Impulse power was only holding us in position.

Chamquee cut power to the drive, hit the jump controls. The lights dimmed, and there was a whine, both unusual, and then the lights came back up.

We hadn't moved.

Chamquee tried again, and this time didn't even get the whine or the dimmed lights. The jump units were dead. They hadn't been overloaded; had that happened, we would have been blown apart. The first attempt had been counteracted, the second fully negated, presumably by use of a highly selective damping field.

The last time that had happened was when the Builders took us into their ship. That had, after all, been the start of the road that had brought me and some of my friends to this point. To the end of the War, or maybe the beginning of it. Maybe. Maybe we'd lost after all.

I tried not to be frightened.

I touched Chamquee's shoulder and jerked my head. She nodded, stood up, let me sit down, and leaned on the back of the big pilot chair as I opened the main ship circuit.

I said, "This is the commander. Our attempts to escape the field have so far been ineffective. Prepare for emergency action against unknown boarders. I am going to make one more attempt to escape the field. Weaponsmasters will begin distribution of sidearms immediately. All corridors are to be guarded, strategic points likewise. Check all ship weaponry for defense against attack from other ships. That is all. Commander out."

I shut the circuit off.

It didn't take long to repeat everything Chamquee had done. It didn't help.

I opened the ship circuit again, sucked my lip for a second, and said, "Situation priority red. Stand by for attack, stand by for attack. Prepare for entry into the core."

I programmed new course vectors into the flight boards, fast, hearing Chamquee shifting behind me. I adjusted the normal space drive board, automatically checked all readouts, and programmed for full thrust.

I hope you're right, Jeweler.

Activation.

Always better to go fast.

We hurtled down towards the core. I gritted my teeth, shut my eyes, swallowed and found my throat was dry.

Entry.

We hit the halo.

Feeling of fire crawling over my body, drawing inside through my mouth and nose, into my lungs, my stomach, everywhere, man into flame, *homo pyrens*.

No light.

Sensation of landing on a pile of foam rubber or maybe marshmallow because of the slow sinking sticky effect while sinking/wallowing.

And . . .

Air was thick and creamy, difficult to breathe, and I tried to scream and clear my lungs. . . .

Pressure, like being wrapped in a tremendous mattress and squeezed by a monster-sized hand.

Talons raking skin ripping senses protesting.

Dry as old bone in a kiln. Skin flaking, mouth paper, hair brittle crystal.

Solarization everything negative in the light.
And . . .

We were drowning.
We were floating sinking drowning choking for air.

And we were suddenly out of it, plunging into black space, a vacuum where no star broke the spread of darkness displayed on the screens. There was nothing, nothing, *nothing*.

Visually, only blackness. Nothing on sensors. Nothing but—

One constant, unvarying level of background radiation.

Heat death.

Nothing but movement now. We could go any direction we wanted, it wouldn't make any difference. It was frightening.

We were lost.

There was nothing to give us any sort of idea exactly what had happened during our passage through the gateway. I was pouring sweat, and breathing in hard, ragged gasps, as though I'd just run five or six kilometers, shaking where I sat, trying to reason out what had happened to us. Chamquee had fallen across me. I could see other bridge crew slumped over consoles or sprawled on the floor. Movement from various of them indicated that no one was badly damaged.

Chamquee came to and struggled to her feet, leaning on the pilot chair for support. Her normal dusty red complexion was returning rapidly. The comboard for this section was showing signs of indigestion, flooded with calls; I guessed that most of them would be of the "what the hell *was* that?" type, and put a hold on all incoming calls. I reached for the switch to make some kind of announcement, when:

*=WELCOME.

The voice was deep, a basso bell, in my mind. Telepathic.

*=THIS IS OUR HOME.

I scowled. I didn't doubt the sincerity, just the owner of the voice. Enemy? Or another mask? Or something entirely removed? I glanced at the impulse controls. They were in the rest position. Builder? We hadn't been attacked since arrival, after all.

*=YOUR CRAFT IS UNDER OUR CONTROL, AND WILL REMAIN SO FOR THE DURATION. WE WILL GUIDE YOU TO WHERE YOU MUST GO.

I looked at Chamquee, who managed to look even more puzzled than she had been. Apart from the fact that this part of it had hardly been expected, despite my misgivings, the situation had been turned completely around. We hadn't yet been attacked. Had we finally encountered the *true* Enemy, the race the Builders called the T'sooli?

I opened all the communications channels, patched in all our communications facilities.

"Who are you?" I said. I barely managed to resist the impulse to lean forward. There was nothing to see. At my side, an emergency com channel beeped for attention. Chamquee answered it, talking quickly and quietly. None of her words registered on me.

*=THE ANSWER TO YOUR QUESTION IS IN YOUR OWN MIND.

"The Enemy," I said. "The T'sooli."

Dark ideas still swirling at the back of my mind, repressed. I didn't need more trouble.

*=WE ARE THE T'SOOLI, THEY WHOM YOU ARE TO DESTROY. WE COMMEND YOU ON YOUR WORK. DESPITE ITS FLAWS AND LOSSES, YOU HAVE WAGED A GOOD WAR.

One or two or a million specters.

"I intend to see the job finished," I said, bleakly.

Silence.

What now? What could we do against them? Our ship was under their control. Looking at the boards surrounding me, I saw other traces. Our whole fleet. Every last ship had been pulled through.

And by the time we worked out some method of getting out from under, it would probably be too late. They could wipe us out like a bunch of rats. *Wham*. The Universal Exterminator does it again.

One way ride into hell.

Hours dissolved—

Part of the blank black spaee suddenly faded away before the ship, became bright, brilliant, shimmering. Another gateway. Sensors were picking up only the radiation output in the visible band. I didn't try to figure it out; I didn't really want to try, not right now.

We went into it. There was a curious twisting sensation, then total normality.

Flaring redness filled the screen segments, showing that the ship was plunging toward a bloated red sun. The bridge lights dimmed, and the image of that swollen stellar mass turned the bridge the color of blood. *Omen*. Eclipsing one corner of the sun was a massive planet, hidden from our monitoring by the star it orbited.

I was startled after the darkness.

I said, "Get me data on the system." That wouldn't be too hard, I thought. We might miss a planet or two, but that was all. Close checking on the giant we could see would be out of the question for a while, that was all.

Seconds passed, and my screens filled with data. I was looking at the system. All of it.

I said, "What about other stellar information?"

Swa's face appeared on my comscreen. She said, "There is none. But for this system, this universe has reached the nadir of entropy. It is dead."

"Heat death," I said, more or less to myself. Swa's vivid face was expressionless, although her antennae twitched slightly at my words. "Okay. What about our other ships?"

"They are following us through the second gate."

"All of them?"

"Yes."

"God almighty." I looked up at the main screen, which remained in its wraparound state. "Okay, fine. That's it for now." I cut the channel.

I settled back in the command chair and looked out into space, wondering whether the T'sooli intended to land us on the planet silhouetted against that dying sun. If that was what they intended, I thought, they'd better have something to counteract gravitational stress on the ship, otherwise we'd end up flatter than a funny preacher's jokes on a Sunday in the Bible Belt. We hadn't determined the mass of the planet yet, but we knew that it was superJovian, with attendant gravitation. Stasis fields could handle the gravity, but the effect of driving the ship into the soup it had for an atmosphere, and the complexities of the gravitational field, would first crush it, then tear it apart.

I watched my boards as controls adjusted themselves, as a new course program appeared on the displays. The image on the screen adjusted as the ship shifted in its track.

We were going down. Our shields snapped on, full strength.

Illusions.

This time an illusion of safety. As though they didn't intend to destroy us. Maybe that was the truth of it, maybe we weren't worth destroying. I couldn't see them bothering to explain everything, like the villain in a thirties pulp novel. Hell, even if they did explain, it was odds-on that we wouldn't be able to fathom it. What motivates supermen, even gods? What does the *mind* a god consist of?

*=KEVVEN TOMARI.

My thoughts ground to a halt, and I sat up ramrod-straight, that bass bell still echoing in my mind.

*=THERE IS NO REASON FOR FEAR.

"Some lack of reason," I said, half-managing a sneer. *Hey, Mas' Lion, jes' lookit dat li'l ol' Mousey-Mousey givin' yo' shit!* I squelched that thought, angry that it had managed to get started. "You've been plaguing our universe for a helluva long time, whoever the hell you are, *what*ever the hell you are. You've been destroying ever since the Builders started their work in our universe. We've built up despite it, and we've gotten just this close to you—and *next* time we'll come closer and come harder, until one day . . . you're dead, man."

Nice angry speech, but I was shaking when I finished it. Bravado sometimes has an effect, but this time, it was useless. Just noise.

*=THERE IS ANOTHER NAME FOR THOSE YOU CALL THE BUILDERS. DO YOU KNOW IT?

Words froze and vanished in my mind, and I scowled at the screen, trying to work out what they were trying to do. As for a name for the Builders, I hadn't heard one. My mnemonic abilities had been boosted a thousandfold, and searching out a fact from my memory was simple. I double-checked against ship files, got nothing.

*=WELL?

"I don't know it," I said, aggressive.

On the screen, the planet was starting to take proper shape and color.

*=THERE LIES WRONGNESS, KEVVEN TOMARI. YOU DO KNOW THE NAME.

I triggered my memory again, automatically, came up with zeroes, and nearly got stubborn about it.

Then the repressed thoughts staged a revolution in my mind, joining arm-in-arm with the grinning specters.

And masks fell.

Illusions faded.

The puzzle went *click-click-click* and became a hideous picture, arranging itself in order, before taking life and dimension, before rising and walking and holding out its hand.

All eyes, staring.

My blood ran cold and my breath caught in my throat. My heart went *thud,* gushed blood through my veins, slammed pain into my mind.

Sudden sharp pain in my shoulder, and I slammed headfirst into reality. Chamzeen's hand was on my shoulder, her sharp nails digging into skin.

Laugh, cry, love, hate.

"Oh God, no," I said. I blinked, rapidly, trying to avoid the tears that filled my eyes. "It's T'sooli, isn't it? *It's T'sooli.*"

*=YES. YOUR FRIEND, YOUR ENEMY, YOUR MENTOR, AND YOUR DESTROYER.

"You sons of bitches. You fuckin' sonsabitches!"

*=YOU ARE JUSTIFIED IN YOUR ANGER.

I was on my feet, lurching.

"Justified *shit!*" I glared into space, fury streaming. "You run us around the goddamned universe, you give us your *toys* to play with, then you stab us in the back to get a laugh out of us. You fucking littleminded bunch of *bastards!*"

My fist slammed into my main console so hard the flesh was ripped and the knuckle chipped. I didn't feel the pain, was barely aware of the blood streaming over my fingers.

*=WE ARE THE BUILDERS, KEVVEN TOMARI.

"I don't give a shit *what* the *hell* you are, motherfucker, because all we are to you is piss-in-the-snow toys."

My knees shook and I almost fell over.

Two screen segments cleared, one to either side of the main image of the planet we were heading for. Images of the Builders appeared, cloaked, shadowed. Builders. Enemy. Murderers. *Janus.*

"My God," I hissed. "My God, you've been using us for millions of years, all of us, our whole universe, and now you have the by Christ gall to *tell* us, for kicks. Well, go on and laugh, baby, and fuck you too."

* = WE TELL THE TRUTH TO YOU.

"*Whaleshit,* man! Nothin' but whaleshit. You hearing me? I don't like it, and I don't like *you,* and I'm gonna cram every bit of your frigging truth right back into your ass where it belongs, dig it? *Every-single-goddamned-bit.*"

I had to force the last bit out through my teeth. My jaw hurt from tension.

* = WE GAVE YOU GOALS TO FIGHT FOR. A REASON FOR ACHIEVEMENT. A REASON FOR BEING. A REASON TO BELIEVE.

"Straw men to take down," I growled. "Straw men. Christ, I hope you had your fun playing your game, baby. I hope you got your kicks. We loved it. Ask anybody."

* = YOUR TASK WAS NOT EASY. NOR WAS IT MEANT TO BE ENJOYED. YOU LOST MANY TO THOSE STRAW MEN.

Friends as well as strangers. They'd killed more than strangers of a thousand worlds, a thousand galaxies.

"Murderers. Liars. You *betrayed* us, you shits. You were playing *God,* man. You *hurt* us."

* = YES. AND WE ARE GODS COMPARED TO YOU. AS OTHERS BEYOND US ARE AS GODS AGAIN, IN COMPARISON TO US.

There was a pause, too short to allow me to start yelling again. It was no use trying to be heard when they were talking. My fingers slid in the blood on the console, and I almost fell over.

* = IS IT NOT TRUE THAT YOUR OWN RACE STRIVES TO THE PERFECTION OF GODHOOD? THAT THE RACES OF EARTH GROW BY PLAYING THEMSELVES AGAINST EACH OTHER? WHICHEVER WORLD YOU CHOOSE, YOU WILL FIND COMPARABLE SITUATIONS. SIMPLY ASK. DO YOUR LEADERS NOT DIRECT DEATH AND DESTRUCTION WHILE STAYING WELL AWAY FROM IT THEMSELVES? DO THEY NOT USE THE HEALTHIEST, THE BEST OF THEIR OFFSPRING, TO FIGHT THEIR WARS? WHEN THOSE ARE MAIMED, DO THEY NOT ABANDON

THEM? WE HAVE NOT ABANDONED YOU. WE WILL NOT. WHO IS THE WORSE? WE? OR THEY? NEITHER? WHO HAS THE MOST REASON TO CAUSE PAIN?

"You're talking bullshit!" I howled, shaking my fist at the screen, splashing blood around.

*=NO, KEVVEN TOMARI. TRUTH. WE HAVE FORCED YOUR RACE, AND OTHERS, TO PROGRESS FROM NOTHINGNESS TO SENTIENCE. IN USING YOU THUS, WE HAVE BROUGHT YOU FROM BIRTH TO THE FIRST STEPS OF INDEPENDENT ADULTHOOD. YOU HAVE NOW LEFT THE DIRECTION OF YOUR PARENTS, AND WOULD WALK ALONE. YOUR UNIVERSE IS NOW YOURS ALONE.

"The hell," I snapped. There was a dull, burning sensation in my damaged hand now, and the fingers were stiffening. The knuckle didn't seem to be broken, but the wound showed white and red. "It isn't *our* universe as long as your bunch are goose-stepping around in it."

*=WE ARE NO LONGER NEEDED TO LOOK AFTER YOU. YOU ARE CAPABLE OF UNDERSTANDING, OF LOOKING AFTER YOURSELF. YOU WILL STUMBLE MUCH AT FIRST, BUT AT LEAST YOU ARE WALKING THE PATH. IT WILL BE YOUR JOB, AND THAT OF YOUR DESCENDANTS, ALL OF YOU, TO TEACH OTHERS TO WALK THE PATH. SOME WILL FALL BACK, BUT ALL WILL, EVENTUALLY, REACH THE END. TOGETHER.

*=IT IS LIKE CLIMBING THE MOUNTAIN. ALL MUST WORK TOGETHER. SOME WILL BEAR THE WEIGHT OF THE ROPE, WHILE OTHERS CLIMB IT. DIFFICULT AT FIRST, BECAUSE THERE IS BUT ONE TO BEAR THE WEIGHT OF MANY. GRADUALLY, THOUGH, THE PRESSURE DIMINISHES, THE BURDEN LIGHTENS, THE TASK BECOMES EASIER. YOU SHALL ALL BE PILGRIMS, HELPING ONE ANOTHER.

*=YOU WILL TEACH OTHERS TO BE LIKE YOURSELVES. YOU ARE FEW, BUT A FEW WITH HIDDEN STRENGTH. YOU ARE FINITE, MORTAL, BUT YOU SHALL HAVE NUMBERS. FOR EACH OF YOU WHO FALLS, TWO MORE WILL BEGIN WORK. AND WHEN YOU ARE FINISHED IN YOUR UNIVERSE, YOU WILL TURN ELSEWHERE.

*=KEVVEN TOMARI. YOU ARE PROOF OF THIS. YOU POSSESS UNDERSTANDING BEYOND NORMAL FOR YOUR

RACE. YOU DO NOT THINK OF YOURSELF AS "BLACK." YOU DO NOT DIFFERENTIATE BETWEEN SUBCATEGORIES OF YOUR SPECIES BY LOOKING AT THEM AS "BLACK" OR "WHITE" OR "RED" OR "YELLOW"; YOU DO NOT BRACKET INDIVIDUALS AS "COMMUNIST" OR "RADICAL" OR "LIBERAL" OR "CONSERVATIVE" OR "REPUBLICAN" OR "DEMOCRAT." YOU GO BEYOND ALL LABELS, ALL SURFACE DETAILS. LIKEWISE, YOU DO NOT CONSIDER YOURSELF AS "HUMAN" AND THEREFORE VASTLY DIFFERENT FROM ANY OTHER SENTIENT. SOMETIMES, YES, THERE IS A PHYSICAL REPUGNANCE, AND SOMETIMES ANGER, BUT NEVER HATE FOR SOMETHING DIFFERENT, NEVER UNTHINKING XENOPHOBIA.

*=YOU JUDGE A SENTIENT BEING BY WHAT IT IS, NOT BY LOOKS OR BY THE RELIGIOUS OPINIONS OR ATTITUDES IT MAY HAVE. YOUR JUDGMENT AND ATTITUDES ARE UNTAINTED BY PREJUDICE. THE ALTRUISTIC TENDENCIES YOU HAVE APPLY WHETHER YOU ARE WITH HUMAN, SHIMO-SH'SASAI, OR LACHALLAN.

"Yeah?" I leaned on a board, on my injured hand, smearing blood over the surface, feeling it sticky against my palm. I managed a contemptuous sneer, although I was mentally offbalance. Which they must have known. "Prove it."

*=LOOK AROUND YOU. A PRETENSE OF MENTAL BLINDNESS IS CHILDISH.

Touché. Chamzeen was fussing around me, her movements as sharp and nervous as those of a hummingbird, and she had a medipak in her hands. Her concern was my smashed-up mitt, which was still dripping blood all over the place, but all my moving and howling and going on had made her wary and jumpy. I stuck my hand out, a little sheepishly, managed what was meant to be a reassuring smile, but felt like a rictus grin, and let her take care of the bleeding and whatnot. I've never had a rep for being a mean mother.

*=THE ONES NAMED BIA AND MOO. THEIR DEATHS AFFECTED YOU DEEPLY. YOU FELT AN EMOTIONAL REACTION AT THE DEATH OF THE "BEACHBALLIUS." THOUGH THAT ONE APPEARED TO HAVE INTENTIONS OF DESTROYING YOU, YOU BORE IT NO MALICE.

I shrugged, difficult to do with Chamzeen holding my hand. "Yeah. So what?"

*=YET MORE. YOU HAVE SHOWN NAUGHT BUT GENTLENESS TOWARD "THE JEWELER." YOU EMPATHIZED WITH HIS GRIEF. YOU RISKED YOUR LIFE TO HELP CHAMQUEE, DESPITE THE PAIN RECEIVED FROM HER. YOU SHOWED KINDNESS AND TENDERNESS TOWARDS NIKOI L'AAN DURING HER PERIOD OF INJURY. YOU UNDERSTOOD AND RECONCILED DIFFERENCES BETWEEN YOU, AND YOU SPENT TIME RESOLVING MISUNDERSTANDINGS WITH YOUR PRINCESS. YOU HAVE SHOWN NO HATE FOR A FELLOW SENTIENT, AND HAVE NOT KILLED OR ATTEMPTED TO MAIM OR INJURE UNLESS THERE WAS NO CHOICE. YOU PAUSED NOT VERY LONG AGO TO CONSIDER WHETHER GENOCIDE WAS JUSTIFIED, OR REQUIRED, IN THE CASE OF THE "ENEMY." YOU DID NOT HESITATE TO DESTROY NON-SENTIENT MECHANISMS ONCE YOU WERE CERTAIN OF THAT ILLUSION.

*=CONSIDER YOUR ACTIONS ON AUREON. YOU PROCEEDED ON YOUR MISSION AS ORDERED, ALLOWING NOTHING TO HALT YOUR PROGRESS. BUT YOU DID SO WITHOUT RECOURSE TO KILLING. YOU MIGHT HAVE LOST YOUR OWN LIFE, BUT YOU STILL DID NOT CONSIDER TAKING THE LIVES OF THE PATROLS YOU ENCOUNTERED. YOU REASONED WITH YOUR PRINCESS WHEN SIMPLE FORCE MIGHT HAVE DISPOSED OF THE KNIFE SHE HELD AT YOUR THROAT.

"Too good-looking to hit," I said, watching the cloaked shapes on the screen. The planet was growing larger and larger. "Some days I come near changing my mind."

*=YOU ALSO TOOK TIME TO ASSIST THE AUREONS DURING THE ENEMY ATTACK, INSTEAD OF IMMEDIATELY FLEEING TO SAVE YOUR OWN LIFE. EVEN ON YOUR OWN PLANET YOU DEMONSTRATED YOUR ALTRUISM AND CONCERN, FIRST IN ASSISTING A WOUNDED FEMALE COMRADE, EVEN THOUGH YOU MIGHT HAVE BEEN KILLED IN THE PROCESS, AND THEN, WHEN YOU WERE BOTH SAFE, RETURNING TO ASSIST LOCAL LAW ENFORCEMENT AGENTS. YOUR CONCERN EVEN THEN EXTENDED BEYOND ASSISTANCE IN THEIR WORK TO PROVISION FOR THE FAMILIES OF THOSE KILLED IN THE BATTLE. WE ARE AWARE OF THE MEASURES YOU

WOULD HAVE TAKEN TO SEE YOUR WISHES FULFILLED.

I made a sour face. "So thanks for rolling my entire life out in front of me, if that's what you're gonna do. Don't you have any shorter method of telling me I was a sucker and a patsy and a dummy and whatever the hell else I was?" Chamzeen's hand was a hot pressure on my forearm. And the Builders didn't bother to answer what I'd said, the high-and-mighty bastards.

*=WHEN BASE 1074 WAS ATTACKED, YOU TURNED BACK TO ASSIST YOUR PRINCESS. YOU DID NOT ABANDON NIKOI L'AAN WHEN SHE WAS PUSHED ON YOU. YOU DID NOT REJECT SHREEKOR. YOU DID NOT LEAVE THE JEWELER IN HIS CASKET. YOU DID NOT HATE CHAMQUEE. AND MORE. NOTHING OF THIS WAS UNDER OUR CONTROL, NOTHING WAS ORDAINED. THE MACHINERY WAS TRIGGERED, NOTHING MORE. IT WAS SELF-DETERMINING, AS WERE YOU.

*=YOU HAVE NEVER FAILED TO HELP, WHEN HELP IS NEEDED. YOU HAVE COMPLAINED—YOU HAVE COMPLAINED IN EVERY WAY THERE IS! BUT NOT ONCE HAVE YOU TURNED AWAY. NOW—

*=WE DEMAND YOUR LIFE AS THE PRICE FOR THE RELEASE OF YOUR COMRADES! WHAT IS YOUR DECISION?

It was so sudden, and so loud, that it shook me a bit. I didn't even take time to think. "What's your guarantee?" I said. I saw Chamzeen shift, saw her eyes on me, her face concerned, her mouth half-open. Some of the bridge crew shifted.

*=THAT WE WILL ALLOW YOU TO LIVE UNTIL YOU SEE YOUR COMRADES FREED.

I sneered. "That makes hash of everything you been rambling about, you patent bunch of assholes." I shrugged. "Could it really matter? I mean, I had it punched into me that I don't *trust,* hear me? Then again, maybe you have some values, some kind of honor system. Maybe. I'm prepared to take it on faith, 'cause I don't have a choice. My life for theirs, whenever you want it."

I waited for it.

There was dead silence for a nervous thirty seconds. Heads and eyestalks turned to look at me, to see whether I'd had my head torn off yet. Chamzeen held my wrist and stared, her triangular eyes fully open, her lips twitching. Compulsive kissers. I wanted to hold onto her for support and courage, but didn't dare. The T'sooli were/was silent, whether they were singular or plural, or what.

Suddenly, there was a bubbling bass river, a telepathic chuckle.

*=DO YOU SEE? YOU WERE SINCERE. OUR STATEMENT WAS UNTRUTH. IT DOES NOT INDICATE OUR DESIRES OR INTENTIONS.

Stiffly, I said, "I was prepared to accept it as fact. I suppose lies are to be expected from you."

There was a feeling of hurt, an emotional pain. I shuddered. Chamzeen squeezed my wrist.

*=YOU WERE PREPARED TO MAKE A SACRIFICE. YOUR LIFE TO SAVE YOUR COMRADES. A NOBLE ACTION, ONE FORCED TO MAKE A POINT. WE ARE NOT SO SO DIVINE AS TO ACCEPT SUCH A SACRIFICE, NOR SO PETTY AS TO TRULY DEMAND IT. THERE IS NO NEED FOR FURTHER PAIN. YOU HAVE ACHIEVED THE STATED GOAL.

*=WHO WERE YOU WHEN YOU BEGAN THIS MISSION, KEVVEN TOMARI?

I glared at the screen, puzzled and annoyed. I didn't like having my life and times and motives unrolled like a bolt of cheap cloth, all over the floor. And I didn't like this question, because it seemed pointless, which made me highly suspicious.

"I," I started, and almost froze, "was me." I suddenly felt very silly, and had to swallow. It was weird feeling that way, when my body was under the impression I was fighting for my life.

*=WHO ARE YOU NOW?

What the hell *were* they up to? I wanted to shout and storm and demand an answer to that. My mind was letting off little explosions of thought, colorful and noisy and chaotic.

All I said was, "I'm me. Kevven Tomari. I, individual. Unstrung puppet. Me."

I thought I was going crazy. I was even willing to help myself along to the funny farm. No such luck. I was stable and unfortunately sane. Damn.

*=BUT YOU AS YOU ARE NOW COMPARED TO YOU AS YOU WERE THEN SHOWS MUCH DIFFERENCE. YOU

HAVE GROWN. ALL OF YOU HAVE GROWN, THROUGH ADVERSITY, THROUGH DISPARITY, THROUGH THE PRESSURE OF NECESSITY.

*=COME, KEVVEN TOMARI. TELL US OUR LIE.

"Lie?" I said.

The memory mat unrolled and shivered and showed me the place to look. I hesitated, briefly, before speaking. Then:

"There is no trust," I said. "That's your lie, isn't it? Your dictum on Soru. I listened, yeah. Got wary. But—"

*=BUT NEVER ACCEPTED IT. EVEN THOUGH YOU WERE UNAWARE OF THE REJECTION OF OUR LIE. ONLY A BLIND CREATURE TRUSTS NOTHING, THE MENTALLY BLIND, THE EMBITTERED, THE EMBATTLED, THE ONES WHO ARE IN PERPETUAL CONFLICT WITH THEMSELVES AND THEIR SURROUNDINGS. THESE DARE NOT TRUST, DARE NOT LOVE, DARE NOT FEEL, FOR FEAR THEY WILL BE DESTROYED THROUGH IT.

*=YOU TRUSTED YOUR COMRADES. YOU PLACED FAITH IN PROPER PLANNING. YOU TRUSTED TO YOUR SKILLS, YOUR ABILITIES, YOUR EQUIPMENT AND ITS CAPABILITIES. BUT NEVER BEYOND THAT. YOU HAVE NEVER TRUSTED BLIND LUCK. HAD YOU DONE SO, YOU WOULD NEVER HAVE WON THROUGH TO HERE.

"Chamquee's fault," I said. "She made me crafty. Hell, I couldn't trust luck anyway. Goddamn situation was too complicated. By the time the parameters finished shifting, luck just kind of got wiped out. And if I didn't trust my people, we'd just get wiped out."

*=INDEED. THIS IS DUE IN PART TO YOUR GROWTH, THIS TYPE OF TRUST. YOUR ABILITY TO ADAPT TO THE DEMANDS OF A SITUATION IS A MAJOR DEVELOPMENT, ALMOST AN EVOLUTIONARY STEP.

*=YOU SEE, WE HAVE FORCED YOU TO GROW AND DEVELOP. BY THE USE OF THE "ENEMY," WE CREATED GREAT ADVERSITY FOR YOU, ADVERSITY WHICH, TO SURVIVE, YOU HAD TO CONQUER. LEFT TO YOURSELF, IN PEACE, WITH ONLY THE BASES, YOU WOULD HAVE GROWN BORED, TIRED, STAGNANT, WOULD HAVE LOST IMPETUS, WOULD HAVE BECOME DECADENT, PROBABLY EXTINCT. THE ATTENTION SPAN OF CHILDREN IS BRIEF. WE NEEDED NOT CHILDLIKE FAITH IN

ORTUNE, BUT A COMPLEX UNIVERSAL SOCIETY CA-ABLE OF ADULT RESPONSE TO NEW STIMULI. YOU AVE ADAPTED TO ADVERSITY, AND CANNOT NOW EASE ADAPTING. YOU ARE TOO AWARE OF YOUR-ELVES, OF THE UNIVERSE AS A WHOLE. YOUR OWN ORK, WHICH CONTINUES AND EXPANDS OURS, HAS EGUN. THE WORST OF YOUR ADVERSITY HAS STILL O COME, AND WILL REQUIRE YOU ADAPT SWIFTLY O PREVENT YOUR OWN EXTINCTION.

*=BUT ACCEPTANCE OF PAIN IS NOT ALL.

*=YOU SEE, THERE ARE BALANCES, MANY OF THEM RECARIOUS, EASILY UNDONE. FOR EACH NEW PAIN, HERE IS SOME MEDIATION—JOY, PLEASURE, THE HRILL OF DISCOVERY, OF CREATION, OF FINDING OVE AND FRIENDSHIP IN AN UNEXPECTED PLACE. IFE IS PLEASURE, EXISTENCE, ECSTASY.

*=CHAMQUEE CAUSED YOU HARM, BUT AS A BAL-NCE TO THAT HARM, THAT PAIN, YOU HAVE HER RIENDSHIP, HER LOVE. YOU HAVE REPAID HER IN IND, WITH YOUR OWN LOVE AND FRIENDSHIP. THE AIN OF GROWTH IS MEDIATED, IF YOU ALLOW OTHER HAN HATE INTO YOUR AWARENESS.

*=PAIN MAY BE BORNE. EVEN WHEN THE PAIN IS REAT, AND CONSTANT, ONE MAY BECOME ACCUS-OMED TO IT. PAIN COMES WITH GROWTH, WITH SUR-IVAL. BUT WITHOUT LOVE OF SOMETHING, WHAT SE IS SURVIVAL? WHY LIVE IN A UNIVERSE WHICH NE HAS NOTHING BUT HATE FOR? AND YOU, OUR HILDREN, WE HAVE HURT YOU, AND FORCED YOU TO ROW. YET WE HAVE NOT DENIED YOU OUR LOVE. WE OULD NOT BE COMPLETE IF WE DID NOT LOVE YOU, OR WOULD YOU BE COMPLETE WITHOUT THAT OVE. OUR PAIN COMES IN FORCING YOUR GROWTH, UT THIS PAIN WILL SOON DIE. OUR LOVE WILL ROW. SO, TOO, WILL YOUR PAIN DIE, YOUR LOVE ROW.

*=LOOK ABOUT YOU. SEE LOVE AND FRIENDSHIP, EE YOUR COMRADES AND COMPANIONS. SEE UNITY. OR EACH WHO SPITES YOU IN FUTURE, THERE WILL BE A THOUSAND WHO WILL KNOW OF YOU ONLY WITH PLEASURE AND JOY.

*=LOOK ABOUT YOU, KEVVEN TOMARI. SEE TH
LOVE SURROUNDING YOU.

"I . . ." I stopped, words frozen. My fury had sort of fade away during the lecture, leaving me standing and feeling absurd and more than a little awed, even while a section of my min was picking the whole thing apart. Chamquee was watching m from her position across the bridge, while Chamzeen was sti holding my wrist. "Okay, that's the way it is. That's the way was brought up. What you did was make me goddamne suspicious of everything. I just don't trust appearances anymore right?" Chamzeen squeezed my wrist. "I kept seeing masks that's all, and for all I know, what I'm seeing now, that's jus another mask, man. Maybe it's all masks, maybe there isn't face to find after all."

The planet almost filled the forward section of the screen now colors swirling in a gaseous mantle. It looked like my stomac felt. Roiling.

*=YOU ARE SUSPICIOUS EVEN OF YOUR PRINCESS.

It wasn't a question at all. They didn't need to ask m questions. They had all my answers ready to surprise me.

I said, "Everything. Doesn't matter what it is." I pulled m wrist from Chamzeen's hand. The medipak was a mild pressur over my knuckles. "Hell, I'm suspicious of me when it comes t that, but that's nothing all that new."

*=YOUR LOVE FOR HER? HER LOVE FOR YOU?

Right out in the open. It didn't sting me as much as expected, even coming from the T'sooli. Or maybe it didn't stin *because* it came from them.

I said, "Okay, so what have we got in common, me an Meheilahn? The first day I met her, it was the knife in the throat and we've been fighting ever since . . ."

I turned introspective at that point, partly because there was slightly disgruntled feeling in my mind, and Chamzeen wa looking at me in a manner meant to shame me somewhat Reflecting, I realized that I hadn't been accurate. I'd bee fighting with Meheilahn up to our showdown in the ship library after that, things had smoothed out. Hell, it was hard to think o any spare time I'd spent without her.

I might have ended up contemplating my navel, but th Builder—even now, I kept thinking of them as the Builders— saved the day.

*=WE ARE NOT GODS, KEVVEN TOMARI. MERELY JILDERS, WE WERE ONCE AS YOU ARE NOW. WE AVE BECOME IMMORTAL, AND OUR HISTORY HAS IUS BEEN RENDERED AS INCONSEQUENTIAL A SPECK S THE SYLLABLES OF THE NAME WE HAVE TAKEN. E HAVE FOUND THAT ALL IS ILLUSION, AND THAT E HAVE YET TO FIND OUR FINAL FORM, OUR DES-NY. THIS IS NOTHING BUT A STAGE, A POINT UPON IE ROAD WE TRAVEL.

*=WE KNOW OURSELVES, YET DO NOT KNOW WHAT E MIGHT BE.

*=WE ARE PATTERN, MATRIX, PLAN. WE, AS YOU, ERE FORCED TO PROGRESS, FOUND THAT OUR ENE-Y WAS BOGUS. WE WERE BITTER, ANGRY, AND WERE ONG IN FORGIVING. IT COST US MUCH IN TERMS OF RIDE, OF VANITY. AND THE LINE EXTENDS TO INFINI-Y, INTO THE PAST, INTO THE FUTURE.

*=WE CAN OFFER YOU THE IMAGE OF GODHOOD, EVVEN TOMARI, WE CAN MAKE YOU AS A GOD GAINST YOUR FELLOW MEN. POWER BEYOND BELIEF. ONTROL BEYOND NEGATION. DESTINY BEYOND IMAG-IATION. YOURS, IF YOU WISH.

I felt like crying something biblical, spiritual, bawling to hell ce a revivalist preacher, getting god and getting taken for cash. had to fight cascades of religious imagery. And more, of urse, but primarily the Bible. Thankyou, Amerika.

"No," I snapped. "I don't want it. It isn't *worth* it."

No born preacherman could have said it better.

*=YOU ARE WISE. YOUR MIND COULD NOT TRAN-CEND ITS LIMITATIONS AND MIGHT DESCEND EVEN-UALLY TO A BRUTAL, COSMIC INSANITY. YOU WOULD NOW ENDLESS ECSTASY, YET WITHOUT THE KNOWL-DGE AND THE ABILITY TO DEVELOP VARIATIONS OF HAT ECSTASY, BOREDOM AND MADNESS WOULD SOON E YOURS. IMMORTALITY WOULD PALL, INFINITE ABIL-Y AND POWER WOULD BECOME YOUR SHROUD. GOD-OOD, OR THE ABILITIES ONE MIGHT ATTRIBUTE TO UCH A STATE OF EXISTENCE, IS DEVELOPED, IS VOLVED, AND IS NOT GIVEN AND TAKEN.

*=WE HAVE AVOIDED THE FALLACIES OF ASSUMED IVINITY. TO BE DIVINE IS TO BE PERFECT. AND BEYOND

THE THREAT OF DEATH, DAMNATION, DESTRUCTIO
BEYOND THE THREAT OF FAILURE, THERE IS NOTHIN
BUT FALSITY, NAUGHT BUT FANTASY. WE ARE MOT
VATED BY THE THREAT OF FAILURE. WE FIND IT MOR
DESIRABLE TO ASSIST IN CREATION, TO RISK FAILUR
IN THE TASK OF GUIDANCE OF CREATURES OF CHANC
—YOU. IF WE HAD FAILED, IT WOULD HAVE BEEN
REASONABLE FAILURE, ACCEPTABLE. WE SEE THROUG
THE EYES OF CREATION, BUT WE DO NOT BLIND THE
AND TAKE CREATION AS OUR OWN.

*=WE HAVE SUFFERED FAILURE, AND ACCEPTED I
AND LEARNED FROM IT. YOU ARE OUR SUCCESS, YE
YOUR OWN SUCCESS TOO. AND WE ARE A STEP CLO
ER TO THE END OF THE ROAD WE ALL ARE WALKING

*=YOU NOW BEGIN THE LONG WALK, AS YOU
OWN SMALL PATH FUSES WITH OUR LARGER ONE.

*=THE FIRST THING THAT IS LEARNED IS THA
ULTIMATE POWER IS ULTIMATE FINALITY. THIS, KEVVE
TOMARI, YOU KNOW. THERE MUST ALWAYS BE NE
ADVERSITY, NEW EXPERIENCE, NEW LIMITATIONS T
EVENTUALLY TRANSCEND. THE ONLY POSSIBL
GROWTH IS THROUGH ALL POSSIBLE OBSTRUCTIO
YOU HAVE, NOW, A UNIVERSE TO DEVELOP. YOU WIL
EVENTUALLY, BECOME ONE WITH YOUR UNIVERS
ONE WITH ALL EXISTENCE ON YOUR PLANE. AND YE
THERE IS STILL MORE TO KNOW, BEYOND THIS, STIL
MORE TO EXPLORE, STILL MORE TO PROVIDE YO
WITH NECCESSARY GROWTH.

*=THE ROAD IS LONG . . . SO VERY, VERY LONG. TH
END IS OUT OF OUR SIGHT, EVEN AS IT IS OUT O
YOURS. YET WE ARE COMPELLED TO MOVE ONWAR
STRIDING NOW, SHUFFLING THEN. SOMETIMES EVE
MOMENTARILY HALTING TO REST. THE PATH WE AR
ON IS WORN, AND NEITHER WE NOR YOU SHALL B
THE LAST. IS THERE AN END TO CREATION? THE CON
CEPT OF LIFE, OF DEATH, OF BEING, ALLOWS N
POSTULATION OF CESSATION, OF ULTIMATE ENTROPY.

"A series of self-perpetuating cycles," I said. I glanced
Chamzeen, who looked steadily at me, her expression as bla
as she could make it. "As one universe, one plane of existenc
dies, another begins. Interlinked. Our method of traveling, a

the shifters and the ships and stuff, it uses the multiverse, doesn't it? Evades physical limitations by changing the plane of reference.''

I suddenly realized that my anger had dissipated. I was fascinated, still awed, but no longer feeling entirely duped, although there was still something of a feeling of betrayal.

*=YOUR QUESTIONS MAY BE ANSWERED NOW BY YOUR COMRADES, AND YOUR MENTORS, THE BASES. TREAT YOUR TEACHERS KINDLY, FOR THEY ARE TRUE SENTIENTS, AND MAY BE HURT. THEIR PERSONALITIES, EACH INDIVIDUAL, ONCE WERE LOCKED IN FLESH. NOW THOSE PERSONALITIES ARE LOCKED WITHIN CRYSTAL MATRICES.

*=WE KNOW YOU WILL FOLLOW US ON THE ROAD. OTHERS WILL COME BEHIND YOU, AND YOU SHALL GUIDE THEM, FOR IN THEM LIES YOUR OWN DESTINY. AND ONE AT A TIME WE SHALL WALK, PILGRIMS TO A PLACE WE DO NOT COMPREHEND, DESPITE OUR EFORTS. IT IS A DARK, MISTY WAY, AND IT IS DIFFICULT TO PERCEIVE THOSE BEFORE YOU, AND BEHIND YOU. THE STEPS GROW EVEN MORE DIFFICULT, THE WAY AHEAD EVER MORE TENUOUS. WE STUMBLE OFTEN, BUT MOVE ON, NOT YET KNOWING WHY WE CONTINUE THIS MOVEMENT. THE ROAD MAY NEVER END.

*=WE HAVE THE FAITH OF CHILDREN, THAT CHILDHOOD SHALL END, AND THAT WHAT COMES BEYOND WILL BE AS INTERESTING TO US. YOU SEE, KEVVEN TOMARI, WE ARE MUCH AS YOU ARE. WE ARE THE PAWNS OF AN INCOMPREHENSIBLE DESTINY, WITH SIMPLE MOTIVES, YET MOTIVES THAT MIGHT BE MORE COMPLEX THAN YOUR OWN. WE LACK PIECES OF THE PUZZLE, OF THE GAME, ALTHOUGH THE GAME CONTINUES REGARDLESS, FORCING US TO ADAPT AND GROW TO WIN. AND, EVENTUALLY, THE SCATTERED PIECES FORM THE PATTERN, THE PICTURE, THE CHECKMATE, THE WIN—AND WE DISCOVER, AGAIN, THAT ALL THAT WAS LACKING WAS OURSELVES.

I visualized the gorilla sequence, unbidden, a sort of associative reflex. Big ape beats on smaller ape, boosts the banana. Smaller ape raises cain and a couple of abels for good measure, bashes even smaller ape, swipes something. Even smaller ape goes huff-huff-huffing over to chimpanzee, bounces up and down awhile on it, rips off something cute. Chimp stalks off to find Cheetah Junior, kicks him out of his tree, and makes off with the booty. Cheetah, Jr., picks himself up, dusts himself off, and screams bloody murder at the trees.

The Builders sensed that, of course, tracing the sequence fully. What else? They knew me, it was impossible not to, just as it was impossible for me to know *them*.

They/It said, *=IT MAY SEEM THAT WAY TO YOU. YET YOU HAVE LEARNED TOLERANCE. THAT YOU DID SO WAS A DELIBERATE PLOY ON OUR PART. AND YOU SHALL BE PATIENT, TOO. WHEN ONE THING FAILS, YOU WILL REPEAT YOUR ATTEMPTS, WORKING UNTIL A BREAKTHROUGH IS ACHIEVED, NO MATTER TO WHAT YOUR EFFORT IS APPLIED.

*=YOU HAVE ALL GROWN, AND YOU SHALL GROW YET MORE. THIS CHILDHOOD, YOUR FIRST, HAS ENDED, AND YOUR ADULTHOOD HAS BEGUN. YET THIS IS BUT ANOTHER CHILDHOOD. AND BEYOND THAT, ANOTHER STAGE OF YOUR CHILDHOOD. AND IN THE END, WE SHALL, PERHAPS, ALL BE AS ONE, AND SHALL GO THROUGH THAT LAST STAGE OF CHILDHOOD TOGETHER. YET, AS WE HAVE SAID, THE ROAD MAY NEVER END. IF THAT IS THE CASE, SO BE IT.

*=AND NOW, YOU WILL LEAVE US, TO RETURN WHENCE YOU CAME, TO GROW ALONG YOUR OWN PATH, UNAIDED, TO WALK THE ROAD AFTER US. AND WE SHALL STRUGGLE ONWARD TO OUR DESTINY, OUR DAWNING.

Over, so soon?

Visual sense reaffirmed itself; I'd started getting lost in the nuances of the Builders' lecture, catching flickering images with my trained but incapable mind. I wasn't much of a telepath, even after Soru; matter of discipline, and maybe even a lifetime too. But the Builders spoke so damn loudly and so completely that the noise in my mind was setting up peculiar feedback, hence the imagery.

On the screen, all colors, swirling, stormy, murderous, non-stellar only by the grace of a fate blasted to splinters by some cosmic LSD, the planet was growing. I wanted to hold out my hands to it to see whether I could feel the heat generated by the miniature fusion fires cycling at the heart of the world.

Growing, growing, changing, changing . . .

The surface peeled and funneled and sprang upwards. There was only a millisecond of warning, and then we were surrounded by gorgeous violence, colors exploding like a madman's fireworks display. Chamzeen gasped and I flinched.

Plunging down to the heart of a world, *falling*.

My boards flickered. Reading the vanishing atmosphere, altering ship position, the infinite distance where it should have been a few thousand kilometers.

Spacegate.

Going home.

I felt tears and fought them and managed to see Chamzeen, saw her stunned expression, her quivering lips.

There was flashing and boiling blue and white at the bottom of the tunnel, and endless black, and the colors of the funnel snatched into the shape of a magnetic field.

''Falling down a hole,'' I said, whispering, watching, caught.

*=THIS HAS NOT BEEN USED FOR A LONG TIME. FAREWELL, OUR FRIENDS, OUR CHILDREN. GROW, PROSPER, PROGRESS. YOU WILL FIND YOUR OWN WAY NOW. YOU HAVE JOINED US ON OUR ROAD, AND MUST WALK BEHIND US, WHEREVER IT MAY LEAD. IN TIME, YOU MAY STAND WITH US, BE PART OF US. WE SHALL EACH HAVE GROWN INTO SOMETHING DIFFERENT, BUT EACH SHALL KNOW THE OTHER.

*=BY THAT TIME, YOU MAY HAVE FORGIVEN US, WITH LOVE, AND FORGOTTEN THE PAIN WE BROUGHT TO YOU.

*=GO WITH OUR LOVE, OUR CHILDREN. GOODBYE . . . AND GOOD LUCK.

The images of the T-sooli, the Builders, faded.

''You canny bastards,'' I said, whispering, respectful, and pretty appreciative. ''You know you taught us too goddamn . . . too well.'' I wasn't going to be able to blaspheme effectively in future, I thought. ''You know we won't ever trust to luck.''

Whisper of a chuckle, whisper of goodbye love.

We submerged in the black, were passed through, were spat out, were *home*.

All the ships in a line, just coming after us. Ahead of us, the central Base of the Builders in our universe, where the armada had massed. Nearby was the big Builders' ship, a gossamer giant.

On our screens, the red sun's image returned. At first, I thought it was a recording, being played back. Nearby, the planet cast its shadow.

Then it flickered and erupted into trilogies of flares.

Nova.

Supernova.

Death.

Heat death.

I stood up, watching, awed, slipped aside slowly and let Chamzeen take my place. I felt sadness, yet elation, watching that massive sun exploding.

It grew, wobbling, explanding, flared out again, pulsed, flares almost touching the giant planet that orbited it, pulsed and licked the planet, flaring again.

There was a blast of white light, a stellar explosion as the atmosphere of the planet, long threatened, long checked, ignited.

A star, being born.

Two stars, dying.

A blazing mass of fire spread across a starless sky, became a torch within a dead universe.

Dying.

I didn't stop the tears, stood watching.

Expansion, red supergiant, pulsing like a bloody heart, dripping flame, stopping, beating languidly.

Collapse, roiling and fighting, imploding, the final stages, from red supergiant to white dwarf in a cosmic hiccup, sloughing mass, crashing to red dwarf, to black star, neutron star.

Implosion.

A brief flash of white light that vanished into itself, a flicker of blue and purple light about infinity black.

Black hole.

And then, nothing.

We had watched a universe die, had seen something beyond a simple description, beyond anything but feelings. Something more had died than a sun, something that was part of us all. Yet it still lived within us. Kinship with the cosmos, kinship with gods.

The screens cleared, and showed space around us. Breath was

a roar as the stars appeared. The Base hung against the glittering background. Nearby, the great shape of the Builders' ship.

We watched, and the great gossamer killer slowly faded, blew apart like a ghost no one believes in.

It was over.

And it was beginning.

Children . . .

I shook myself into some semblance of a stable mental state, watching as Chamzeen deftly flicked her fingers over the boards, putting us into a stable parking orbit around the big Base. I glanced at the tally of surviving ships, didn't register the numbers. Not enough, not enough, but . . .

Enough.

I leaned against the command chair, suddenly feeling tired, immensely tired. My legs hurt from standing stiffly and watching the screens. Chamzeen twisted in the command chair, her movements as lithe, as delicate, as impossible as they'd ever been. She took my wrist, gentle, warming. I sat down on the arm of the chair, grinned wearily.

"Still got a lot to do, y'know, sweetheart," I said. "Lot of good ol' folks in that thar uni-voise. Lot of nasty types too. We got to go love the lot of 'em."

Chamzeen pressed her lips against my palm, then laughed.

"We have been waiting for this, Kevven," she said. "We have many things to do, ourselves. Many places to go. You will see."

"I will see," I said. "I will see. Yep. I can't help it. Shit, what do I do, now I come fitted with Panavision? Blink sideways?" I chuckled, felt silly, and realized the tiredness was screwing me up.

"Kevven?" Chamzeen said.

I looked at her, saw her eyes, pupils wide and glinting, intent on me. "Hmm? What, what, what can I do for you?"

She smiled and managed to look fresh rather than devilish. "At one time, I frightened you."

I chuckled, shook my head. "Yeah, well, that's the way it goes." I looked at her carefully. "Hell, no, I'm not frightened of you now. Hardly ever was. And now . . ." I hesitated, words stinging the lining of my throat, coughed them up and got them out. "Now, I love you. I love you so much I . . . I can't say how much."

So easy. And so true. My pulse was careening.

Chamzeen closed her eyes, still smiling, madonna-like. Finally she said, "Later. It must be later, then. But soon?"

I bent, kissed her. Ritual had died with that sun, with the leaving of the Builders. I said, "Soon."

She buried her long fingers in my hair, not even tugging, so expert that I could have purred. "I love you beyond being, beyond soul, Kevven. There are things I must teach you . . . must teach Meheilahn. Your children too, if you permit."

I smiled. "Anything. Always." There was an echo, some of that feedback, neatly pigeonholed for easy reference. "I give you my tomorrow."

She didn't hesitate. "I give you my life and soul."

I straightened up. "Don't fade away, Chamzeen."

She laughed. "Be careful. My love for Meheilahn, too, do not forget."

"Yeah." I touched her shoulder. "I'll be back when I've slept awhile. Or whatever." My teeth ached as I stretched. "See you in however long it takes."

I left the bridge and went down an automatic route, trying to work out what the hell I was going to do, whether I'd see Shreekor first, or Nikoi L'aan, or the Jeweler, or . . .

My mind went blank just before I hit my quarters. Meheilahn was standing outside the door, waiting.

I stopped and tried to say something, and choked on the first word.

The masks had all come down, the illusions all faded.

Many faded ages before, I had passed through Missouri, USA, Terra, beginning a journey that words couldn't describe. I had been shown myself, had been shown tomorrow. Missourians would approve, because their motto is "show me."

I have never told Meheilahn how much I love her.

ABOUT THE AUTHOR

STEVE E. MCDONALD has published several short stories in ANALOG and is a free-lance book reviewer. Mr. McDonald resides in Jamaica, West Indies.